The Most Glorified Strip of Bunting

cGill

TWO RAVENS
PRESS

Published by Two Ravens Press Ltd
Green Willow Croft
Rhiroy
Lochbroom
Ullapool
Ross-shire IV23 2SF

www.tworavenspress.com

The right of John McGill to be identified as author of this work has been asserted by him in accordance with the Copyright, Designs and Patent Act, 1988.
© John McGill, 2007.

ISBN: 978-1-906120-12-2

British Library Cataloguing in Publication Data: a CIP record for this book can be obtained from the British Library.

Designed and typeset in Sabon by Two Ravens Press.
Cover design by David Knowles and Sharon Blackie.

Printed on Forest Stewardship Council-accredited paper by Biddles Ltd., King's Lynn, Norfolk.

About the Author

John McGill was born in Glasgow and now lives in Orkney. He has taught English all over the place and has published a collection of short stories, *That Rubens Guy*, and a novel, *Giraffes*. His stories have featured in a number of anthologies and have been broadcast on BBC Radio 4 and Radio Scotland.

To Morag

THE UNITED STATES NORTH POLAR EXPEDITION (1871-1873)

Charles Francis Hall	Commander
Sidney O. Budington	Sailing Master
George E. Tyson*	Assistant Navigator
Hubbard C. Chester	First Mate
William Morton	Second Mate
Emil Schumann	Chief Engineer
Alvin A. Odell	Assistant Engineer
Walter F. Campbell	Fireman
John W. Booth	Fireman
John Herron*	Steward
William Jackson*	Cook
Nathan J. Coffin	Carpenter

SCIENTIFIC CORPS

Emil Bessel	Surgeon/ Scientist
R. W. D. Bryan	Astronomer/ Chaplain
Frederick Meyer*	Meteorologist

SEAMEN

Hermann Siemens	Joseph Mauch
Frederick Anthing*	G. W. Lindquist*
J. W. C. Kruger (Robert)*	Peter Johnson*
Henry Hobby	Frederick Jamka*
William Nindermann*	Noah Hays

ESKIMOS

Joe (Ebierbing)*	Interpreter/ servant
Hannah (Tookolito)*	Interpreter/ assistant
Puney*	Hannah's child
Hans*	Hunter/ servant
Christiana (Merkut)*	Hans' wife
Augustina, Tobias, Succi*	Christiana's children
Charlie*	Child, born 12.8.72

*Those members of the expedition marked with an asterix were cast adrift on the ice floe, 16th October 1872.

THE 2000-MILE DRIFT OF THE POLARIS SURVIVORS

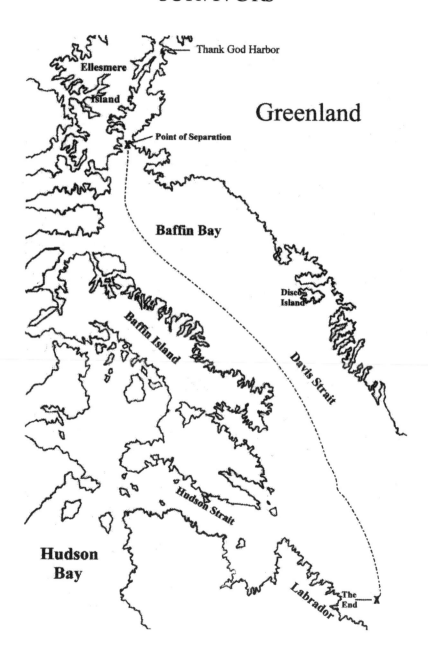

Thank God Harbor

Ellesmere
Island

Greenland

Point of Separation

Baffin Bay

Baffin Island

Disco
Island

Davis Strait

Hudson Strait

Hudson
Bay

Labrador

The
End

CONTENTS

PROLOGUE
CHARLIE POLARIS MAKES UP THE NUMBERS

The eskimos must have known Christiana was pregnant, must have helped her with the taboos, but they said nothing till the morning of 12th August, when Hannah told Captain Budington that her friend would need the cabin to herself for a few hours.

He summoned Bessel and Bryan, and between them, doctor and chaplain, they tried to enlist Hannah as go-between. Hannah was strong. A transatlantic celebrity, she had taken tea with the Queen of England and the Prince Consort, bought corsets in Bond Street, promenaded the length of the Strand under an umbrella, lunched with senators on Capitol Hill. She was a householder of Groton Connecticut whose English was surer than the doctor's – notwithstanding his ladylike hands, his monstrous erudition and his heap of academic distinctions – but in this affair she was Tookolito again, and Christiana was Merkut: savages. The doctor and the chaplain considered an appeal to the captain and through him to the native husbands, but Hannah's flat square stance and tight unaccommodating grin made it clear that this would have been a futile gesture.

Bryan was distressed. 'I'd foolishly entertained the thought that their years of contact with civilisation might have delivered them entirely from their barbaric practices, but it seems not.'

Dr Bessel, for whom the Americans were hardly a notch above the natives in the matter of civilised management, shook his head and smiled. 'Not in an affair such as this, Reverend. We should have guessed – she has been avoiding some food; there have been looks.'

The chaplain's voice became still more anxious. 'There is even a danger, of course, that if the child is female …' It was their custom during conversation to take no more account of the eskimos than of the dogs, but now they looked at Hannah, assuring themselves that she had heard, had understood.

She had, and her grin widened.

The sailors, too, grinned. Christiana, four and a half feet tall, plump as a late-summer walrus and permanently enveloped in fur, had fooled them. The skat players were sitting in the open air, enjoying the sun. Kruger placed his cards between his lips to

1

free his fingers for counting, then solemnly informed them that the conception had been on the very night that their great leader Captain Hall had given his last breath, screaming of murder.

'Celebrating,' Lindquist said. One or two snorted, but most were uncomfortable with his quip, and he did not expand upon it.

Christiana's sweet fishy rancidity made the sailors heave at anything less than five yards, so the doctor's admonition to avoid the eskimos' cabin was superfluous. The news of her confinement, however, caused a general buoyancy of spirits: everyone laughed, and there were even small splutterings over bear-soup for Tyson – navigator, acting ice-master and permanent Yankee prig – when he reminded them of his theory that the natives were God's Arctic Joke: half-man, half-seal, little and well-spread so the ice would bear their weight; brown and slant-eyed so the seals would accept them into their midst; evil-smelling to repel the mosquitoes. (In their turn, the eskimos called the *kabloonas* half-men, and wrangled over the precise composition of the other half: the exact proportions of moondust, water, fox-essence and assorted shits.)

Hannah helped Christiana to arrange the oxhides in the cabin then left and sat in her tent on the shore, patching Joe's britches. In the soft summer air with the glass high and the mercury almost up to freezing, the routines continued: dogs, boats, sledges, journals, clothes-mending, snow-melting, temperature-reading, sample-collecting, chess, checkers, skat, gossip, target-practice – but it was hard for them not to steal glances, not to listen, however wide a berth they gave the cabin. Harder still to steer clear of it in their talk. Tyson, joining the circle of card players, elaborated his thesis, his solitary joke, that some tribes of eskimos were descended from *Phoca vitulina*, the small Greenland seal. While he was drawing his explicatory diagrams in the snow, Hans and Joe appeared on the southern ridge, squat and seemingly no taller than the dogs, returning from the morning hunt. The sailors roared and the gossip, to Tyson's prudish discomfiture, became coarser.

'*Guckt mal!*' Kruger said, pointing toward the ridge. Then switching to English in deference to Tyson, 'Look, Mr Tyson: two fat seals.'

Unable to conceal his pleasure, Tyson smiled, and Kruger

continued: 'But it's not just their outline; think about their smell.' The sailors groaned. Jamka compared the stink of Hans' family unfavourably with dead fish, whale's bowels, singed hair, rotten pork, and the lingering farts of Jackson, their black cook. Lindquist measured Christiana's sexual allure against that of a female bearded seal, and found it wanting.

'Yet she has a nice way with lice,' Kruger said, pinching his finger and thumb together, noisily sucking them, then swallowing with a small burp of satisfaction.

'And nose-pickings.' Jamka's gross mime had entertained them often enough before. Tyson felt the heat of anger on his cheeks – against their happiness, their solidarity, their vulgarity, their un-American accents; against his own folly in beginning the trend in the conversation. He knew well enough that the attempt to ingratiate was ill-founded, that they would finally despise him for it, would return to German and mock him as soon as he left the circle. He watched Hans and Joe, still more than a mile distant, plodding methodically through the patchy snow, and let his attention drift, but the jibes rattled in his skull.

'Her clothes are not changed from summer to winter to summer again.'

'They feed girl-babies to the pups.'

'She sucks her own hair.'

'She throws her pap over her shoulder like a knapsack.'

'Have you seen her with a caribou prick?'

'I wonder which is the father?'

'No point in asking, they're all under the skins together: they wouldn't know themselves.'

'They're worse than the dogs.'

'They do it like the dogs.'

'They do it *with* the dogs.'

'Mr Tyson's right – they're like seals.'

'Only louder.'

'Ah, louder – the grunting and the squealing – *ugh ugh ugh ugh.*'

'*Aa-ee aa-ee aa-ee.*'

Unable to divert them, shamed by the approach of the hunters, Tyson excused himself, rose and walked toward the observatory. He tried to focus on other things, but was no more able than the tittle-tattlers to resist the compulsion to cast his eyes in the direction of the banked-up *Polaris*, or to banish images of what was happening in the deep recess of the eskimos' cabin.

Sounds carried. Already across the mile of rock and moss flecked with snow that was hardly thick enough yet for serious sledging, he could distinguish Hans from Joe as they urged the dogs home. And as he rounded the stern of the *Polaris* he could hear – nothing new, as familiar now as the ice itself – raised querulous voices from the captain's quarters. Here too, notwithstanding the three inches of Yankee oak, distinctions were easy: Captain Budington hot, slurred, offended, bristling; Dr Bessel frosty with contempt, somehow superior and holding the initiative despite his uncertain command of English; Pastor Bryan whiningly apologetic, conciliatory, appealing to their gentlemanly instincts.

If the *Polaris* was not a happy ship, the unhappiness had little to do with the encroaching ice, the splits in her sides, the waterlogged hold. For a winter and a spring she had housed the thirty-two northernmost people on the planet: all of them, except the two eskimo women and their four children, armed; most of them angry, resentful, ready to switch at the latest real or fancied grievance from one grumbling faction to another. In the blackness of November they had laid their dead commander a bare two feet under the gravel, and with him they had buried all sense of common purpose. They had waited nine months for the ice to release its grip on their vessel, some hopeful of a push northwards toward the Pole, others dreaming only of New York and foaming beer and women's arms. Throughout these months dancing auroras, wheeling constellations, the high Pole Star itself, had illuminated and mocked the squabbles of cliques, counter-cliques and cliques-within-cliques – shifting alliances of Yankees and Germans, officers and men, sailors and civilians, white men and natives; with Jackson the cook – remote, indeterminate and unaligned in his blackness – a bitterly silent faction of one.

Tyson walked faster, trying to shut his ears to the discord. There was a thin hope that Meyer, who would be setting the chronometers in the observatory, might offer respite of a sort from the coarseness of the men, the complex intertwined loathings of the officers, the fathomless insouciance of the natives. He was the most Americanised of the Germans, a man who had served in the Army of the United States as well as that of

4

Prussia, somehow intermediate in the three-man scientific corps between the comfortably Pennsylvanian Reverend Bryan and the irredeemably European Dr Bessel. Exasperatingly for Tyson, he veered capriciously from clannish and insubordinate solidarity with his compatriot Bessel to a soldierly Yankee bluffness that had once or twice hinted at an invitation to friendship.

The noon transit recorded, the fine adjustments to the chronometers made, he looked pleased enough at Tyson's arrival. He nodded toward the ship, shrugged his shoulders, pushed a stool in Tyson's direction, offered his medicinal flask. Tyson sipped. He expected gossip, and hoped it would be about the officers, but Meyer, like the sailors, was preoccupied with the dirty miracle that was coming to pass in the forward cabin.

'It's not without interest, waiting to see whose nose it will have.'

Tyson needed the companionship. 'They're the strangest creatures on earth. In twenty years I've never approached an understanding.'

Meyer laughed. 'Sooner understand the whales. Sooner talk to the icebergs.'

'And sooner civilise them.' Tyson was becoming happier. He looked at the flask. Meyer, responding, found two glasses and poured an inch into each.

'Yet I believe she spent two years with the great Doctor Kane,' he said.

Tyson nodded. 'At least two. That's the strangest of all – Kane was a gentleman, and he adopted them as friends.'

'The celebrated Doctor Kane,' Meyer said. 'The great Doctor Kane and his Noble Savages.'

Tyson pointed at the door, in the direction of the ship. 'That Noble Savage is quite up to strangling it if it's a girl child.'

Surely not?'

'Quite up to it,' he repeated. 'Sometimes they feed it to the dogs, keep the head as proof to show the others.'

Meyer sighed and shook his head slowly. Tyson sighed. They were both happy now. Here, in the squat stone observatory there was always hope of escaping for a half hour or so the creaking rancour of the ship. Here a man could sit on firm earth, answerable only to the stars.

It was a little after one when Hannah heard Christiana's call

5

and went to the cabin door. She paused for a moment, staring across the ice, before she entered. It was not a propitious time for a birth: daylight was waning again, the circling sun visibly lower each day, the temperature dropping fast. Budington heard the call too. He unlocked his cabinet and brought out three bottles of rum, and when the two women appeared amidships to tell him that the child was a boy he thanked God in his drunken fashion and summoned the men with the ship's bell. They gathered on the deck and cheered, and Christiana acknowledged by showing them the head, snug against her left breast, unequivocally attached to its body. Chester, the first mate, proposed that the new member of the United States North Polar Expedition be named in honour of their dead commander, Charles Francis Hall, and the sailors, Germans and Yankees alike, hurrah-ed again.

If Budington was taken aback he had wit enough to disguise it: he stroked his beard, nodded, gave his blessing.

And if the women had a notion of their own, if they had a real-human-being name in mind for the child, a hint picked up from his emergent cry or a commemoration of some dead relative, they kept it to themselves. Dr Bessel raised his glass and offered a further suggestion. 'Perhaps we might also remember our little ship. Perhaps the little fellow could be Charles Francis Polaris.'

The suggestion made them laugh, but there was solemnity in the moment too. Tyson proposed a less portentous "Charlie Polaris," and a further, louder, cheer signalled the sailors' approval.

Hans and Joe arrived bowed with seal meat, exhausted, curious about the raised voices. There was backslapping for them both and lewd congratulation for Hans as they were dragged on board for the ceremony.

Smiling, bewildered, Christiana yielded up the naked thing, her fourth child, to Hannah, who passed it to Bryan. At twenty-six Fahrenheit, the ritual had to be briefly performed. Within seven minutes Charlie Polaris, the world's northernmost baby, was duly baptised, the dead captain and his soon-to-be dead ship duly commemorated, the rum duly drunk.

The afterbirth and the cord, tidily severed by Christiana with the short razor-teeth that had more than once yanked boots and socks from the renowned Doctor Kane's frozen feet, were given by Hannah to the dogs, before she scrubbed the oxhide and buried the mother's clothes.

CHAPTER ONE
QUESTING: THE AMERICAN WAY

As the *Periwinkle* she had plashed through muddy rivers, tugged, snorted, liberated errant steamers from shifting banks of sand. Reborn for the ice and renamed for the constant star, she was better furnished for the voyage to the Polar Sea than any ship had ever been. With Yankee oak and steel went Yankee ingenuity, Yankee science. Lightrigged and fat below, she was no greyhound of the waves, but the American Way to the Pole did not ask for greyhounds. Beyond the berg-littered whaling grounds of Baffin and Melville, with the mountains of Ellesmere lowering on the port horizon and the glaciers of Greenland on the starboard, she would brace herself for the Yankee charge through the heaving pack of Smith Sound, and the thundering Neafles and Levy engines would show their worth. Prodigies of compact power and Philadelphian know-how, their boilers happily devouring coal, wood, bones or whale-oil, they drove a propeller that could be unshipped in two minutes to be raised through a snug groove clear of the ice-nip. And in the Sound it would be cut, slice, bash and cut and bash again, asking no favours of ice or wind or current, not seeking to blend or conciliate, but only to drive the nose of the *Polaris* northwards.

A time would come when others would plant themselves in podgy bathtubs in the crazy project of being borne god-only-knew-where, praying that the ice would kiss and caress them to the Pole without mangling them in its embrace, ready to allow the pack four, five, six years – as long as its vast slow drift required. But the *Periwinkle-Polaris* was shaped for battle, and when Charles Francis Hall heard reports that the Arctic springtime had been kind, that ice conditions were the best in living memory, he opted for the warlike route, the beeline to the top of the world. Her iron-plated solid white oak bows met in a sharp vertical stem, the knife-edge that would carve her a passage through Smith, Kane, Kennedy, the channels that divided the frigid deserts of Ellesmere Island from the Greenland glaciers, through the drifting mass of berg and floe and pack to the uttermost margins of land, then beyond the tip of Greenland to the Polar Sea. Thence, with sails unfurled, she would cleave the waves and carry the three dozen

questers singing and dancing to the still-point of the globe where
her namesake, the hub star of the wheeling heavens, would wink
down on them along a line plumbed to the earth's centre.

There were further wonders of Yankee invention: slung
from her stern was a spring-operated buoy that would carry an
electric light a yard above the waves – a glittering beacon to guide
separated mariners back to mother-safety through the Arctic dark;
and stowed amidships a folded canvas boat hardly heavier than
Captain Hall himself, yet fashioned to carry twenty men should
need arise.

There was food for two and a half years. Augmented by fresh
meat from the native hunters, it would comfortably stretch to
four. The beef was delicately corned, no rank scurvy-breeding
salted Texan stuff – Hall had insisted upon that. He knew beef,
as he knew pemmican, wheat, flour, biscuit, coffee, molasses,
figs. When it came to food, he could rightly tell the Secretary of
the Navy that no previous expedition had been so lavishly or so
cunningly provided for.

But when it came to men, he lied.

He lied to George Robeson, Secretary of the Navy; lied to
Ulysses S. Grant, President of the USA; lied to Mary, his wife;
lied to himself and God. A naval commander who had never read
a chart in earnest, a leader of a scientific expedition who barely
knew a spectroscope from a psychrometer, he felt the burden
of every ounce of the *Polaris's* four hundred tons, every cent of
Congress's fifty thousand dollars, and lied.

'The officers and crew of the ship are all I could desire,' he
wrote to Robeson, and the bite of the polar bug might even have
convinced him it was true, as it had convinced others that cloud-
banks were fabled lost continents, curt inlets the passage to Japan,
prancing reflections the Open Polar Sea.

He was but the latest in a long line of dreamers; in the pursuit
of their personal Grail – the Passage, the Pole, King Solomon's
Mines, Frobisher's Gold, the bones of Sir John Franklin – their
eyes had been the least serviceable organs, had seen what their
fevered yearnings had wished them to see. In justification of the
pounds and dollars, their promises had become ever more vain-
glorious: we'll be back by Yuletide with gold enough to plate the
Tower of London; we'll plant these Stars and Stripes at the top of

the world; we'll name a continent for your granddaughter, a strait for your mistress, a headland for your pug. And the thousands of monies demanded titles in keeping: the Cathay Company, the Company of Adventurers, the United States North Polar Expedition. Always, for the searcher, the weight of bigger men's and women's dreams: for Frobisher, the pleasure of the Great Queen Bess, the greed of the Thames merchants; for Franklin, the confirmation that Britannia did indeed rule the waves; for Hall, the awesome charge of confirming that the Republic, emerging from her five years of fraternal slaughter, was indeed preserved, was a United States, singular and great among the nations of the earth, her unity proclaimed, the handshake between Grant and Lee at Appatomax consummated and blessed by the unfurling at the Pole.

Heavier still the millstone of Science. He had asked for a hundred thousand dollars and been granted half; but even at fifty thousand, a single dream is overpriced. 'I never will be satisfied in voyaging and travelling in the Arctic regions until I shall reach that spot of this great and glorious orb of God's creation where there is no North, no East, no West,' he told his journal; but between Hall and that satisfaction a mighty tonnage of discovery was deposited, as if Galahad and Percival had been required to analyse dragon's blood, measure the pulse-rates of besieged virgins, chart the bottoms of enchanted lakes. A loner in his bones, happiest chewing narwhal fat in a dripping igloo, he had become the servant of the National Academy of Sciences, the whipping-boy of geographers, oceanographers, astronomers, geologists, natural philosophers, chemists, meteorologists, botanists, ornithologists, entomologists, zoologists.

Too much, far too much for a blacksmith, a failed backwoods newsman. So he puffed his small achievements in articles and letters and public lectures: he had single-handedly plugged up the false Northwest Passage. Frobisher's Strait, the supposed Gateway to the Orient, he had discovered, was a humble inlet of Baffin Island. It would be for him, Charles Francis Hall, to navigate the real Passage, after he had unravelled the fate of Sir John Franklin and charted the Open Polar Sea. And it was he, Charles Francis Hall, who had sledged and mapped the unconsidered northwestern tip of Melville Peninsula and so brought to an end

9

the five hundred-year enterprise of charting the outline of the American continent.

Grand claims for the Cincinnati hack. The learned scientific officers of the *Polaris* sneered and made withering asides in English and German, while the sailors who knew the fogs of Bergy Hole and had listened to the grinding of the floes and the detonations of the crumbling icebergs, laughed and said they were damned fools alike, the commander and his scientific corps.

'The officers and crew of the ship are all I could desire.' On the Friday night before they left Washington Navy Yard he might have bloodied the narrow patrician nose of Dr Bessel, his Chief Scientific Officer, except that the satisfaction of his anger would have cost him the Expedition. Sipping champagne with the assembled senators, scientists, editors and curious wives, the doctor paused in his delineation of the scientific objectives to sling his scholarly pebbles: 'Our Captain' – always the capital C, the hint of speech-marks around the word, the derisive tilt of the head, the half-smile – 'of course, in his previous ventures, has been of a mind to put more faith in the testimony of the natives than in mere scientific observation or deduction. I am not sure if the Casella theodolite or the prismatic compass have claimed much of his attention hitherto – I believe he is a subscriber to the view that science has much to learn from the children of nature.'

The communal snigger reached Hall, and their glances brought sweat to his brow, whitened his knuckles. They knew his touchiness well enough – a scant two years before he had shot dead the whaler Patrick Coleman for precisely this offence, this questioning of his credentials. In five slow strides he was among them and facing Bessel, and none doubted that the scholarly doctor's throat was at risk from the blacksmith-fingers. But he smiled, offered a suggestion of a bow, and said: 'Doctor, they and their forebears have existed on those desolate shores since a time before all written history, before science. Their survival has depended upon an intimate instinctual knowledge of the configuration of land and sea, the behaviour of animal and fish, wind and weather. Children they may be, and sorely deprived of the blessings of civilised commerce and particularly of religion, yet I consider it arrogant presumption on our part to suppose that they can teach us nothing about the region they inhabit. In

my experience, subsequent scientific observation has invariably
served to confirm their accounts of Arctic topography.'

'Precisely so.' Bessel looked around the circle, inviting the guests
to smile with him. 'What need, then, of instruments? What need
of fifty thousand dollars? Give an eskimo a sextant and he will
beat it into fish-hooks, no?'

'And catch fish,' Hall said.

But he would not be inveigled, would not abandon his grin,
would let the doctor have his fun. Enjoying the moment, Bessel
gestured toward the table where the expedition's books and
instruments had been arranged for display, and said, 'Yes, the
instinct for survival – give him a copy of Bowditch's Navigator
and he will eat it. Uncooked!'

The joke was not lost on the editors, who knew that Hall's
maritime credentials were reputed to rest on this and only this: that
he had memorised *The New American Practical Navigator* from
cover to cover. They knew too that he was prey to ungovernable
rages, and had escaped the charge of murder only because Repulse
Bay, where Patrick Coleman had raved for two weeks before dying
from his bullet-wound, was outwith all civilised jurisdiction. When
he said nothing and maintained his good-humoured demeanour,
one of them asked if he would look first to his scientific corps or
to his native friends for confirmation that the chief aim of the
Expedition – the Pole – had been achieved. Or perhaps, suggested
another, he would trust to his own instinctual knowledge of these
things.

His smile became a laugh, and he pointed upward. 'I shall look
for the Pole Star, gentlemen, and I shall find it – straight above
my head. And mindful of the stellar parallax, I shall invite Doctor
Bessel to agree with me that it is above his head too, or virtually
so.' They laughed, the crisis passed, and they turned contentedly
to matters in which all could concur: to the decades of English
failures in the polar regions; to the British admiralty stuffshirts
who mulishly refused to acknowledge that minus fifty Fahrenheit
required alterations to rules of precedence, authority, dress and
language; to the manifest superiority of Yankee science, New
World democracy. Yet Hall the unschooled blacksmith, even as he
joined in the mockery, felt the day coming when he would yearn
for the godlike authority of a ship-of-the-line captain, sustained

11

by the full panoply of leg-iron and lash, musket and yardarm.

In the weeks before it left Brooklyn, the *Polaris* became an unhappy ship, divided into mutually contemptuous factions, with barely the half of her complement seriously stirred by the grand object of her fifty-thousand dollar expedition and barely the quarter remotely convinced that her captain was capable of achieving it.

Hall, the Captain who was no captain, enjoyed the love of Tyson, who would have been his ice-master but had been taken on too late for that and ranked as mere assistant navigator; of much of the forecastle, where his soldierly plainness was preferred to the hauteur of the scientists; of the eskimos, with most of whom he had shared blood-warmth and chamber pots under caribou hides in temperatures low enough to freeze mercury harder than steel. But for his sailing-master Budington, once a friend but now inveterately hostile and in abject thrall to the bottle, the whole affair was damned nonsense, no matter whether it was reckoned as exploration or as science; and the German sailors, already suborned by their better-educated compatriots in the scientific corps, laughed at every attempt by the commander to claim patriotic and religious significance for a mere voyage to the ice and back.

For Hall, there were early intimations of the horror to come: on 20th June – the very day of their departure from the Navy yard – Meyer the meteorologist, a sergeant in the Signal Corps well accustomed to the military regime, skirted insubordination in the curtness of his refusal to help him with the preparation of his papers for publication – the precious account of five years spent in search of Franklin on and around King William Island. And when Wilson the chief engineer jumped ship at New York, followed by the cook and two others at New London, his despair drove him to share with Tyson a budding fear, not only that they might be denied the Grail, but that their safe return was less than assured.

CHAPTER TWO
DRIFTING: TYSON BLAMES THE DARKNESS

On the floe there is an assumption of shared authority between Tyson, assistant navigator, with twenty Arctic summers and thirteen winters in his bones; and Meyer, well-seasoned sergeant-signaller, meteorologist, scholar – a Prussian who can command the sailors in their native tongue. There is no dispute that Tyson is the ranking officer and Meyer his second, but in two years of trying they have failed, except during brief and soon-forgotten moments of communication, to soften their mutual dislike, and co-operation is difficult.

For the first few days, however, command has fallen naturally to the eskimo men. The first desperate need is shelter against the gales, and the construction of that shelter is their business. As masterbuilder, Joe is God. His instructions to Hans are peremptory, virtually wordless. He places his left hand on Hans's shoulder and with a sweep of his right defines a raised part of the floe fifty paces distant, toward the southern edge, then a flat area immediately north of where they stand. Hans barks at Christiana, who reaches under a bundle of oxhide for his snow-knife. He tests its edge in the snow, then moves to the hummock. The sailors, accustomed to smiling at his waddling short-legged gait, watch in silent admiration as he fashions the first block with a mere half-dozen rapid cuts. It is a perfect oblong, two feet by one and a half, and its six-inch thickness will shield them against winds that would penetrate their britches and their boots and kill them within a few hours.

While he cuts, Joe and the women begin a slow dance on the snow of the flat area, smoothing it. Johnson and Jamka join them, laughing at the solemnity of it, the near-religious rituality of the shuffling steps. When they have prepared an area some forty feet square, Joe takes his position at the corner nearest Hans's quarry, surveys the site for a moment, then stoops, and with the rounded end of his snow-knife draws a fifteen-foot circle in the snow. He sniffs the air, nods, and piles snow into the windward half of his circle till he has raise it a foot above the rest. Hans delivers the first snow-block and watches with professional interest while Joe sets it in its place and presses it hard down until it stands firm in the circumference of the circle. They leave it and walk together to the quarry. Joe cuts with an unhurried deftness that makes Hans seem clumsy. Within five minutes they have a tidy row of ten blocks, and shame has driven the sailors to the quarry bearing an assortment of knives and spades. Their first efforts are laughable and useless, but some, under Joe's patient instruction, gain enough skill to cut serviceable blocks, and they organise themselves into a proper work-gang.

Joe returns to the site with the crucial second block. Lovingly, he shaves and bevels it then sets it against the first, gently easing them both inward, glancing upward to calculate the slope, picturing the spot where the last block, rounded to fit the hole a foot above his head, will enclose him in the dome. He works his knife under the second block and removes a thin sliver of snow from its bottom edge before he raps it down hard against the first. He steps into the circle and the sailors deliver a steady supply of blocks, laughing as the little man gradually disappears behind the spiralling wall.

Hans instructs the less skilled masons in the simpler task of pointing the cracks with fine snow. In their eagerness they are clumsy, and more than once a heavy body stumbles against the structure, undoing the builder's handiwork. Yet before an hour has passed, Hans is shaping the last block, and delivering it to Kruger, the tallest of the labourers, for him to place gently into Joe's upstretched hands. When Joe's face appears at the bottom, grinning through his square doorway, they cheer, and Kruger pats his head.

Then three times more, with no pause, no discussion, he works the miracle, and the women prepare the interior of each dome as it is completed, squaring off the raised sleeping area, cutting the niches for lamps and implements, shaping the ice-windows, the fireplaces, the doors. After five hours, four huts are completed and habitable. Joe is ready enough to continue his labour, to complete the connecting passages and the outhouses, but Tyson orders him to rest.

And so, after a meal of bread and pemmican and coffee flavoured with chocolate, they spend their second night on the floe warm in their bellies and secure against the weather. The sailors' hut is larger than the others, but still offers room for them

14

to sleep only in tight-packed rows, herrings in a box, unable to turn, barely able to stretch. Only in the very middle of the floor is it possible for them to stand upright, and then only two or three of them at a time. Yet that night they sleep well, and in their exhaustion and joy at the accomplishment of the collaborative task, they consider it paradise.

And a week into their drift, with Joe continuing as architect and masterbuilder and Hans as his bricklayer, they have built their ice-village on the large floe and have rescued their belongings from the small one. In the brief moments of rest they have time to admire its snug intricacy: connected by a labyrinth of ice-tunnels are a store-house, a cook-house and four dwellings: for Tyson and Meyer, for the eight sailors, for Joe and Hannah and Puney, for Hans and Christiana and their brood of four. With food, they can live forever, no matter how low the mercury sinks.

It is difficult to know who are the forsaken ones: the fourteen aboard the crippled and wind-tossed *Polaris*, or these nineteen who inhabit a fragment of the pack some three miles in circumference. They are carried southward at an average rate of eight miles per day, faster or slower depending on whether wind and current are in harmony or in opposition. But current predominates, and it is always southward, always sunward, always toward Baffin Island and the Davis Strait, where the Scotch, English and Yankee whalers are thickly strewn in springtime. The floe is perpetually buffeted by bigger, higher, harder, faster-flowing icebergs, and relentlessly nipped and squeezed by the scouring pack. At any moment it might be shattered, sprung as if dynamited into a million fragments, and every second it shrinks, its edges at once rasped by the pack and melting as the water grows infinitesimally warmer.

Their ship, for all they know, is lost; their shipmates dead.

In their disharmony they mirror the disharmony of the *Polaris*, of the entire venture. Tyson is the solitary Yankee, as far as he knows the last living white American of an expedition that was to claim the North Pole for These United States. Herron the English steward and Jackson the black cook are his uncertain allies. Meyer, his fellow-officer, has long-since abandoned the attempt at closeness, and regards him with a settled contempt that stops just a curse short of plain mutiny. On every issue he sides with the Europeans – Kruger, Jamka, Lindquist, Johnson, Anthing – and on most he is the fomenter of bitterness.

For the Eskimos – Joe and Hannah with their adopted daughter, Hans and Christiana with their small tribe – Tyson is the last piece of Captain Hall. Their loyalty to the dead commander, through Tyson, keeps them on a piece of ice where they expect some day to be eaten.

Meyer, the man of education, the scientist, resents his inferiority of rank, and compensates for it by assuming a tone. Close confederacy with Dr Bessel from the outset has trained him, allowed him to perfect his technique and refine his sneer. His European accent has returned, snuffing out Maryland, and with the men he uses only German.

On the seventh day, Tyson wakes into a sudden panic, stirred by the echoing crack of and thud of axes on wood. He crawls to the doorway, and his movement wakens Meyer. In the grey light there are only ill-defined outlines to be seen, but it is enough. 'Dear God,' he says.

Meyer emerges from the hut and kneels beside him. 'Dear God, Meyer,' Tyson whispers.

Kruger's huge lumbering form is unmistakable. The two others, he guesses, are Anthing and Jamka. They have been hard at work for some time, and the object of their attack is now hardly recognisable as the twenty-foot whaleboat. Trying to rise, Tyson notices for the first time that Meyer is holding him by the left arm, a little above the elbow. In response to his frown, Meyer says, 'They're cold, Tyson. They need fuel for their fire; they need to cook their food.'

Tyson groans. 'The boat, Meyer. Dear Christ, the boat.'

Meyer nods. 'They see no need for two boats; they expect to be off Disco Island within two weeks. Heat is what they need now: they must stay alive for two more weeks.'

Tyson relaxes, no longer straining against Meyer's grip. He fights against the tears of rage. 'What have you been telling them, Meyer?'

'Nothing but what I believe to be true.'

Tyson groans. Their ignorance will destroy them all: abjectly he recalls the comic despair of Hannah as night after night she has tried to instruct them in the mysteries of the eskimo lamps that she and Christiana have improvised from pemmican tins, with canvas strips as wicking; but the management of the flame is beyond them – either they set the blubber ablaze, or drive themselves coughing from the igloo, taking flight from the black smoke, weeping the soot from their eyes. And now this.

Kruger has noticed them. He pauses in the act of raising the axe above his head. Theatrical in his defiance, he silently invites Tyson to admire, to intervene.

Meyer maintains his hold on Tyson's arm. 'The wood will give them two weeks of heat,' he says. 'They think by then they'll be walking to Disco. You must understand their view of it, Tyson.'

If there is a grin on Kruger's face, it is hidden behind his beard and the enveloping gloom. He brings the axe down on the whale-boat, demolishing the last of her planks. Tyson turns back to the doorway, and Meyer releases his arm. Inside the igloo, Tyson covers his face with his hands, shakes his head. 'Meyer, you must speak to them. You must save the other boat.'

Meyer risks a smile. 'I think they understand the need to keep one boat whole.'

'They understand nothing, Meyer. You must speak to them: you must speak German.'

In the formality of his tone, Meyer signals the end of the discussion. 'I'll speak to them, Mr Tyson.'

But as the days pass undifferentiated in their bleakness, they talk again. In the closeness of the igloo, under their shared oxhide, with nothing to be done, with Tyson too thinly dressed to venture forth and Meyer prevented by gales and fogs from making observations, they talk about everything, and as their world makes no distinction between night and day, sea and sky, work and rest, so their conversation makes none between the grossest matters of personal hygiene and the sublimest mysteries of creation.

Meyer the signaller-scientist is eager to distance himself from the seamen, the natives and Tyson alike; and science – much of it his rehash of Bessel's assertions – is the provider of distance.

Tyson, virtually naked when they parted from the *Polaris*, his spare britches stolen on the first night of their drift, stands in his ragged sealskin at the mercy of every draught and worries for his testicles. But there are moments of intimation even for him: icebergs, rendered unstable by the grinding pack, topple with shock-waves that rattle the million tons of their floe; clouds clear to reveal the myriad twinklings of the clearest firmament ever seen by human eyes; ghostly paraselenes – phantom moons – cancel hatreds and bring the whole company together for brief minutes of shared wonder; and night upon night they hear, not in their ears but in their hearts and bones, the silken music of the aurora. They watch it dance, and Meyer taunts Tyson with the glory of it.

'I suppose you regard it as a manifestation of the divine.'

Tyson does. 'Don't you, Mr Meyer?'

For Meyer it proclaims the failure of the North Polar Expedition, and Tyson does not disagree – but the scientist needs an argument.

'I question the wisdom, if not the existence, of a deity who has to patch and mend. He pitches this benighted land into endless night, then comforts the bears and the eskimos with pretty displays of electrical discharge.'

Tyson raises his hand toward the shimmering green and yellow curtain that sweeps across the southwestern sky. 'I feel no need to question this,' he says.

Meyer laughs and there is a hint of German, a delicate lacing of Doctor Bessel, in his reply. 'Not even to ask why He troubled to make the darkness and the desolation in the first place?'

Tyson wonders if the theological speculation will continue when the flesh has properly wasted from their bones, whether Meyer will still be interested in metaphysical pointscoring when they have eaten the last dog and are turning to the sledge-lashings and the lamp-oil. 'Precisely in order that he might make the display. This might be as close as we are allowed to looking him in the face,' he says.

Meyer has uncased his sextant, but begins now to pack it again. 'You might ask him in your prayers to spare us the divine front tomorrow. I can get no bearing on Cassiopeia tonight.'

With scant confidence in either the observer or his instrument, Tyson listens to the music.

Meyer prods: 'I find your view interesting, and typical of the seafaring breed. Didn't our late commander express similar sentiments?'

The barb is double: Tyson the superstitious sailor, Hall the Captain who never had a ship. Tyson controls his anger, measures his speech. He remembers Hall on the deck of the *Polaris* a year ago, on just such an October night as this, raising both hands to let the light stream through his fingers. He recites, as Hall did then:

Anon, as if a sudden trumpet spoke,
Banners of gold and purple were flung out;
Fire-crested leaders swept along the lines,
Which from the gorgeous depths, like meeting seas,
Rolled to wild battle.

'Yes, pretty,' Meyer says.

Tyson smiles, raises his arm again. 'Captain Hall knew this better than any civilised man on the globe.'

Meyer clicks shut the sextant-box. 'Agreed, but he hardly could be said to know it as a civilised man should. His knowledge was like that of the natives. If I understand Christiana correctly, it's the dancing souls of her ancestors.'

'The Captain always regretted their persistence in clinging to their pagan beliefs and practices.'

'Yet his own beliefs were hardly more advanced than theirs. And we'll say nothing of his practices, except to mention his relish of rotten blubber.'

'The Captain saw that here, as nowhere else in the world, the firmament does indeed show the handiwork of God.'

'Ah, Mr Tyson. You see the hand of the Creator; they see their dancing grandparents; the man of science sees an excitation of molecules.'

'Excited by whom?'

'The question does not interest us, since we have as yet no instruments that can detect the hand on the switch.'

Instruments. Tyson recalls the observatory at Thank God Harbor, seventy-nine degrees north: transit Instruments, sextants, theodolites, thermometers, anemometrers, psychrometers, hygrometers, barometers, chronometers, magnetometers, clinometers, pendula, dipping needles, spectroscopes, electroscopes, prismatic and magnetic compasses, isogonic charts. He plays his trump. 'I remember Doctor Bessel losing his way between the observatory and the ship – four hundred yards, I think – and Joe Ebierbing rescuing him, then Hans saving his ear with his hot savage breath.'

Meyer dismisses it as a cheap shot, and laughs. 'For the scientist, the true glory of the aurora is that he can observe its effect on the needle, measure it, and begin to realise that all things are connected – magnetism, galvanism, light itself – they are fluids that differ only in degree, not in kind. And rather than sit in dumbstruck awe, he strives to unravel the mystery, to find the connections.'

Tyson hears Bessel again in Meyer – the book-talk, the teasing intonation, the supercilious elongation of syllables, the pauses that seem designed to allow the slow understanding of the ignorant sailor to catch up. He presses home his advantage. 'Hans blew on his ear, remember? If he's still alive, he can thank Hans that he still has two ears. And your own eyelids froze solid on your way to the observatory, did they not?'

'That hardly proves ...'

'And you took twenty-eight hours once to walk to the Captain's grave. A single mile.'

Meyer concedes the preliminary skirmish, moves to the main campaign. 'The men are pushing me to do something.'

'What?'

'They want us to make for land soon, to the east, to the Greenland shore.'

Tyson sighs. 'We would all be dead before we were halfway there.'

'I can't agree. The wind has been steady northwest for seven days. If our point of separation was Northumberland Island, as I believe it was ...'

Tyson shakes his head. 'Meyer, I know Northumberland: there are jagged hills, a glacier. I've seen Northumberland.'

Meyer bristles at the affront to his competence. 'Mr Tyson, I made two observations, in perfect conditions, only two days before, on the thirteenth.'

They have had this same argument more than once before. Tyson would like to end it peremptorily, by a simple assertion of rank, but from the outset the scientists have succeeded in obscuring

20

distinctions. He sighs again. 'Did you have the almanac? Did you make the corrections?'

'Of course.

'Then there was something wrong with your instruments. The island we saw was Littleton, I'm sure of it.'

'You trust your sailor's nose above the finest instruments?'

'My sailor's nose and my man's eyes. They've been twenty years in these parts, and they know that the ice takes more heed of current than of wind, no matter how strong.'

Meyer stands up, and they begin to move toward the igloo. Tyson points to the west. 'We've been drifting *westward*, Meyer: on that I would stake my life. And in their present shape, the men would be dead within two days if they headed east.'

Meyer sees the opening. 'Their present shape is a result of your starvation rations, which they see as unnecessary.'

Tyson's tone becomes urgent. 'You must support me on that, Meyer, or we're all dead.'

'They think without the natives they could move faster.'

'Without the natives their end would be even quicker,' Tyson snorts. 'Surely they can see that? Surely they can't be so blind?'

He expects that Meyer will be the main source of the trouble that lies ahead, more dangerous than the worst of the sailors. From even before the separation the signaller has been suffering from swollen gums, rotten breath, stiff joints, fatigue, outbursts of wild melancholy – yet he has disdainfully refused Hannah's prescription of seal's blood. If the scurvy seems to have passed, Tyson worries still about its legacy – Meyer will read the sextant for what he wishes, for what he needs to see and what the men demand that he sees, and will use the comforting readings to consolidate his power. Already his position as quartermaster and his command of German are a threat to Tyson's command.

They complain bitterly about the distribution of the food. Risking everything, Tyson has mustered them after a week of reckless free-for-all and announced a regimen: eleven ounces, all told, for each adult, and five and a half for each child, to be measured by Meyer on scales improvised from a broken aneroid barometer and two pasteboard boxes, using lead shot for weights. They grumble: the diminutive eskimos need less than six-foot sailors; Charlie Polaris, permanently suckling at Christiana's ample breasts, needs nothing; the total allowance is too small. Tyson has no German, but he knows that Meyer has been filling their heads with stories of the eastward driving gales, convincing them that the Greenland shore is within reach, the call for Spartan economy unnecessary and womanish. Yet there remains, even after the year of licence that followed the death of Hall, a faint vestige of naval discipline. Weaponless and virtually naked, Tyson has raised his voice, reminded them of orders, invoked Hall's memory, pleaded his own Arctic credentials, and temporarily subdued the revolt.

The eskimos too, though staunch enough in their allegiance, question the need for providence. Two pounds of pemmican, six pounds of bread, four pounds of canned beef – any one of them, man woman or child, could devour the day's supply for all nineteen of the castaways at a sitting. Only *now* matters – and eating *now* ensures no leftovers for the bear, no scraps to be carried away by the next gale. Short rations are a notion as alien to them as the Holy Trinity. On the very night of Tyson's announcement, Eeka and Friedrich, the two thinnest dogs, are reported missing; but Joe and Hannah laugh at Tyson's concern and look toward Hans's igloo. There, Christiana has already scraped the skins and is drying them for child-mittens; Augustina is tickling Charlie Polaris' cheek with Friedrich's creamy tail, while Succi chews solemnly on the eyeballs and Charlie Polaris sucks the marrow from a leg-bone. Tyson knows the pointlessness of remonstration: Hans has managed the dogs, and now that they are of no use, too weak for bear-hunting, simply an extra pair of mouths, he feeds them to his family.

Tyson has argued the need with all of them. With fourteen cans of pemmican, one drum of dried apples, eleven bags of bread, thirteen hams, and no work to do, no exertion that will burn away the nourishment, they can live till midwinter – if the natives can eke the provision out and hold scurvy at bay with some fresh game. Not till then will they start to die.

The day of the killing of the dogs is the last day of the sun. The morning after is clear, but even by climbing a hummock Tyson fails to see the disc. The night that has fallen will last three months – longer, he fears, than some of the men. The need for seals is urgent. Without blubber there will be no fuel for their lamps or their stoves. Raw meat will do them no great harm, but the problem of thawing their drinking water will become desperate. Tyson has known similar deprivation before, but never with such a crew as this. For a year, they and their drifting shipmates on the *Polaris* have lived in lawless anarchy, with loyalties extending no further than the bound of the immediate clique at best, but more often stopping at the self. Eruptions of spite have been their daily routine, tetchy boredom their accustomed state. The camaraderie of the lower deck, which should sustain them now that their lives are in extreme peril, is utterly wanting. As Captain Budington once raided the liquor store, so they now raid the food supplies. Two months' rations of chocolate have been reduced overnight to a few crumbs, and Tyson lacks the authority either to institute an enquiry into the crime – often enough dealt with as a capital offence in such circumstances – or to set a watch against further depredations.

Their drift, mercifully, is toward the retreating sun. On 27th October they see the western shore nine miles off, and Tyson guesses it to be the unmapped coast of North Lincoln Land, the southernmost part of Ellesmere Island. Meyer shakes his head but offers no alternative. Joe and Hans have returned stoically empty-handed from the hunt, and hint at a drive for the shore. The men, wishing to believe that it is the opposite Greenland shore that is more attainable, respond sullenly to Tyson's urging, asking Meyer to confirm that what they see is indeed land. Meyer shrugs, refers them to Tyson, who is already by the boat, preparing for the heave. They position themselves slowly and their effort is halfhearted and truculently sluggish. By the time they have the boat launched, a thick fog has descended. Tyson, heartsick in the knowledge that his command has been further weakened by the failure, orders a retreat to the huts.

The effort lays them up. Under the oxhide, Tyson and Meyer achieve a measure of solidarity in their shared sickness. With neither dogmeat, like the natives, nor purloined supplies, like the sailors, they suffer most. A yard of movement costs Tyson an agony of groans, and he fears to remove a moccasin lest the toes come with it. Meyer shivers, loses all feeling in his limbs, endlessly tests his loose teeth with his tongue, prods his ulcers with his gloved fingertips. Hannah crawls through the connecting passage to minister to them, offering dog-broth from the last three animals. She rubs Tyson's shoulders under his ragged shirt and he yelps, doglike, with the pain and joy of it. She softens blubber with her teeth for them both to suck. She pounds Meyer's thighs with the sides of her hands; his penis stiffens and in his bouts of fevered sleep he dreams of Joe, the jealous husband, crawling through in the night to smother him with a sealskin.

Sometimes, warmed by the broth, touched by her cheerfulness, they laugh. Tyson recalls plump lecturers in Washington and New York assuring gawking audiences that the eskimo igloo is as cosy as their own parlours, and wishes them here to share this forty-below blackness. Then the bloodwarmth fades and they range through their intertwining grievances, rive themselves with anger and spite and overlapping paranoiac fears.

The small kindnesses survive. Tyson instructs Meyer in the benefits of freeing his arms from his upper garments to let them share the warmth of his body. And the ceaseless search for animal warmth, for a proximity of flesh under the buffalo and ox blankets, overrides mutual aversion. They apologise for sudden unguarded coughs, shifts in position that stir the air, recalcitrant knees that bruise unfleshed ribs.

In their recollection of the sixteen months that passed before the separation – the five in which they variously shared, envied and despised Hall's sublime dream, and the eleven of imprisonment under Budington's increasingly drunken and arbitrary regime – they differ most. Meyer has become habituated to scorn of the dead Captain, has shared in the men's jokes. As Hannah returns through the tunnel to Joe and Puney, he smirks at Tyson's groaning appreciation of her skill.

'I believe she performed such services for Captain Hall many times, in the privacy of their igloo on Baffin Island.'

Tyson is indignant, but exhausted. 'Both Hannah and Joe were devoted to Captain Hall.'

'Obviously. I'm thinking of the time when she saved his feet, you remember? When she took him under the bearskin and massaged his feet with her own for some hours.'

Hall has described the episode often enough, with a fervour and innocence that clearly marked its sexual ingenuousness, but the men have come to snigger at it. Tyson spurns the challenge,

24

and Meyer goads him further.

'I've read the Captain's account, and very affecting it is – he wished to enlist me as his amanuensis and literary assistant.'

'I recall,' Tyson says. 'But he changed his mind.'

'I refused,' Meyer sneers. 'It was hardly a job for a scientist.'

A sergeant, Tyson thinks. But there are other things, life and death things, and he wants to avoid a quarrel. 'You would earn my gratitude if you spoke to the men.'

'On what matter?'

'On the matter of economy, of husbandry. On the need for preserving supplies, if we are to see this business through.'

'I think you've made your view plain enough. What can I add to it?'

Tyson's anger is rising. 'You can speak to them in German. They refuse to respond to me.'

Meyer senses an advantage. 'It's hardly a matter of language. A starving man has no language. You may have forfeited your right to be listened to by showing too much favour to your native friends.'

Sensing Tyson's wrath, he adds, 'In the men's view.'

Tyson will not fight. 'That's where I need you: where we must work together. Explain why we need the natives.'

'To rub your shoulders?'

'To find meat. We'll reach the Strait, and there's meat there, but only they have the knowledge to find it and the hands to kill it. Dear God, the men can't even light the lamps!'

'There's the trouble. The men don't look to the Strait. They don't plan to be on this floe that long.'

'They must plan for it.'

'They expect soon to be due west of Disco, then they will cross the ice, to food and drink and women and double pay.'

'You must disabuse them of that. Disco is out of the question. You must make them understand.'

'That will not be easy. They think your strictures about short allowances are unnecessary.'

'Meyer, some of them can hardly walk. And think of your own condition.'

'Precisely. But on fuller rations they'd be stronger – can you see their reasoning?'

'Disabuse them, for God's sake.'

'I don't know if I have the power.'

'They must have the truth, Meyer. Disco is not in the reckoning, we're drifting south and west. Have you put the Greenland coast into their thoughts?'

'I've told them only what I believe, from the direction of the wind and my observations. I think the Greenland coast might be quite near.'

'Oh, God.' Tyson heaves himself into a sitting position. In the sputtering glow of the blubber-flame, Meyer looks already a corpse. 'On shifting ice, with a battered sextant, no chronometer, no almanac, no correction tables, no companion to verify the observation times, there can be no calculation of longitude that's better than the naked eye and guesswork.'

Stirred by the further affront to his professional skill, Meyer tries to rise, but his strength fails. He settles back to recover his breath for speech. 'On the contrary. I got an accurate reading of the lower culminations of the Pole Star and of Gamma Cassiopeiae only three days ago. You can read my notes: I've made the corrections.'

'How?'

'Mr Tyson, after a year of constant observation, four times every day, there isn't much need of the almanac. I have most of the corrections already in my diary, or in my head.'

'Damn your diary, Meyer. I've seen Carey Island, bearing south-east – sixty miles from us and sixty more to the Greenland coast. Any thought of Disco is suicide.'

Offended, Meyer becomes formal. 'Well, sir, we'll see if the men are prepared to put their trust in my instruments, or in your nose.'

'The men hear only what they wish to hear, and only in German. There's no double pay for corpses. They're past all reason.'

'I will observe the lunar transit tonight, if the sky is clear,' Meyer says, managing through the pain in his gums to muster a petulance of tone that closes the conversation.

Petulance, rancour, recrimination. Tyson has read the stories, mulled them many a night with Hall in the lamplight – Frobisher, Hudson, Fox, Ross, Parry, Franklin, Kane – and together they have traced the thread of bitterness: always, always, the mutinous murmurings, the recriminations, the wranglings over command, the factions. Always the official reports stuffed with lies.

'The darkness, the monotony of diet, the ice-wind, the Place: white men are not welcome,' Hall said. 'With the eskimos it is a sudden flare, a frown, a blow, and then they are either laying out a corpse or embracing and passing round the maktak and laughing about their moment of folly.'

'Like children,' Tyson replied.

Hall shook his head. 'They know. In this place, things cannot be allowed to fester, it's a luxury that cannot be afforded, and a lesson the white men can never learn. I had hoped that this expedition might be different.'

In his sad smile Tyson read resignation to death, conviction that he would never again walk the Connecticut shores.

Meyer is snoring fitfully, feverishly. It ought to be different, Tyson thinks. He recalls the nights at Thank God Harbor when the interludes of truce occurred, when the grand distinction of being the most northerly men on the planet and the awesome joy of charting the glittering heavens created a freemasonry of belonging that made friends of enemies; when the principal chronometer was shielded more tenderly than their own cheeks from the shocks of wind and cold. He recalls the nightly attempt to consummate the perfect reading, to capture the millisecond of a stellar transit; tries to envisage the isosceles triangle – man, star, man – whose base is two feet, whose equal sides are a million million miles; smiles at the joke of parcelling and processing the light that has travelled those miles, correcting it for aberration and mutation and refraction and dip and hoping it will some day add a dollar to your pay if it demonstrates another second of northing. Now, through Meyer's damaged and wobbling sextant it will complete the joke and kill them all. Meyer jerks out of sleep, unaware of his lapse. 'The moon is always easier,' he says.

Tyson is not sure if his companion is aware of what he is saying or merely rambling. He reminds him that the thermometer reads minus thirty, sixty-two degrees of frost, and that neither of them can take ten steps without pain.

'The moon is always easier,' Meyer says again.

'Someone is stealing the chocolate,' Tyson says. 'And the bread.'

27

The change of theme startles Meyer into wakefulness. 'We can't keep permanent watch,' he says.

'No, but we must speak to them. Speak to Kruger.'

'You've never liked Kruger, Tyson. You've made that plain from the beginning.'

'Herron saw him with the chocolate in his sleeve.'

'Then you have your man, don't you?'

Of the men on the floe, only Tyson is weaponless. Issued with pistols and rifles on the *Polaris* as a counter to boredom, the sailors have strutted the ice, potshotting at birds, seals, whales, foxes, icicles, stars – expending hundreds upon hundreds of balls and generally hitting nothing. Meyer knows that to confront the thief is beyond Tyson's power: a mere request to be shot. He goads. 'The men see no more reason to share the chocolate than the natives to share the titbits from the seals.'

Tyson sighs. 'Joe sat twelve hours at the breathing-hole.'

'The heart should have been counted as part of his ration. And the eyes. He gave them to Hans's brats without consulting the men.'

Tyson's irritation penetrates to his bones. They have covered this ground before.

'Joe is out every day, however low the mercury, however strong the wind. He sits ten or twelve hours on the ice, waiting for an animal to rise, while the men play cards and trade fantasies about double pay and the rum and the women at Disco. In God's name, Meyer!'

Meyer interrupts. 'He has his relief, as the men have not. Hannah is less ugly than the generality of her kind, even if she smells as strong as the worst.'

Tyson cannot comment on the offensiveness of the remark. As often as any of them, he has remarked on the assault to the nose that the white man suffers when he enters an igloo. Of them all, only Hall had been able to endure it, had indeed revelled in it. Remembering Hannah's tireless attention to them both, stirred by the guilt of ingratitude, he makes a small effort in defence of the natives.

'Niceness of toilet can hardly figure large in their minds, any more than in yours or mine in our present condition.'

'Indeed. And I'm reminded that the men have been more *fleissig*, more busy, than you give them credit for. Some of them, under the direction of our good little Hans, have been enlarging their living quarters. They tell me there is now ample room, if I want to share with them.'

They both now recognise that it is an important moment, signalling the end of whatever gentlemanly distinction had been maintained during the month spent on their five hundred acres of ice. Now it will be Tyson and the natives in permanent opposition to Meyer and the German seamen, with Herron the Englishman and Jackson the negro frightened and trapped somewhere between. Isolated, inescapably bound to the eskimos, he will hear his assertions of rank ringing hollowly against the engulfing bergs; the men will act as they please and Meyer, his prickliness increasing, will encourage them in their folly and offer nothing to counter Kruger's criminal influence. Since the *Polaris* may have gone to the bottom with their fourteen shipmates, he is on the cusp, and his is the final voice. His response now will determine whether the United States North Polar Expedition is to continue as an enterprise sanctioned by Ulysses S. Grant and wrapped in the sacred flag, or whether it will become an ungovernable rabble, a cauldron of competing appetites.

Yet he knows that shared body-heat and a handful of agreeable memories are not enough; it cannot last with Meyer. He tries to make the best of it.

'It might be advisable. There is folly hatching, and you might be the voice of prudence.'

Meyer laughs at the prim word, sniggers through his ulcered gums at its jar against the ghostly music of the Arctic sky, the grinding of the pack, the gnawing of their empty stomachs.

Tyson presses. 'They've already broken up one of the boats for fuel. If they break the other, we're dead.'

'That's not the way they see it,' he repeats. 'They expect within a few days to be within striking distance of Disco.'

'That expectation will kill us all, unless...'

'You've made your opinion on that matter clear. I tell you, I had a good sighting on Gamma Cassiopeiae. I know where we are.'

'You'll kill us, Meyer. Before God, you'll kill us. Make sure, at least, that they preserve the boat.'

'Don't worry on that score. They're sailors.'

'And for God's sake, remind them that without Joe and Hans we would all have starved by now.'

'A difficult proof. They see two women and five children – all of them a hindrance when we make the drive for land, whether east or west.'

'They're frightened. They think Kruger wants to kill them, eat the children.'

Meyer tries to laugh again, but the effort hurts his joints. 'I don't think we've come to that pass, yet.'

'Move in with them, Meyer. Do what you can, and remember we're Christians.'

'There's room for you too,' Meyer says.

'I think Joe and Hannah would like me to move in with them.'

The moment come, Meyer cannot refrain from marking it with a jibe. 'Yes, and Hannah will maybe warm your feet for you, as she did for Captain Hall.'

UNITED STATES NAVY BOARD OF INQUIRY, ON BOARD
USS TALAPOOSA, OCTOBER 11TH, 1873 GEORGE
ROBESON, NAVY SECRETARY, PRESIDING

Testimony of John W. Booth, Fireman

Q   Was Captain Budington drunk at the time you were beset
in the ice?

A   Yes sir, he was. Not on rum, but on the doctor's alcohol.

Q   How do you know that?

A   The doctor caught him at it, and they had quite a tussle
together.

Q   How do you mean, a tussle? Do you mean violence?

A   No, sir; not serious violence, to speak of. I believe the
Captain might have taken him by the collar, and raised his
voice.

Q   How did you know of this?

A   Everyone knew of it, sir. It was no secret.

Q   In your opinion, was his drunkenness a cause of your being
beset?

A   No sir, it was not.

Q   Then what do you think was the cause?

A   The ice was the cause, sir. The ice was the cause of
everything.

Testimony of Noah Hays, Seaman

Q   Did you ever see Captain Budington drunk?

A   Captain Budington was drunk very often, every day after
the Commander died.

Testimony of William Morton, Second Mate

Q   To your knowledge, did the Captain ever drink?

31

John McGill

A   He did, both before and after Captain Hall's death.

Q   And did you see him drunk?

A   Captain Budington, if he drinks at all, must get drunk.

Q   You mean he drank with a purpose to get drunk, or he has a poor head for drink?

A   I mean both, sir.

CHAPTER THREE
QUESTING: DOUBTS AND LIES

Charles Francis Hall lived the eskimo life longer than any white man on the planet, and lived it with a relish that set him apart from the rest. He had started, like Kane before him, with a search for the bones of Franklin's men – the hundred and twenty-nine British seaman who had disappeared with *Erebus* and *Terror* in 1845 on a mighty quest for the Northwest Passage. Better than Kane, he found a few, and for a while entertained hopes of turning up some more with the living flesh still on them – a sailor or two gone native in King William Land, waiting for Christian succour. There were bones, spoons, scissors, snuff boxes, bits and pieces by the sackful, and a million stories of battles, burials, cannibal feasts, all of which he believed.

After seven years among the Inuit and four thousand miles of dog-sledging, he became a thing of the north, oppressed by the softness of the Connecticut sun, affronted by the tenderness of roast beef. He breathed easiest in the fetid intimacy of igloo life, inhaled loudly the rankness of soot and year-old blubber and unwashed humanity when others retched at the first whiff. Invited to share a blanket with unsorted groups of men, women, boys, girls, he did so, losing his sexual delicacy after the first eight or nine occasions. Joe and Hannah had been his Man and Woman Friday for eleven years; he had made them the most famous eskimos in the world, and with their help he persuaded Congress and the President to part with thousands of dollars in the hope that the Sacred Banner fluttering at the top of the world might help to heal the wounds of Gettysburg.

With three days of August left, the hopes of the United States North Polar Expedition were high. The *Polaris* stood at the entrance to Kane's Basin, her prow about to cut the seventy-ninth parallel, and the way ahead clear. Budington, ice-master, drunkard and one-time friend, addressed the officers' conference and made his play plain enough: he could not be responsible for the safety of the ship beyond Foulke Fiord, already a week south of them, and recommended a retreat to that haven, where the vessel could be made secure and preparations made for those who felt the need to dash for the Pole by sledge. Hall kept his voice soft, but fell into his customary high tone and reminded the ice-master that they should all feel such a need, that the sole (Bessel coughed at the word and he acknowledged the polite objection with a nod) or, at least, the primary object of the expedition was the placing of the Stars and Stripes at the still point of the turning globe, and that Providence had afforded them the opportunity to do so now, in 1871, by laying on conditions more favourable than anyone had recorded in the last forty years. Eighteen years before, in this latitude, Kane had seen a prodigious moving rampart of ice bearing down on the *Advance*, while only that morning Bill Morton had reported from the crow's nest dark channels of clear water wending Polewards beyond the horizon, and dark skies far to the north.

Budington straightened himself in his chair, shook his head. 'Morton sees what he wants to see, as he saw what Kane wanted him to see. I know ice, Mr Hall. It is not simply a matter of watching.'

Hall turned to Tyson for support, and the assistant navigator entered the fray willingly. 'There has been some groaning, but Mr Budington must have experienced a thousand times worse, in ships less able to withstand the squeeze. I find his fears ...'

They waited for his word, for the accusation of cowardice that would have sparked a proper fight. He looked to the commander for encouragement, found it in his eyes, and said, '... puerile.'

Budington's fist struck the table, shaking the glasses. Hall laid a conciliatory hand on the ice-master's sleeve, but did not rebuke Tyson. 'Think, Sidney,' he said. 'A generation might pass before the ice is as friendly again: a hundred years might pass. We are perhaps singled out to be the first and only men to sail the waters of the Open Polar Sea. I cannot believe that even you are unmoved by that prospect, that your heart does not quicken at the thought.'

His hand remained where he had placed it, and under it, Budington's fist tightened. 'Am I to take it, sir, that you add the charge of cowardice to the insults you have already heaped upon me? Do you share Mr Tyson's contempt for my judgement?'

Hall smiled, but when he spoke, his tone was formal. 'No, Mr Budington, you are not to take it. Your advice has been received, and considered, and respected. But consultation with Mr Tyson,

Mr Chester and the scientific officers has persuaded me that the opportunity to take the *Polaris* into Kane Basin and possibly to the Polar Sea itself is not to be spurned. We owe it to the President and to the nation.'

Budington looked to Tyson, then back to Hall. They had already had their arguments about the limits of Tyson's authority, and he was sober enough not to re-open old wounds. 'That being the case, sir, I will inform the engineer.'

Hall lifted his hand from Budington's sleeve. 'I thank you, Mr Budington. My confidence in your capabilities is absolute, and you are assured that you will receive full credit for the achievement when the *Polaris* ploughs waves unploughed by any vessel before her.'

Budington nodded his bitter thanks. The officers stood, and he and Tyson stepped back together, ready to leave, but Hall asked Tyson for a further five minutes of his time.

With Budington and the others gone from the cabin, Tyson sat again in response to Hall's silent gesture, but he felt no relaxation in the air until Hall had assured himself that the ice-master had climbed the companionway to the quarterdeck. Even then, the commander spoke in lowered tones.

'I need you, George.'

'Sir?'

'I've been too indulgent. The man should have been returned to Brooklyn in irons before we left Disco.'

It was not Tyson's place or prerogative to join in criticism of his superiors. 'I think he has the safety of the ship and crew at the front of his mind, sir.'

Hall acknowledged the soft rebuke, smiling at Tyson's stubborn generosity. They had both sailed with Budington before. 'I don't doubt it, not for a moment. But we are not mere sailors, are we? And this is not a whale hunt, still less a pleasure cruise.'

Tyson accepted the invitation to presume on their friendship. 'It might be to our advantage, sir, to have someone who speaks for the ship and crew, if only to provide a cautionary voice.'

Hall shook his head, 'You mistrust my enthusiasm, George. Do you think me a Don Quixote?'

'No, sir. For my part, if we can take the *Polaris* to the Polar Sea; or to the Pole itself, I want to be there with you. But there are some who …'

Unsure how far he might take the presumption, he waited until Hall urged: 'Tell me the whole of it, George.'

'… are less fired-up than others. Less enraptured, and less committed to the goal.'

Hall sighed. 'Queer sort of explorers, eh?' They laughed. Tyson nodded at the papers strewn over the Captain's table, and risked a small joke.

'I might have thought you'd be in a hurry to lay the ship up, in order to pursue your literary endeavours.'

Hall spread his stout fingers on the papers. 'These? No, George; these are simply notes, jottings of the day's events. I left the papers at Disco.'

Tyson frowned. 'Your book?'

'My book. Five years of my life. I left them with Governor Smith.'

Responding to Tyson's frown, he said, 'Yes, I had hoped to fill the void of the polar nights by writing up my Franklin search, but the events at Disco gave me cause for doubt.'

'What manner of doubt, sir?'

'All manner. Mr Meyer could not see fit to assist me. He complained that his duties as meteorologist would not allow him the time.'

Again, Tyson felt the coaxing, the hint that he might overstep his authority, join in criticism of fellow-officers. Meyer too, the unspoken argument ran, should have been clamped in irons, but he would have taken the Germans with him, and the expedition would have collapsed in ignominious failure before the first ice-berg. So he stayed, diligent enough in performing his scientific duties but shamelessly insolent, overtly fomenting trouble and encouraging insubordination on the lower deck.

'Besides,' Hall continued wryly, 'my roughness of style has been frequently remarked upon, and I reckoned the comfort of my study in Groton would be more conducive to the composition of a masterpiece. There will be work enough in the next two years.'

With that there could be no demur. But in the calculation of two years, Tyson saw the certainty of failure. The crew of the *Polaris* was not the stuff to endure two years of ice. Dutifully, he made his encouraging noise. 'The *Polaris* has already taken us past Kane's winter quarters, sir. Before the month is out, we might be standing on the shore of the Polar Sea.'

'We ought to call it Tyson's Sea, George, but the Secretary of the Navy might feel slighted. Look.' He pushed a piece of paper to the edge of the table, turned for Tyson to read without lifting it. 'My dispatch from Tossac to the Secretary. As pretty a piece of prevarication as you'll find.'

Tyson read, imagining Mr Robeson's Yankee pride as he handed it to the President: a message full of hope – mild frustration over the price of dogs, manly rage at the refusal of the Dane Jansen to join the expedition – but also joy at the signing of the eskimo Hans, Kane's famous and trusted companion, for three hundred per annum; at the swelling heaps of coal; at the harmony and good health of all aboard.

Laying the paper back on the table, Tyson thought only of what was not there: the sailing-master's raids on the liquor store at Goodhavn; the unconcealed abuse of the commander by Bessel and Meyer, his chief scientists; the periodic refusal of the German sailors to show him the respect due to a commander of a vessel of the United States Navy; their mockery of his religious fervour, his language, his inexperience, his insufficient education; the offers of resignation, whispers of mutiny; the threats of Captain Davenport to take half of them back from Goodhavn in the USS *Congress* in hard iron and ineradicable disgrace. A sorry catalogue. He had looked forward himself to a share in the getting-up of Hall's book about his adventures among the King William Land eskimos between '64 and '69, had enjoyed the prospect of having a small hand in a new *Robinson Crusoe*, better than the other because its fantastic escapes and its sublime wonders would be unadulterated truth. Now, as Hall's face relaxed into unguarded and patent misery, he realised that as far as his captain was concerned, the North Pole might have been a far-flung asteroid, so firm was his premonition of failure, so low even his expectation of seeing Navy Yard again, of handing Ulysses S. Grant a pebble from the most northern shore in the world.

He looked at Hall's sunken shoulders and saw a dead man. And in his captain's death, he saw his own.

CHAPTER FOUR
DRIFTING: JOE AND HANNAH LET THE CHECKERS DECIDE

Joe sits. Cassiopeia wheels. In the thin moonlight, in the sharp silence, the harpoon is better than the Springfield rifle. Six hours he sits, though he does not count hours or particularly mark Cassiopeia's quarter-circling of the Star.

He has sat, this Joe, on gilt-surrounded plush, sipped tea with the Empress of India, sucked partridge bones with the Prince Consort.

Now he perches on his ice-stool and time is not circling stars but the chants he composes to the rhythm of his own slow heartbeat. Under him he feels walrus and narwhal and the variegated seal tribes – the Greenland, the ringed, the thunder-headed oogjook – and he selects one, a small shiny spotted Greenlander, and enters him and bloodtalks to him. He sees the heart which he will remove and eat the instant the seal is on its back by the hole, as his payment for the frozen hours. He chews a piece of flipper, spit-softened by Hannah, and his chewing too finds the rhythm of his silent chant as his heartbeat tunes to the seal's pulsing blood:

Come to the breathing hole, little brother,
Come to the breathing hole, little friend,
My harpoon-head is worried.
Let me see your head here, above the ice,
Little bowl of blood-soup, little blubber-feast, little shitbag,
I'll chew your heart, Tookolito will lick your liver,
Puney will suck your warm eyes. Yes – the breathing hole,
little friend,
Show your nose to the moon, little brother.

There is no wind, no grinding of the ice. But there is movement up high, a dance of moonlit clouds and a noise of starsong that slips under his chant. He sleeps with eyes and ears open, focused on the two-inch hole. Eyes, nose, ears, fingertips – they work unbidden, like his singing blood, and his mind is free for pictures, memories, anticipations.

Hannah's wise feet, famous for having massaged Captain

Hall's frozen ones and thereby saving his toes. At lectures in five states she bowed to the applause while Hall introduced her and her feet, pronouncing her real name with romantic slow emphasis: Ladies and gentlemen – *Tookolito*.

These feet are cleverer than the ladies and gentlemen or Hall or Budington or Tyson or the scientists can ever know. Joe makes pictures: in the sweet blubbery warmth under the bearskin her toes coax and tease his oosook (which even now in his half-starved state rises to the memory, salutes their cunning) while his fingers and hers meet between her thighs in the warmest haven in the igloo. Beside them, Puney grunts her irritation and hunger and Captain Tyson knows nothing.

Tyson has told him the temperature is minus fourteen, forty-four degrees of frost, too cold for the hunt. But he has gone because the wind has died and because Puney has sobbed, and because there is a clear sky and moonlight too bright to be wasted. The moonlight is sharper, reveals more than the hour and a half of noon twilight. Within an hour his heart and fingertips are synchronised to the ghostly frolickings under the ice while his head roams free. There is a parade of feasts in his skull – deep red oogjook soup, delicate sweet walrus liver, a comically small chewy oosook from Nanuk the ice-bear, blankets of maktak fresh from the whale, warming the gums and the throat. Then satiation, and Hannah laughing under the skins as she steers his oosook from her ribs to friendlier shores.

It is not only Hannah who fills his head: there is Nananuak, ten years younger and still unbreached when Utak, her angakok, offered to procure her for him, urged him to throw Hannah out because her children always died and she was no longer fresh fat, no longer a merry fuck. He was cited the example of Ugack, his mother's brother, twenty-wived and still a fearsome hunter after sixty-eight winters, and he was tempted, but Hannah howled and reminded him of England, of their proper Christian marriage in Mr Bolby's house, of strolling down the Strand with his umbrella, of the Prince Regent's groaning and glittering table. Then she offered the blandishments of more and better in the United States, among senators and newspaper proprietors and crinolined wives and the President. Finally she knitted him socks of American wool and made his oosook dance and sing time after time through two rounds of the midsummer sun, telling him he was a mighty hunter whose thunderstick would be wasted on the skinny slut Nananuak.

Hannah knits and reads books and drinks weak tea and stirs the tune of *Rock of Ages* into her spring-chant and laughs imperiously, in the face of Joe's nervous anger, at Utak or any other witch-doctor. Their gilyas and their spells hold no fear for her – a woman such as she is not a trading-good, nor will she share his juice with the first smooth-skinned virgin slut who happens along. She laughs still, but in the laugh there is the sorrow of a woman whose children die, mixed with a light wheeze that reminds him of the importunate whimpering of the pups at the igloo door. Sometimes too there is a faint hollow rattle that tells them both she will die young. They have accepted this, as he accepts now that with Hall dead, the ship gone, Mr Tyson unable to command the sailors, they will all die young, and Charlie Polaris will not witness a full cycle of half-year night, half-year day.

Tyson and Meyer will not save them. They argue over latitude and longitude, the reliability of the battered sextant, the skill of Meyer's readings. Neither deigns to consult the Real People but Joe and Hans know without compass or sextant that in a few days they will be at the latitude of the beach where Joe's people often camp, and within striking distance. Hannah knows too, and knows what is in the Real Men's minds.

Natchek: the little seal. Through the sole of his right foot he feels the stirring, the pulsing of its heart, quicker than his own now but still in harmony. He feels the urgency and the pain in its lungs as it smells out the breathing-hole. His left hand involuntarily moves to his ankle, checking that the harpoon line is still attached, still secure. After six hours of somnolence, in forty-six degrees of frost, his body can still react on the instant to the glint of moonlight on the seal's nose. If it has smelt him, as it doubtless has, still it needs to breathe.

The half-second of nose is enough for his feet, his fingertips. He strikes hard, not straight downwards, but at the gentle slant that will increase his chance of holding the seal. The harpoon-head is his only one, the sailors having destroyed the others to make infantile throwing spears; to lose it now would kill them all. He drives it neatly through the skull to the back of the neck and into the ice. In its death-thrashings the hundred-pound beast might break the shaft and sink to perish under the ice, beyond his reach. Feverish in his speed now but cool and unhurried in the precise drill of what has to be done, he grips the shaft in his left hand, his knife in his right, and digs. Twelve cuts of the knife widen the hole enough for him to heave the head clear of the ice-surface, and the fear of failure in his heartbeat begins to soften, to transmute. There is a singing joy in his ribs as he drags the writhing body on to the ice. On its back, its belly catching the moonlight, its lungs rattling in their final exhalations, the seal looks piteously small, hardly a meal for himself and Hannah and Puney, though he knows it will be cut into eighteen pieces. He tunes into the last throbs of its blood, apologises to its drifting spirit. The heart still flutters. He kneels on the ice and presses with both hands on the white chest, stopping the pulse; with the last flicker his own fever subsides and he begins to calculate.

His by right, that heart; his, by all the justices under the stars. Kneeling by the carcass that will be solid within half an hour, he is beset by hunger, by the urge to slip his knife into the chest and remove the heart whole and transfer it to himself. The thought fills his mouth and throat and belly; the knifepoint hovers over the whiteness.

Then new pictures come: Kruger, eternally bitter, waving his cocked pistols, promising a bullet each for Joe, Hannah, Puney, all of them, threatening with his eyes to eat Charlie Polaris, pointing out the empty chest cavity of the seal and calculating the weight of the missing heart as the entire eskimo share. Nothing for Hannah, nothing for Puney, nothing for Hans and Christiana. Frightened by the pictures, he loops his line around the seal's flippers to drag it whole back to the huts, where he and Hans and their families will have to be content with their unfair portion.

They will, however, allow him the eyes for Tobias and Puney. That little, the infants' moiety, they still concede, laughing at the barbarity of it, marvelling at the contentment on the children's faces as they suck. With the handle of his knife he presses out the left eyeball into his mitten. For Tobias. As he picks out the other he smiles, picturing Puney's happiness when he pushes it between her lips.

It is three or four in the morning but everyone is awake, there being no day, no night. The joy when they discover that the hunt has been successful, that meat is being dragged across the floe, changes to accusatory disappointment at the sight of the little Greenlander: hardly seventy pounds of it, they calculate. Kruger unhitches the body and checks it, assuring himself that the chest is intact, the organs still there. He organises the share-out, for which Joe and Hans are allowed into the men's hut, the house they planned and built. Acknowledging Joe's dexterity, he hands him the knife, points to the meat. Joe swiftly removes the brain, liver, heart. Kruger takes the knife and cuts them each into sixteen pieces, fourteen for the adults, two to be shared among the four children. There is no ration for the infant Charlie Polaris and no concession to Christiana, the suckling mother.

Lindquist, using the ladle fashioned by Hans from a bear-bone, scoops the blood from the body cavity into a pemmican tin, which is passed round the circle of men. Excluded from this circle, resentful that their women and children are denied the warmth-giving soup, Joe and Hans know that to protest would be worse than useless – perhaps fatal. The thick blood raises the spirits of the men and the mood becomes festive, with a conviviality that almost extends to the natives. Jamka holds the tin aloft, shapes as if to drain it in a single swallow, as he might have done at the beer festival in Kiel. He toasts Joe. 'You are a clever little fellow, Joe. I hope your little lady rewards you well.' The sailors laugh, and Lindquist lewdly rocks his shoulders and mouths Joe's noise – *ei-ei-ei* – while Anthing responds with Hannah's *aaoo-aaoo-aaoo*; their igloo-joke. Through the laughter there is grudging acknowledgement that this Joe, this half-starved savage, is their provider for as long as they remain trapped on the floe, and their admiration for his prowess is genuine enough.

The cry is taken up – *aaoo-aaoo-aaoo*. It continues to grow louder and wilder until Tyson, querulous in his distaste, orders Linquist to call the names, reminding him not to neglect the absent women and children. Within five minutes Joe has sectioned the meat and removed the skin. Kruger arranges the portions on the shelf and lifts them singly as Linquist calls the names in random order. The children are called as 'pair one' and 'pair two.' As soon as their share has been issued, Joe and Hans crawl through the passageway to Hans's hut. The women have already boiled water over the lamps. For the two families, the pleasure of smelling the cooking meat is part of the meal. They wait patiently enough, staying their hunger by chewing pieces of old leather from the floor of the hut. Hans and Christiana happily concede the seal's right eye as Puney's titbit, female though she is, and she and Tobias lie on their backs and suck loudly.

Next door the sailors, unskilled in using the blubberlamps and driven by their hunger, devour their portions raw, pausing only to compare, and to complain of imagined injustices in the division of the meat. Tyson crawls into the eskimos' hut, offering his portion for the pot then squeezing into the space made for him between Joe and Hannah, the warmest refuge in the igloo. Puney swallows the last of the eyeball and crawls across the skins to curl into his lap, shaping her body to fill the hollows.

'I'm so hungry, Mr Tyson,' she says, and falls asleep.

The three pounds of sealmeat more than doubles their fare for the day – their sad scraps of ham, pemmican and biscuit – so the sense of expectation is strong, the excitement palpable. There will be rich scalding soup followed by tender meat. The entrails they will allow to freeze for later, when the pangs begin to hurt again.

Puney snuggles deeper into Tyson's chest. Her smell – grease and blood and urine and sweat – comforts him. She wakens and Joe reaches across to put a piece of blubber into her mouth. Idly she picks her nose, sucks the stuff from her finger to mix it with the blubber, whimpers. There was a time when Tyson might have retched, might have chided her, but it is long gone. Privation, as the sailors have frequently remarked, has not levelled them. Tyson's skin hurts where it is stretched across his fleshless shoulders and hips. Offered a mirror, he would refuse to look. The eskimos, who have had more fat on the frames to begin with, who keep a supply of fresh water melted from the ice for constant sipping, who have eaten dogs, flippers, lice, birdclaws and the sooty residues of oil lamps, are still on the edge of plumpness, still oily. But they cough and spit perpetually, and Hannah rattles. A meal that might once have been riotously enhanced by Joe's account of the hunt, the blood-chant, the final thrust of the harpoon, is taken in a silence punctuated only by coughs and belches and farts. Warmed by Puney's body, his ache stilled by the juice of the blubber, Tyson

43

settles back against the iglerk – Hans's neatly sculpted ice-couch
– and drifts into the customary dreams of beefsteak, beer, linen
sheets, soft white arms.

After soup and tender stew, Joe and Hannah and Puney and
Tyson crawl through to their house. Tyson, despite Hannah's
warning, has eaten too quickly – causing indigestion and a fear
of bowel trouble in the night. After seven hours at the breathing-
hole and the effort of killing, dragging and butchering the seal,
Joe should be ready for sleep, but he wants checkers. Hannah
shakes her head, but reaches for the sealskin that serves as their
board. 'White for you,' she says.

The white pieces are disciplined, almost uniform, carved
from seal-bones. The black are a ragged army of stones, charred
bones, buttons, wood fragments. As with most things of the
brain, Hannah is quicker. She might win all the games, but does
not choose to, having her own reasons for losing the round half
of them. While the Germans next door play skat for imaginary
fortunes in silver dollars and golden crowns, Hannah and Joe let
the brief tussles and skirmishes of the checkerboard determine
the tactics of their night's sport under the ox-hides. And sport
it still is: if Hannah has wobbled through marble halls in silken
gown and crinoline and Joe has tapped his gentleman's brolly on
the pavement of the Strand, still they have not forgotten that a
meal, even such a meagre one as this, must be celebrated, and
that under the hides they are Ebierbing and Tooklotito – he of the
thundering oosook, she of the welcoming warm ootchook, and
not Captain Hall nor the Prince Regent nor the shy Mr Tyson
can silence the music they make together, or still the dance. Joe,
white, enters another trap, allowing Hannah's button to capture
two of his bones and breach the double corner.

'Ei-ei-ei,' he says, dropping his head. 'I'm a poor sort of hunter,
a poor little hare-shit. The seals laugh at me under the ice.'

She slaps his knee. 'No, no. You're a mighty warrior, a bear.
You feed your family well.'

He shrugs. 'I did once. Now I'm old; my knife is blunt.'

'No, little bear. Your knife is sharp, and your harpoon always
finds the mark.'

'Ei-ei-ei. Find yourself a younger man, with sharper tools.'

'Young men are tasteless. I like my maktak well matured, well rotted. Every woman does.'

'You should warm Mr Tyson tonight.'

Tyson recognises his name, tries to read their faces as they giggle and look in his direction. Succeeding too well, he looks down.

Hannah pouts. 'I don't think Mr Tyson is interested, I don't think the *kabloona* is skilled with the harpoon.'

Joe persists in his ritual self-deprecation. 'Ei. Maybe you should visit next door. Hans's belly is cold.'

She snorts. 'Hans is not a man yet. He can't find his way to the katak, he gets lost in the entrance-tunnel.' Laughing at her own joke, she coughs, splutters, coughs again and loses control of her chest until Tyson thinks she has to burst, so wild is the hawking, the wheezing, the spitting. But she recovers, laughs at Joe's feigned anger as he resigns from the game, sets up the pieces again with herself as white.

Their sojourns in brick and stone have taught them that the *kabloona* at once despises and envies them, is repelled and intrigued. The things they revel in most are the things he most despises; for their most inconsequential attributes he reserves his highest praise. In turn, they draw limits around their admiration for the *kabloona*. Locomotives and gaslight and Buckingham Palace notwithstanding, there are things they, the Real People, know better. The passageway between the igloos is a chaos of filth – bones, tatters of clothing, spent cartridges, broken knife-blades, cast-off lids from pemmican tins. The *kabloonas* can never appreciate the difference between the ordered clutter of the eskimo igloo and this dangerous detritus that can cut, maim, infect, kill. In 'going native' they have abandoned their nautical tidiness, forgotten how skilfully each had once ordered his square foot of the lower deck, but have gained nothing of the assurance of the Real People, who can reach out in the dark and find whatever is required – knife, tobacco, chamber-pot, fish-head, lampwick, louse-trap, nose-rag. For Joe and Hannah, despair has turned to amused resignation. 'You might damage your crinoline in that passageway,' he tells her.

Their marital jokes have acquired layers: Hall has made Hannah famous by describing how she appeared at his tent door in wildest Baffin resplendent in crinoline and muslin gown to offer him tea, strong or weak. The sailors know the story and tease her with it; she herself has come to view it sardonically, has asked the Boston ladies how they imagined their fashion-sense might fare in a gale at forty below, and has long since put the crinoline to good use as needles, spoons, checker men, backscratchers. When it was whole they laughed over its function – was it fashioned to keep the man in? Occasionally, in a fit of irritation and contempt, she cleanses the passageway and marvels at its filth. 'They call us dirty,' she says.

The dull ochre glow of the blubberlamp is generous to her features. Even the Germans remark that by the yardstick of her kind, she is comely – no pudding. But the laughter lines and pain lines have over the years filled with soot, and so have her lungs. In daylight, her face is a sad tattoo; yet she smiles. The sailors might refer in their jokes to her bovinity, but she beats them in checkers, stitches their boots with unnatural skill, speaks English better than the best of them, reads, talks familiarly of Mr Gladstone, General Grant, house prices in Groton. Her hair, the glory of even the most slatternly eskimo female, is lustreless and unbrushed because still, for the luck they will need if they are to survive their drift, she adheres to the taboo – no combing while the men hunt seal – and either Joe or Hans or both will be hunting most hours of the day. If she smells of rottenness, so do they all. With the constant prospect of the floe breaking up, the line of water appearing through the middle of an igloo, not even the eskimos undress for sleep. They will wear, all nineteen of them, the same underthings for the seven months they will need to reach the whaling-grounds.

Yet, under the hides, they find ways; Ebierbing and Tookolito find ways. The checkers decide, the loser in seven games to take on the work of easing off britches and undershirts, assuming the uppermost position, disposing the limbs. She compromises her superior skill in answer to the need: if the hunt has been successful, his muscles will glow and the blood-soup will grant him strength to overcome the exhaustion and the rheumatism, swell and stiffen his harpoon-shaft till her stubby fingers can hardly encircle it; so she will let him win, confirm his manliness and his superiority to all of them – Tyson, the Germans, Hans. And their couplings are not bound by bizarre *kabloona* notions of rationing: only sleep brings an end. Cast adrift to the virtual certainty of death, with each choice grimmer than the one before – to be crushed between icebergs, to starve, to drown, to be killed in a hopeless defence of their children against the hunger-crazed sailors, to be brained in the night and have their hearts and livers ripped out for food – they squeeze and suck and devour the moment. Small concessions are made to the presence of Tyson, the thickness of a buffalo hide from their threshing; a dampening of giggles, a slowing of buttocks, stifling of grunts. But Hannah can never fully subdue her gasp, her *au-au-au*, at the moment of release. Always, that has come from somewhere else, somewhere beyond her management. That *au-au-au* escapes the ox-hides and the buffalo-hides to sweep through the passageways, through the kunitchook of Hans's igloo, through the snow-cement itself to the sailors' quarters, where they bellow and joke dangerously about the little sow with the knowing smile. Hans, permanently exhausted and in perpetual expectation of being killed and eaten, hears it and groans. Joe is more than his match at everything that becomes a man. If Christiana remarks upon it – and for the moment she has the delicacy to avoid doing so – he may have to hang himself.

UNITED STATES NAVY BOARD OF INQUIRY, ON BOARD USS TALAPOOSA, WASHINGTON DC, OCTOBER 11TH, 1873, NAVY SECRETARY GEORGE ROBESON PRESIDING

Testimony of Captain Sidney O. Budington

Q   Do you admit the general charge of drinking made against you by the officers and men?

A   I do, but I deny that I was ever incapacitated for duty in consequence.

Q   Were you conscious that the men talked of your drinking?

A   I was not. I believe it was no great matter.

Q   Do you admit that the doctor caught you in the act of surreptitiously drinking his alcohol, which you had taken from his stores, and that you had an altercation with him about it?

A   I remember I went aft to get something to drink, and he was there and made some offensive remarks. I made nothing of it, but just took him by the collar and told him to mind his own business.

Q   Was not the alcohol put on board expressly for scientific purposes?

A   Yes, sir.

Q   Then what did you drink it for?

A   I was sick and down-hearted, sir, and had a bad cold, and I needed some stimulant. That is, I thought I did. I do not suppose I really did.

Q   Were you in the habit of drinking alcohol?

A   I make it a practice to drink but very little, but during the voyage I was not myself, my health was not perfect, I was conscious of a heavy responsibility for the safety of the men.

Q   Did you experience difficulty in your relations with Captain Tyson?

A   No particular difficulty. Mr Tyson is of a carping and critical disposition. He was a man that was rather useless aboard, and he was in the habit of complaining bitterly about the management generally, but we had no particular trouble – none to speak of. I got so that after a while I did not pay much attention to him. I think no-one did.

Testimony of Emil Schumann, Chief Engineer

There was no disorder on the ship. There may have been in the forecastle, but I did not know it. I am so constituted that I would not have heard any, if it were to take place; I would go away. I did see Captain Tyson drunk like old mischief: I saw Captain Tyson when he could scarcely move along.

Testimony of Hubbard Chester, First Mate

Q   Did you ever see Captain Budington drunk?

A   I saw him once or twice in a condition that we could call 'boozy.' I have seen him boozy when I thought there was nothing else on board, and I wondered where it came from.

Q   And was drinking a general practice among the officers?

A   I think the doctor's preserving alcohol was not always put to its proper use. I believe Mr Schumann, the Chief Engineer, had made himself a key to the cabinet, and that he used it very often.

Testimony of Nathaniel Coffin, Carpenter

I never saw any of the officers drunk on duty, but I more than once saw the Mate, Mr Chester, under the influence of alcohol, on duty or off.

CHAPTER FIVE
QUESTING: A CARPENTER CALLED COFFIN

Henry Grinnel, merchant and shipping magnate, was the arch-sponsor of Arctic exploration, the whipper-up of public and congressional interest, the provider of ships and dollars and high-flown sentiment. It was largely thanks to him that America knew about the disappearance of Sir John Franklin and his crews and gave a damn about the North Pole and the Northwest Passage: his money had sent Kane and Hall to the ice, and his speeches and letters to the newspapers had made them famous. Three days before they sailed from New York he reminded the officers and scientists of the *Polaris* that the banner which would flap at the Pole was the most glorified strip of bunting in the world. In thirty-eight it had been carried by Lieutenant Wilkes closer to the South Pole than any Stars and Stripes before or since. Subsequently, De Haven, Kane and Hayes in their turn had unfurled it ever and ever closer to the top of the globe. Receiving it, Hall shed unashamed tears at his own conjuration of the scene, less than a year hence, when the officers and men of the *Polaris* would salute it at the Pole, the crowning jewel of New World exploration. Among those same officers were a few who eyed each other over the rims of their glasses as they toasted him, sharing their silent sneers for his childishness, wincing at his sesquipedalian excesses, spitting on his dream.

Already in New London Connecticut, the last of the United States, the sneers were becoming public. On Sunday July 2nd, the Baptists of New London left after a service on board the *Polaris* that again stirred Hall to his marrow and caused him to draw his big blacksmith's hands across his cheeks, while Dr Bessel once more orchestrated the contempt.

At St Johns Labrador, where they bade farewell to the continent, they needed a week for engine repairs. Hall sent Tyson, Chester and Morton to scour the inns for a carpenter to replace Mr Coffin, who had taken sick in New York. But here where the glory of the Stars and Stripes was of no account and the tetchiness of the Arctic pack too well known, they were greeted at best with sympathetic beers and shaking of heads, at worst with guffaws and mock condolence for the coming loss of their vessel and their lives.

Reporting their failure to Hall and the other officers at dinner, Tyson aired his suspicion that the denizens of the St Johns waterfront had been suborned by the sailors of the *Polaris*.

'I surmise, Sir, that we were expected, and our purpose known, and that their minds had been encouraged to view our expedition, and our offer of employment, with disfavour.'

Grimly, Hall nodded. 'There are elements in the crew…' He would happily have left it there, but Bessel, wishing to know which elements he referred to, dabbed his beard and sat straighter in his chair, ready to be offended. Hall, however, could not yet risk the open quarrel. To damn them here, on the mainland of America – Bessel for a meretricious pedant, Budington for a drunkard, the whole man-jack of them for traitors to the Sacred Cause – might have been the release his simmering anger demanded, but there would never have been another fifty thousand dollars. His voice maintained its conviviality, its measured courtesy. 'It cannot have escaped your observation, Doctor Bessel, that there has evolved among the crew a manifest tendency to align themselves in certain factions, and to display feelings of special affinity, principally on the score of national affiliation.'

Bessel shrugged. He removed his napkin from his lips to reveal his customary half-smile.

Hall smiled in return. 'You might also have observed that some of the sailors are less than cordial in their support for the main object of this expedition.'

Bessel's eyebrows arched, but he said nothing, waiting for Hall to enlarge.

'I refer, of course, to the attainment of the ninetieth degree of northern latitude.'

In the six seconds of silence that followed the battle lines were drawn: Hall and Tyson, quester knight and squire; Bessel and Meyer, agnostic man of science and assistant researcher. Caught between were Budington the ice-master, drunkard, coward; and Bryan the astronomer-chaplain, a professional conciliator, staunch enough in his Yankeeism, but devoted to his science.

Bessel would not be the one to raise his voice first. 'Is there not some danger in concentrating on that single object, Captain?' Into the title, pronounced with slow emphasis and a miniscule raising of his eyebrows, he injected the full dose of his scholarly

51

contempt.

Meyer nodded his agreement, but Hall ignored him. 'What manner of danger, Dr Bessel?'

Bessel became the Heidelberg professor delivering his lecture to admiring students. He spread his white nervous fingers. 'We are at the mercy of a multitude of unforeseeable, incalculable agencies – so many that it would be unwise to rate our prospects of reaching the Pole as better than remote. Mr Budington knows that the ice conditions in the polar regions can vary most profoundly between one year and the next.'

Hall spoke before Budington could acknowledge the appeal to his authority. 'We all know that, Doctor. We know there are few certainties in this world in general, and even fewer in the Arctic.'

'As a scientist, sir, I like to speak rather of probabilities. At my best reckoning, the probability of our achieving the ninetieth degree is not high.'

Tyson and Hall together shook their heads, but the doctor continued: 'It is important then, that we place great emphasis on the scientific achievements of the expedition, quite independently of the attempt on the Pole. Then, whatever the outcome, we can never be accused of failure, or of squandering the funds of the United States Congress.'

Hall's smile was real, an offer of comradeship. 'Agreed, Doctor. We will trumpet the work of the Scientific Corps to the nation and the world, Pole or no Pole.'

He raised the decanter. There was a second of deliberation before Bessel offered his glass for recharging. 'I don't speak of trumpeting, Captain Hall,' he said. 'Only of utilising our unique opportunity for research and scientific achievement.'

Hall vigorously nodded. Bessel accepted this as encouragement to continue. 'The Pole, I might dare to suggest, is of symbolic interest only.'

Too much for Tyson. He brought his fist down on the table with a thump that rattled their glasses. 'Oh, but what a symbol, Sir!'

'Indeed, indeed, Mr Tyson,' Bessel said, assuming the patient tone of the expert addressing the layman, 'but it is of no intrinsic scientific interest. Our study of the conditions that appertain in the land, sea and sky of the high Arctic is in no way dependent upon our reaching it.'

Tyson flushed. He looked to Hall for leave before he spoke. Hall offered a tolerant frown, a smile. Tyson unclenched his fist. 'But are you not a man as well as a scientist, Doctor? And are you not an explorer, not stirred by the thought that you'll place your foot where no foot has been placed before, and where none might ever be placed again?'

'Mr Tyson, it is stirring enough for me ...' he looked to Meyer and added, 'us ... to sound ocean depths that have never been sounded, and to assist, however feebly, the advance of scientific knowledge. The Pole is a chimera, a poetic fancy. To dwell on it, to become obsessed with it, might even hinder us in our scientific pursuits.'

Tyson was puzzled. 'A poetic fancy?'

Patiently, warmly, moderating his sneer, Bessel enlarged. 'As a scientific – or, shall we say, an *astronomical* concept – it does not have to be discovered, or even investigated. It is fully understood. Indeed, for all you know our Inuit friends might have been dancing around it for the last thousand years. You may find your Holy Grail, only to have your boots and your compass stolen.'

They all laughed. Tyson forced a smile and the fight was postponed. Bryan proclaimed that he was a scientist, but no whit the less of an adventurer for it. He would rejoice in the evidence of the divine handiwork every time he gazed at the starry vault, but his heart would quicken in that moment – he lifted a peach from the bowl in the centre of the Captain's table and held it between the index fingers of each hand – when he cowered under the infinitely gentle, infinitely mighty tip of God's forefinger. When the respectful laughter subsided, they allowed him his serious moment. He faced Hall as he spoke, but the words were for Bessel, Meyer, Budington. 'I am too, a servant of the United States Government, and like all of us I have committed to memory the paragraph of the Navy instructions which obliges me to be, sir, under every circumstance and condition, under your command and subject to the rules, regulations and laws governing the discipline of the Navy.'

So they sailed. Budington, who loved neither the science nor the poetry, and who was smarting from a public dressing-down about his invasions of the liquor cabinet, grumbled already that there was too much damned ice for his liking.

And Hall lied. From the farther side of the Davis Strait, it became easier. At Holsteinborg, Greenland, there was scant coal and no reindeer skin and the *Congress* had not yet arrived with promised stores, but there was good news from the returning Swedish Polar Exploration Party: Baffin and Melville were clear – hardly a score of modest bergs sat between Holsteinborg and Upernavik, the best season for years, confirmation that they would enjoy the most favourable ice conditions ever recorded. Not since Parry's record thrust of 1827, eighty-two degrees, forty-five minutes north, had the Pole beckoned so plainly.

A comfortable day's sailing brought them to Disco Island, where all the resentment gathered into one ball, where the United States Government might have saved the greater part of its fifty thousand dollars, where Hall lied loudest and finally bent himself in two to salvage his dream. When Budington renewed the liquor raids, the reprimand was private and muted and comradely – an appeal to duty, to patriotism, to their once-warm friendship. But when Hall, flushed with the good news from the Swedes, proposed that they abandon Jones Sound, the western passage along the shore of Ellesmere Island, and take the direct route, the northern route, the manly route, the American route, between Ellesmere and Greenland, Meyer loosed his bound-in sarcasm with such violence that even Bessel his mentor was taken aback.

'So the whole expedition, the whole scheme, is to be imperilled for a rumour?'

'No, Mr Meyer,' Hall said. 'For the well-founded report of our Swedish friends, with full documentary and scientific corroboration.'

Meyer would not retreat. 'Sir, how often have we heard from Mr Budington that ice conditions are a matter of hours, of days? A change of wind can blow your documentary corroboration to oblivion.'

Freshly reconciled with his commander, freshly aware of his derelictions, Budington said nothing, and Meyer snarled. 'Will the plan change again if we come across a kayak, and an eskimo who reports a fine coconut harvest from the shore of the Polar Sea?'

The unbridled insolence left Hall with no choice.

'Mr Meyer, you are relieved of your duties and confined to your cabin pending the arrival of the USS *Congress*.'

Their blood had hardly begun to cool when that arrival happened. With the supplies came the reassertion of naval discipline. All hands were mustered and informed that Meyer was to be placed in irons and delivered to a court martial.

This was the defining moment: Hall registered the shock on the faces of the German seamen, and as Dr Bessel stepped forward to speak, he touched his arm, stopping him, before addressing the Commander of the *Congress*. 'Captain Davenport, my earnest hope is that such extreme measures might be avoided. Mr Meyer has expressed his opinion in a manner which he may now acknowledge as excessively zealous.'

Bessel moved quickly to support, to affirm that the Scientific Corps, after long discussion with the commander, recognised his supreme authority and was clear in the precise demarcation of its responsibilities.

The glances that passed between Davenport and Hall did service for a thousand words. Davenport was offering him the chance to abandon the expedition, to return to his family as an honourable failure, and setting against it a poetic horror: the transport of a shipload of rankling disaffection to uncharted waters where the only certainties were that nerves would be stretched to their uttermost tension, loyalties tested far beyond any challenge they had yet faced, desperate effort demanded of bodies enfeebled by privation and minds soured by resentment.

With a nod hardly perceptible even to himself, Hall chose as he had to, wrapped himself in his grand lie, and secured his coming fame as the northernmost corpse on earth.

The bargain closed, Davenport did his admirable best, invoking the full might of Congress and President and blasting them with Navy Discipline, just as he knew an earlier breed of captain had blasted sullen tars with the Articles of War.

The last murmurs of discontent were stifled in a tearstained service conducted by Dr Newman of Washington, whose prayer jerked at the heartstrings of the most cynical of the scientists:

Oh hear us from Thy throne in glory, and in mercy pardon our sins, through Jesus Christ our Lord and Saviour. Give us noble thoughts, pure emotions, and generous sympathies for each other, while so far away from all human habitations. May we have for each other that charity that suffereth long and is kind, that envieth not, that vaunteth not itself, that is not puffed up, that seeketh not her own, that is not easily provoked, that thinketh no evil, but that beareth all things, hopeth all things, endureth all things; that charity that never faileth.

May it please thee to prosper us in our great undertaking, and may our efforts at this time be crowned with abundant success. Hear us for our country, for the President of the United States, and for all who are in authority over us. And hear us for our families, and for all our friends we have left at home; and at last receive us on high, for the sake of the great Redeemer. Amen.

In his report to the Navy Secretary, Davenport fell in with Hall's game, reporting only that he had 'made a few remarks' to the officers and crew of the *Polaris* before bidding them farewell, and that perfect harmony prevailed on board the little craft when she left Goodhavn. The cheers of the *Congress's* crew echoed among the bergs as the *Polaris* steamed out of Goodhavn harbour. The dozen hovels of Upernavik, then the seven of Tossac, were the last they would see of Christian settlement, of waterpipes, of chimneys.

Jansen the Dane, who had tried to reach the Polar Ocean with Hayes ten years before, had grown high and mighty as the governor of the snowfields: he was not inclined to offer his services as a humble seaman, and demanded exorbitant heaps of dollars for his dogs, but Hall's rage cooled when Chester arrived with Hans and Christiana, their three children, their myriad pups, their tents and tools and cooking pots. Searching out familiar faces, Hans found none, and Morton had to work hard – pointing to the scars on Hans's hand and reminding him of how he got them in a powder explosion on the shore of Smith Strait – to convince him that under the grey whiskers he was indeed that same Bill who had sailed with him under Dr Kane twenty years before and had claimed the first sight of the open Polar Sea.

The sailors made faces and asked Morton if Hans had smelled

as bad twenty years ago. But the unforced jollity of the reception given to Hans and Christiana by their compatriots, Joe and Hannah, restored Hall to bouncing optimism again, and his hand did not tremble over his final dispatch to Robeson from Tossac:

1.30 pm. The anchor of the Polaris *has just been weighed, and not again will it go down until, as I trust and pray, a higher, a far higher, latitude has been attained than ever before by civilised man. Governor Elberg is about accompanying us out of the harbour and seaward. He leaves us when the pilot does. Governor Lowertz Elberg has rendered to this expedition much service, and long will I remember him for his great kindness. I am sure you and my country will fully appreciate the hospitality and co-operation of the Danish officials in Greenland as relating to our North Polar expedition.*

2.3.5pm. Governor Elberg leaves us, promising to take these dispatches back to Upernavik, to send them to our minister at Copenhagen by the next ship, which opportunity may not be till next year. God be with us. Yours ever, Charles Francis Hall.

Tyson brooded. On the bottom at Upernavik, in six sections, lay the principal parts of their vaunted oil-and-bones boiler, rejected as unnecessary by the Chief Engineer Schumann, and heaved over the side amid high jollity by Kruger and Anthing. He knew that a protest to Hall would have been useless, that until civilisation was safely beyond his telescope, the Captain would hear nothing that might hint at trouble; knew too that Schumann would take instantly to his high horse – from the saddle of which he spoke only German – at the first inkling of a complaint.

Now, when the coal ran out, there could be no steam, and the exquisite Neafles and Levy engine would be useless weight.

The *Congress* had delivered the last coal and provisions at Goodhavn. Tyson's commission, signed by the Navy Secretary, made his appointment as Assistant Navigator official, legitimised his seat at the Captain's table and his voice in the officers' deliberations. And stepping across from the storeship was Nathaniel Coffin, the carpenter they had lost to a bilious attack in New York and had failed to replace in St Johns. Noticing his downcast face as they threaded northward from Tossac, with the icebergs pink in the gathering dusk and the masthead of the *Congress* still breaking the southern horizon, Tyson understood his fear and addressed him as an old acquaintance.

'I guess you might be sorry you didn't stay right where you were on the *Congress*, Nathaniel. Or maybe I don't read your thoughts aright: maybe you have a hankering after the ice.'

'You read them aright,' said Nathaniel Coffin.

UNITED STATES NAVY BOARD OF INQUIRY, WASHINGTON DC, DECEMBER 24TH, 1873, GEORGE ROBESON, NAVY SECRETARY, PRESIDING

Testimony of R, W. D. Bryan, Astronomer and Chaplain

Q   Were you ever aware of discord between Captains Budington and Tyson?

A   Not in regard to business aboard the ship, sir. There might be a want of some cordiality on occasion, but after a short time they would be very friendly. They knew each other a long time.

Q   Did you ever see Captain Budington under the influence of alcohol?

A   I must confess that I did, occasionally. I think however, some excuse might be I made for him; so little liquor seemed to affect him so much, and he was not always well.

Q   Did you see other officers under the influence?

A   I know that the engineer had made a key to the doctor's closet, where the preserving alcohol was stored, and that he made use of it, and for all I know lent it to others. I think some of the men had a store that they could reach by crawling through the engine shaft. I have heard that it is a common thing for sailors to establish such a cache.

Q   Was there drinking among the officers before Captain Hall's death?

A   If there was, it was not open, sir. I cannot recollect any.

Q   Then the situation worsened after his death?

A   It did.

Q   Was there no attempt made to stop it?

A   I cannot see how it could have been done, sir. The only way it could have been stopped, I believe, was by taking all the liquor on board the vessel, and all the preserving alcohol, and throwing every last drop overboard.

Q   Did you ever speak to Captain Budington on the matter?

A   I did not, sir. It would not have been welcome.

Q   Nevertheless, did you not feel a responsibility?

A   I felt one, indeed, sir. But after the death of Captain Hall my position was weakened.

Q   How so? In what sense weakened?

A   Captain Hall, as you know, was a man who felt his religion, and lived it. His religion meant much to him.

Q   And Captain Budington was not strong in this matter?

A   He had not the same conviction, sir. That is, I do not believe he felt it as strong. I believe he saw it as a private matter for each of the men.

CHAPTER SIX
DRIFTING: KRUGER BLAMES TYSON'S FRIENDS

The six can split conveniently into two skat schools when tempers and cooling of feuds allow. All of them cheat, and each justifies it by assuming that the others are even shadier than himself. They joke about it – call Jamka *Bubenkönig* for his facility in turning up jack-trumps, and Kruger *Nostradamus* for his awareness of everyone else's cards. But with morsels of stolen chocolate at stake, then mountains of imaginary dollars; with pistols within five inches of every hand; with the galloping paranoia of men whose choices seemed limited to lingering death by starvation or sudden violent engulfment by the ice, there is a danger of flare-ups that go beyond the unwritten limits, and a general relief that sealskin mittens prevent ready access to triggers.

Five weeks into the drift, under daily instruction from the eskimo women, they have mastered the pemmican-tin lamp sufficiently to have some light and a little warmth in their snowhouse. The spare sails of the *Polaris* have been put to good use in lining the walls. The smaller whaleboat and the two eskimo sledges are long-since consumed and Kruger, now unassailably the spokesman for the lower deck, has bowed – literally, mockingly – to Tyson's desperate request that the twenty-five footer be spared. 'We will only burn it when we see the chimneys of Disco, Mr Tyson,' he has promised. 'That will be our signal.'

This Kruger has a proper presence. In his bitterest reflections Tyson concedes the fact; allows his bloodiest vengeful fancies to be palliated by small twinges of admiration, tweaks of kinship. Even as the crew of the *Polaris* were banking up their little ship in September 1871, the captains of the New England whaling fleet were formally abandoning their thirty-two vessels to the ice of the Beaufort Sea, on the opposite side of the great Canadian archipelago. It was to be marked down as the year of the Great Disaster, the destruction of an industry, and among the thousand men who battled through the ice to the rescuing ships were hundreds whom Tyson and Kruger might have claimed as shared friends. If they had never till now sailed together, still they had served under the same captains and scrubbed the same decks. Tyson knows Kruger as a man named with affection and respect in the waterfront taverns, a man always first to volunteer where the action is thickest. If he now whines, if he now succumbs to ungovernable tantrums, so too does Tyson. If he now plots the slitting of children's throats, so Tyson lovingly envisages the bashing to pulp of a shipmate's skull, and recognises that each of them is infected bone-deep by the explorer's disease. It is something they all share – a thick compound of guilt and delusion and murderous suspicion of everyone around. The strange unnatural death of the leader, the loss of their ship, the failure of their quest – these are the stuff of a sour brew; failure and death and darkness oppress their spirits as scurvy attacks their flesh.

Their bellies warmed by mock-turtle soup and ship's biscuit, they settle into the two hands: Kruger, Jamka and Nindermann north of the lamp; Anthing, Lindquist and Johnson south. Stakes are high: an imaginary dollar per point. In the furthest corner by the stove, Jackson and Herron clean up from the dinner and make space for their backgammon board. These two speak little, and the rattle of the dice is virtually the only sound from their square yard of the igloo. Shut out from the German clique, afraid to be seen as allies of Tyson and the natives, they stare silently into each other's eyes, acknowledging some bitter secret, some shared agony. According to the talk, Hall was killed by coffee, and that coffee was prepared by the one, delivered by the other.

Tyson has told them it is Thanksgiving, hinted at some kind of acknowledgement, some kind of service, but nothing has happened yet.

'Thanksgiving what for?' Anthing asks.

Jamka growls across the lamp, 'For all this, man. For lice and frozen toes and sometimes an inch of seal's prick to suck.'

'And don't forget this.' Kruger pats his chest, where the bulge of a stolen loaf, not thawed yet, is just visible.

In the absence of Meyer, who has crawled through to the eskimos' house at Tyson's invitation for a strategic discussion, their talk is freer than usual.

'And also this.' Jamka flourishes the blank notebook he has stolen from Tyson's bundle. 'At least this one will be put to some good use.' He opens it and pencils in the columns for keeping the scores, toting up the dollars.

A noise in the entrance tunnel stops the conversation, and

Jamka shoves the notebook under his leg. Meyer climbs in, bringing cold and powder-snow. Tyson is behind him and before either speaks it is clear there has been disagreement, ill temper. Space is made for them to sit. They recover their breath and Tyson nods to Meyer as a sign that he might have the first word. Meyer marks the formality of the occasion by speaking in English.

'Gentlemen, I have been able to make some quite reliable observations, and I am of the opinion that we are now crossing the seventy-fourth parallel, that we are past Cape York and well into Melville Bay. I think we are in longitude sixty-seven fifty west, and drifting eastwards toward the Greenland shore.'

He pauses, letting them imagine. Then he looks toward Tyson, whose expression is enough to indicate the depth of their disagreement.

Jamka breaks the silence. 'When shall we reach Disco?'

Tyson shakes his head, but it is still Meyer's floor.

'I calculate that we will be approaching the latitude of Disco Island within three weeks, and that the time will then be right for an attempt to reach it with the boat and whatever provisions we can carry. But I have to tell you that Mr Tyson does not share my opinion.'

Anthing mumbles, *'Zum Teufel mit Mister Tyson.'* The German, a clear breach of protocol, causes momentary embarrassment. They all recognise the bitter importance of decorum now, when the decisions which will determine the manner of their deaths are to be made.

Jamka restores discipline. 'What is his opinion, we wish to know?'

Kruger interposes. 'Are we supposed to go with only one boat, all nineteen of us?'

Tyson erupts. 'We have only one boat because you ...' He spreads his arms to indicate all of them, but it is clear that Kruger is the object of his rage, 'have burnt the other. And God help us all if the last remaining one is damaged.'

Meyer, at once ingratiating himself with the men and preserving the show of naval correctness, says: 'It should be entirely possible for us to make the attempt, all nineteen, as long as Mr Tyson and the natives are willing.'

The mention of the eskimos, Tyson will later realise, is

calculated: out of the sullen silence comes Kruger's scream, killing protocol. 'Willing *arsehole*! Who cares if they are willing? Are we willing to risk our lives dragging the savages and their females and their cubs? By ourselves we can do it, but dragging women and children, we are feeding the fish.'

'And Hans is sick – the fat one is sick,' Anthing says.

Tyson and Meyer have foreseen this argument, have conducted their own rehearsal of it. Meyer shifts backwards, allowing Tyson the floor. Tyson stands silent for a moment. He looks around the circle, but in the dimness of the blubberlamp he cannot meet their eyes.

'I will not speak of Christian duty, or the behaviour proper to a man,' he says.

'Good,' a voice interjects.

'I will say just this: I think Mr Meyer is mistaken in his reckoning of our latitude. I think we are seventy miles further north than he estimates – and drifting west, toward Baffin Island. It is the current that determines our direction, not the wind.'

'And what instruments do you have?' Kruger asks, then adds a sardonic 'Sir.'

'I have none.'

The sudden candour starts a ripple of uncomfortable laughter. Kruger is momentarily taken aback, but he recovers his anger. 'Are you relying then, on advice from your friends?'

Tyson, mastering his own rage, speaks softly. 'I am relying on twenty years' experience of these waters. You have burned our boat and our sledge and all the wood that might have served us to build more. To unshelter ourselves in this season and attempt to drag the women and children across the ice would be sure and certain death for us all, yes…'

Even as he flounders, trying to shape the rest of his sentence, he realises his mistake. It is Jamka who leaps in: 'Then you can do what you like, and you can take the natives off our hands.'

Now the silence is taut. Through their anger, they feel still the need for caution, for measurement, in the exchanges that must follow.

'If you take the boat, it will be death for whoever is left behind,' Tyson says. 'They will never be able to escape from the floe once open water is reached.'

Kruger reassumes command. 'So the way is clear. Without the natives we can reach Disco. With them, everybody dies.'

Tyson's anger begins to give way to his fear. He turns to Meyer, looking for help, and receives none. He pleads now, evading Kruger, reaching out to their separate consciences. 'Have you all forgotten that every last scrap of fresh food has come from Joe or Hans? Without them the half of us would already be dead, of hunger or the scurvy.'

Kruger is prepared for this. 'Have you forgotten that the starvation rations have been your idea? If we allow just a single month more on this stinking floe we have plenty – especially if we let the fat people hunt for themselves. That's how they live, that's their way.'

The murmurs of agreement are small, hesitant, tentative. They know without reminding that for most of what stands between them and instant frozen death – the shelter, the tight-stitched moccasins and shirts, the heat of the lamps, the invigoration of the seal's blood soup – they are beholden to the eskimos, the men and the women in equal measure; but they know too that if their lives and their prospects of food, double pay and girls in Disco are to be hazarded by the women and children, then the women and children must go, and that will require shooting the men first.

Despairing, Tyson urges them to look at each other, observe their emaciation. 'The strongest of us could not wrestle with a kitten,' he says.

'Because of you. Because of your starvation rations.'

He sighs. 'I have to work on the reckoning that we might be on this floe until spring, when we reach the whaling grounds, and when there could be a chance of reaching land on the western side. We must preserve our food, our fuel, our ammunition and our boat.'

This is not the counsel they want to hear.

'Long before your spring the half of us will be dead,' Johnson says.

Tyson does not deny the possibility. 'There will be more game, much more, as we travel south,' he says.

But the prospect of the bleak Baffin coast set against the dwellings and the rum of Disco, angers them.

Anthing finds voice first. 'You are proposing two hundred miles

65

across broken ice, in darkness. The boat would be destroyed in six hours.' He mimes the crushing of the boat with his hands. 'Matchsticks.'

Tyson shakes his head. 'It will not be darkness then. The daylight will have returned, and I think we might drift within forty miles of the land.'

'We see it, Mr Tyson,' Kruger says. 'Nineteen bodies drifting into the whaling grounds. Perhaps some old friends of yours will lift them, no?'

'I believe with God's help we can all come through,' Tyson says. 'But we must stay together, and we must work together.'

Again Kruger laughs, inviting the others to enjoy the absurdity. Tyson's shoulders sink.

'We are all dead, then,' he says. He turns and steps toward the doorway. Seeing that Meyer intends to stay with the men, he pauses for a final word.

'Someone is making raids on the stores. The bread is disappearing.' He waits, but no one speaks. Attention has become focused on the kitchen recess, where Jackson and Herron sit apart, their eyes cast down. Herron coughs, creating a space into which it seems for a moment that he might throw the accusatory remark that will initiate the bloody last act of the North Polar Expedition ... but the silence holds, and it is Tyson who finally speaks. 'It is not within my power to compel. I cannot drag the man to trial; I cannot have him shot, as he deserves. I can only appeal.'

'Have you consulted your friends?' Johnson asks. 'In the game of pilfering they have much to teach us.'

Tyson dismisses the suggestion. 'Even if their loyalty and their sense of duty failed them, they would be too afraid.'

Johnson assumes an innocent curiosity. 'Afraid?'

'They are already afraid for their lives.' Nobody laughs at the implication of Tyson's remark, and he is too frightened to enlarge upon it.

'Then it must be the dogs,' Kruger says.

There are no dogs left. Turning from the calculated insult, Tyson stoops to leave the hut. Once more he hesitates, allowing Meyer the opportunity to accompany him, but the sergeant-signaller makes no move.

'Dead,' Tyson softly says.

When they sense that he is clear through the tunnel, Meyer, keeping to English out of some obscure sense that the business remains official, says, 'I think he means for the best.'

'Except that he's a fool,' Johnson says.

'A fool who might kill us all,' Kruger adds, 'and not only by starvation.'

His remark has the planned effect. 'What do you mean?' Anthing asks him.

The circle tightens, shutting Herron and Jackson out. 'I don't trust his friends,' Kruger says. He has switched to German, but keeps his voice conspiratorially low. 'I wait to have my throat cut in the night, and I think he might encourage them.'

Jamka agrees. 'Hans must be watched. Remember, he's killed already.'

They know the story well enough: how Hans, on Hayes's expedition, set off with Sonntag the astronomer, their fellow-German, in search of eskimo settlements, and returned alone with a cock-and-bull story of Sonntag falling through the ice and disappearing before he, gallant Hans, could reach the hole. And how, in the same expedition, he sent his fellow savage Peter off to his death by spinning him yarns about how the white men planned to eat him for their Sunday dinner. Encouraged by their nods, Jamka continues: 'They are afraid, as he says; so they might be tempted to strike first. They are worried for their young.'

'I don't think so,' Meyer says. 'Remember, they have seen much of civilisation. They are not ordinary eskimos.'

If the observation is calculated to calm the sailors, it fails. They laugh and begin a raucous bandying of images: Christiana biting the cord to separate herself from Charlie Polaris; suckling the six-year-old Tobias, her breast thrown upwards to his mouth while he drapes himself across her shoulder; Succi idly cracking lice in her teeth; Hannah mending the pemmican tin with a plug of masticated blubber and dogdung; Hans licking the sooty dregs of the lamp, scooping out the dog's brain and devouring it with childlike relish; Puney, the pretty one, solemnly sucking her seal's eye titbit; the nightly circling of the korvik – the chamberpot – in the blackness of the igloo; the bucking under the buffalo hides, Hannah's squeal, Joe's grunt. They talk, and they laugh, roaring themselves out of all fellow-feeling for the savages, eliminating every last twinge of gratitude, lathering up their hatred and their fear of death until there is a momentary danger of the murderous raid being put into effect on the instant. Missing the nuances of the German, but unable to mistake the tone, Herron and Jackson are frightened. When they look to Meyer for reassurance, he smiles. 'We must remember that we are in the service of the United States Government,' he tells the sailors in English, 'and that Mr Tyson is the ranking officer.'

They hear the irony. Nindermann laughs. 'Yes, and he looks every inch a commander. Have you seen his britches?'

At the separation from the *Polaris* Tyson was left with nothing but the clothes he stood in and a bundle containing a spare shirt and a pair of deerskin socks. Kruger has stolen the bundle, and now that his clothes are worn and holed Tyson owes his survival to a coat that Hannah has made him from fox and dog and seal skins.

'A gentleman,' Jamka says.

'His hohtuk barely covers his arse,' Anthing laughs. 'She made it eskimo-size.'

They abandon the skat. A domestic rail against Congress, Ulysses S. Grant, the North Polar Expedition, Charles Francis Hall and the last surviving envoy of all these things, George Tyson, will fill an hour more beguilingly, and with smaller risk of quarrels. Even Jackson and Herron are drawn in, readmitted to the lower deck for the comradely rant.

Jamka gestures toward his own crotch. 'But you can see through the holes – in one area he's far from eskimo-size.'

Meyer tuts, but shares in the laughter. Enjoying the attention, Jamka turns his fire on Hannah. 'Unless the little louseball female can make him grow.'

They enjoy the image for a moment. 'Pscha!' Kruger says. 'I've been close to her – the smell!'

'The soot.'

'The grease.'

'The noise – *aaoo-aaoo-aaoo*.'

When the convulsions subside, Nindermann takes the stage. 'You forget, my friends – the little louseball, little Hannah, is a friend of the Queen of England. She drinks tea with Albert of Saxe-Coburg.'

'The dear Prince is dead,' Jamka reminds him.

'Ah, yes, but he poured the tea for little Hannah and little Joe.'

'Weak tea,' Jamka says.

'Pheasant-brains on toast,' Johnson says.

Food is a perilous theme. Jamka stops laughing, lowers his voice. 'Have you noticed his voice when he calls the numbers?'

Yes, they have noticed. He elaborates. 'They have a code, a trick of the voice, some bastard plan.'

Nindermann is sceptical. 'How can that be? The savages have no say.'

'I don't know the trick, but I'm positive there is one.'

They all agree that if it were possible to rig the sharing out of the meat, Tyson, preferring the seal-people to human beings, would contrive it.

'We're only *kabloonas* – he doesn't care a shit for us.'

'Everything is for his louseball friends.'

'They eat the dogs – the seals.'

'And get bigger biscuits.'

'Eyeballs for their damned young.'

'Their damned young will be the death of us all.'

Meyer, who has kept discreetly quiet, now has his moment. 'That, dear friends, is my fear. My real fear.'

They wait, knowing his reluctance is all show. He continues: 'He knows we cannot reach the Greenland shore or Disco dragging the women and the young, that to save ourselves we have to abandon them, and he wishes at all cost to avoid that.'

Kruger is interested. 'Really? '

'Really.'

'He thinks your observations are wrong.'

'That's his method. He pretends to know more; he talks of his experience in these waters. But I've tested him. His navigation is like Hall's: it consists in memorising a few sections of Bowditch.'

'How have you tested him?' Kruger asks, and silence falls as they wait for Meyer to reply.

'He isn't a scientist. In geographical knowledge he's closer to the natives even than Hall – he relies on his nose, his animal instinct.'

Kruger needs to be sure. 'But how have you tested him?'

69

'In a hundred ways.' Meyer feels their alertness; senses that his next few words could spark the mutiny. His hesitation is real. In their desperation to understand, Herron and Jackson scan the circle of faces.

'How?' Kruger repeats.

Meyer shrugs, allowing the possibility that his remarks are of no great consequence. 'I've deliberately pointed to the wrong star. I point to Alpha Cassiopeiae and call it Delta – and he makes no objection.'

'Bastard,' Jamka says, and no-one knows if the remark is ironic, a sneer at Meyer.

'All the time, in the observatory, he used to ask questions that showed the depth of his ignorance, stupid questions that no-one with the slightest knowledge would ask.'

'Shithead,' Jamka says. 'What did he ask?'

Meyer decides that Jamka is his main audience.

'The isogonic chart was a Pharaonic mystery to him, as were Kirchhoff's maps of the solar spectrum – he held them upside down.'

Jamka's voice is a growl – he may be acting, twitting Meyer, whom he has never liked. 'Arsehole,' he says. 'Upside down?'

'And he handled the Casella theodolite like a spade. The man is a whaler.'

Jamka has exhausted his store of curses. He digs Nindermann with his elbow, and Nindermann is suddenly serious. 'And he wants to kill us all – he tells us we have to sit on this shit-ice till March, till April, feeding on two ounces a day, praying for a seal to pass by, waiting for his friends to meet us in Baffin Bay.'

'We'll be gull-food before that,' Anthing says.

Kruger's anger has been climbing. His voice is a high whine. 'I won't let the bastard kill us for the sake of a few louseballs.'

He begins to rise, but Meyer lays a hand gently on his arm. 'Be calm, Robert. He is the senior officer.'

'I shit on the senior officer,' Kruger says.

'He has the authority of the United States Government. He can hang you.'

'I shit on the United States Government, I shit on General Grant, I shit on Brooklyn.'

They like this. Their right to survive outranks the President's command, and they feed Kruger's rage.

'They would cut our throats in the night.'

'Fry our livers in seal-fat.'

'They eat their grandmothers.'

'Hans is a murderer of white men.'

Meyer disengages. 'My friends, they are human like us. We are all men.'

'They're not human like *me*,' Kruger snarls. 'Are you sure your observations are good?'

Meyer nods. 'In three weeks we'll reach the latitude of Disco – at a distance of less than sixty miles west.'

Now Kruger's voice is a low murmur, more dangerous by far than Jamka's theatrical growl. 'His sarcasm, always sarcasm, and always suspicion, and always complaining.'

Anthing recollects. 'Folly Bay. That's what he called the bay where we lost the boat. He wanted to write it on the map, the bastard.'

Meyer laughs. 'A very *superior* whaler.'

'A superior arsehole.' Anthing wants Meyer to go through now to Joe's quarters, to collar Tyson, to confront him with the reality of their situation.

Meyer laughs again. 'Friend, I've spoken to the man till my jaw ached. I've reasoned with him, threatened him, tried in a hundred ways to educate him. Always it gets back to his friends – he will not do anything that might endanger them.'

'Piss on his friends,' Anthing says.

Johnson growls. 'Stinking louseballs.'

Jackson and Herron find themselves unconsciously edging closer together, sharing their fear, their helplessness, but saying nothing. Any intervention now, any hint even of English, might unleash the anger, and the mere attempt to move in the direction of Tyson's hut could be their deaths. It is Meyer's recklessness that frightens them most: as he feeds the bitterness of the men, so they in their turn feed his long-germinating resentment against Tyson. His laugh now takes him to the edge of hysteria. 'The concept of magnetic moment was completely beyond his wit, and his pronunciation of "syzygy" was grotesque – the man is a whaling clown. Yet I spent hours in the observatory, frustrating useless hours, trying to instruct him. I felt a kind of duty.' He stresses the final word, knowing that for the sailors it reeks of Tyson, Congress, the Navy – everything they revile most.

'Duty be damned.'

'Duty is a stinking bitch.'

'Tell my belly about duty – tell my arse.'

Meyer leans forward, making a silence. When he speaks his voice is low, and he smiles. 'And now,' he says, nodding his head slowly, 'now he corrects me. He tells me my observations are wrong.'

'Why didn't you tell the stinking arsehole and his friends to piss off and walk to Canada?' Anthing says. 'Why do you let him kill us with his four stinking ounces?'

Meyer sighs. 'My friends, I've tried.'

They wait for more. Meyer puts an inch of seal gut into his mouth, chews, groans with the pain of it. 'You may be right – he may be killing us,' he says.

Milder than the others, Lindquist says, 'He has to be told.'

'We're not going to be killed for a pack of louseballs,' Kruger says.

'He has to be told,' Lindquist says again, appealing to Meyer.

Meyer raises his hands. 'I've tried. Dear God, I've tried.'

'I'll tell him.' Kruger is loud now, on the edge of tears. 'I'll tell the arsehole.'

'It won't be any good,' Meyer says. 'He has only one thing on his mind, only one aim. He won't listen to reason.'

Kruger raises his pistol, a heavy colt that seems small in his huge mitt. 'I'll put something else on his mind.'

Herron now sees the full horror of what is afoot, understands the game Meyer is playing with his smiles and sighs and protestations. Encouraged by a small pressure on his arm from Jackson he rises, ready to remonstrate. But Meyer too has risen, and it is he who speaks first, using English. 'I don't think the weapon is a good idea, Robert.'

There is a moment of hideous expectation when it seems that Kruger will cock the pistol, but while he considers the thing, trying to decide whether Herron or Jackson should be his first target, the alarm of the others gets to him. He tucks the pistol into his jacket and shakes his head. 'I don't plan to use it – only to underline my point. Don't think I would shoot the bastard, Mr Meyer.'

'Even for underlining, Robert,' Meyer says. 'Remember: the natives are armed, if Mr Tyson is not. And they are nervous, and more accustomed to the darkness than you.'

They are speaking German again, but Herron recognises the lowering of tension, and sits down.

Kruger coughs loudly, wipes his mouth with his hand, passes the pistol to Meyer. Meyer places it on the snow-bench.

'Speak to him by all means,' he says. 'That's your right, and you should speak with as much force as you can summon. But I suggest you don't mention my name, that you tell him you're there for the men.'

'For the men, yes, for the men.' Kruger suddenly addresses Herron. 'Do you want to come with me, John?' he asks.

It is a difficult moment for the steward – his invitation to the clique, to solidarity with his shipmates, to safety of a sort. He looks first at Jackson, then Meyer, then back to Kruger.

'No, Robert,' he says. 'I think you should leave off now. I think it's better you should sit down.'

Kruger makes his soft growl, and turns toward the tunnel. Crawling into the two yards of darkness that separates them from the natives' and Tyson's quarters, he growls again, this time shaping a word: 'Arsehole.'

Always first, Hannah hears him. She grips Joe's arm, disturbing the checkerboard as she crosses on her knees to be close to him. Tyson, who has been huddled by the lamp with his journal, drops his pencil.

Kruger peers into the darkness, trying to locate the faces, pinpoint the weapons. He sees Joe's harpoon and snow-knife propped against the wall on his right, closer to his own hand than to Joe's. Hannah has picked up her ulu, her curved knife. It is small, and at distance almost valueless as a weapon.

He eschews greetings. 'The men are not happy,' he says. Tyson rises from the rugs, sits on the snow-bench. When he speaks his tone is friendly. 'That's hardly surprising, Robert, when we consider what Providence has visited upon us. I'm not in a state of highest bliss myself, I confess.'

Kruger bludgeons his passage through the irony. 'They think you are lying to them.'

Tyson stands. In order that they can both be upright in the

hut, they must come together in the centre. Kruger is half a head the taller.

Tyson speaks with painstaking slowness, in a tone that asserts his rank and raises the Stars and Stripes above Kruger's head. 'I'll overlook your insolence and subordination for the moment, Robert, so that I might hear some explanation of your remark.'

Responding to the lowered voice, Kruger smiles bitterly, assumes a conversational tone. 'Shit on your explanation. You've lied to the men. You've kept food from them to keep your friends happy.'

Conscious of a stirring behind him, Tyson motions for Joe to remain in his seat. He takes a short step back in order to look Kruger in the eye without straining upward in a manner that he feels, obscurely, might diminish his authority. 'You're raving, Robert, and the best counsel I can give you is that you go back to your quarters and consider your apology.'

'Damn your apology. Shit on your apology.' Kruger's hands twitch, but still he baulks at the final mutinous act, will not lay hands on an officer. His voice rises in pitch, stopping short of a scream. 'You know shit-nothing about the stars; you only want to protect these louseballs.'

Heedless of Tyson's warning, Joe edges toward the doorway, where his Danish rifle is leaning, loaded for bear. Tyson, gambling on the presence of a last shred of naval discipline, lowers his voice still more. 'You're raving and insolent and insubordinate, and my only regret is that indiscipline in the crew has come to such a pass that I'm not able to clamp you in irons. But your insolence will be reported, mister.'

'Ha!' Kruger flaps his arms. 'Reported to the stars? You don't know the stars! You don't know nothing! The men need more food.'

'We all need more food – your ration is the same as mine.'

'They say you cheat, you give more to *them*.' As his arm stretches to indicate the eskimos, Joe reaches the rifle.

Tyson maintains his voice at a level hardly above a whisper. 'If they say that, they're lying. Or being lied to.'

'We'll be abreast of Disco in three weeks – Mr Meyer has taken observations.'

'And I disagree with his findings. If you try to reach Disco in

February you will all die, that I'm sure of.'

'Then at least' – Kruger's voice becomes a proper scream now – 'we'll die like … '

Tyson helps him. 'Like men?'

'Yes, like men. Your way is to starve us like dogs!'

Tyson smells danger, but also advantage. He becomes gentler, almost paternal. 'My way is the *only* way, Robert. In April the Scotch and the Americans will be in Davis Strait, and we'll be in the correct latitude.'

For a moment there might be a possibility that Kruger will respond to the tone, will embrace him, cry on his shoulder.

'But we'll be dead!' He shouts.

'Some of us, maybe. But I trust not. In the Strait we'll find bears and seals and plenty of birds. If we keep our heads now, and conserve our stocks as much as we can, there is a chance for all of us. Any other way is certain death, let me promise you that – whether you take the women and children or not.'

Kruger spits in the direction of Joe and Hannah. 'Damn them.'

Catching the hint of indecision, the failing resolve behind the bluster, Tyson gambles again. 'I find your cowardice still more offensive than your insolence, Robert. I find you a disgrace to the flag you sail under, and to the memory of your dead captain. You've attacked my honour – now make good your charge, or return to your quarters and consider your apology.'

Kruger thinks. Tyson calculates. In ordinary circumstances, Kruger would be sanguine enough about his prospects in a brawl with Tyson or any other Yankee. But now, lingeringly contemptuous of Meyer and his observations, emaciated, enfeebled, trapped in a dim eskimo hut with Tyson and the feverishly alert Joe whose cunning and alacrity with harpoon or rifle he has witnessed often enough, he wavers. When Tyson takes the half-step that brings their bodies into contact, he breaks.

'Shit on you, Tyson! You're killing us all.'

Suddenly bitter in his triumph, Tyson shouts, 'I could have *saved* us all when we broke from the *Polaris*. If you had listened then we could have reached the shore, but now there's no hope of that – now we can only work together, save our food, trust to our courage and to God – and to Joe's harpoon.'

Kruger is shaking, and the futile attempt to control his twitching limbs brings tears to his eyes. Tyson speaks now as if to a petulant youth.

'Dear God, Robert, have you forgotten who sheltered you after your ship was lost, when you would have died in an hour? Have you forgotten who has brought us our only fresh meat? The scurvy would have killed us all by now.'

Kruger has indeed forgotten. Gratitude has been the first casualty of hunger. For him, as for all the seamen, hope has rested on Disco, on the possibility of dragging the boat to the Greenland shore. Tyson's assertion that the feat is beyond their strength is a sentence of death, and Tyson is their executioner, the focus for all their misery and rancour. Kruger remembers the pistol he has left behind, despairs, and returns to the old tune.

'The men say you favour the natives: you give them the best meat, the best fuel.'

'And how in the name of God can I achieve that, Robert? You commandeer all the meat that they bring in, and you divide it yourself.'

'He eats the heart and the kidneys, yet still he gets his full share – you make no allowance.'

'*Once* he took the heart and kidneys, and that when he'd spent nine hours at the breathing-hole, with the mercury at minus twenty, while you slept and played cards.'

'They take half of every animal.'

'They capture the whole of every animal.'

'Their job. That's what they're paid for.'

The evocation of job, pay, is a blunder. Even for Kruger, it conjures up duty, teamwork, rank, the Navy Department, Ulysses S. Grant. He stands, trembling, making no attempt to dam his tears.

Tyson seals the victory. 'And remember, mister, what *you* are paid for. Go back to your quarters, play your card game, tell Mr Meyer I would like a word with him at his earliest convenience.'

The stand-off is over. Kruger sobs. Tyson helps him to turn, to ease his shoulders back into the blackness of the tunnel.

'Mr Tyson,' Hannah says, 'that sailor is big trouble. That sailor wants to kill us eskimos.'

Tyson cannot deny it, and knows they have won a mere

skirmish, bought a brief postponement. He puts his arm around Puney's shoulders. 'We won't let him do that, Hannah. Joe and I won't let him harm you. But fear not – the next time he comes through he'll carry his apology.'

Joe ferrets beneath the hides, finds a bundle of dog-fur, lays it in front of his knees to unwrap it. The Smith and Wesson is pristine, glinting yellow in the lamplight.

'You take that, Mr Tyson,' he says. Tyson lifts the pistol in both hands. Until this moment, he has been the only unarmed man on the floe.

Joe says, 'When him come through with him apology, you shoot him in him head, Mr Tyson.'

While he crawls through the tunnel, Kruger reassembles himself, tries to recover his swagger for the sailors.

'I've told the arsehole,' he says.

They see the tearstains on his cheeks. 'What have you told him?' Anthing asks.

'In February we take the boat to Disco, and damn the louseballs.'

'I hope you were reasonable with him,' Meyer says. 'I hope you were not violent, not threatening.'

'I told him he was a shit-liar.'

Meyer winces. 'How did he respond?'

'He looked for an apology, and I damned him to hell, him and the louseballs.'

'Then you may not have been wise, Robert,' Meyer says. 'I think next time you see him you should apologise. I think it would be good strategy.'

'Damn him,' Kruger says.

'Yes. Still, it might be good strategy.'

The others murmur. 'We don't want questions; we don't want them to take our double pay,' Jamka says.

Nindermann supports him. 'We should try to keep him on our side. He's the officer.'

'And when the time comes, he'll eat the eskimo piglets with the rest of us,' Johnson says.

Above, the sky clears, the stars sing, the aurora dances. In Meyer's thermometer the mercury sinks to minus forty and freezes.

CHAPTER SEVEN
QUESTING: THE ICE-MASTER HAS COLD FEET

When the fog lifted at eighty-one degrees, thirty-five minutes north they saw that the charts were useless. Hall rolled his account of their campaign against the ice into a copper cylinder and, sighing, dropped it into a patch of clear black water. He wrote down nothing of their complex bickerings, though these were no less a threat to the safety of the expedition than the icebergs themselves. This foggy wilderness of grumbling ice should have been the *Polynya*, the Open Polar Sea, the rippling paradise of dancing narwhals and darting swallows that Morton had descried from Cape Constitution twenty years before, providing consolation and justification for Kane's strife-racked expedition and sensational headlines for the New York press; but days of east-and-west steaming in search of leads had revealed only a tight channel, eighteen miles at its widest extent, between harbourless cliffs. Hall called it Robeson Channel, at once granting the Navy Secretary his small niche in history and consigning Morton's discovery to the fat directory of Arctic Follies. When they came within reach of either shore, they launched the small boats or scanned with the telescopes in search of a bight that might offer a protected anchorage for bedding the *Polaris* and beginning the winter programme of sledge and boat journeys – preparations for a spring dash to the Pole.

In semi-disgrace, denied his alcoholic solace, Budington grew first sullen, then truculent, then desperate. With the scientists determinedly offering no opinion, he looked to the sailors for his claque. In thirty years of Arctic travel, he told them, he had never seen ice of such thickness, never heard grinding of such rank malevolence. The odds were strong that they were already doomed, and every mile northward took them closer to the inexorable disaster: the *Polaris* would be cracked like a nut then pulverised, and their bodies delivered to the seals and bears. The promise of the Open Sea was a diabolic trap – in swift seconds there could rise from the flatness of clear water an ice-mound twice as high as their mainmast. Within minutes the hull would be gripped from below and held fast until the million tons of the mound crashed upon the decks. The favoured ones would be those on the upper decks, whose deaths would be instantaneous and unenhanced by thought. His plain terror combined with the capricious fog, the banshee howl of the north-eastern gales and the remorseless growling of the pack to unsettle all of them and start the quick snowball of panic rolling in the minds of the more timid sailors.

When the *Polaris* complained loudest in the grip of the ice, they unloaded provisions, and loaded them again when the timbers relaxed and she sighed her relief from the pressure. The icebergs, which offered the most immediate threat, were also their main shield against the gales and the driving pack. Yankee engineering, Yankee carpentry, Yankee fortitude, were tested to their groaning limits. Unannounced squalls hurled them broadside against the ice-field with a violence that threw them from their bunks, broke crockery and bones. More terrible still was the squeeze – across her beams, stem to stern, top to bottom or all at once – that set the little ship singing, screeching, wheezing, howling in every nail.

On the first day of September 1871 they hoisted the propeller into its clever groove, and Budington stormed cursing from Hall's cabin, abnegating all responsibility for the safety of the ship and crew in the absence of an instant assurance that the northward thrust was here ended, that the sole navigational object was the discovery of a safe refuge where the *Polaris* could be fastened and banked for the winter. Faced with the united opposition of Hall, Tyson and the first mate Chester, and denied support by the scientists, he had drained his rum and slammed his glass to the table with shattering force. From the alley-way, addressing the officers but raising his voice for the seamen to hear, he declared the futility of reasoning with men whose thirst for glory had obscured their judgement. Hall followed him into the passage, took him by the arm, appealed as he had done a dozen times before to his manhood, his patriotism, his captain's pride – not, however, to their long-dead friendship – and returned to inform the others of the failure of his efforts. He asked Tyson and Chester, as they finished their drams, to allow him three hours for consideration of their plight, then to reconvene.

When they met again at three in the afternoon he uncorked a bottle and invited them to toast and congratulate themselves on the comfortable passing of the eighty-second parallel, well beyond the furthest northward reach of any prow of any nation in the history of geographical discovery.

'But now it's all up,' he said. He spread his arms, placed his clenched fists on the table. They read the gesture as an invitation to debate. Tyson looked to the mate for encouragement, and received it in the form of a slight nod. 'I've been aloft within this half-hour, sir. There's clear water ahead.'

'I don't doubt it, George.'

'Two or three degrees further north, sir – it would reflect great credit on you.'

'My credit is of no moment, George.'

Chester attempted the other tack. 'The flag, sir, the Sacred Bunting. The President.' He spread his arms.

Hall's smiled widened, grew sadder. 'Friends, I've thought hard My head aches with thinking. Tomorrow I'll assemble the crew for the sabbath service, and after prayers I'll inform them that here we begin our search for an anchorage. We are five hundred and fifty miles from the Pole, and in the year to come we shall do the utmost our strength permits, by sledge and boat, to cover every one of those miles. The Great Cause is not abandoned.'

Tyson bit his tongue. Hall saw.

'I read your thoughts, George. I read them. You see another two hundred miles – an anchorage within striking distance.'

Tyson blushed. 'I'm thinking only of the expedition, sir. And of you, and of the hopes invested in us by … '

'By the nation,' Hall says.

'By our friends.'

'Yes, our friends, God bless our friends.'

Tyson saw a chink. 'Even Bessel supports us. Even he's for a push north.'

Chester assisted. 'Mr Tyson and I have shown them the water clouds, as far north as the glass can see – Mr Bryan and Dr Bessel are convinced that our duty lies there.'

'If only the ice-master and the men were likewise convinced,' Hall said.

On the seventh of September they found an anchorage on the east side of Robeson Channel, in thirteen fathoms, leeward of a grounded iceberg. Budington announced that here, in this secure spot, they would house the ship with canvas and bank her up with snow. If his advice were not taken, if winter quarters were not established here, he would not be answerable.

Bryan read their latitude as eighty-one, and reckoned they had been fifty miles, almost a full degree, further north.

At the service, Hall christened the berg Providence Berg, and the anchorage Thank God Harbor.

UNITED STATES NAVY BOARD OF INQUIRY, WASHINGTON DC, JUNE 5TH, 1873. GEORGE ROBESON, NAVY SECRETARY, PRESIDING

Testimony of George Tyson, Assistant Navigator

Q   Did you discern a notable change in discipline after the death of Captain Hall?

A   I believe everyone did, sir.

Q   How do you mean?

A   From the beginning Captain Budington had consorted with the men, circulating among them as an equal. I must say, he was a disorganiser from the very commencement of the expedition.

Q   How do you mean? How did he disorganise?

A   Well, sir, he associated himself with the crew very much, cursing his commander, blaming him, and speaking slightingly of him.

Q   Was it Captain Hall of whom he so spoke?

A   Yes, sir.

Q   In what way, particularly?

A   In his own way. I could not describe it to you.

Q   What seemed to be the ground of complaint, if any?

A   His ground of complaint was that the Captain was not a seaman. On the most frivolous things, he would be among the crew, complaining of Captain Hall.

Q   Was he insubordinate to the Captain in any way?

A   Oh no, sir; he was very subordinate to the Captain in his presence.

Q   Did you have differences of opinion with him?

A   I did, sir.

Q   And did you make these differences of opinion clear to the crew?

A   Not to the crew. Not for my part, sir, though I cannot speak for Captain Budington on that.

Q   Did you accuse him of cowardice before the officers?

A   Never.

Q   Did you in any way impugn his competence, or question his authority?

A   I do not think so, sir. I did once, at a meeting of the officers and scientific crew, use the word 'puerile.'

Q   'Puerile?'

A   Yes. In reference to his reluctance to advance the ship in a northerly direction. I believe he was much offended by this, but I felt it my duty to speak plain.

UNITED STATES NAVY BOARD OF INQUIRY, ON BOARD USS TALAPOOSA, WASHINGTON DC, OCTOBER 11TH, 1873, NAVY SECRETARY GEORGE ROBESON PRESIDING.

Testimony of Hubbard C. Chester, First Mate

Q   Did you think Captain Budington insubordinate to Captain Hall at any time, or disrespectful to the principal aims of the expedition?

A   I think Captain Budington to be a good whaling captain, but I do not think he has enthusiasm for the North Pole. As to Captain Hall, I think Captain Budington depreciated him, using improper language to the seamen on the main deck. He did not speak respectfully of the commander or the expedition, neither when he was drunk nor sober. His idea was that the enterprise was all damn nonsense, and he thought the scientific work was nonsense too. He regarded the whole thing as foolishness.

Testimony of William Morton, Second Mate

Q   What caused you to resign your charge of the provisions after the death of Captain Hall?

A   I thought it would be an unpleasant situation.

Q   And how?

A   I think Captain Budington lacked firmness.

Testimony of Noah Hays, Seaman and Coal-passer

One day I was over at the observatory with Dr Bessel; I was there a good part of the time then, in the winter. He appeared to be very light-hearted, and said that Captain Hall's death was the best thing that could happen for the expedition. The next day, he was laughing when he mentioned it. I was much hurt at the time, and told him I wished he would select somebody else as an auditor if he had any such a thing to say.

Testimony of Captain Sidney O. Budington

I did say to Seaman Noah Hays some such thing as, 'They will do for the devilish fools on the sledge-journey,' in regard to some carpenter's shavings, and that as Captain Hall was about to set out on such a journey. The Captain overheard my remark, and took some offence at it, I recall. As ship's captain, I perceived the safety of the ship and the crew as my primary responsibility. My language was not always nice; perhaps not always well-chosen.

CHAPTER EIGHT
DRIFTING: TYSON DINES

For Tyson, the testimony of the firmament is neither the childish fancy nor the nursery picturebook mocked by Bessel and Meyer, but stark proof. The aurora is the brushwork of God, and no rival exegesis passes muster. As successive days offer mere gradations of grey for the eye and a grotesque symphony of growling ice and howling wind for the ear, only the wilfully blind, the perversely deaf, can stand beneath the sudden gratuitous glory of the dancing light and deny that here, in this desert, the Creator has at once stretched his canvas and tuned his harp.

The need to urinate wakens him. He feels a new silence, the end of three days of gale, and resolves to venture outside, to piss under the stars as becomes a man. He crawls into the kunitchuk, the tight entrance tunnel, and wriggles toward the sky. Before he has covered half the length there are intimations of light, and when he timorously pokes his head into the night he gasps.

Brushwork?

Canvas?

The Almighty's tablecloth.

Only the eskimos are ever unequivocally awake. For Tyson and the sailors, with neither day nor night, with no cycle of work and rest, the days are endured in a flickering dance between sleep and waking, between plump dreams and the gnawing grey reality of hunger, cold, bleeding gums, aching joints, paranoia. The dreams are of food and drink and sex, and the freer spirits recount them to the others, record them in their otherwise humdrum diaries. They have eaten peacock-pie, drunk champagne, parted the white thighs of the Empress of all the Russias. And now Tyson, half-asleep, his bladder relieved, his oosook safely stowed against the minus-fifteen of the Arctic midnight, receives an invitation to dinner from the God of the wandering Israelites.

Southward, the Smile. The frozen indigo frown of the horizon has melted. Luxuriating in the unwonted stillness he stands staring at the sky and drifts through dreams: the effect of forty minutes, when the frown becomes apricot laughter, seems instantaneous. Above the Smile, lapping to the zenith and beyond, the undulations of colour drown the Pole Star itself. Eastward, silver fingers deftly nip the corner of the tablecloth, delicately shake, and the cloth unfolds – flickering green and yellow, rippling southward, upward, till Swan and Lion and Dragon and Bear and Charioteer and Winged Horse are all awash, all new, and nothing is familiar, nothing is what it has been. At the zenith the green is flecked with purple, crimson, blood-scarlet; the blood of Christ drips and trickles to the horizon, stains the glittering gown of the Almighty. The fingers shake again, rippling the cloth from the left hand to the right, and the shimmering hem becomes three-layered: purple and scarlet below, melting above into a gossamer haze of soft pink. Behind the translucent cloth, the crimson-dapple of the divine robe, the silver fingers of the Creator.

Tyson's feet are bloodless; his toes in extreme danger. Five minutes more might mean the loss of his nose, his ears, his penis. The warmth of the golden heavens is dream-warmth, chimeric, the ice's invitation to easeful death. He shakes his head, says aloud, 'No, no,' and summons the will and the strength to turn back into the kunitchuk.

But the Smile holds him yet. He stares southward, waiting. There is no music beyond the quickening drumbeat of his heart against his ribs, the dull vibration of Hannah and Joe making heat under the skins, a faint chorus of snore from the sailors' igloo, yet he sits in a vast dome of glittering stillness and listens.

And the Smile widens, and the Lord God of the wandering Israelites addresses him in a courteous drawl that hints at the slow stateliness of a Louisiana planter.

'Peacock pie,' God says.

Tyson has never chewed peacock pie. He anticipates its gamey warmth in his nostrils, feels its oniony feathery sting in his throat and his belly. There are persimmons too, and there is cream.

'Cognac,' God says, and Tyson's dead toes become warm. Again, the passing of a half-hour is an instant.

His body begins to die. Peacock feathers betoken ill-luck, someone once told him, and only the hen is good eating.

The voice of that someone, captious and jarring, jerks him into awareness. The cloth is gone, the blue-black sky telling the old stories again. His eyes flit from the Dipper across the Pole to Cassiopeia, all familiar. His legs hurt and his feet have disappeared. In the south a straggle of floating streamers indicates

87

where God had spread His grin. As Tyson watches, the Smile returns for a moment of avuncular solicitation. Maintaining the warm Louisiana drawl, God says:

'Pecans.'

Awake now, Tyson knows that he might already have lost his feet, might die. Into his head drifts Dr Bessel's favourite word.

'Coruscation,' he says to the sky.

Gasping with the pain of it, he turns until his knees are in contact with the ice and begins the long crawl through the entrance tunnel

The lamps are dowsed, and in the blackness of the igloo there are no distinctions, no proprieties. The mound of buffalo and reindeer skins that covers Joe and Hannah and Puney fills most of the space. Tyson finds his corner – two buffalo hides, one walrus, most of a bear. Under their weight he still freezes, and below his knees he feels nothing.

Maybe this is death, he thinks. The memory of the Smile, the absence of all sensation now below his knees, the sudden un-earthly clarity of the pictures in his head – these, he thinks, might portend, might signal, might be a finish. Dying duly concentrates his mind. If his forty-two years are reviewed, they are done in a rapid flick of the pages that takes him to the final chapter, the moment when he was pitched into the wonderful: ten o'clock of the night of fifteenth October 1871. Engraving it in his skull, on his tombstone, he capitalises it:

THE SEPARATION

There was prelude enough. Hall was almost a year dead, Budington had long abandoned any pretence that his ambition reached further than escaping the embrace of the ice and getting the ship south. Tyson and Chester pleaded for a final hike, an assault on the 83rd parallel, splitting into two groups of four, following the land as far north as it would take them, depositing caches for the return journey. He assured them that the first relaxation of the ice in Polaris Bay would be his cue for weighing anchor, insisted that northward forays were confined to recovery-trips for jettisoned equipment. The *Polaris* had been nipped and squeezed and stretched and battered till she leaked at every seam, and the sailors were refusing to man the hand-pumps while there was an ounce of coal for the boiler.

At the centre of discontent in the forecastle was Kruger – baptised Johannes Wilhelm Christian, but called, for reasons forgotten even by himself, Robert. For Tyson, he embodied all that was best and worst in the maritime breed: a well-salted seaman, possessed of reckless self-sacrificing courage that had placed many a shipmate in his debt, but an inveterate ranter and whiner about trifles. He would hurl himself joyfully at growling icebergs or threshing whales, yet he seethed and plotted murderous revenges if he fancied himself slighted by a stray remark or cheated of a biscuit. His colourful career was encapsulated in his accent – thick Pomerania laced with Brooklyn, Connecticut and Edinburgh. He had skipped from a Rostock herringer to a Leith merchantman and from that to a string of Dundee whalers; then in '62 to the *Orray Taft* whaling out of New London, a vessel Tyson himself had sailed in, signing off a Scotchman to join a Yankee because there were enough of his countrymen aboard her for the making of a skat school. At intervals regular enough in the ten years since then, Tyson had spoken a ship in the whaling grounds and found him among the crew, a prized boatsteerer, but a man never settled, never raised to the quarter-deck, denied advancement by the taint of devilment, a madness that seemed inexorably to produce at least one episode of violence or near-mutiny on every voyage.

In the time before Hall's death, the romance of the polar quest seemed to grip him as it gripped none of the other sailors and few of the officers, and Hall loved him as tireless flogger-up of merriment. If he laughed at the High Ideal and ludicrously pantomimed the planting of the Sacred Banner at the top of the world, still his reduction of these things to a jolly sailor's prank made them seem all the more possible. That he was incontinently hated by Budington, whose stomach sickened at the mere thought of a further mile northward, had raised him to the highest peak of Hall's affections.

But during the year of disintegration in Thank God Harbor, with the officers openly bickering and the men released from virtually every duty and given over to aimless cavorting, gambling, and shooting of guns, it was Kruger who suffered the most terrible falling-off. The reckless bodily courage remained, but it was now

89

untempered with humour or sociability. As all of them succumbed to dark-induced paranoia, his irascibility over small things grew savage and murderous, and the sailors became nervous in his company, afraid that any transaction – even an exchange of greetings – might unleash the monster. For Tyson, it seemed that Kruger might stand as the epitome of what has afflicted everyone – their moral disintegration personified.

On the afternoon of 12th August, two hours after the christening of Charlie Polaris, they broke out of Polaris Bay and charged full-steam into the ice-litter of Kennedy Channel.

There were three days of slow southward progress; they reached the 80th parallel before the ice gripped them again and they secured the ship to a floe, an immense five-mile disc of southward-drifting pack.

The summer was dying, and the light with it. Their floe dragged them slowly, two miles each day, through snow, sleet, rain, dripping fog, into the wide expanse of Kane Basin. South and north they saw the dark clouds that announced open, ice-free water, but here the pack enfolded them in a crushing hug. Most of the coal had gone to the donkey-engines, pumping the hold dry – work that could have given purpose to idle hands. The last sections of the oil-burning boiler, useless weight, had been left behind at Polaris Bay. When cracks appeared they fired the *Polaris* up for a spurt, a Yankee charge, or took to the ice and dragged her through, but after five weeks of drifting, steaming, sailing and manhauling they found themselves still locked in nervy companionship with the great floe.

The growling in the ice worried Tyson, stirred him with the need to prepare for the worst. Grudgingly, as if scared to admit the possibility of losing the ship, Budington let him have poles and canvas from the hold and with Joe's help he built a shelter on the floe for the ammunition and emergency provisions.

By the end of September, summer was truly over, and it was clear even to Budington that they would have to winter there, in Kane country. The thought was almost too much for his raddled nerves. The public, fed on tales of high romance by the New York and Chicago newspapers, and the politicians, no less seduced by Kane's own bright-purple accounts, knew virtually nothing of the real horrors of the events that had taken place here twenty years ago, when Kane had taken the *Advance* into the ice, ostensibly in a search for the remains of Sir John Franklin but secretly setting his sights on the North Pole. Hall himself had happily fed the legend in his fundraising lectures – had conjured up scenes for patriotic Boston housewives, sensation-thirsty journalists, factory-owners eager to associate some thimbleful of their millions with Yankee heroism: eighteen men, minute specks in a seething, crashing hell of floe and berg, dragging their tiny brig ever closer to the Pole, culminating in the moment when Morton, a new Columbus-Cortez-Pizarro, left Hans in charge of the sledge and climbed a headland – Cape Kane, he christened it – to gaze upon the glittering Polar Sea.

Budington and the sailors, who had lived with that same Morton and that same Hans for two years, know the real story: the grisly catalogue of scurvy, frostbite, treachery, mutiny and murder, with the fragile Dr Kane faring better than his men only because he acquired a taste for rat's blood.

Budington's ill-subdued panic was shared by many of the sailors, who read the flagrant terror in his face and who knew too well that there was no prophylactic against the vagaries of the ice; that their floe, dragged in one direction by the wind, might meet face-to-face a million ton berg, tide-borne in the opposite direction, and be instantaneously shattered; that the spiralling central pack might sweep the *Polaris* to the edge of the fixed shore-pack and slice her from stem to stern.

Scurvy had delivered its calling-card: Meyer's gums began to bleed, his joints to ache. Tyson prescribed a daily cupful of seal's blood. With seals in plentiful supply, they enjoyed a strengthening eskimo-menu, but the season of autumn gales was upon them and their southward, sunward drift was not fast enough for them to evade the darkness. 'The Polar night is upon us now,' Bryan portentously informed them over the breakfast table on October 15th, whilst to port and starboard the ice rehearsed its attack. Driven by a northerly gale, the floe jammed between grounded bergs, and the squeeze began in earnest. The little schooner herself proclaimed that this was not the day-to-day pressure they had endured for the last two months, but a proper death-hug. Steep-sided, not flared like a whaler, she relied on her strength, and while the nip was even, she bore it nobly – screaming and growling in

91

every plank but unbreached, like an egg squeezed evenly in the hand. But as she was lifted and dropped, lifted and dropped, there was an ever-present danger that a sudden stab would crack her sides.

In his starboard-side cabin Tyson was roused by the rapid elevation of the entire ship and ran out to the deck. The pack had risen above the gunwales. The sailors had gathered on the port rail. In the darkness they could not see the lowering berg that pressed on their floe, but they could feel its presence, and their panic swelled.

A push from the floe lifted the port side still higher, then the ice retreated and the *Polaris* dropped again. Lindquist and Jamka had been knee-deep in seawater in the starboard alleyway. Now they were left dry as the flood rushed across the deck. Schumann, the chief engineer, suddenly engulfed in the port hold, ran aloft to tell them it was all up with them, there was a leak in the stem and the ship was splitting apart. They had to make for the ice on the port side. Tyson delivered his news to Budington, who was in the galley with a bottle of rum and no glass. Through his drunkenness and his fear, Budington tried to reassume his captain's authority.

'Dear God. Dear God.' He drained the final inch of liquor, stood, sat, stood again, lifted the empty bottle to his lips, slapped it on the table, shook his head at its emptiness.

'Dear God.'

Tyson grabbed his wrist. 'The men are dropping everything over the side, Captain. Most of it's lost, running under the ship. They need your presence. We require your orders!'

Budington stood again.

'My orders, Mr Tyson? My orders? On the ice! Everything on the ice!'

Tyson tried to drag him aloft, but he shook himself free. 'The books, man. I must save the books.'

In the waist, the sailors had not waited for orders. Frantically they hurled flour, rice, pemmican, corned beef, coal, clothing, sledges, boats – everything that had been gathered on deck for the emergency – over the side. There was a two-foot crack between the *Polaris* and the main floe, but the hawsers were holding. Screaming above the gale, Tyson succeeded in forcing some of the sailors over the side with himself and the eskimos.

Hannah organised, securing the biggest sledge under the ship so that they could load it. In the driving sleet, in almost complete darkness, Tyson worked hour upon hour, passing barrels, boxes, cans, bundles, to unseen hands, while the *Polaris* rose and plunged, pounding the ice beneath her to mush. He knew that some of the men had retreated to the heart of the floe with their personal necessities, felt them cowering in the roaring dark, afraid of the ship and its wild pummelling; but the time for recrimination would come. As far as he could see, Budington had stayed below, but he heard the piping tones of Dr Bessel, fighting to maintain order on the deck, striving to turn blind flapping into disciplined unloading. He knew too that Meyer was on the ice, struggling in the face of his own feebleness to muster the men and to offer relief to Hannah.

And still there was time for thinking. In the midst of everything, while the storm shrieked and the ice grated and the ship pounded the ice to porridge, his mind roamed. Not two nights ago, he had dreamed just this: the *Polaris/Periwinkle* lifted and flung against a fearsome precipice of ice, bursting apart, tossing them all into the pack. As he watched his dream-self then, so he watched his real self now. This will end, he told that self, this will end and there will be a time when coal is burning in a tiled grate and the scents of woman and roses and pipesmoke tickle his nose and silk rustles and tea tastes sweet and all of this screaming horror is a traveller's tale. This will end, the voice in his head said, this will end as all nightmares end, and we will laugh. There was even time to chide himself for harbouring unchristian thoughts about the scientists, time to admire the cool determination of the little doctor, the courage of the meteorologist; and thought to spare for Hannah, expertly stacking the provisions under the heaving side of the ship, precise and neat and careful with the prospect of instant death upon her.

In four hours of frenzied toil they transferred half of the ship's stores to the ice, with the sledges and the two whaleboats.

At last the pressure eased. There was a lull in the gale and the *Polaris*, listing to port but unsplit, ceased her groaning. Budington appeared at last by the rail, and Tyson climbed aboard to consult him.

'How is it with the leak?' he asked.

'There is no leak – no more than there was before,' Budington told him.

'Dear Christ,' Tyson said. 'Then we have to bring it all back – the ice is breaking up; we might lose everything.'

He did not wait for Budington's orders, but stopped the sailors from throwing anything more over the side, and leapt back to the floe. His rage outstormed the storm. He found Kruger and dragged him across the floe to the whaleboats, all the while screaming at the indistinguishable figures that they must reclaim what they could and return it and themselves to the ship.

Then with a rumble different in kind from all that had gone before, the floe began to crack under their feet.

All of them, on the floe and on the ship, felt the change. Budington's fear was fresh-kindled. Waving both arms, he called on them to retreat, to drag themselves and the provisions further from the ship into the middle of the floe. They were still dragging when the ice exploded under them. The *Polaris* righted herself, ripped her portside fastenings from the floe and began to drift. In the storm-battered blackness, lit only by their few lanterns, it required less than two minutes to place her utterly out of sight for the people on the ice. At the edge where she had parted from the floe, Tyson seized the corners of a bundle of oxhides, and dragged it clear of the water. The weight of it exhausted him, and he crumpled to the floe while Christiana fell upon the hides and unrolled them to release Augustus, Tobias and Succi. Her fourth child, Charlie Polaris, was naked and asleep in her parka hood. In the darkness, men were crying out from fragments of the floe no bigger than tabletops. Tyson recovered, grabbed the arm of a man – Jamka it was – and dragged him to the bigger of the whaleboats. They launched it and paddled toward the cries, screaming into the wind. Four of their shipmates clambered aboard. From the other boat, Kruger and Anthing rescued two more.

Finally, by four of the morning, with the *Polaris* three hours gone, the cries ceased and they were all on the main floe, though none could tell how extensive it now was. There was no hope of erecting a shelter. They huddled into a single knot of bodies under the hides and canvas in what they hoped was the secure centre of the mass.

Freezing in his tattered sealskin, Tyson walked the floe and watched for the meagre dawn.

Now, three months gone, as he waits to die, he rolls himself into a ball under his blankets and recalls that dawn of the sixteenth – a hesitant easing of black into grey that served only to reveal the hideousness of their predicament: nineteen miserable souls perched on a heaving cake of ice, staring in disbelief across the jagged wilderness of the pack in futile search for their lost ship, their fourteen drifting comrades. They might have made land, but the sailors would not respond to his orders. There is melancholy satisfaction in the thought that his death will be followed by bloody anarchy, a miniature war whose outcome will be the deaths of all nineteen of them.

But his arms refuse to die. They drag him toward the central hump of the igloo, fight through the intricate tangle of skins and find living flesh, Joe distinguishable from Hannah by a hint of hair on his back, Puney skinnily naked between them. The natives – he has never fathomed how – retire fully swathed in parkas and britches and socks but contrive in the night to undress themselves completely for the maximum of body-warmth and for drying off their clothing. And five, six times in the night they will discharge bodily functions with the merest ripple of disturbance, a momentary unravelling of the skein of interlocked flesh, then an instant repair. Should crisis arise – a cracking of the ice, a sudden hurricane, a marauding bear – they will be instantaneously alert and dressed – not a presence in the snow-world, Tyson thinks, but a constituent part of it. His entry under the hides, the intrusion of chill, causes no alarm, but an easy somnolent readjustment that places him between Hannah and Puney in the deep bloodwarm core. Without waking, Hannah eases off his shirt, drops it clear of the hides and embraces him, her hands over his heart, her belly and chest tight against his back. Returning warmth brings realisation: there is no longer an easy drift into nothingness, but a tearing agony in his limbs; no longer acceptance of death, but fear for his feet. He groans, and Hannah's clasp tightens.

'Feet, Hannah. My feet,' he says.

'Feet, Mr Tyson,' she whispers in his ear.

Warm now, the skin on his belly acknowledges her hands as they travel downwards. Her fat fingers undo the cord of his britches, work the hard-frozen sealskin past his knees. He feels nothing on his skin, but hears the screaming of a pain that seems to originate in his legbones.

Her famous fingertips begin at his knees. After the weeks of privation he is barely fleshed and even her butterfly pressure starts jagged pains. However light the touch, however tender the rapid fine rubbing on his calves, he fears for his shinbones, fears that unguarded as they are by muscle or fat and brittled by cold, they might snap.

Hannah knows. The bones will not snap but the quickening blood will bring feeling and with it white pain and a tearing in his brain that will make him want to die.

He has legs again, calves and knees and thighs, but knowledge of them brings renewed fear.

'My feet. How are my feet, Hannah?'

Her mouth closes on his ear. 'Hannah's feet, Mr Tyson: Hannah's feet. You wait; you don't be afraid.'

He surmises, but cannot feel, that his left foot is between her thighs, his right in her hands.

'Hannah's feet, Mr Tyson.'

As the pain recedes and his terror eases, he tumbles into sleep and watches her eating his right foot. It sits in front of her face, upright on a tablecloth of blinding variegation, gently steaming. She plucks the toes singly, beginning with the little one, popping each into her mouth until she arrives at the big toe. She bends to it, smiles, licks it, laughs, nibbles. Her teeth are two curved razor-edges. She bares the bone of the big toe and his cry of terror wakens him again. Puney whimpers her irritation. Joe farts. Hannah's breathing is a soft hollow whine; every fifth or sixth exhalation ends in a delicate rattle. He has a foot again, his right foot, but as yet no toes. He realises that his feet are naked for the first time in eight weeks. As her hands resurrect the toes of his right foot, so her thighs bring blood and life and agony to his left. Press and ease, press and ease. There is still fat on her thighs, and knowing that, he knows that the foot has survived, is still connected to his brain.

'Toes, Hannah,' he says.

She breathes into his ear. He is no longer aware of her smell, having lived in it for two months. She enfolds him in her blubbery flesh and imparts a new motion, hardly motion at all, that resonates in his every bone. He is being rubbed and squeezed and pounded along the full length of his body, yet there is no movement that an observer could detect and no sound above their synchronous breathing. His toes return, each distinct in its fiery agony. He welcomes the pain, celebrates the reinstated wholeness of his body, allows his mind to voyage again.

That dawn, that morning of the sixteenth. A layer of snow on the oxhides had helped them to stay warm. Excluded, Tyson had not asked for a skin because he was afraid of the consequences of a refusal, the admission that discipline and camaraderie were irrecoverably at an end, that the courtesy they would have extended to a stranger or an enemy might be denied a shipmate.

Over the year since Hall's death, as a corollary of his pique at Budington, he had repudiated his own authority, lost the habit of command, and now he paid the reckoning. He could not order, but merely plead that they rise, shake off the snow, make ready the two boats, transport themselves and the supplies to the Greenland shore. The floe had been cracking, there was a serviceable east-ward lead, but the northerly gale was bringing new ice. The men rose grumbling and slow. Those who had rescued their bundles wanted to change clothing. All wanted a fire, coffee, cooked meat. Tyson's importunacy, far from bringing home the perilousness of their situation, confirmed his status as a whining fool, a chronic fault-finder, a nag. Meyer, his only hope for an intermediary, was exhausted, unable to stand. Jackson the cook, who shared his dread, was despised as a negro and as Budington's favourite, and enjoyed smaller authority even than the eskimos, whom no-one would think of consulting. In the night the gale had softened to a near-calm, but now it rose again, cutting them through their wet clothes, driving fresh ice before it, closing the leads between the jammed floe and the shore.

It was mid-morning, nine o'clock, before they launched the boats, and Tyson knew the effort was hopeless. They hauled up again, spent, despairing, and bitter in their loathing of Tyson, Budington, the United States Government, the North Pole.

And while they were re-establishing themselves on the floe, Tyson scanned the horizon with the telescope and saw the *Polaris*.

She was eight miles above them, ploughing the mush-ice under both steam and sail.

So corrupted was his authority that even his cry, 'The ship! The ship!' provoked scorn and at best a half-hearted effort to raise colours, assorted rags on tied-together oars. Watching the speck of the ship disappear behind the land, their rancour swelled. Kruger claimed that Budington, in his fanatical loathing of Tyson, would be content to let them all perish. Seriously considering the proposition, Jamka countered that the captain's love for Jackson the cook and Puney the native filly would bring him to their rescue.

Tyson avoided the fight, enlisted Anthing and Nindermann to erect a tent on the western side of the floe as protection for the supplies. From there they saw the *Polaris* again at anchor behind the tongue of land, ten miles to the north. Tyson's telescope confirmed the melancholy news that she was stationary, her sails furled, the air above her funnel clear.

But he found strength at the sight, became an officer again, ordered them to make the boats ready – abandoning everything but food – and drag them the quarter-mile to the open water. With Joe and Hans and Jackson he ran for the eastern edge, reached the lead, and turned to find the eskimos gone. He cursed them for cowards, then realised it was not fear of gale or sea or ice that had taken them back, but fear of leaving their women and children with the sailors. He sent Jackson back and watched, screaming his rage at Greenland, while the new ice closed. When the sailors arrived with the boat it was crammed above the gunwales with food, clothing, coal, pots, walrus tusks for peddling on the Hamburg waterfront, everything that could be lifted from the ice.

But there was no rudder.

Tyson howled, and Kruger laughed. They made the useless gesture, launching the whaleboat into the ice-gruel, pushing her from the floe, attempting to row, but the wind was now a hurricane roaring full into their faces and they were rudderless and exhausted from the drag across the floe. The attempt to raise a sail almost capsized them, and Tyson ordered them back to the ice. He saw through his rage the folly of remonstration, the pointlessness of nagging the darkness. He dragged an oxhide to the thickest part of the floe, wrapped himself in it and collapsed, for once heedful of nothing beyond his own exhaustion, his own frozen limbs. He was instantly asleep, and within ten minutes the sailors and the eskimos had formed their hide-village around him.

He dreamt of sea-monsters, and their throttling tentacles became Joe's hand, shaking him awake into the drab grey dawn. The ice had cracked in the night: across a hundred yards of heaving sea they watched the boat – still laden with their provisions, their clothes, the greater part of their canvas, their guns and powder, the eskimos' kayaks, all that might keep them alive till the whaling grounds now that the *Polaris* and the Greenland shore were alike impossible – drifting ever further from them on the main floe while they stood on a bobbing fragment less than two hundred yards in its widest girth. The gap widened as they stared, the main floe swept eastward by the wind and the driving bergs, their fragment buffeted southwestward toward the frowning cliffs of Ellesmere Island. He mustered the eskimos and Jackson to the sides of the other boat, but the sailors, egged on by Kruger, pleaded exhaustion, the wind, the fragility of the smaller boat, the nearness of the *Polaris* and their imminent rescue, the likelihood that change of weather would bring them back closer to the lost supplies without their stir, without the risk to their lives – anything rather than another venture upon the heaving water. Desperate for the kayaks, Hans and Joe strained at the sides of the boat, and screamed for help. Some of the men were roused, and the boat was dragged to the edge, but again the struggle to launch her into the gale was fruitless.

If there were those among the sailors who shared with Tyson and the eskimos the conviction that the defeat was a sentence of lingering death, they allowed themselves to be comforted by Kruger's laughter. Better the solid ice than the raging sea in a cockleshell, he told them – better erect their beacon here, where Captain Budington would be sure to see it, and be sure to move heaven and earth to rescue his Inuit filly.

There was a sliver of relief in Tyson's despair. Convinced that they had seen the last of the *Polaris*, he saw too the futility of ranting at the loss of the boat, the provisions, the fuel, the kayaks. Lacking those kayaks, the eskimos would be crippled in their search for food. Scurvy and starvation would make short work of them, and the best they could hope for was that the floe remained large enough to bear a few of their corpses into the whaling ground to be found in the spring and offered decent burial by Christian sailors. That prospect, offering a curtailment of his ordeal, he found almost bearable.

But the boat came back to them, the food and the kayaks were recovered, the agony was prolonged; and now, two months into their drift, the floe has lost a tenth of its ice. The edges of the platform have frayed, and each of them has lost flesh in proportion.

Hannah's rhythm is becoming faster, her breathing deeper. There is a storm in his ear, a ferocious tightening of the pressure on his ribs.

Tyson's knowledge of women is meagre, his shy couplings with Mary his wife in their polite bed thinly augmented by a handful of fleeting waterfront encounters in New London and St Johns. Female nakedness is an alien plant, and he shudders at the enveloping flesh of Hannah, whose sex has hitherto impinged on his consciousness no more than the sex of the huskies. The pore-to-pore contact thaws his skin until he can distinguish the contours of breast and belly and thigh, the prickling of her pubic bush. His brain thaws too: the storm in his ear becomes again Hannah's silken voice, breathless and urgent, and he recognises with horror her little gasp, her *au-au-au* of pleasure-pain, monstrously foreign in its abandon, its femaleness, its paganism, its innocence, its solicitude. Her hands release the pressure on his ribs, her suddenly relaxed fingers encounter his engorged oosook, pinning it to his belly.

There is no work. Tyson merely adds the weight of his right hand to Hannah's fingers and by some obscure reflex, some communication of mutual need, the plump clever fingers close.

In a matter of seconds the eruption of the long dormant volcano happens, far more pain than pleasure, raking him with a sharp agony from toes to skull.

She is asleep, gently snoring, but her fingers, with a life of their own, close gently on his shrunken oosook, offering motherly comfort. Tyson's aches become indistinguishable, his body a single pain. Now that his toes are safe he fears for his teeth, grown slack in their sockets. He ventures a hand to his mouth: only the canines seem confidently bedded – the rest dance at his touch, the gums throb, and there is a soft warmth of blood. The irony is not lost on him: standing between him and perdition are hard biscuit, endlessly tough pemmican, rock-solid sealgut, all of them beyond the strength of his teeth. He relies utterly on the eskimos, whose cooking softens the meat and whose teeth, in the days when there is no fuel-blubber, can do the work of mastication for him. There will be a time, not far distant, when he lies as helpless before Hannah as a hatchling in a redwing's nest.

Hannah, most wonderfully, has found Joe's thighs. Joe has been twelve hours at the breathing hole, has failed to make a kill. Now she warms him; now through their shared exhaustion they make new warmth, when the only need is warmth.

Night upon night they have made that warmth. Often, stirred to wakefulness by their dance, Tyson has crawled to the lamp, worked on his journal. Writing is bitterly exhausting labour. The occasions when he has risked the removal of his glove for easier control of the pencil stub, trusting to the lamp to fend off frost-bite, have been catastrophic, almost costing him his fingers. Now he fumbles with the stub in his mitten, scribbles blindly. To limit himself to the bare log of events would leave a void. Nothing happens, so he frequently expands the account, gropes toward the lyrical, essays the scientific, the metaphysical, the theological. Irony besets him in this too – the realisation that here, in the throes of a bizarre adventure, playing out a drama that will be ranked among the most thrilling of desperate episodes in the sublimely desperate history of Arctic adventure, their chiefest problem, outweighing even that of filling their bellies, should be the preservation of their mental equilibrium in the fight against eternal paralytic boredom.

Sameness. Outside the subdued cavorting of Joe and Hannah, only the flickering of the blubberlamp or the occasional squawk of a sleeper battling through bad dreams relieves the black silence of the igloo.

101

UNITED STATES NAVY BOARD OF ENQUIRY, ON BOARD USS TALAPOOSA, WASHINGTON DC, OCTOBER 11TH 1873, NAVY SECRETARY GEORGE ROBESON PRESIDING

Q   According to your recollection, what attempts were made to find and rescue the party which was stranded on the ice floe?

Testimony of Hubbard C Chester, First Mate

During the course of the day, October 16th, I was up and down the mast-head at intervals of ten or fifteen minutes, in all perhaps an hour and a half. I saw a piece of floe with supplies on it, but no men. I do not recall anyone else climbing the masthead, but someone might have done in my absence.

Testimony of Dr Emil Bessel, Chief Scientific Officer

I believe that a constant search was maintained during the day of the 16th, but no sign of the party could be seen. I cannot understand how it was that we failed to see them, while they could distinguish the smoke-stack of the *Polaris*, or so I have heard.

Testimony of Emil Schumann, Chief Engineer

I climbed the mast-head twice, but saw nothing. I think no-one was aloft at four of the afternoon, when it is said they saw our smoke-stack.

Testimony of Noah Hays, Seaman

I do not know that we looked for them right away: our first concern was for the safety of the ship, for it seemed she might be sinking. I was at the wheel, and my attention was turned mostly toward the shore. I scanned the horizon two or three times to the southward, using a marine-glass that lay by the wheel, but I saw nothing of our companions. I believe Mr Chester climbed the mast once or twice, but there was no continuous watch. I think once he called out that he saw something – not men, but some provisions – but most concluded it was black ice, some fifteen miles off, and anyway, it was not in our power to reach it, in the thickness of the ice.

Testimony of William F Campbell, Fireman

I climbed the mast at ten o'clock in the morning. I saw some provisions on a small floe, but no human beings. I had a cat on board the *Polaris*, taken all the way from Washington. It stayed with us two winters before it ran away at Hakluyt Island, as we came down in our boats. The eskimos had never seen a cat before, and were much interested in it. They have a name for it in their language, though they do not have the animal.

AT WASHINGTON DC, NOVEMBER 6TH 1873

Testimony of R W D Bryan, Astronomer and Chaplain

The separation was entirely an accident, unless someone maliciously cut the rope, which I cannot believe was the case – that any member of the crew could have been of such a hostile disposition. The morning after, Mr Chester came down from the mast-head to report that he could see a piece of ice with provisions, but no sign of people. No-one else went up then, unless perhaps Mr Hobby when I was not present; we were satisfied that wind and current had carried them southward, out of our reach, and we were much grieved by this.

CHAPTER NINE
QUESTING: THANK GOD

At Thank God Harbor, eighty-one and a half degrees north, there was industry, and with it came comradeship, communication, even laughter.

The *Polaris* was tightly bedded, the decks housed in canvas, the whole structure banked with snow. Entry was gained eskimo-style through a narrow tunnel that required all but the natives and the petit Dr Bessel to stoop. All talk of pushing the ship further north was dropped, satisfying Budington and reassuring those among the sailors who had been more susceptible to his whining. They joked now about the *Hansa*, lost a year before on the other side of the Greenland icecap from where they now sat, whose crew was rewarded with double pay after a perilous drift through the eastern pack. The scientists Bessel, Bryan and Meyer eagerly set about establishing their laboratory-observatory while Hall, recovering his famous ebullience and his contagious optimism, hurled himself at the preparations for the sledge trips that would, he assured them, point the route for the spring dash to the Pole. His unforced forgetfulness of all that had marred the first three months of the expedition – the contempt and insubordination of his scientists, the drunkenness and unconcealed hostility of his ice-master, the indiscipline of some of his sailors – won him a smattering of respect and a heap of affection.

Among the Real People, the complicated fiction was maintained that even here, in their ancestral hunting-grounds, Hall was the father-protector and they the vulnerable and occasionally wayward children. If somewhere in his heart's core he acknowledged his dependence upon them and kept a tally of the occasions when they had saved his life – as often as not at clear risk to their own – still to the listening world he presented them as his faithful pets, distinguished from dogs or horses less by their intellect or their possession of an immortal soul than by their odour and the repulsiveness of their features. That repulsiveness he remarked upon as frequently and as loudly as the most intolerant of the men. Justifying his openness to the mildly distressed Bryan, who pleaded the equality of christianised creatures in the Maker's eyes, he assured the pastor that, insofar as he was privy to the workings of their savage minds, he was convinced that they returned the contempt of the *kabloonas* with one hundred percent interest. 'In rating one of us – even the most refined, even, shall we say, the young Dr Bessel himself – as somewhere below the lowest of his sledge-dogs, Joe would be making what to him would be a frank and entirely uncontentious judgement, Mr Bryan.' Touched by the pastor's sadness, he added, 'There might be a time, indeed, when he rightly rates you or me below a pound of rotted sealmeat.'

He slapped the pastor's arm and laughed, as he laughed often during the rapidly darkening October days.

There were occasions with beer and stories when flickerings of amiability lightened even Budington's ingrained surliness, though he growled his irritation whenever Hall hinted that the Pole might still fall within the reckoning of the expedition, that Congress still might get the full return on its fifty thousand dollars. If the scientists were no less scornful of their commander's dreams, they happily humoured him in the closeness of the eight-bunk cabin and in front of the seamen. Contempt for Budington ran deeper, and they ostentatiously offered him no support when he snorted his opinions about the folly of the entire undertaking and boasted that only his good sense had prevented their loss of the ship and death from starvation. Amid the complex inter-weaving of loyalties, Bessel found himself with a foot in Hall's camp, driven by their shared sense that the Republic was indeed owed some recompense. They jollily exchanged heroes, agreed that Ulysses S. Grant was the Bismarck of the New World and Otto von Bismarck the Grant of the Old, and that their utmost exertions in the quest for the Pole were no less than these master spirits of the age, unifiers of nations, deserved. Shut out by this poppycock, Budington renewed his assaults on the liquor store, and the doctor announced that he was compelled to lace his alcohol stock with tartar-emetic, well aware that he was striking not only at the ice-master, but at the chief engineer, Schumann, his countryman, who had filed himself a key and developed a taste for preserving-spirit and ether.

Hall's pride in the Stars and Stripes that fluttered at eighty-one degrees thirty-eight minutes north was not diminished by the discovery of hooks, arrowheads, spoons and other intimations that they occupied ground recently enough home to a sizable eskimo tribe. The savage presence here no more ranked in the chronicle of human achievement than did the numerous traces of bear, fox and musk-ox.

Bellies were well-filled; hands and feet blessedly warm. The Greenland oxen proved easy to kill and unexpectedly tastier than their fat musky Labrador cousins, and their hides, stretched and softened and stitched by Hannah and Christiana, made luxurious moccasins, gloves, pants, blankets. Hall, who was no sailor, rejoiced in the coming confinement of the ship, and his infection of the men with boyish hope, with easy optimism, with pride in what they had thus far achieved, progressed rapidly. Responding to the warmth, Bryan became his intermediary with the sailors, and between them they fashioned the sabbath services as an instrument in the forging of the *Polaris* crew into a family of sorts. On the last Sunday of September he invoked their high cause with such unaffected passion that most of them wept. He assured them also that there were in future to be no differences whatsoever between the fare offered to the forward and after messes, that they should all live together in brotherly equality and love, and after the service Siemens was enlisted to pen a letter of thanks, signed by them all and delivered secretly to his cabin. In his delight at reading it, Hall embraced Tyson, and asked him to stand by while he scribbled an instant reply:

> *Sirs,*
> *The reception of your letter of thanks to me of this date I acknowledge with a heart that deeply feels and fully appreciates the kindly feeling that has prompted you to this act. I need not assure you that your commander has, and ever will have, a lively interest in your welfare. You have left your homes, friends and country; indeed you have bid a long farewell for a time to the whole civilized world, for the purposes of aiding me in discovering the mysterious, hidden parts of the earth. I therefore must and shall care for you as a prudent father cares for his faithful children.*
>
> *Your commander,*
> *C.F.Hall*

United States North Polar Expedition, in winter-quarters, Thank God Harbor, Lat. 81 38'N, Long.61 44'W. Sept. 24th, 1871.

He blotted and folded the note, then opened it again for Tyson to read.

'George, we'll yet do something for our grandchildren to be proud of.'

Smiling, Tyson handed back the note.

'Do you approve?' the captain asked.

Tyson did.

But a week later, when Hall ordered him to start feeding up the dogs for the sledge-trip, the attempt to beat Parry's 82 45' north, he was abashed to have his request to take part refused.

Hall patted him on the shoulder. 'George, you know I'd like nothing better than to have you along, and I know you're Joe's and Hans' man for the job. By God, you're the dogs' choice too!' He lowered his voice. 'But you know my problem.' He nodded toward Budington, who stood on the ice directing improvements to the protective bank. 'I cannot trust that man. I can rely neither on his loyalty, nor on his seamanship. The thought that you are here to monitor both will be of immeasurable comfort to me on my journey.'

Chester the first mate was chosen as his companion, travelling with Hans on one sledge while Hall and Joe took the other. Tyson contented himself with supervising their preparations, meticulously weighing out food, feeding dogs, cutting harness lines; and responding with eloquent silence to Budington's rumbled asides about the folly of the venture.

The rancour of the ice-master was scrupulously impartial; he condemned the sailors as indolent dogs, the scientists as pompous dilettanti, the officers as damned fools. The eskimos, for whom he had preserved whatever exiguous grain of human affection was left in his system, he nevertheless routinely dismissed as fouler than the vermin that infested them.

There were almost-moments: October began in pellucid stillness – the feeble rays of the sun that was about to leave them cast a beneficent glow over the basin, the Arctic monster slumbered, and their laughter became song. The sailors found their squeeze-boxes, and Jamka proved the dabbest of hands on the doctor's violin, transformed into a fiddle. Anthing's mellow tenor offered relief from the raucous shanties. At the doctor's importuning, he acquainted himself thoroughly with every syllable and note of beautiful miller's daughter, abandoned spinster, bereaved king, winter traveller; and for the young refined physician-scientist the overheated deck of the *Polaris* became a drowsy chintzy Weimar drawing room, heavy with the aroma of Franconian wine, while the shaggy heads of the sailors metamorphosed into the delicate coiffures of perfumed girls fanning their cheeks and sighing over sad hearts in snow:

Ich will den Boden küssen
Und seid ihr gar so lau
Dass ihr erstarrt zu Eise
Wie kühler Morgentau.

Hall too sighed and wiped a tear, then led the men thunderously in the Battle Hymn of the Republic, and that finished, recited the valedictory words of the Navy Secretary, which he had long committed to memory:

'*Wishing for you and your brave comrades health, happiness, and success in your daring enterprise, and commending you and them to the protecting care of the God who rules the universe.*'

Thoroughly alive, thoroughly himself again, he apologised to the English contingent before his rendition of his favourite ballad:

The British shot flew hot,
Which the Yankees answered not,
Till they got within the distance they call handy, O!
'*Now,*' *says Hull unto his crew,*
'*Boys, let's see what we can do,*
If we take this boasting Briton we're the dandy, O!'

Thwarted in his desire to travel with Hall and the eskimos, Tyson threw himself into the construction of a storehouse.

Hall had gained a scant five miles of east when he made camp and sent Hans back to the ship with a letter requesting the items he had overlooked in the loading of the sledges – his bearskin mittens, his Greenland sealskin gloves, lancewarp and dogline, sealskin britches, candles, onions, files, candlesticks, a single snowshoe, a gill-cup, a fire-ball, whip handles, a coffee-box, sinew, sealskin boots. Hannah was required to stitch him a watch-case with neck-thong, and Puney was enjoined to be good.

Aiming for a hundred miles in two weeks, he achieved fifty. There was much christening: the wide beautiful bay where they made their outermost camp he named for the Rev. Newman, and in naming it, he recited the second prayer which that good pastor had composed for them:

Almighty Father in Heaven, thou art the God of all ages, climes and seasons. Spring and autumn, summer and winter obey Thy command. In the tropics Thou dost cause the sun to send forth floods of light and heat upon plain and mountain, until the earth burns like a furnace; and here in this far-off northern clime Thou givest snow like wool and scattereth the hoar-frost like ashes. Who can stand before Thy cold? But Thou art our shelter from the stormy blast, and our cover from the storm.

They named the southern cape for Senator Sumner, the northern for J. Carson Brevoort; and from their camp they scanned north to the limits of land, from where, Hall announced, he could descry his spring-route to the Pole. At Cape Brevoort they deposited a cylinder. There was food aplenty – ox and bear and wolf, rabbit and goose and partridge. In the comradely warmth of Joe's igloo Hall sucked on goose-bones and became again the Cincinnati newshack, fashioning headlines and lofty anthems of praise for their triumph of next year, smacking his lips to simulate the popping of the champagne corks at ninety north. Once, they came close to disaster: settling for the night on the floor of Joe's expertly fashioned airtight igloo, they found themselves suffocating. The failure of the kerosene lamp alerted Hall to the problem. 'Kick down the door!' he called to Joe, and recovering their breath, they laughed at their folly.

But Hans, who smelt as keenly as a fox, was not happy. Assisting Joe with the building of the final igloo, he stood within the circle of ice-blocks and pointed to where the commander sat alone like a rock deposited by the ice on the headland.

'Why does the Captain not help? The Captain likes to help,' he said.

'The Captain is tired. The Captain is thinking,' Joe said.

Hans was not mollified. 'The Captain likes to help.'

And on the last outward night as the wind rose and bitterly howled around the igloo, Hall ceased in mid-conjuration of their arrival at the Pole, listened for a moment then dropped his shoulders in a melancholy slump, as if the prospect of returning to the ship had already drained his spirit.

'Mr Chester,' he told the mate, 'I have a son, Charlie. Eleven years old, and I have been in his company less than three months of that eleven years.'

Chester gruffly offered comfort. 'The life, sir. The explorer's life.'

'A dog's life, Mr Chester. I look at Joe with little Puney, not even his blood-child. I watch her settling her head in his lap and I envy him. I look at Christiana with little Succi at her bosom; I watch her lick the child all over, like a mother-bear, and I envy them. I envy the poor savages, Mr Chester, and I think of my little Charlie, fatherless.' He shook his head. 'My wife will be destitute.'

'No sir, she will be rich: the celebrated wife of the greatest explorer of the age. She and you and your son will sit down to dinner with presidents and kings.'

'Like Hannah and Joe.' Hall shook his head slowly, mustering his sorrow. 'Chester, my arms ache. My chest aches.'

The ice of Newman Bay heaved and snarled, offering no westward passage for the dogs. Eastward loomed the vast unscalable Greenland icecap. To the north the land rose and fell in thousand-foot ridges well beyond the strength of dogs or men. Hall announced that in the morning they would travel in the only direction that offered itself – south, back to the *Polaris*.

They found her tight in her snow-housing, and their welcome on all sides was warm. Tyson embraced both captain and mate, and Budington's handshake seemed an offer of something. Hall reddened, drew a mitten across a tearstained cheek, and settled in his chair.

'Gentlemen, is there coffee?' he asked.

CHAPTER TEN
DRIFTING: THE REAL PEOPLE TALK LIBERALLY

On the matter of staying alive, the Real People are not practised in disagreement, not fluent in argument. Not only are these things luxuries they can ill afford, but their collective sense for the nuances of weather and the whims of their food supply render them unnecessary in all circumstances save the bitterest extremity. But Joe and Hannah, Hans and Christiana are tainted, have cast some of their Reality adrift. Primarily, there is a taint of love: Hans in Kane and Joe in Hall have come across *kabloonas* distinguished enough from the generality of their kind to have made possible a connection of sorts. Kane the eater of rats, Hall the swiller of bear's blood – each strove to become more real than the Real People, condescended to learn a smattering of language, approached fleshly contact. And with the particular loves came a general something else – compounded of fear, greed, loyalty, pity, admiration, curiosity. Joe has promenaded Broadway and Bond Street swinging an umbrella, Hans has fondled a Winchester carbine wonderfully fashioned in New Haven Connecticut. At times the greed predominates: how few eskimos have counted dollars, dressed their wives in calico, paid taxes, become creditors of the Government of the United States of America!

For Joe, a New Englander and a man of property, these things count mightily. Furthest from him in their debate, Christiana yearns for her kin. They require no sextants to tell them their position. Shorn of the clutter of *kabloonas* and dollars and the United States Navy they would be in a predicament hardly worse than is faced by most families of Real People or by whole tribes twice or more in a normal winter – a few days journey from safety, facing a battle against sea and ice that might peremptorily finish some or all of them. Uncontaminated and unencumbered, they would not find food the all-encompassing preoccupation it now is – would fill all their bellies for two days with a single seal, a few handfuls of dovekies, a pair of foxes. A bear would secure them. Now, eight hours of vigil by the breathing-hole, even if it is rewarded with a kill, affords them mere scraps, a trickle of blood, a goad to their hunger

The Navy food, of which they receive less than their fair

111

portion, is barely digestible and delivers no warmth. Christiana is frightened of the sailors and feels more at risk from their assaults than from the ice, but having made her case and had it rejected by the men, she maintains the silence that becomes her as Hans's wife.

Yet Hans's authority is waning. In what matters most, success in the hunt, he has been soundly outdone by Joe, whose skill, enhanced by a firmer command of English and an intimacy with Hall that has sometimes approached man-to-man communication, has earned him a grudging respect from the *kabloonas*. Hans recognises that the verdict of the seals outweighs his longer experience of the region and his deeper acquaintance with American sailors and polar questers. He acknowledges Joe as the senior man, their spokesman, and relies upon him for intelligence of how the *kabloonas* are thinking – not only their schemes for escaping the floe or for eating or abandoning the children, but their views on the prospect of extra payment for their drift. In his turn, Joe relies without acknowledgement on Hannah's rapidly developing comprehension of German.

Christiana complains loudest and with most cause. She is the most abused: even Hall the Inuit-lover has designated the daily contemplation of the repulsive features of the eskimo as a horror to be reckoned with alongside the cold, the hunger, the icebergs and the mosquitos in making polar exploration unsuitable for all but a particular breed of strong-stomached voyager, and for many of the sailors she has been the daily verification. Habituated in their distaste, hardly recognising her humanity, they have denied her the courtesies they might have considered due to her sex. Expecting nothing from them, she has borne the insults and has dutifully stitched for them because Hans has told her she must. But in the year since Hall's death, when simple discourtesy has sunk into gross and leering contempt, she has suffered bitterly. She aches for her family, yearns to escape the cadaverous faces and the sickly odours of the *kabloonas*, doubts if Hans, whose failings in the hunt have resulted in sullenness and lethargy, will ever again present an oosook mighty as a bear, a thunderstick too fat for her stubby fingers' encirclement, will ever again love her four times in a single April afternoon.

Worst of all, Tobias is sick. She prises his lips open, pushes in a morsel of pemmican, but his tongue instantly rejects it. She chews the meat to soften it, inserts it again, holding the mouth closed, but he will choke rather than swallow it. He is no better with biscuit, corned beef, sealskin. A scrap of bread is taken and chewed, but he whimpers with the pain of swallowing. Naked, he is grotesque, swollen-bellied, as ugly as a half rotted seal-corpse. He has till now tolerated only fresh seal-meat, and there is none left.

There are myriad seals beneath them but mid-November offers no sun and barely a hint of twilight. When the moon is obscured hunting is virtually impossible.

As fear and anger grow, tempers wear thin. The women point to the whining children and provoke the men, question their manhood, laughing contemptuously, conducting ironic debates about who has the feebler husband. On November 10th, a thin trickle of moonlight entices the hunters out. Days of blizzards and drifting snow have transformed the floe and they have to negotiate unexpected mounds and ridges, but they find breathing-holes. Hans arranges his gear and settles for the long vigil while Joe, seeking relief from his companion's carping, searches further across the floe. He finds a hole so barely covered with new ice that he smells the seal's blood, hears its heartbeat. The seal is no less aware of him, and waits, listening to his blood-chant, swimming in circles under the hole while Joe perches hour upon hour on a stool of ice and the powder-snow gathers upon him until he becomes a mound indistinguishable from the thousands of others on the floe. Wind and snow and darkness thicken. For fleeting moments he escapes his trance and returns to the here-and-now of grumbling stomach, numb toes, the shaming prospect of Puney's whimper, Hannah's sorrow and ill-disguised contempt when he returns yet again empty-handed.

After eight hours he nods to the seal, acknowledging its victory. Then the wind brings a sudden whiff of bear, a thrilling onset of hope for a meal, mixed with the fear of becoming one. He rises from his crouch, rotates his shoulders, directs himself toward the huts. In this darkness he cannot pursue the bear, but their paths might cross. Confident that he will have outlasted Hans at the breathing-holes, he returns in a direct line – an hour-long wade through soft drifting snow into a wind that is rapidly becoming a gale.

The women are together in Joe's and Hannah's hut, with Tyson dozing between them. Their joy at his arrival melts into fear when they realise he is alone.

He reacts with irritation, in English. 'Damn fool.'

Christiana howls, and Tyson is roused. Taking in the situation, he groans. To walk alone out into the gale would be folly even for a Real Person, but he in his threadbare shirt would die within five minutes. Yet something must be done.

Expecting nothing, Tyson and Joe crawl through the filth of the connecting passageway to the sailors' quarters. Christiana's keening has penetrated the walls, so that some of the shapes in the blackness are of men sitting upright. Tyson's surmise that a direct appeal for help is less likely to fail than an attempt to borrow clothing is well-founded. Several of the sailors half-humorously offer to accompany Joe on a search for the body, though in the end they agree that one is enough for a fat native, and Johnson is selected. Tyson's fears for Hans, for whom he has no real affection or admiration, are virtually cancelled by his relief in finding that not every human tie has been severed, not every laugh stifled.

Johnson is happy enough at the interruption to the deathly boredom of skat and food-talk and sex-fantasies, and there is a ring of rough jollity in his voice. 'Come then, *kleiner* Joe: maybe we might shoot a bear or two or three.'

With the wind behind them and a hint of moonlight diffused among the clouds Johnson can see six yards ahead and Joe ten; Joe leads. They cover a quarter-mile in the first half-hour, then Joe stops, signalling Johnson to do the same.

The bear is ambling directly toward them, its moondusted whiteness defining it against the enveloping darkness.

'Nanook,' Johnson says, in an awed whisper. Assuming the authority which is inviolably his on such occasions, Joe signals him to be still, be silent. They are upwind from the beast, so he knows it will have their scent, will be drawn by hunger and curiosity to seek them out.

And it grows bigger in their sight, shambling and busy and clearly hungry, clearly attached to them along a scent-line. Johnson has never shot a bear, but knows well enough he has to find the head, put a ball into the small brain. To wound a charging nanook, even with the heavy ball from his revolving colt rifle, would merely enrage it, redouble its ferocity and consign himself to instant dismemberment. Joe is armed with Hall's single-shot Jennings; there is never time for a second shot when the quarry is seal.

'Hit him head,' he tells Johnson, but what faces them, growing by the second, has no head, no neck, no shoulders, no features that distinguish themselves from the grey-black mass. Joe touches Johnson's elbow.

'Wait.'

'Dear Christ, it's jammed,' Johnson says.

The revolving chambers, unspun through months of bitter frost, are ice-clogged. Johnson drops the weapon. If his intention is to turn and run, his legs do not receive the message. He throws his arms upwards into the blackness and yells, '*Heilige Jungfrau!*'

Joe thrills. Their salvation depends on his single bullet. There is no rush, no *kabloona*-panic: he removes his right mitten, sinks to his hunting crouch and raises the rifle.

Johnson yells again, a wordless cry of pure terror, and the bear stops. Motionless at five paces it becomes a target worth the risk of the single bullet. Unflurried and happy, Joe aims for the head. When the bear calls out, the shock almost drives him into squeezing the trigger. He hears the Real Language: '*Ebierbing! Ebierbing!*'

Exhausted and two-thirds asleep from his long night on the floe's edge and his hard hike to and from the breathing-hole, and drunk now with the prospect of bear-soup, Joe does not make the immediate connection. The bear-voice that rattles in his head throbs too in his veins, tunes to his heart as always on the hunt, establishing the blood-bond between him and the animal he will presently eat. It is Johnson who realises first.

'*Jungfrau! Hänsel soll's sein!* Little Hans!'

The rifle falls from Joe's hands and he stands up. Johnson laughs. Hans sinks slowly to his knees, slumps forwards until his head is resting on the backs of his hands, and thus, in the attitude of a praying Muslim, falls asleep.

In the men's hut there is sympathy from some, scorn from others when Johnson regales them with his version of the story – a version which conceals nothing of his own terror.

If he'd had any shit left, he would have shit himself, he tells them. 'And the little man's face – by God, he might wake up without a nose.'

'An improvement,' Kruger says.

'But he won't be able to kiss his little wife: they kiss with the nose,' Jamka says. He rubs his nose and loudly smacks his lips. Something has happened, and although it has brought no food to their bellies, everyone is a scrap happier.

But not in Hans's igloo, where the saving of Hans's nose is as nothing to the saving of his spirit. Tyson crawls through the tunnel with Joe and Hannah to offer comfort. Hans is a trembling fat mound of abjection, his body bare to the waist, his shoulders heaving with shame and misery, his head plunged between Christiana's exposed breasts. Hearing their arrival, he looks up and mumbles: 'Tippak.'

Joe has anticipated the need, has already filled a pipe for him, and now they all light up and Hans's sobs become deep puffs and the discipline of holding the hot smoke for maximum effect calms him. He recognises Tyson's silhouette, feels his sympathy.

'Him Peter and Joe want to shoot poor me, Mr Tyson,' he says.

Tyson tries to laugh. 'They took you for a bear, Hans. They meant no harm to you, little man.'

Hans' self-pity swells. 'Them two want shoot poor me. Them two.' He releases the smoke in a slow sigh. Christiana reaches from behind with her short arms to rub his cheeks with her knuckles. She worries for his nose. Opening his mouth for the pipe, he says, 'Poor Hans, him better hang him.'

Ah, poor ruined, dollar-rich Hans! There was a time when the utterance would have been real and dangerous, when they would have shrugged, made two or three gestures toward dissuasion, cajoling him back to a proper respect for his manhood. And those failing, they would have helped him to order his affairs, eased his taking-off for him, kept clear while he knotted the walrus-hide rope, grieved loudly while they cut him down to give his body back to the wind and the bears.

But their cajolement now is ritual and insincere and joyless because they do not reckon seriously with his despair. This wretched Hans is forever in limbo and forever dollar-corrupted and forever imprisoned by his fame. Twenty years ago, a mission boy at Fiskenaes, he was engaged by Kane in the *Advance*, and even then, nineteen and unacquainted with *kabloonas* beyond the Danish missionaries, he bargained: fat, sly, stupid, mother-fixated youth, he held out for two barrels of ship's biscuit and fifty pounds of pork, to be paid in advance to his mother. Kane took him on board and made him famous, as Hall was to do for Joe and Hannah. Through Kane, he became the mixture that the magazine subscribers loved: mighty hunter, rescuer of dying comrades, grovelling Man-Friday – but lovelorn homesick boy withal. He had sunk to the snow in Kane Basin and sobbed his yearnings for his maiden left behind in Etah, that same Merkut-Christiana who now rubbed his cheeks; had wished for death and been restored to laughter by his heroic commander; had shared with Morton the first sight of the fabled Open Sea. Even his final desertion of the expedition, his flight to Merkut's arms while his comrades battled with the storms of the Davis Strait, had been forgiven and forgotten in the sad romance which followed: his six years of waiting, climbing his headland time after time to scan the water for a Yankee ship.

And when Hayes came with the *United States* he signed on and became once more a player in the great game. The drama was hot again: there were mad dogs and a crippled ship and the suspicious death of Sonntag the astronomer with Hans as the only witness. And Merkut too became a famous little eskimo, packing the infant Tobias in her hood and declaring she was for home, she had had enough of the shit-smelling *kabloonas* who disinter her uncles' corpses and talk of shipping them to some New York museum, who scrub her with carbolic, wrinkle their noses at her smell, expect her to serve their every domestic need as she serves the needs of stupid dumb Hans. That same Hans filled his pipe and lit it and waited for her to come back and when she did he cuffed her hard once on the side of her head and offered her a piece of seal flipper.

Now in his fortieth year, he wishes again to die, sobbing into her hunger-shrivelled breasts and jabbering of hanging himself, and it is neither a Real Person nor a *kabloona* who speaks but a literary creation, concocted by Dr Kane for sensation-starved readers of the *New York Herald*.

Tyson joins the others in coaxing him, offers consolatory

117

slaps.

Poor as they are beside Joe's, Hans's hunting skills are still crucial to their hopes of surviving the drift. Joe has found him an irritating time-server, but still he acknowledges that the danger of his being shot was real enough and he sees plainly, even in the gloom of the ill-lit hut, the patches of discolouration on the cheeks, the dead flesh that must be resurrected.

The almanac informs them that winter officially begins on 2nd December, and on that day Tyson sets the daily ration at a reduced six ounces of bread, eight of corned beef, two of ham – a diet that obliges them to spend their days in virtual motionlessness under their buffalo robes. If the cloud lifts there is a thin strip of twilight in the hours either side of noon, but the temperature never rises above minus twenty, fifty-two degrees of frost, and the wind is seldom less than a gale.

The sailors play skat and tell dirty stories and dream of banquets and routinely curse the natives for their failure to deliver meat.

'The seals are singing and dancing under our arses,' Kruger says. 'Every night I hear them.'

'And Tyson gives half our rations to the louseballs,' Jamka says.

For their part, the Real People need no almanac. The seals are laughing and farting, but it is too dark for the hunt. When Hans traps a fox it furnishes a thin bite for each man where it might have been a full modest meal for his own family. They can talk liberally, since not even Tyson has gleaned more than an essential few scraps of the Real Language; and their talk is of leaving while they can still smell land.

Christiana dreads what might befall the children: at best, that they will be abandoned at some stage when the drift has borne them impossibly far from land; at worst, that the rapidly shrinking stocks are entirely consumed before they reach the breeding grounds of the bladdernose, and the sailors slaughter them for food. Her lingering loyalty to Hall has dwindled to nothing in the year of anarchy since his death, and the months of unchecked patronising contempt from the sailors have embittered her against all *kabloonas*.

Countering, Hannah pleads for Hall's memory. The *kabloonas,* his children, will die like so many before them if the Real People abandon them on the floe. As usual, it is her quiet authority that prevails.

'They gave you the sail,' she says, raising her arms to the canvas-lined walls of the hut, invoking the sailors' one act of cheerful generosity.

'Look,' Christiana says.

She places her hand flat against the naked belly of Tobias. He moans in his sleep, feeling the pain. 'He can't eat the pemmican: he can eat only seal, and they take it.'

There is no answer to this. She senses victory.

'They stole Joe's seal yesterday. We got nothing. The child got nothing.'

Joe says, 'They are sorry for that. They say I cut up the seals now.'

Christiana will not be mollified. 'Because they can't do it. They lose the blood.'

Her misery rises, her voice become a wail. 'They want to shoot poor Hans.'

In the darkness, Hans's stooped shoulders indicate his feeble-ness – the shoulders of a man no longer assured of his position. Christiana unleashes a bitter torrent. 'They cannot make tea, cannot light a lamp, cannot catch a bird or hunt fox. Now that they've destroyed one of the boats, they waste all the oil. However much we teach them, they cannot learn.'

'They can boil water now,' Hannah says. 'I taught them.'

Christiana snorts, summons her energy for the next outburst, but plays into Hannah's hands. 'They lie and fart and do nothing. When they do move, they shout and shoot and scare the food away.'

'Yes,' Hannah says. 'They are Captain Hall's children. He brought them. If we go, they will all die.'

The simple truth silences them for a moment, but the decision cannot be long delayed. Now and for only the next two or three days there might be a prospect of reaching the Greenland shore. Thereafter the bleak and foodless western shores will be the closer, though still impossibly far off. Hannah will not go, and Joe will not go without Hannah and Puney, and Hans will not go without Joe. Christiana wails, then tightens her lips in bitter silence.

Tyson has jaloused little of the detail of their argument, but the tone is plain enough even through the unintelligible jabber of the Real Language. He reads Hannah's authority, Christiana's fear, Hans's despair, Joe's pliant misery. Nominally in command of the sailors, the plenipotentiary of the United States Senate on the floe, he has nevertheless thrown in his lot with the seal-people, and insofar as the floe might one day become a battlefield, he must be their defender to the death. That office becomes dramatically official when Hans, in the full flush of terror from his narrow escape, crawls to him and presents his six-shooter, fully loaded.

'Mr Tyson, you shoot bad man in head, you tell him he's no good man and shoot his head.'

The bad man, Tyson surmises, is Kruger. Tyson now has two loaded pistols – a double exhortation. His gums throb when he laughs, and the small effort of rising to take the Colt 45 wrings a soft groan from his throat as the stabs of rheumatism cross his shoulder blades. He lifts the pistol, draws comfort from its weight, nods his commitment to the Real People. He will try to deliver them all from their agony, but above all he will deliver the eskimos, though it cost him his life.

With the diminishment of the rations hunger is transformed from a gnawing irritation to a violent agony. Hans and Joe shoot a dozen narwhals and lose them all to the sea. Tyson marvels at Hans's skill in working the kayak across mushy ice to retrieve a seal shot precisely in the brain by Joe – skill beyond the wildest dreams of any of the sailors. He reckons that Hans works at a loss, that the effort he expends in securing the animal is not repaid by the pitiful remnant he will receive as his share of meat and blood. Stiffened by the Colt, he resolves that there will be an allowance of food for the hunters, above their normal portion. Let Kruger object.

Yet his blood boils against the natives too. On a day in January when the mercury drops to minus forty-two and freezes, Hans returns from the hunt alone, having set out with Washington, their last dog but one.

'Him run away like I don't know how,' he says. Two days later Joe returns empty-handed with Patch, the last, who flops to the ice in pained exhaustion, unresponsive to a seal bone which Tyson dangles at his nose, and dies after a half-hour of agonised whining. He is the first natural fatality since their separation from the *Polaris*: a bad omen.

Without the dogs, their hope of bear-meat recedes, and Kruger curses the eskimos. Hans feels Patch's stomach, satisfies himself that the death has been caused by a blockage of seal bone, then opens the chest and consumes the heart in two rapid swallows. The piteously thin meat that clings to Patch's bones he strips off and feeds to Succi, Augustina and Puney. Tobias retches and cries when Christiana tries to tease his lips open with a piece of it.

Miserable in his rags and tormented by rheumatism, Tyson has no occupation beyond the painful scribbling of his journal. While the Eskimo men scour the floe for meat, he folds the perpetually whining Puney in his lap and stares in wonder at Hannah's stern housewifery as she makes their daily tea. With short precise blows of her fist she pounds the ship's biscuit into powder, then mixes it with their communal ration of pemmican. She stirs the mixture in a pemmican-tin half-filled with melted salt ice. There is a pin-prick leak in the tin which she stops with her finger then plugs with chewed sealskin. When the hideous concoction – their 'tea' – has warmed to a sickly tepidity, she pours his cupful and hands it to him first, absurdly recognising his authority as captain and head of the house. She sees the pain of his effort to lift the cup to his mouth and shuffles across the floor to help him. She holds the cup to his lips.

'Nectar, Hannah,' he says, swallowing the vile soup. Its thin warmth is sufficient only to bring home the awful misery of their predicament. 'Dear God, Hannah, what will become of us?' He tries to laugh, but the effort again hurts his gums and his ribs. She pats him maternally on the back. 'Maybe Joe and Hans will bring a big seal home, Mr Tyson. Maybe an oogjook. Maybe you'll be fat again, and maybe Hannah too.'

'Dear God,' he says again.

She pours the last of the mixture into his mouth and sets the cup down.

'Where do you hurt bad?'

'Everywhere, Hannah. I ache in every bone and every joint. And where I don't ache, I itch and suppurate.'

She places her hands flat on the oxhides. 'You lie down here,' she says. 'You lie down, Mr Tyson.'

121

She helps him to roll over, lie on his belly.

'You shut your eyes.'

Closing his eyes, he sees with his bones, feels the soft rising and falling of the floe, and floats. He hears the eternal scrape, scrape, scrape of Puney's knife on the icewall, her chronic soft hunger-whine, her little rattling breaths.

Then Hannah pounds him with the edges of her stubby hands, softly at first, but gradually increasing the force, as she has pounded the pemmican some half an hour ago.

Her knuckles are now hardly more fleshed than his own, her fingers no longer plump, and for a moment there is a racking agony of bone on bone, a pain that explodes bright yellow in his skull. He feels himself drifting into oblivion and wonders if it is death. Hannah knows the white man's ailments, knows where the disease is mere cold, requiring a hard pounding that will bring blood back to numbed tissue, and where it is the creeping death of scurvy that can not be cured in the absence of fresh meat but only eased, only soothed by the slow circling witchcraft of finger-tips. She sits astride his buttocks. She raises his shirt, shakes her head at the revealed emaciation, the pitiful jagged soot-blackened tracery of vertebrae and ribs, scabs and ulcers. She warms her fingers at the lamp, then allows the tips to trace their pattern of healing sorcery, transferring their warmth with feather-touches to his inflamed joints, his brittling bones, his dying spirit.

He groans. If this is death.

Her weight when she lifts her own shirt over her head and lowers herself to him – even that, all shrunken breast and hollow belly – is insubstantial, fleshless. He drifts into sleep, and when they hear the heavy hand-and-foot tread in the tunnel that signifies not one of the Real People but a sailor, he is unable to react.

Kruger rises from his knees, but has to stoop to avoid touching the roof of the hut.

'I disturb,' he says, mocking them.

'No,' Tyson says.

'You are not well, Mr Tyson.'

'I'm well enough, Robert.'

Hannah moves to allow him to rise. She makes no move to cover her breasts, and Kruger stares through the flickering lamp-light. He takes Tyson's arm, helping him to rise.

'Little Joe and little Hans have brought a seal,' Kruger says, 'but perhaps you are not able to come out.'

'I'm able, Robert.'

'A small seal,' Kruger says.

'That's unfortunate,' Tyson says.

'We have agreed that Joe shall cut it, under my eyes, and yours.'

'Good.'

'But if you are not well, or if you are too busy...'

Hannah pulls on her shirt. One day, Tyson feels, he will strike or strangle or shoot Kruger, but for the moment he can do no more than silently fume.

CHAPTER ELEVEN
QUESTING: COFFEE

To get the beauty of their coffee hot, they drank it in quick gulps, like beer. Hall had been known to down two quarts at a sitting then smack his lips and laugh and ask for more.

Budington served him his first cup, welcoming him back from the sledge journey, placing a chair for him at the captain's table. Hall sniffed the steam and was touched.

'A fresh brew, Sidney – did Jackson have none on the stove?'

Budington's lips came as close to a smile as any of them had seen since leaving New York.

'Fresh for you, Commander.'

It seemed that only the steaming mug in his hand prevented Hall from embracing his old friend. 'You are kind, Sidney; you are very kind.' Both men had tears in their eyes, and there was a fever in Hall. The sledge party had achieved a mere fifty miles when the hope had been for two hundred, but he had convinced himself that he had seen the Way, and night after night in his dreams the Sacred Bunting had fluttered at the Pole, the President's champagne had popped.

He poured out his joy to Tyson, Budington, Meyer. Then he calmed himself for the solemn announcement: 'Gentlemen, I believe it shall be accomplished. I believe we shall do it.'

Tyson smiled, nodded; Meyer raised a friendly eyebrow with barely a hint of mockery; Budington poured more coffee into Hall's mug.

This was the Hall that Tyson liked. They shared their enthusiasm, deepened their friendship as they conjured images.

'I've seen the way, George: the highway to the top of the world.' Even Meyer, the eternal mocker, was touched. He smiled. 'Fascinating, Captain Hall. Have you been able to form an opinion on the open polar sea?'

Hall nodded. 'Ice, Mr Meyer. We saw it clear as our hands in the moonlight – endless clean ice. I suspect we might be able to skate the last two hundred miles to the Pole.'

Tyson, infected with the fever, was not the one to mark the deep groaning exhaustion under his commander's intoxication. 'Sir, let me offer to carry the banner.'

The request was heartfelt. Tyson wanted his share of the grand adventure, did not wish to be permanently confined to quarters as resident spy against the ice-master. Hall reassured him.

'Oh you shall, George, you shall. I promise you now, before these witnesses, you'll be the first man to stand at the end of the line that's plumbed to that Star. We'll plant you there.'

Their eyes followed his, and the line of his outstretched arm. It was a clear moonless night with the Arctic firmament in full display; they had to search to find the Pole Star, not isolated in these crystal skies but modestly twinkling among a thousand companions, with a diamond-dusting even in the black deserts of the Little Bear and the Giraffe. They responded with good humour to the solemnity of the moment, stirred by his boyish wonderment. Meyer proposed sealing the bargain with a sip of something stronger than coffee.

Hall laughed. 'Gentlemen, feel at liberty, but for myself I'll make do with another cup of Mr Budington's exquisite brew.'

Budington poured the coffee then opened the liquor cabinet and took out the Jamaica rum – his own favourite. Tyson accepted a discreet tot, Meyer a large one. Budington poured himself a measure that stopped only at the rim of his glass. Hall cleared his throat, hollowing a silence, re-establishing the sanctity of the occasion.

'My friends,' he said, 'my good friends, my comrades on this desolate shore, I invite you to raise your glasses and drink to the crowning success of our great goal, the accomplishment of the sacred mission which our God and our President have entrusted to us – I give you the North Pole.'

They drank, and even Budington mouthed the words of the toast before draining his glass and reaching for the bottle. Hall placed his coffee cup on the table with a loud thump that startled them. He drew his hand across his mouth, wiping his beard with the palm, then with thumb and index finger he drew the tears from his lower eyelids. With finger and thumb together on the bridge of his nose, he lowered his head, and his massive shoulders rose and fell in a profound sigh.

'My friends, my friends ...'

His head rose and the smile died with his voice. He looked at Budington, at the empty coffee cup, at Budington again, then at each of the others, scanning their faces in turn. Tyson leapt to his feet, knocking over his chair. Budington remained seated, but leaned back a little, the better to view what was happening.

Tyson's arm enfolded Hall's shoulders, preventing him from slumping forward to the table. Hall's face was purple, his breath suddenly laboured and desperate.

'Are you unwell, sir?' Tyson said.

Hall's lips were pursed, the tip of his tongue protruding. 'I think – I think, gentlemen, a bilious attack. No cause for alarm; I've swallowed the coffee too quickly.' Tyson began to ease him toward the door, to the cabin that he shared with seven of them.

'Lend a hand,' he called to Budington, still immobile in his chair. Meyer was already on his feet, ready to run for the doctor.

'A basin, perhaps,' Hall said.

They knew that it would require a half-hour or more for Meyer to fetch Bessel from the observatory. In the heavy heat of the cabin Hall's breathing became still more strained. They lowered him to his bunk, began to undo his clothing. 'I would be obliged ... I require a basin, gentlemen,' he said.

When Meyer and the doctor arrived he was in his woollen undergarments, which were sodden with sweat. He had filled two basins with vomit. At the sight of Bessel his eyes widened in frank terror. He tried to rise from the bunk, but his head fell back to the bolster and his right hand came up, trembling, the fingers spread, in an attempt to ward off the doctor.

'That man ... I cannot ... these men ... don't let them!'

Bessel was no longer the supercilious intellectual, but the doctor with his patient. He looked into Hall's eyes, spoke softly. 'Come sir, you require help, you are not well.'

Hall shuddered. 'That man...' He tried to raise both arms, but the effort was beyond his strength, and he plunged into unconsciousness.

And now the doctor was brisk, and they made room for him. Tyson stared at Budington.

'He's raving,' the ice-master said, turning to walk through again to the dining area, where the half-full rum bottle stood beside the empty coffee cup.

Bessel enlisted Tyson and Meyer. 'His pulse is violently irregular, and we must reduce the fever as quickly as possible.'

They toiled for half an hour, feverish themselves in the thick warmth. Unable to administer a drug, they poulticed his legs, blistered his neck, cooled his head with icy water.

And he woke cooler, but white with exhaustion and terror. He tried again to fend the doctor off, but was unable to move his arms. Yet he turned his head, seeking escape, as the doctor bent to speak in his ear.

'You have suffered an apoplectic shock, sir, and I think you are paralysed, at least on your left side. You will recover, but you must calm yourself, you must rest.'

He could not, would not, be calm. His tongue twitched toward words, but only with his eyes could he utter his fear when the doctor approached his lips with castor oil. He tried to resist swallowing it, and the croton oil that followed. Then, straining desperately as he slipped again into coma, he said, 'Hannah.'

The eskimos were more distraught than any of the others. Hannah howled for the dying leader, and all of them trembled at the prospect that after his death there would be no expedition, a collapse of order – and guns everywhere. From their cabin they listened to his cries in the night, wild mad accusatory cries: they were shooting at him, forcing his feet into poisoned stockings, breathing blue gas at his head, corroding his legs with mustard baths, injecting him with strychnine. The unholy alliance of Bessel and Budington was killing him. The seven other sleepers in the captain's cabin suffered in the fumes of tartar-emetic, corrosive sublimate, laudanum. They spent as little time as they could in their bunks. He rejected each in turn as a watcher, and the very mention of the doctor's name threw him into a frenzy of impotent panic. For two days Bessel treated him from afar, advising Joe, Hannah, Tyson and Chester.

Madness invaded even his lucid moments, and his paranoia thickened. Joe and Hannah were obliged to taste his food, even from cans opened before his eyes. Tyson was enjoined in desperate whispers to survive, in order that the truth might be carried to Washington, that the homicidal conspirators might receive their punishment. Indiscriminately he demanded pills, swallowing them wholesale; Bessel created a stock of bread-pellets for Hannah to administer, calling them caffeine, morphine, digitalis. To Joseph Mauch, his amanuensis, he dictated his crazed dying messages, his promiscuous accusations against Budington and the scientists.

A week into his sickness they knew he would not recover and Bessel informed the assembled hands that, the leader being incapable of movement or of rational speech, command of the United States North Polar Expedition now fell upon Captain Budington. Their eyes turned to the ice-master, who stood, for once sober, at the doctor's right side. Sensing that something, some statement of intent, was expected of him, he said, 'It is my solemn promise, now that the matter is within my power, that none of you shall die of starvation.'

Hannah wept. Hour upon hour alone with the dying man in the eight-berth cabin she embraced his feet, knowing that this time her ministrations were for herself, that there was to be no resurrection of the stiffening flesh such as had been accomplished half a dozen times in the past. For long stretches she slept, and only the melancholy duet of their breathing disturbed the silence: his stertorous rattle, her silver whine.

Or he spoke, babbling of the past, of Baffin, where she presented herself new-washed in her crinoline and muslin and offered him tea, weak or strong; where she massaged his feet into painful life; where she buried her dead baby under a stone. And of Puney, whose breath also whined: 'Budington will love her, Hannah. God damn him, Budington will preserve her, look to him, Hannah.'

Conscious of his Hippocratic responsibility, Bessel engaged the as yet unslandered Bryan as emissary. The parson-astronomer spoke tenderly into Hall's left ear: 'I beseech you sir, to allow the doctor to treat you. He wishes to inject you with quinine.'

Hall tried to raise himself, but fell back again. 'God damn him, Bryan, he calls it quinine.'

The pastor was distressed. 'Sir, he is preparing the medicine now, before my eyes. I implore you.'

'I trust you, Bryan,' Hall said. 'Only you and Hannah. Only Hannah and Joe and you.'

He closed his eyes. Bessel heated the crystals of quinine, dissolved them in warm water.

'Have an eye, Mr Bryan,' Hall said, as Bessel injected the solution into his left leg.

He summoned a meeting: Budington, Bessel, Bryan, Schumann,

Tyson and Chester crowded around the bunk.

'Remember the man is dying,' Bessel whispered to Budington, who nodded. They propped him up on a bolster of rolled ox-skins. Bessel dabbed his brow with a damp cloth, gave him water to sip, arranged his coverings. He had regained most of the sensation on his left side, but his speech was muddy and the effort of moving his tongue made him sweat.

'I'm obliged to you, doctor; most obliged. You have been very kind to me, and it has been recorded.'

Bessel stepped back. Hall searched the dimness of the cabin till he found Budington.

'Captain Budington,' he said.

Slowly, with head determinedly bowed, Budington stepped into the glow of Hall's lantern.

'I am here, sir,' he said.

'The Pole, Captain, the North Pole.'

The silence was tense. For Budington, the very words 'North Pole' had been for uttering only as a sneer, and he had long since abandoned any pretence of taking them seriously. Yet he was neither fool nor monster.

'I am listening, sir.' He stepped forward, allowing Hall to lower his voice, speak with reduced strain. Hall painfully turned his head toward the glass by the side of the bunk, and his left fingers twitched. Budington held the glass to his lips.

They had been friends. Hall sipped. 'You are kind, Captain.' He sighed, summoning his strength for his last speech. 'Command passes to you in the event of my death.'

If there was a pause to permit solicitation, disagreement, reassurance, Budington did not make use of it. Hall's voice was a taut whisper. 'I ask you to swear.'

'Swear, sir?'

'Swear that you will strive for the Pole, not give up, not return until you've achieved ...'

A silent, complicated negotiation: Budington's eyes passed around the circle, pausing to establish communication with each of them in turn, saving Bessel till last. And from each he received wordless complicity, guilty assent, permission to palliate the suffering of the dying man.

'Sir, I shall do my utmost – we all shall do our utmost.'

'To reach the Pole,' Hall pressed.

'To reach the Pole.'

'The ninetieth degree of northern latitude.'

'The ninetieth degree of northern latitude.' Budington was sweating as heavily as his commander.

'Your solemn promise, as a sailor.'

'My solemn promise.'

It was the second solemn promise he had made that month, and not even the demented invalid believed it. Hall asked them to leave, except for Tyson, then sent for Joe and Hannah. He asked Hannah for morphine and she placed one of Bessel's bread-pellets between his lips. He swallowed it with an effort that made him groan, and motioned for Tyson to approach.

'Your hand, George,' he said. Tyson gave him his right hand. His grasp was feeble, yet desperately importunate.

'George, those men are murdering me.'

'No, sir.'

'Yes. The doctor and the captain – they've plotted against me against me from the start. They've tried to destroy the Expedition.'

'I'm sure they have not, sir.'

'I've heard them, George. I've seen them. Chester too, he's in it.'

'Captain, I think you're deceived. The doctor has ministered to you daily.'

'A mask, George. He despises me.'

'No sir. If he despises anyone, it's Budington. I think he's as set on the Pole as you yourself, and I think you will yet shake hands with him on that sacred spot.'

'Ah, you're kind, George. But they're out to murder me. I see their eyes, hear them whispering. I trust only you and Hannah.'

'All of us, officers and men and natives, want nothing but your speedy recovery to health, sir. I think you should rest now.'

Hall's eyes widened. 'You must come through, George. You must tell Washington, tell Robeson, tell the President.'

Tyson tightened his grasp on the trembling hand. 'As for coming through, I intend to do that under your guidance, sir.'

Hall's face twisted in mingled pain and misery. 'Ah, George. Tell them. From Greenland's icy mountains, by God, tell them.'

Tyson released the hand, and looked to Hannah for help. He stepped aside to let her approach the bedside.

Hall clutched her hand. 'My papers, Hannah: I entrust them to you. With Mr Tyson here as witness.'

'Lie still, Cap'n Hall, sir,' she said, easing his supporting bolster from under him, letting him sink back on his pillow.

'That man must not have them, Hannah.'

She placed her hand on his brow. 'Sleep now, Cap'n Hall. Rest now.'

He slept.

On November 5th, when Bessel tried to bathe his feet with mustard-water, he raved of poison and murder and threshed his feet, overturning the basin. The night after, while Mauch was sitting by the bunkside, he leapt abruptly from his bunk, rousing them all.

'I require Budington and Hannah,' he shouted. His voice was suddenly clear, his tongue freed from the grip of the paralysis. While these two were fetched, Hays fought through a blizzard to the observatory, where the doctor was writing up his weather reports.

Hall stood solidly by the side of the bunk. Dressed only in a flannel nightshirt and shrunken by his days of sickness, he seemed a child beside the burly ice-master; but his voice was firm, his enunciation bitterly precise.

'You've killed me, Sidney. He has killed me, Hannah. This man, once my dear friend, has murdered me.'

Bessel arrived and offered a quinine injection.

'Water,' Hall said.

He sipped, then agreed to go back to his bunk on condition that Hannah remain by his side.

For an entire day his rattling breath and sudden wild outbursts destroyed their rest; then came a blessed three hours when the breathing eased and became regular, so that when it stopped at three in the morning, the effect was as of a sudden explosion, and no-one in the cabin was in doubt that the end had come.

Morton spoke first. 'I think the doctor should be brought, and the captain.'

Bessel listened at Hall's chest, felt his throat and pronounced him dead. Budington nodded slowly. Again he felt the pressure of eyes, the expectation that something had to be said, and that he was the one to say it. He raised his head and looked around the company. In the moment that followed he might have been working to formulate a fitting few sentences, might have fleetingly considered a prayer, a blessing, a tribute.

But the ice-master had gone to bed drunk, and his bitterness at Hall's accusation still rankled, so that when he finally found words they were reckless chilling words, his revenge on the dead leader, the lost friend; and they ushered in a year of bleakest chaos for all of them.

'You shall not be starved to death now,' he told them. 'A stone has been lifted from my heart.'

UNITED STATES NAVY BOARD OF INQUIRY, WASHINGTON DC, JUNE 5TH 1873, NAVY SECRETARY GEORGE ROBESON PRESIDING

Testimony of George Tyson, Assistant Navigator

Q   Did Captain Hall ever talk rationally after his sickness began?

A   I think about the third of November, after he had been sick seven or eight days, he appeared to get better; he talked rationally and went to writing his log, and our hopes were raised that he might be recovering his health. But he still appeared to be thinking on one subject – he thought someone was going to injure him; he seemed to think somebody was going to poison him.

Q   Did he accuse anybody when you were by?

A   Yes, sir, almost everybody; and when I was absent he might accuse me for aught I know. He accused Captain Budington and the doctor of trying to do him an injury, even of trying to kill him.

Q   Do you know what became of Captain Hall's papers after his death?

A   As far as I knew, Captain Budington took charge of them, sir.

Q   Were they not certified and sealed up?

A   To my knowledge, no, sir.

Q   Did not you mess with Captain Budington?

A   Yes, sir, we messed with him.

Q   Did not you know what he did with the papers?

A   I saw some of them. I know many remarks were made about them; I understand some were burned.

Q   And which would they be that were burned?

A   I took it to be those that related to private matters between Captains Hall and Budington, sir.

Q   You mean matters of disagreement between them?

A   Perhaps, sir.

Q   Was there no advice that the papers should be sealed up?

A   I did myself; I advised that they should be sealed, boxed, and screwed down, and suggested it to Captain Budington.

Q   And his reply to this advice?

A   He did not make any remark whatever, or merely his usual 'Damn his papers.'

Q   We have heard of the burning of some papers of Captain Hall's, and you have spoken of burning. While he was delirious, did Captain Budington get him to burn up some papers?

A   That I cannot say, sir; but he told me he was glad the papers were burned, because they were much against him; and that he had asked Captain Hall to burn them.

Q   And were they burned?

A   Some were burned, sir, but whether by Captain Hall in his sickness or by Captain Budington afterwards, I cannot say. I know only that Captain Budington spoke of his satisfaction that they were gone.

Q   Did you take it that these papers related to captain Budington's drinking, and his theft from the doctor's cabinet?

A   I did.

Q   Did you think they had a bearing on his capacity to perform his duties? Did you think they made mention of his failings?

A   I do not know. I heard it talked of on board the ship, and I supposed it to be the truth.

Q   Did you ever hear Captain Hall speak on the matter of his papers during his sickness?

A   Yes, sir. He asked that they be entrusted to Hannah.

Q   To Hannah? To the native woman?

A   Yes, sir. I believe only Hannah had his full trust when he was sick.

Q   And did he make this request in your hearing?

A   He did, sir. When Hannah and I were alone with him.

Q   What did you make of it? Did you suppose it to result from rational consideration of his circumstances?

A   I saw it as part of his sickness, sir. He was anxious and afraid, and not in his right mind.

Q   Did you inform any other officer of the request that the papers be put in the keeping of the native woman?

A   I informed Mr Bryan, and together we reckoned it not proper that it should be taken seriously.

Q   This before or after Captain Hall's death?

A   After, sir. We considered that it was not Hannah's place to be burdened with such a responsibility.

Q   And later, did you ascertain what became of these papers?

A   I did not, sir. I knew only that Captain Budington took charge of the box.

Testimony of Frederick Meyer, Meteorologist

On the night of the separation I saw the japanned box containing Captain Hall's papers sitting on a table in Captain Budington's cabin.

CHAPTER TWELVE
DRIFTING: JAMKA COUNTS HIS TOES

In the early days of their drift, with bellies full and minds un-alert to the true horror of their predicament, they were young men freed of all but the last thin remnants of adult authority, set loose upon an adventure that would end soon enough with rum and girls and double pay, so they joked and boasted and counterboasted and gambled recklessly for stolen chocolate and masturbated more or less openly. Jamka's kerchief, put to use in the relative warmth beneath his blanket, then removed and smoothed to freeze solid overnight into a brittle scarlet square that he claimed might have been used to chop firewood, became a regular breakfast jest.

For two weeks, under Meyer's scientific assurance that they were drifting toward Disco and the Greenland coast and hopeful of rewards from the President for their ice-ordeal, they were raucous, dismissive of Tyson's fears, untroubled by guilt as they pushed fragments of the whaleboat and the sledges into the fire and almost shameless in their pilfering from the store hut.

Now after a Thanksgiving feast of frozen entrails and ancient seal-skin, a Christmas banquet of a mouthful of ham floating in seal's blood, a New Year toasted in weak pemmican tea, they laugh sparely and bitterly. There is to be no drama, no grand duel between the officers, no terrible moment of revelation about their latitude, but something worse: a slow and sour acceptance. Meyer has won their allegiance by telling them what they wished to hear, what he and they wished to be true. He has set his scientific credentials and his sextant against Tyson's eskimo-instincts; speaking in German, he has ridiculed Tyson's English as well as his seamanship, his religion, his priggishness, his britches. Now, enfeebled by hunger and scurvy, he is less arrogant, less loud in proclaiming his optimistic message, but still unwilling to admit defeat. Closer to death than any of them, he offers a poor target for the sailors' rage, so that Tyson for being correct is hated the more savagely. The creeping paranoia begins to gallop. They watch and listen for comings and goings, knowing that movement is more likely to signal thievery than mere pissing, anxious that the crime should be in the service of the group of disaffected sailors rather than the individual.

But movement itself, as the polar night deepens, becomes rare.
Whilst earlier they might blast dovekies with random buckshot,
they are aware now that none of them can command the stealth,
patience, endurance or precision of the eskimos, that their
cavortings on the ice can only warn the seals, lessen the already
slim prospect of Hans, or more probably Joe, making a kill. After
eighty days of utter sunlessness, with fresh food provision never
exceeding a rate of a single small seal each week shared among
the nineteen of them, the jokes have all but disappeared. The
darkness and the swathes of oxhide are mitigation of a kind: in
full light they might surrender to the hideousness of what they
would see around them – men in the prime of their youth reduced
to festering cadavers, the ashy grey of their skin relieved only by
the blackness of ulcers, the yellowness of running sores. Yet the
same darkness can only thicken the despair of each man as he
groans under chronic dull aches, punctuated by racking agonies
in every joint, charts the disintegration of his body, shudders at
the thought that a morsel of ship's biscuit will prove too much
for teeth that rattle in bleeding gums.

The dreg of life that remains is spilled and wasted in rancour
and recrimination: against Tyson, the carping tyrant; against the
eskimos, his pets, still comparatively fat, still with a sheen of oil
on their skin; against Meyer, the Little Count, whose bland assur-
ances they now know for delusion, and who seems the likeliest to
die first and so mark the beginning of the end of the adventure.

Then something happens. On the 19th of January, Herron
the English steward crawls through the tunnel into a stillness
that makes minus twenty-eight feel almost mild. In response to
some vestigial need for propriety, he walks fifty yards through the
moonlight toward a dimly silhouetted hummock. Rounding it, he
senses a yellow taint in the indigo of the southern sky. Obscurely
stirred and a little frightened, he forgets bladder and bowel and
griping gut and climbs nine slow painful steps to the top of the
hummock. He peers southward into the gloom, squints at the
unaccustomed brightness of the horizon. His brain, like his body,
functions slowly, and it is a full minute before he realises what
he is looking at.

And he laughs.

In the dead stillness, his laughter carries, bounces among the crowding icebergs, penetrates the thick walls of the huts. Jackson, who is thawing the day's water over the blubberlamp, crawls through the tunnel, sees him darkly outlined against the sky, and runs to join him on the hummock. Herron is sitting now, crumpled into a trembling ball of laughter, clutching his ribs. Jackson smiles, unaware as yet of the cause of his friend's condition, but beginning to share the wonderment.

Then Anthing and Lindquist are there, and close behind them Tyson, and they climb the mound and stand, the five of them, staring in silent amazement as the yellow sliver grows until it is three-quarters of a full disk.

'I saw the beginnings of it, four days ago,' Tyson says. 'But I wanted to wait, to be sure.'

He thanks God, and invites the others to do the same. Ready for once to humour him, they allow him his prayer, his thanks, and when he further pleads that the fresh light guide Joe to a successful hunt their *Amen* echoes long and loud in the ice.

Anthing cannot resist a comradely blasphemy. 'Amen, amen, amen, *Arschloch*,' he says to the sky.

The profanity is received in the spirit intended, and their wonder grows as the prayer is immediately answered. While the celebrants are still on the mound, Joe and Hans come toiling across the floe from the north, dragging a fat seal – two days' supply of fresh meat, warming blood, oil for the lamps. By the time they divide the carcass, all have seen the sun, and the sailors are benign. Jamka watches while Joe makes his rapid cuts and when the liver is removed he nods and says, 'You take that to the little ones, Joseph.'

But the return of the light does not mean an end to winter. February brings a succession of days when fine gale-driven snow confines all of them, including the natives, to their beds. There is consolation for Tyson: the days of blizzard see them drifting rapidly and, even by Meyer's admission, incontrovertibly beyond Disco and out of reach of the Greenland coast, and with the vision of rum and girls faded they are more willing to accept the need for conserving stocks. On the third of February Tyson declares these to amount to three bags of ship's bread – four hundred pounds in all, and five forty-five pound bags of pemmican – in total a third less than he has reckoned they should have by this date. Secretly he appeals to Herron for help in curbing the thefts, and Herron says, 'Robert is the man – he encourages them, and they're scared of him.' Approaching Jackson for confirmation of Kruger's guilt, he is sullenly rebuffed. 'I don't see nothing, I don't hear nothing, I don't know nothing, Mr Tyson.'

As Kruger's complaints grow more strident, so his authority among the sailors weakens, becomes a matter of fear rather than fellowship, and this brings increased danger. In his desperation, he seems ever closer to the point when he will resort to open and violent revolt. The time is not far off, Tyson feels, when the pistol will provide the answer – but he must first win the men's minds against both Kruger's insurrectionary murmurings and Meyer's false hints that land, western land now, Baffin Island or the Canadian mainland, will soon be attainable.

The slow shift of power in Tyson's favour continues in the strengthening sunlight. Meyer is the sickest of the adults on the floe, and with his bodily strength has gone much of his arrogance and most of his authority with the men. While they might accept the accuracy of his earlier observations in preference to Tyson's guesswork and be impressed by his sextant and his rote knowledge of the almanac, his claim now that the Strait is a mere eighty miles wide at the sixtieth degree, set against Tyson's experience as a whaler and against their own recollection of the northward journey, earns their ridicule and open contempt. They begin to laugh at him, to use his nickname *Gräflein* – Little Count – before his face, to imitate his piping voice, his habitual sneer, his Americanised German, his Germanised American. Tyson stops short of endorsing their scorn, but takes secret comfort.

And there is a resurrection of sorts: the glimmer of daylight stirs them to spring-cleaning. They attack the canvas linings of the igloos, beating the clinging frost of their frozen breath from the walls to the oxhide carpets then dragging the hides into the air and shaking them free of ice, frozen blood, bones, the accumulated filth of their four-month drift. Performing this, they observe the grotesque grandeur of their ice-city. Surrounding bergs are sculpted by wind and water into mosques, palaces, Gothic cathedrals, pink and green and golden in the low slanting sunbeams. All about them the narwhals plunge and dance and at night the shanty-town vibrates with their frolicking; a single carcass would furnish them with weeks of meat and fuel, but they sink on the instant a bullet pierces their hide, and the native harpoons have long since been destroyed and fashioned into useless spears for profitless sport.

Yet hope grows, and as if Herron's laughter at the returning sun has stirred a sleeping thing, they begin fitfully, hesitantly, spasmodically, to laugh. Gallows-tinted and hollow, it is nevertheless laughter. That they jest about eating the eskimo children obscurely reduces the likelihood that they will one day do it. That they joke about starving to death seems to offer the possibility of escape. Jackson the chef has minced and parboiled three seal-flippers for lunch, and they send formal compliments. Jamka raises a piece on the point of his knife preparatory to pushing it into his mouth. 'Until now, Mr Jackson, I have insisted on a mild zigeunersauce with my seal-flipper, but this...' he touches the ugly morsel with his tongue, but still withholds it from his lips '...this is truly exquisite.'

'Agreed.' Linquist pretends to burp. 'The delicate suggestion of soot, lampoil, dog ... and something else.'

'Shit,' Jamka says.

'Shit, yes. We eat shit.'

'I think there is also some nose, some nigger-nose,' Johnson suggests, and even the eternally sour Kruger laughs and points toward the cook.

'Nose, nose – look at his nose. Mr Jackson has become a white man.'

All of them, the eskimos not excepted, have suffered 'the skin of the nose' and other unbecoming effects of frostbite. In Jackson's case, the sunlight has revealed patches of whiteness under his blue-black outer skin, and these have merged. His nose is entirely white, a lantern-glow in the centre of his face, beckoning to them from the kitchen alcove.

Jamka swallows. 'No, we won't find these flavours in Copenhagen, but they say the beer there is cheaper.'

They have accepted that Disco, Greenland, Denmark, are faded dreams now – jokes. They are alive to the ironies of their plight: discovering that the combined strength of three of them is barely enough to shift Hans's little kayak across a hundred yards of the floe, they accept in their hearts if not in their bluster, that the ferocious February gales which confine them to the hut are in fact preserving them, that an attempt to drag the boat landwards would kill them – the Little Count first, then the rest, one by one. Nor do they need Tyson's prompting for an appreciation of the eskimos' view of the situation.

'Hänsel brings home two weeks of food for his wife and his young, and we take it from him and hand back a few scraps,' Linquist says. Meyer, who spends twenty-three hours of each day on his back, reminds them that Hans has been paid three hundred dollars as a hunter, a provider of fresh meat for the expedition.

'A job which he performs badly, like a clown.' Jamka adds. 'He thinks we should pay him a hundred dollars for every piece of seal. He thinks he is the donkey that shits gold.'

Kruger growls softly, 'And so we can't kill him. Little arsehole.'

Linquist, intrigued by his discovery of the paradox, wishes to expound it: 'They think they would have a better chance without us, and we think we would have a better chance without them. And we're both correct.'

'And both wrong,' Jamka says.

Kruger is still growling. 'Very funny. Very comical.'

Lindquist has been thinking. 'Then there is the boat. It's too heavy; it will kill us to drag it across the ice, yet it will kill us to leave it behind.'

Kruger controls his rage. Logical nitpicking is not his strength. 'What you mean, shitbag, is that we die, boat or no boat, wind or no wind, eskimo or no eskimo, food or no food. We die.'

He looks toward the wall that divides them from Joe's hut, where Tyson sleeps.

'That shitdog knows it. That shitdog has done this to us.'

Meyer's loss in authority has as yet done nothing to raise Kruger's estimation of Tyson. He continues his vituperative rants, and if there are some who feel the injustice, none is yet brave enough to cross him, none dares fall foul of his murderous rage. And they sense it quickening, growing ever more dangerous. In the shamed silence that follows his remark an onset of creaking and groaning reminds them of the most savage paradox of all

– that the same currents which bear them hourly into lighter skies, warmer seas, abounding game, carry within them the destruction of their platform. Already a third smaller than when they were first cast adrift, it threatens now to disintegrate; it is no longer simply wearing at the edges, but cracking: suddenly, unpredictably, explosively. Their little conglomeration of houses, erected on what they took to be the thickest part of the ice, could drop into the sea with not five minutes of warning; instant perdition for all of them.

Their first sighting of land is scant comfort. Westward, shimmering and ethereal in a pink sunrise-sunset, there is a headland. Tyson guesses Cape Siward, forty miles distant, and tries to win their support with comforting images of eskimo settlements, game, and within a month or two, English and Scotch whalers.

But not yet. The gale and the eternal heaving of the ice prohibit the attempt. He offers a plan: a bid for Shaumeer, sixty-five degrees north, as soon as there is a remission in the gale. In one month the bladdernoses will be thronging the ice, the easiest of kills. Winning their support, with Meyer sick and silent, he dares to propose a reduction in bread and pemmican rations to a single meal per day, and is astonished to find them agreeing at once, with Kruger surly but acquiescent.

They are among the dovekies now – fat sluggish little birds that even the sailors can bring down with buckshot or clubs. Less than bite-sized, they nevertheless allow a saving of bread, and make a soup that offers a hint of flavour, an illusion of heat.

When March comes in they can begin to talk about winter being over, begin to think of New England, Missouri, Pomerania, Bavaria, firesides and women and beds with sheets. But seals are scarce and the gales undiminished in their ferocity, and they wait for Meyer to provide the first of nineteen deaths.

'*Lieber Gott,*' Jamka says as they sip their dovekie soup. He pulls something from his mouth. 'Jackson, let me see your nose.'

In the feeble yellow glow of the lamp, pictures form slowly. Jackson's nose is white, raw, swollen, but intact. Their speculations range through human and non-human anatomy, till they conclude that it is a piece of random seal-gut from the bottom of the soup-pan.

'I don't care a shit,' Jamka says, returning it to his mouth.

The spring equinox approaches, but there have been no seals, and rations are cut to five and a half pounds of bread and four of pemmican for the eighteen bodies; Charlie Polaris is not assigned a share. None of them has escaped the ravages of frostbite and most are receiving the early intimations – the twingeing limbs and bleeding gums – of scurvy. The mercury plunges to minus twenty-five. Meyer licks a smudge of blubber-refuse in the bottom of a pemmican tin, painfully musters some saliva, swallows, lies back and makes his pronouncement: 'My friends, I think I'm beginning to die now.'

It is not the ineluctable truth that transfixes and silences them; only the frank articulation of it. They are all dying, their flesh visibly rotting on their bones, but Meyer will die first, and he has announced the imminence of the event. The silence for once is uncomplicated by guilt or spite or greed or accusation. Drawn together by fear unalloyed with resentments or rivalries, they ponder what it is to be mortal. The first small utterance comes from Jamka, who is sitting beside Meyer. '*Mensch, Mensch,*' he says, patting the sergeant-signaller lightly on the shoulder, but addressing all of them and the encompassing wilderness. The comforting word invites them to feel and taste and smell, as they begin to die, what it has meant, being human. Lindquist intones, '*Was es ist, was es ist, was es ist, ein Mensch zu sein.*'

'We eat shit,' Jamka says. '*Man ist, was man isst.* We are shit.'

And as they begin to wallow in their gloom, as they count their ribs and whimper with self-pity, as each reads his own wretched fate in Meyer's, as they settle into dying, Tyson's cry comes drifting on the wind: 'All hands! All hands! Oogjook!'

And behind him, still shy and half-apologetic through his excitement, Joe's penetrating treble: 'Oogjook! Oogjook!' Johnson, first through the tunnel, comes nose to nose with Tyson, who grips his shoulders. 'We need all hands, Peter, we need every damned hand.'

Joe stands ten paces from the hut entrance, waving frantically, a little seal-man, comical in his agitation. He holds his arms at their widest extent from his sides, palms toward the hut, conjuring bulk, fat, food. 'Oogjook, Mr Peter,' he says to Johnson. 'Plenty big.'

Big. All except Meyer assist in dragging the gigantic carcass to the huts, and all sweat. They measure him at nine feet from the whiskered nose to the ends of the hind flippers. The moment is important. Meyer drags himself through the tunnel to share it, and they stand, a solemn dozen, in a silent circle around the body of the great bearded seal. The blood has already frozen hard at the single hole in his head, through which Joe's ball has found the brain. In his immensity, they think, he might sink their floe.

'Seven hundred pounds,' Tyson tells the silence. 'Forty gallons of oil.'

They have been virtually pagan for a year and a half, and there is an awkwardness now when thanks are due and they scarcely know how to deliver them. Sensing their need, Tyson dredges for a psalm:

The people asked, and he brought quails,
And satisfied them with the bread of heaven.

Only Jackson and Herron and Meyer, the English speakers, fully understand. Jackson reverently touches the hind flipper with his foot. 'That sure is some mighty fat quail, that sure is some monster quail, Mr Tyson. Oh, sweet Jesus.' It is the longest utterance he has made on the floe.

Then Meyer laughs, gasping at the pain in his gums and his ribs. 'And a lot of bread, Jackson. A lot of manna.'

'Oogjook!' Jamka shouts. He slaps Joe on the back. 'Oogjook, little Joe.'

Joe nods. 'Oogjook, Mr Peter, plenty good, plenty hot.'

Jamka falls on the oogjoook, rubs his face in its rapidly cooling hide.

Joy gives them the strength to haul the monster to the entrance tunnel, and even in their hunger-madness they are prudent enough to leave the initial butchery to Joe and Hans, so that no drop of blood and no dram of oil will be lost.

As the hunters swiftly remove the blanket of skin and blubber, the sailors cut themselves titbits of flesh, with no squabbling. Soon the huts resemble the ghastly aftermath of a slaughter, and blood-spattered men are singing and dancing, drunk with the joy of feasting. Some, overcome by exhaustion, collapse to the floor to enjoy the agonies of digestion. As Joe steps from the reeking carcass with the huge liver cradled in his arms, Jackson reaches out to receive it.

'Don't you go wasting that, Little Joe. I'll make one devilish good fricassee with that.'

Joe does not release the meat. 'No sir, Mr Jackson; this no damn good, this give you plenty damn belly-ache.'

Herron, friendly enough, intervenes. 'Ah, little Joseph, you want to keep that whole damn monster liver for you and little Hannah, eh, with maybe a slice for Mr Tyson?' Joe turns to Tyson for support. Tyson knows from his whaling days the danger of the oogjook liver.

'That's killer stuff, John. He was a full-grown bull: his liver is poison through and through, like the bear's.'

Herron pauses to examine the meat. He prods it, marvels at its blood-rich sheen, its hot smell. 'You're joshing us boys, Mr Tyson.'

Jamka comes to join him in probing the liver. 'That looks like a pretty damn fine piece of liver,' he says.

Tyson, acknowledging Joe's silent appeal, shakes his head briefly, then offers a final small warning: 'It'll make them sick, Jackson. It might kill some of you.'

The cook says nothing. He will fry half of it in its own fat; stew the rest.

From the north comes a week of unrelenting hurricane that sets the pack heaving, crashing, grinding. A berg that has been grounded is unseated and capsizes in a vast eruption of fragments that alter their landscape from flat desert to jagged cordillera. Tyson yearns for a belly-laugh. 'I think there was never a party so destitute of every element of merriment as this,' he confides to his journal. But he is not entirely right: if joviality has died in the space he shares with Joe and Hannah and Puney, there is still, from the men's quarters where he is an unwelcome stranger, the low rattle of self-mockery and gibbet-laughter.

Confined within doors by the gale, sated with oogjook fat and liver, the sailors lie and burp into the darkness. The fresh blood has warmed them, eased their cramps, subdued the inflammation in their joints. Hours pass during which the howling of the gale obliterates speech and the incessant burping and intermittent farting mark the limit of their communication. But in the interludes they laugh.

'Fred,' Jamka appeals to Anthing, 'I would beg you, as a friend, to pull off my socks for me.'

'As a friend, dear Friedrich, I would be happy to oblige.'

'So kind, so kind. I wish to count my toes; I have not counted them for some days.'

'I trust you will find you have ten – five to each foot.'

'Yes, but I wish to know how many are still attached to the feet.'

'Ah.'

'And you, as my dear friend and namesake, you may have the loose ones. I bequeath them to you.'

'So kind. The nigger can pickle them for me and arrange them on a bed of Mecklenburger sauerkraut. You might even like to join me for dinner.'

'I think not. To eat one's own toes, that I find a little barbarous.'

'I understand. Let me promise then, before these witnesses, that you have first claim on any toes of mine – or on any other appendages which separate themselves from my person.'

Kruger comes in. 'I think he would choose death before eating that nose of yours, Anthing.'

Meyer is growing stronger from the infusions of blood-soup, but the effort of laughing makes him gasp. Jamka rolls out from under his buffalo skin and stretches his legs until his feet are within Anthing's reach. Propping his head on his bundle, he brings his face into the glow of the lamp.

'Dear Christ,' Anthing says. 'Dear God in Heaven.'

His alarm penetrates the howl of the wind, finds the others.

Abandoning tact, he says, 'Friedrich, your face is coming to pieces.'

In their state of perpetual fear for their shrivelling bodies, it is the worst thing he could say. Jamka cries out his anguish, singing a grotesque duet with the wind, then as Anthing bends toward him, bringing his own face into the circle of lamplight, he laughs hysterically.

'Yours too! Dear Jesus, we're falling to pieces! We're rotting

146

on our bones.'

Movement is always difficult in the eskimo-space of the hut, but soon all but Meyer have crawled into the yellow glow and there is a chorus of anguished revulsion as they stare from face to face. Meyer sits up and cries into the darkness, 'In the name of God, what's happening?'

Jackson is the most gaudily altered. Only a few pitiful shreds of outer skin remain clinging to his cheeks. His predominant hue is a purple-tinged grey, and reflected in his wide-eyed terror they see their own. The braver spirits begin to explore, and discover it is not only their faces that have suffered: hands, feet, chests – everywhere on their bodies the skin is hanging in dead strips. On noses and cheeks the new affliction has merged with he old, the frostbite, to create Gothic horror. Then Kruger confesses, 'I've been as sick as the devil this two days, from both ends.'

They all have. All except Meyer, who has avoided the oogjook liver, have been creeping on to the storm-racked floe for would-be secret vomitings and desperate evacuations into the wind. Hearing their groans, Meyer, who has taken on Bessel's medical mantle, has told them that frequent and painful alvine discharges are to be expected from the engorged stomachs of men who have been starving. Yet they know this to be something else, some fresh affliction, and no one protests when Herron finally voices what they have been afraid to admit.

'That damned liver, that damned oogjook. We're poisoned.'

All are indeed poisoned, but each feels singled out as the special victim of the poisoner, as each has felt particularised for special insult, special deprivation. The skat has long since been abandoned – officially because they are unable to spare the fuel that will give them sufficient light, in fact because of the danger to their lives. It matters nothing that Meyer, unofficial medical consultant, can explain it all as a concomitant of hunger – each cherishes his grievance, sees himself as an object of persecution: every cough has become a calculated spit in his direction, every hesitation, every smile, an act of sarcastic denunciation. Each, convinced that he alone has preserved his balance while the rest have succumbed to creeping idiocy, that he has begun to see with aquiline clarity while the rest have gone purblind, is haunted by dreams of being attacked, dismembered, devoured. Kruger,

147

admitting to a nightmare in which he feasted upon their several heads, now carries an aura of dread, and some have half-earnestly considered cutting his throat while he sleeps, in prophylactic self-defence.

Conversation has become a dice-game in which the object is to fend off thoughts of death, images of bones picked by ravens and terns. They exchange tediously similar happy dreams: taverns and ale and plump girls and soft-quilted beds and gardens; food in infinite variegation – game pies, gherkins on vollkornbrot, cream cheese, spanferkel dripping fat, rollmop herrings, fruit tarts, wienerschnitzel – their mouths move in silent sympathy as they feverishly concoct images and smells – become poets, sigh, weep, groan, yearn tearfully for mothers and sisters and wives and sweethearts and children. They masturbate, whenever strength permits, with as little attempt at concealment as the despised eskimos in their love-tumbles. And when the dice fall badly, when the images will not be fended off, they laugh bitterly and begin to compare and catalogue their symptoms, minutely itemise each prick of doom.

They scan their bodies head to toe, inch by inch, checking each manifestation against Jamka's list.

He begins with his snow-blindness.

'Since the sun returns I go out to see the sky and shoot the little shit-birds, and what's my reward? What do I get? My eyes are like hot onions in my head.'

'Mine too,' Anthing says.

'And mine,' Lindquist adds.

'I'm completely blind,' Johnson says.

'They burn like hot coal,' Nindermann says.

Jamka's 'Ha!' dismisses their afflictions as mere fleabites. 'My nose, my ears – when I walk into a warm room, they'll drop off.'

Kruger offers ironic comfort. 'Have you seen them? You'll be handsomer without them.'

Jamka ignores him. 'And my teeth. I could pull them out with my fingers, except that my mouth is so painful. Wherever my tongue goes it finds an ulcer.'

'I don't think you can have my daughter,' Anthing says. 'She prefers men with mouths.'

Jamka has taken the floor from Kruger. 'I have to sleep on my back because I can't turn over without opening a sore. My bones are sticking through everywhere – on my shoulders, on my hips, on my arse.'

Kruger regains the platform: 'What arse? We have no arses. No eyes, no noses, no arses, no brains.'

'And dear God, my feet!' Lindquist cries.

Herron crawls through to the eskimos' quarters and humbly, with a hint of grace, admits to Tyson that he was right. 'No more damn liver, Mr Tyson, unless it's a young one.'

Tyson laughs bitterly. If he dies on this floe, as he surely will, it will not be from hunger, but from rage, and from the monstrous curse of always being right.

The March gales, fiercer than ever, threaten a swift end to their trials. Sinking again toward death and feverishly pellucid in his dreams, Meyer sees and hears the others from the moon: eighteen black specks in a surging white wilderness, eighteen feeble heartbeats in a roaring chaos of wind and wave and clashing ice. The wind screams from the unattainable Pole, ripping through the mountains of Ellesmere and the churning packs of Robeson Channel, Hall Basin, Kennedy Channel, Kane Basin, Smith Sound – the American Way. The Great Humboldt Glacier calves into the pack of Peabody Bay, dropping a myriad of bergs which drive the pack against the cliffs and capes of Ellesmere; grounding, they form immense barriers against the southward-driven floes, force them upwards into fantastic sculpted mountains, ever shifting, ever rising and falling and grinding themselves into ice-porridge.

And on the night of the eleventh, their floe is summarily shattered. Their cagey negotiation with death becomes at last an open, desperate fight. Throughout the night they have lain shaking, sensing a new urgency in the tumult of the pack, as if the very epicentre of the icequake were under their bodies. There is too a new sharpness, a new immediacy, in the detonations in the night, as the floe begins to fall apart. They wait for the floor to open beneath their rugs, for their tiny village to disappear through the gap; but the wind abates and the day breaks clear and cloudless and they find themselves still whole, still roofed, but bobbing amongst bergs and heaped fragments of the floe on a platform hardly seventy by a hundred yards in extent. Twenty steps from

Joe's front door is the lapping of open sea.

They watch while Tyson whistles to an oogjook, and Joe finds its brain with a single shot.

Again, irony abounds: there is sea everywhere, and they are sailors; there are seals and narwhals and birds, and they have bullets to spare. But they are eighty miles from firm land, on a dancing shelf that might explode into a million fragments at any moment. Their boat has been providentially spared, but would be quickly splintered if they tried to launch it. Two seals per day is sufficient ration to keep them alive, and the eskimos are almost able to maintain this rate of supply as the drift carries them into the breeding grounds of the bladdernose. They capture the pups, kill them softly with their feet pressing on their chests, catch the milk from the stomachs for stirring into the blood-soup. Health improves. Eyes cease burning, running sores heal, cramps and joint-pains ease, teeth set firm again into gums. But the fear of slow death from hunger is now replaced by the acute terror of instant engulfment in the freezing waters. By the last day of March they have passed the sixtieth parallel, are south of great cities: Christiania, Stockholm, St. Petersburg. After a night of mad gales they find themselves tossing and rolling in open sea three miles east of the main pack, on a piece of ice smaller than a suburban garden. Even if summary destruction from stray fragments of the pack or careering bergs is evaded, it will not support them for more than another two or three days, and there will be no sleep for any but the children. Their boat is built for six men. If they are all to survive, it must do service through eighty miles of tempestuous water for twelve, with two women and five children. And it must carry their tents, blankets, weapons, ammunition, cooking utensils, and as much food as they can risk.

As ever, it is Kruger who voices the horrific thought. 'If we all go, we all die.'

He looks toward the huddle of eskimos. Sensing his mind, they tighten their circle, drawing the children inwards. Puney, Tobias, Augustina, Succi, Charlie Polaris: spared from being eaten by the sailors, they are now to be cast on the waters. And before that can happen Joe, Hannah, Hans and Christiana – the four most famous Inuit in the world – will have to be shot.

CHAPTER THIRTEEN
QUESTING: THE NORTHERNMOST CORPSE

Coyly, Tyson resorted to dashes even in his private journal: 'When I was in, he accused ____ and ____ of wanting to poison him.'

Ranting, foaming, threshing, riven by paranoiac delirium, Hall had scattered accusations like buckshot. Though fear of Bessel and Budington featured most often in the rants, he had been as likely in his interludes of calm to thank the doctor for his tender ministrations, or to revert to the days of warmest friendship with the ice-master, declaring their brotherhood in underscored capitals and begging the old whaler to share with him the joy of planting the red, white and blue at the top of the world.

At the doctor's suggestion, Nathaniel Coffin suspended work on a set of sledge wheels in order to make a coffin. The wheels were never to be fitted.

There were tears and noise for their dead leader and for themselves, imprisoned in darkness. Not only the *Polaris/ Periwinkle* was rudderless now. Hannah had lived with bitterest sorrow, had laid dead parents and children under rocks – but never had she suffered such as this, for Hall had been father and child to her in equal measure. She did not roar as she might have done, but her soft keening drifted on the November winds and filled the blackness and unnerved the sailors, until the younger ones unashamedly howled their misery and their self-pity into the night. They too had known him as Father Hall, and most had enjoyed moments when they were fired up by his boyish trust in the glorious conclusion of their adventure.

Though stones had been lifted from a couple of hearts, palls of guilt and misery had descended on others. Young Noah Hays, sickening for his Indiana farmyard, shook in his grief and even the brutish Kruger shared a part of it and embraced him.

Two feet into the gravel of Polaris Bay, Tyson's pick struck the adamantine undersoil. It would be the shallowest of graves, hardly more than those that the eskimos afforded their corpses. Hall's propped-up head faced eastward around the brief circle of the eighty-second parallel. In the cortège, a final vestige of hierarchy was preserved: Tyson, leader of the grave-digging party, walked in front with a lantern; Budington, the officers, the scientists and the chief engineer preceded the coffin, which was dragged on a sledge by four of the sailors; Anthing lit their way with a second lantern; the younger sailors followed the coffin and the eskimos brought up the rear. Half a mile seaward, in Hall's converted stateroom on board the *Polaris*, Jackson and Herron cooked a thirty-pound stew of musk ox. Tyson and Anthing flanked Bryan while he read the service. Noah Hays, Hall's most passionate acolyte, whom they jokingly called 'Little Hall,' fixed his eyes on the yellow lantern-spots, and watched as they blurred through the film of tears. One Star-Spangled Banner hung limp at half-mast on the flagpole of Bessel's observatory; another draped the coffin and a third enshrouded the stout body. The darkness was not total: through the boreal glow – yellow-pink and unearthly – the Dragon and the Bear and the Charioteer quietly twinkled, directing some of the sailors' eyes to the faint speck of the Pole Star, not quite overhead.

Then followed an old story. The little commonwealth of Thank God Harbor could not bear the death of its Cromwell. The inter-weaving hatreds now spread unchecked, and the United States North Polar Expedition was not only leaderless but purposeless, for Budington's only grails were his snug fireside in Groton Connecticut, his plump smiling Sarah, his claret-rack.

There were councils, discussions, token-talk of sledge and boat trips, food-caches, a spring dash for the Pole, but the old whaler left no-one in doubt that the first hint of a relaxation in the ice would mean a drive outwards into the basin then south for the whaling grounds and home. And anyone foolish enough to be drinking champagne at the North Pole when that happened could build himself an igloo there and wait for the next Ship of Fools to come to his rescue.

Lamely, conceding in his tone the injustice of his remarks, Tyson reminded him of Hall's last plea that they must press on to the Pole, raise the Sacred Bunting at the still point of the turning globe. Budington bridled his scorn, but shook his head. 'Captain Hall was my good friend, a friend of nigh on twenty years, but I cannot be bound by the ravings of a sick man whose mind was manifestly deranged.' With an outstretched hand he appealed to Bessel for support. The doctor's shrug was equivocal, and he said nothing. Budington continued, 'My responsibility is for the ship and the crew – my only priority is their safety.'

Master not only of the ship, but of Hall's keys, he no longer had to filch the scientists' preserving alcohol, but could breakfast on a porridge of biscuit dissolved in rum. Yet he needed Bessel's approval as a seal of legitimacy. 'Dr Bessel, you have an entire winter in which to complete a course of scientific observation in a part of the globe never before visited by civilised men – I surmise that you look forward to the work with relish, and in the accomplishment of it will do credit to your illustrious profession.'

He rose before the doctor could reply. 'I have to speak to the men,' he said. 'If you gentlemen will kindly excuse me.'

The men were not easy. Before them stretched the months of Arctic darkness that they knew well enough destroyed the spirits, tortured the nerves. The United States North Polar Expedition was national in name alone and naval only in the minds of Washington officials. Led entirely by civilians and crewed by men of disparate patriotic allegiance and the feeblest of dedication to the Flag, it began to fall apart long before the sun reached its southern terminus. Not for Budington, the hardnosed New England whaler, the programme of capers, the props against the darkness; not for him the amateur theatricals, improving lectures, newspaper production, religious observances that Kane, following the examples of Ross and Parry and Franklin and other British commanders, had instituted for the moral and corporal well-being of his forward cabins. And if the stupidity of life under navy orders was thereby averted, so too was the discipline, the comradeship, the security, the comfortable brotherhood of the military regime. 'Suit yourselves,' Budington told them, issuing firearms to each and every one, 'you'll not starve now, my friends.'

They thanked him for the proffered freedom, but did not love him for it. And nature itself, as it will, harmonised with their misery. With Hall three days under his pebbles, the first aurora of the season came not with the shining robes of angel-choirs, but a hesitant flickering, a dull ochre that reflected the pallor of their own joyless faces.

Then the puppies began to die.

There would be a vomiting, a whimpering, an agonised howling,

153

a bleeding from the anus, a final hideous protrusion of bowel. If the men did not strangle them and dispose of the corpses, the older dogs would devour them and spread the disease further. When Noah Hays, still tearful over the death of the commander, made known his distress, Budington brutally offered him a belaying pin, to spare his thumbs. Jamka, always the most skilled in the handling of the dogs, growled his sympathy, patted Hays's shoulder, and relieved him of the duty.

For the sailors the talk was of the weeks and months to come – months of endless gloom, with an officer corps descending into drunken animosity, recrimination, indecision. The bug of sarcasm infected the middle-rankers: Chester, Tyson, Schumann and Morton liked neither the senior officers nor each other. Caught in the rancorous maelstrom, Bryan, the pious and amiable chaplain-astronomer, despaired and retreated into silence. On the nineteenth of November, a week and a day after the interment, he conducted the last Sunday service. Budington, having sat through the hymns and prayers in pouting silence, stepped forward to make the announcement that in future each of them could pray for himself if and when he saw fit. It was a gesture that might have been intended as a counter to hypocrisy, yet it was seen by most as a spiteful trampling on the memory of the commander, his one-time blood-brother. In the dismal silence that followed the dispersal of the men, the officers were grim. For Hall, the sabbath service had been the week's fulcrum, the hour when all differences were overlooked in communal submission to the Greater Power, and his faith in it had touched even the sceptical hearts of the scientists.

'We were not prepared for this, sir,' Bryan said.

Budington looked toward the cabin as he spoke. His rum bottle was already on the table.

'I did not consider it a matter worthy of preparation, Mr Bryan. A simple act, of no particular consequence.'

Bryan, always anxious to avoid strife, nevertheless persisted. 'If you were disturbed, sir, by my too frequent allusions to the purpose of our expedition ...'

'Purpose, Mr Bryan? My purpose is to save the lives of these men, and if possible, to bring this miserable ship back to civilised waters in one piece. That is the only purpose that I concern myself with.'

He stood up, cutting the conversation short, while Bryan frowned and waited in vain for the other officers to offer support for his cause.

'I wish to rest, gentlemen,' Budington said. 'I think you have work.'

Using a fist-sized rock, Jamka crushed the skulls of five puppies, then lashed the bodies together with a length of rawhide. Official responsibility for all fuel and kindling lay with Noah Hays, but Jamka, sparing the grief-stricken boy, went straight to Jackson the cook. 'Put them in your stove, William, but save the rope,' he said.

Jackson, always isolated by his colour, descended into a pit of mute and lonely depression. Attempting to discharge something of his pastoral duty, Bryan offered a sympathetic ear to his worries, but elicited no response beyond a deferential shake of the head.

'But my poor William,' he said, 'you're plainly suffering, and that distresses all of us. Can I prevail upon you to speak to the Captain?'

The headshake now was violent, the courtesy transformed into frank terror. Bryan placed a hand on his arm. 'Maybe to Mr Tyson, then?'

'Maybe, sir,' Jackson said.

But before he would unfold to Tyson he exacted a solemn promise. 'You say nothing to nobody, Mr Tyson. Not nobody, not till we get back to New York, leastways.'

'Nobody, Will. You have my word.'

'Captain Budington sent me out, Mr Tyson.'

'Sent you out from where?'

'He come into the galley and he say, "Will, this-here coffee, he's too old; the commander needs it fresh." And he sent me out.'

'And where did you go?'

'Nowhere, only out on the deck; and Captain Budington come out with the coffeepot, and he say it's good fresh coffee, like the Captain need. But I don't know, Mr Tyson.'

Tyson waited, but Jackson said nothing more. 'What don't you know, Will?'

'I don't know what he done, Mr Tyson. It wasn't Captain Budington's way to make no coffee. He never made no coffee before. And he say, 'This coffee, this fresh brew, he's for the Captain only, them there eskimos and Mr Chester, they can have the old stuff.'

'Dear God, Will,' Tyson said.

'Amen, Mr Tyson. And that ain't all. When Captain Hall was sick, Captain Budington told Hannah to feed him bread pellets, and he told her they come from the doctor, only they don't come from no doctor, they come from hisself.'

'How do you know this, Will?'

'I know, Mr Tyson. I seen him, he threwed the doctor's bread-pellets clean away, clean over the side, and he give Hannah his own bread-pellets. I seen him in the galley, rolling those pellets, when I come back from feeding the dogs. He look me in the eye and say, "Medicine, for the Captain." But he ain't happy I seen him; he don't look good.'

'Will,' Tyson said, 'have you spoken of this to anyone else?'

'No, sir. I'm scared, Mr Tyson. I'm scared Captain Budington kill me. I don't say nothing to nobody 'cepting you, and I'm scared he might still kill me because of the things I seen.'

'No, Will; he'll not harm you, but he might speak to you; he might ask for your silence. He might find some way, some story, and ask for your support.'

'Oh, sweet Jesus!' For a moment, absurdly, it seemed that Jackson would run. Tyson patted his shoulder, spoke softly into his ear. 'Remember you're not alone now. You've shared.'

'But only you, Mr Tyson. Don't nobody else know nothing.'

'And it stays that way for now, Will. Until New York. And if he asks for your silence, or your support, promise it.'

For the eskimos, the miserable weeks to come were as nothing to the miserable Now, but even in the depths of their sorrow they coped better than the sailors because they had the comfort of sex. As the funereal stillness gave way to storms that rocked the ship and made hunting impossible, they retreated to their cabin, to the nakedness of semi-hibernation in which the children slept and ate and the adults slept, ate and sorrowfully copulated.

Hannah trembled for the onset of the *piblokto* – the November madness. Always in her own sinews she had felt the stirrings when the blackness fell upon them and the sea began to lose its war against the ice, always there were the headaches, the restlessness, the twitching in the limbs. For Christiana, she knew, it was still worse. Her friend had known Novembers when she could not safely sit within reach of her knife, when she howled at the kiss of moonlight. And they both waited in dread for the madness and the sickness to pass from the dogs to the *kabloonas*. Already the infection seemed to be taking hold of Noah Hays, mingling with his grief for the lost leader and his fear of the lengthening night and his loathing of the drunken ice-master to make a bitter soup of lunacy. They knew stories of naked women climbing moonlit icebergs, the heat of their crazed bodies keeping them alive and melting the bergs themselves. Now they imagined – and their own grief for Hall magnified the image – the disease passing from Hayes to the others, and they saw them running naked with their rifles in frenzies of destruction. In her terror, Hannah crawled under her buffalo robes, in part a terrified creature of the Arctic desert, in part a woman of the world who knew danger when she saw it. Hall had entrusted to her the metal box containing his papers, but she had not yet found the courage to face Budington and demand the custody of it. She retreated naked under the robes with Puney and when Joe came to them she enfolded him with arms and legs, shackled him, drew him into her spread thighs.

Joined, they slept through the dangerous hours of the full moon, rocking only as the northern gales caused the *Polaris* to rock in her icy fetters.

Separated from them by a draped canvas, a courtesy from Hall they had been too polite to refuse, Hans and Christiana, less assimilated despite Hans's mixed blood and his unrivalled experience of the *kabloonas*, were even more unhappy, more scared.

For Christiana, nothing was right. The men had returned from a trip, had been half a moon gone, but there were no spoils. And now Father Hall, the great provider, was dead.

Hans, succumbing to another of his fits of despondency, wanted to leave. If there had been a time when that would have started Christiana packing it was over now, as was the time when she might have silently submitted to his rebuke, his roundhouse cuff on her left ear. For her thighs and breasts he had once deserted Kane: now with Hall gone, there was still less to hold him to the *kabloonas* than there had been then. But she knew that the time was wrong; listening to the gathering darkness, she knew that it was not the moment to be starting a journey.

Whatever the sailors might say, she was a virtually silent lover. Suppression of love-cries was the custom in the enforced closeness of the igloo, and the suppression became part of the joy, so that a tight secretive winter fuck became memorable in a manner that a springtime rut, a daylight-fed free-for-all, never could; for there was the riotous love of dancing noses and nipples and thighs, of shared youth and joy in the return of light; and there was the greater, quieter love of bone-deep sorrow, tuned heartbeats, entwined lives – shared everything.

Miserably he whispered in her ear 'Eih, eih, I'm a useless limp-prick! I'm an inoosoot, a framework man for fooling the walrus, I'm empty, empty bearskin-pants!'

'Hush,' she said.

With Hall dead, the North Pole a faded mirage, the *Polaris* nothing more than a cramped hovel for twenty-four frightened *kabloonas,* these four, the most famous eskimos on the planet, came nose-to-nose with their mongrelism. Despised, or at best patronised, even here where their knowledge outstripped all the white man's science, they were permanent outcasts. Twenty years before, Hans had quietly left Kane's party as it toiled southwards after two years of desperate privation. It was not a desertion, because he had arrived at his latitude, Merkut's latitude (she had yet to receive her Christian name) while the *kabloonas* had other preoccupations. He had stolen none of their meat; had simply shouldered his rifle and his harpoon and had walked across the ice to the Etah settlement and Merkut's plump arms. But now the sea would harden and the moon would point the way and they would not take it. Tethered hounds that they were, and dollar-steeped, they would share the sufferings of the white men, follow them to whatever grisly fate awaited them.

'Oh, it's a poor man, it's a poor sad sekajook that can't stock his own larder, can't feed his own children.'

'Hush, mighty hunter.'

'Can't satisfy his own wife.'

She hushed him again and they tightened their embrace and listened for a while to the sounds that crept under the curtain:

Joe's regular soft grunt – *ng, ng, ng* – mixed with Hannah's gentle whistling sigh and Puney's dream-whimper. One of the sailors called out, his voice coarse and suggestive and directed at Joe, but unidentifiable through the thick wood of the bulkhead. Hans and Christiana laughed, sharing the joke, and his oosook stiffened.

Like their eating and sleeping, like their singing and dancing, their lovemaking was infected by the *kabloona* and his dollars. This was November – *toosarfik* – the time of listening, of storing fat and sleeping and slow heartbeat and ears and noses tuned to the thickening darkness and the songs of the dancing auroras. Not the fucking time, not for making children who would be born as the sea froze and the darkness coiled to engulf them again and the birds left and the fat bears crept into their scooped-out dens.

Yet the men were home from the chase with stories of their journeyings on the ice-edge, and the women welcomed them, puffed their male vanity for them, encircled them in legs and arms.

Christiana lay under Hans. Their soft bellies merged and she shut her eyes to dream while he nosed her, travelled the contours of her body on the routes she liked: her forehead, her right eye, her left, her cheeks in turn, her chin, her throat. Then her eyes again: their flutterings under the lids excited him, quickened his heart and his breathing. She turned her head and he lifted the thick hair to expose her right ear and enclosed it with his lips, warming it with his breath until her heart found the same rhythm as his. She began to make her rapid sharp gasps – her *e-ih, e-ih, e-ih*, and her legs involuntarily tightened around his waist while his fingers sank deeper into the soft meat of her shoulders. Again and again and again he kissed her cheeks, brows, throat, and finally her nose. Lightly he featherbrushed it with his lips, then his tongue fluttered across it and his teeth softly, softly, touched the tip of it and she grew hot and crushed him in the grip of her arms and her thighs, squeezing the breath from his body. He began to thrust, growing inside her, and she drummed her heels on his muscular buttocks and her *e-ih e-ih e-ih* grew faster, higher in pitch and a little louder, a little sharper, penetrating the seams of the floors and walls.

But he soon shrank again, and after two minutes they rested, relaxing their embrace, and laughed softly and listened to Joe's contented snore creeping under the curtain. Joe and Hannah did not make strong babies – they had already buried two – and the whine in Hannah's chest signalled that she too would soon die. Poor Joe.

'Poor tired hunters,' Christiana said, tightening the grip of her thighs again, holding him off, teasing him, laughing at his rising anger till he laughed too, and understood, and rolled from her.

Half a moon, fourteen sleeps, had passed since they had last made love. But they had eaten well after a kill, and celebration was called for. While she settled comfortably on her back with her thighs parted, he took his position on her right side and propped himself on his left elbow so that his right arm was free. And his hand, seemingly of its own accord, but responding to her unspoken directions, journeyed, visited, discovered. His fingers trod the deep valley between her breasts – still plump and full after three children and after the weeks of hunger – and tripped lightly, rhythmically, up and down her throat. He was a good dancer. Aroused, she took his hand in hers and eased it back to her breasts, to her nipples. He resisted, exacting his little revenge, his hand stronger than hers. His fingers descended the valley again to the gentle rise of her belly. She released a long slow sigh and let her hands drop, fingers clenched, to her breasts; she stilled her panting breath and relaxed into an easy moan. On the film of her sweat his fingers glided cunningly, insisting on nothing, careless and nonchalant as they brushed against her tight knuckles, squeezed her nipples, lightly tapped her chin.

Captain Hall, dead Father Hall whose hovering spirit blessed them, had had a famous weakness for eskimo women's breasts. She had felt his stare more than once as she suckled Tobias, and knew from Hannah his custom of apostrophising them, reciting poetry at them, extemporising hymns in praise of their milky amplitude. She knew too, though she could admit this only in the circle of women, how loudly Hans would proclaim the glory of her endowments during the rounds of boasting in the hunters' igloos, uninhibited and coarse in the happy fellowship of the chase; how he liked to draw her twin-mounds in the snow with his harpoon-point, making the others laugh when he capped the monstrous caricature with vast fountaining nipples. These things she knew without being told, for there was a fellowship of the sewing circle too. Had she not made the needles pause with her song in celebration of his mighty oosook? Had she not rocked the igloo with her air-drawing of his boundless spouting anissarpok – an ejaculation that could accommodate a whale, that filled her to bursting?

Not all men were the same. Joe, Hannah had told her, was a good lover but not a mover, not a thruster. He had done service, she said – and she was no weaver of fantasies – two and three and even four times under the blanket with Hall beside them in his bearskin pants and woollen shirt, knowing nothing, nothing at all, of their love-dance. And that tale had intrigued Christiana, stirred her. The knowledge that even now he was lance-rigid beyond the curtain, that even in his sleep and his paralysing grief he would be locked between Hannah's thighs these six hours or seven, made her pulse rush and her nipples swell and her ootsook flutter. All outwith her control, her throat throbbed to the rhythm of her *e-ih, e-ih, e-ih*. Never loud, never given voice, that *e-ih, e-ih, e-ih* still penetrated the well-caulked inches of white oak and ran along floors, through bulkheads, forward to the forecastle, where the sailors listened and tutted their disapproval yet secretly blessed it, and found it medicine to their grief.

'Dear God, the little seal-bitch is dancing again,' Jamka said.

They listened, softly laughing through their sorrow, and embraced the liberty that was offered them, the freedom to speak. 'Aaaah, I can't hold any longer,' Kruger said. 'I'm bursting.'

'We used to watch the stallion and the mares, in Pomerania,' Jamka said.

The communication was wordless now, though the quick breaths might edge into laughter. His fat strong fingers stroked her ribs the underside of her breasts, then he covered her nipples, each in turn, with his palm, caressed them with soft circular insistence till she trembled everywhere, till the high *e-ih e-ih e-ih* became a low moan that had tears in it and yearnings for happier times. He kissed her in every inch of her flesh: head and ears and eyes and nose, but never lips, never quite consummating the *kabloona* kiss; shoulders and breasts and belly and thighs, but never ootsook, never the wiry thatch or the moist petals down there where still after twenty years she would not allow his hands, would gently, with a soft reproachful laugh, deflect his clever insinuating fingers

161

if they should stray from her thigh.

Then she needed him as he needed her and there was power beyond their imaginings in the merging of their needs, their hungers, their yearnings, their griefs. She opened her thighs to receive him, raised her heels to press them on his strong buttocks, and released her breath in an endless sigh as he summoned all his cleverness to enter her katak, her welcoming tunnel, with the slowness and the terrible drum-tight patience of the hunter at the breathing-hole. And as he eased inwards, the combined strength of his hands pulling on her shoulders and her heels pressing on his rump locked them tight, bone on bone, with the upper ridge of his oosook hard against her mound. He thrust deeper, to the uttermost limit, to the edge of her womb, and they remained locked and motionless for an exquisite moment, with no grunting and no sighs, until they began their slow, slow rocking, their man-and-wife dance, so slow the robes scarcely lifted, betrayed nothing.

Hot. While the temperature on deck sank to minus forty and the ice tightened its grasp on the *Polaris*, they made heat, and the infinitely gentle creak of their dance on the planks of the ship reached the sailors' cabin, where Kruger hushed his deckmates and they lay in tense sniggering silence, listening for the end.

Her release came first, as it always did. The fluttering in her ootsook grew stronger and quicker and yet lighter, making her laugh and cry together, then it deepened, spread – through her thighs and her knees and calves to her drumming heels, which pressed still harder on his buttocks, clutching him, urging him. Then her breath was expelled in a whistling shuddering sigh, and her hands on his back tightened, squeezing the breath from his ribs, and he too sighed – *aaaahhhhhh* – and his explosion rocked them both, throb on throb, pulse on pulse, and her eyes in the darkness widened at the power and the wonder of it. His expiring groan rumbled through the joints of the *Polaris* as it creaked incessantly under the remorseless pressure of the pack.

And as her womb received the seed that would make Charlie Polaris, the corpse of Charles Francis Hall, imprisoned in the permafrost of Thank God Harbor, began its long slow rot.

True to their fears, the *piblokta* was not only an affliction of the Real People. Barely three hours after seeing the coffin lowered into the gravel, Nathaniel Coffin, the carpenter who made it, began to cry at the stars.

'I'm next,' he told them. 'They've poisoned the dear fool, and now it's my turn.'

A visionary, a Catholic, a hesitant latecomer to the expedition, he had never meshed with the company in the forecastle, had allied himself with the natives, and insofar as distinctions of rank permitted, with Hall. On the pretext of mending a cabinet hinge he had entered the cabin and found the commander asleep, but raving of murder, and the air heavy with a sickening bittersweet smell which Mauch later told him was tartar-emetic.

Now, bitten to the heart by the *piblokta*, he himself saw it all and raved: a murderous conspiracy of heathens had quenched the soul of Hall and was turning now on him, Nathaniel Coffin, for the continuation of the Devil's work. In the general collapse of comradeship, in the dark drunkenness that enveloped them without sparing even the pious Bryan or the upright Tyson, his madness was not particularly remarked until they had to search for him, prise him from hidden dark recesses of the ship, curled and frozen, struggling against their ministrations and screaming of death and devils. Everywhere he smelled murder, saw toxic vapours. In his boundless paranoia he saw each of them in turn as his would-be assassin: the sailors, the officers, the eskimos, the dogs, the House of Congress, the President, the dead Captain Hall.

In deepest January with the mercury long frozen at minus sixty and the gale above fifty miles an hour he left the ship, carrying his hammer, his saw, his chisels, and no food.

Roused by something, Joe peered into the blackness, thinking of bear. He lifted his Remington rifle from its resting place outside the door and gave chase, and forty yards from the ship he came upon the carpenter, slumped on his knees, facing westwards toward the frowning mountains of Ellesmere. He was ten minutes from death. Joe called for help and was joined by Jamka, and together they dragged the carpenter to the *Polaris*. There he was rubbed back to life, but not to health. Opening his eyes to find himself staring into those of Dr Bessel, he howled his terror, and his body jerked and writhed in a futile attempt to escape the doctor's touch.

'Him loco crazy,' Joe said. 'Him say him walking back to New York.'

UNITED STATES NAVY ENQUIRY, ON BOARD USS TALAPOOSA, WASHINGTON DC, 11TH OCTOBER, 1873, NAVY SECRETARY GEORGE ROBESON PRESIDING

Testimony of William Morton, Second Mate

Q   Did you know of Captain Hall's suspicion that there were some aboard who wished to injure him?

A   Yes, sir. He spoke of it many times in his delirium.

Q   And did you hear that he mentioned anyone in particular?

A   I believe he mentioned almost everybody, sir, but the doctor and Captain Budington were most frequent.

Q   Did you hear him mention them by name?

A   I did, sir, but he named others too.

Q   Which others, within your hearing?

A   I have no definite recollection, sir, but it seems he suspected everybody at some time, except perhaps Hannah.

Q   But you are clear that the captain and the doctor were most often mentioned?

A   That was no secret, sir.

Testimony of Henry Hobby, Seaman

Q   Did you know that there was any talk of foul play in the matter of Captain Hall's death?

A   I know there were a couple of officers who were greatly relieved by his death.

Q   Which officers do you mean?

A   I know that Captain Budington was one, and I think Dr Bessel was another.

Q   Did you hear them say so?

A   No, sir, I did not.

Q   Then how did you know they were of such a mind?

A   I could see it by their manner, sir, and I could hear it in their voice, and it was talked of by everybody.

Testimony of Henry Siemens, Seaman

Q   Did you see Captain Hall during his sickness?

A   No, sir. I asked Captain Budington for permission, but never had the privilege. I asked Dr Bessel about Captain Hall, and he told me he would not get over his sickness. This was before he got so very sick the second time.

Q   Did the doctor seem certain in his opinion that Captain Hall would not live through his sickness?

A   The second time, yes sir, he did.

Testimony of Nathaniel Coffin, Carpenter

Q   Did you see Captain Hall during his sickness?

A   Yes, sir, I saw him twice.

Q   Under what circumstances?

A   I had a piece of furniture to fix, and made that an excuse to go into the cabin. And another time Mr Morton asked me to go in and open a keg of tamarinds. The captain was asleep on both occasions, and I was ordered not to disturb him.

Q   Why did you feel the need of an excuse to enter the cabin?

A   There was concern among the men sir, and we were never told much of Captain Hall's condition.

Q   Why was there concern? Did you hear of any suspicion of foul play?

165

A   There was a deal of talking, sir, and I asked Hans, the native sledge-driver, what he thought of the Captain's illness.

Q   What did he tell you?

A   He said the Captain had travelled hard on their journey, and was much fatigued by it. While they were building snow-huts the Captain stood idle in the cold, and that did not do him any good and was not like his usual habit. Then I overheard Mr Mauch talking with Hayes, and he was something of a chemist,

Q   What did you hear him say?

A   He told Hayes that the alcohol they burned in the cabin had tartar-emetic in it, to prevent pilfering for the wrong purpose, and that the fumes of it acted as a poison when burned. He said he thought that hurt Captain Hall.

Q   Did you speak to him on this?

A   Yes, sir. He told me the same thing – he thought it had a great deal of effect on Captain Hall's health.

Testimony of William F Campbell, Fireman

Q   Was the coffee that Captain Hall drank on return from his sledge-journey made purposely for him?

A   Yes, sir, but several others had some of it at the same time as the Captain.

Q   Did you see Captain Hall during his sickness?

A   I did, several times, but was not permitted to speak to him. I heard that the Doctor told the men when he was first sick that he would never get over it.

Q   When he was first sick, you say?

A   Yes sir.

Q   And when the doctor spoke thus, what name did he give Captain Hall's sickness?

A   I did not hear him directly call it anything, sir. But the men talked of an apoplexy.

Q   Did you hear poisoning mentioned?

A   There were some whispers among the crew, but I did not know their source. They might have come from the captain himself, because it seemed a part of his sickness that he thought there were those who were minded to do him harm.

Testimony of R W D Bryan, Astronomer and Chaplain

Q   Did you suspect that Captain Hall's illness might prove fatal?

A   No. The Doctor had said that if he had another attack he would die, but at the time I could not believe it, the captain being such a strong man. The doctor asked me to assist in persuading Captain Hall to take a dose of quinine, which he was refusing. I did so, and watched the doctor prepare the medicine.

Q   What did you see him do?

A   He had little white crystals, and he heated them in a glass bowl. Then he heated the water, apparently to dissolve the crystals, That is all I know about any medicine. It was given in the form of an injection under the skin in his leg.

Q   Did you ever hear Captain Hall speak rationally during his sickness?

A   The night before he died, as he went to bed, he seemed very rational indeed; I remember this very distinctly. The doctor was putting him to bed, and tucking his clothes around him, when the captain said, 'Doctor, you have been very kind to me, and I am obliged to you.' I noticed that particularly, because it was a little different from what he had been saying before to the doctor, and his manner as he spoke was very gentle.

Q   Did you know of any statements from the officers that the death of Captain Hall was an event not entirely unwelcome?

A   I had heard that both Captain Budington and Dr Bessel had expressed relief, as though they had been under some kind of restraint which was not pleasant, and they were glad it was over.

Q   Did you hear this directly from either of them?

A   No, sir. I do not believe they would ever have expressed such sentiments directly to me.

Q   Did you not mess with them?

A   I did, sir, but I found they had little to say in each other's company. Their relations were never cordial, not from the beginning and particularly not after Captain Hall's death.

Q   Yet they agreed in their view of Captain Hall's sickness, and of his death?

A   Perhaps, sir, but I never heard them speak of it. It may be that they had their own different reasons.

Q   And what might these have been?

A   That I cannot say, sir.

CHAPTER FOURTEEN
DRIFTING: THE FLOE BREAKS UP

The rising sun of 2nd March reveals what sixty hours of blizzard have hidden: the flat desert of the pack has been refashioned into a tormented jumble of fragments, piled and jammed together like the rubble of Gomorrah. Accustomed to the roar of the wind, they find themselves shouting into the big silence. Remarks intended as secret confidence are heard across the floe. There is open water all around and cracks in the ice which bring seals to the surface. Joe and Hans shoot from the front door and the sailors gorge themselves, eskimo-style, on fresh meat. They lie on their backs on the rocking ice, revelling in the pain of stretched stomachs, shouting at the sky, competing for the loudest groan, the most resonant and protracted fart.

As food becomes a smaller preoccupation, fear for the condition of their floe deepens. Tyson feels the pressure of their anxiety and cherishes a scrap of relief that through it all there has been preserved at least some remnant of naval order: they expect him to lead them, and contemptuously ignore Meyer and his sextant. Their wild blasting at the game produces nothing, underlining the necessity of keeping the eskimos, the hunters at least, alive. On 21st March, Joe and Hans leave them to their sport and trek a mile across the ice to the breathing-holes. Within two hours they have returned, dragging seven carcasses, and Hans ruefully confesses that six of them were the reward for Joe's marksmanship. The meat warms them, and as the sun passes into the first point of Aries and the mercury rises to fifteen above zero, the first basking bladdernoses are sighted, and laughter once again becomes possible. In a single wonderful morning Joe kills three fat females and Hans one – twenty days of plump rations. Tyson's courage is fed by the clear recognition that the eskimo men are their mainstay, and he addresses the sailors with fresh candour about their plight, about the prospect of rescue. He chooses the moment when they are best prepared to listen, as they receive their bloody portions of bladdernose and marvel at Joe's easy skill in the dismemberment of the monstrous body.

'We are now in the grip of the strong tides off the mouth of Hudson Strait, and the wind is mostly in the north, so we plough the sea at above ten miles each day. The prospect of finding open water increases every one of those days, but so does the prospect of this floe being crushed in the movement of things. I think we must get the boat ready, and watch for the chance to launch her at a moment's notice.'

'And when we've launched her, where are we taking her?'

Jamka's question is not the real one, not the one their eyes are asking, but Tyson is thankful for the chance to talk.

'We're not far from sixty degrees north.' He looks to Meyer, who nods in confirmation. He speaks louder now, for both of them, for the officers. 'We're east of Cape Chidley, in Ungava Bay, and somewhere across there –' he waves his arm vaguely westward '– is the coast of Labrador.'

Jamka is unimpressed. 'Somewhere?'

'We can never be sure of our westing. It might be two hundred, three hundred miles, might be less.'

Kruger, always more dangerous than Jamka, breaks in. 'Then we're shit; we're food for the fishes.'

'No.' Tyson waves his arm again. 'We're in the whaling grounds. I've been here, Robert, and so have you. The season is beginning, so we can have good hope of rescue, but we must take to the boat soon, if only to find a safer floe.' He pauses to let them take in the view – the wild variegation of the pack, the encroaching bergs, the steel-grey sky.

Kruger's voice, lowered, brings them a desperate step closer to the real question.

'So when do we leave, Mr Tyson?'

Tyson knows the need for care. 'There is no open water within a mile. To launch the boat is out of the question until there is more movement in the ice, but that could be today, tomorrow... We have to be ready.'

'No, no! Shit-ready, shit-no!'

Jamka has jumped to his feet and is suddenly screaming, hurling his mad rage at the sky, at the water, at the pack, at everything – but finally at Meyer, who sits five yards from his left knee, propped against Herron.

'You told us! You took your readings!'

Feeling their eyes, isolated by Jamka's scream, Meyer sinks lower until his nose almost touches the ice. Although there has been some firming of flesh, some return of colour, he is plainly the weakest of them, the one whose death will mark the beginning of the final chapter. The new direction of things shocks all of them, even Kruger. Jamka steps into the silence he has made for himself. Something is expected of him. He points at the sunken figure of Meyer and his voice is still high, and thickening with tears. 'You said we would walk to Disco, you said he –' He swings his arm to indicate Tyson '– was lying to us, and giving food to his friends.'

Tyson frowns, takes a single step toward Jamka, and laughs.

'Now?' he says, and can think of nothing more, can only laugh that his hour of triumph should come, his officer's dignity be restored, at this moment, as the ice melts under their feet and the bergs close in to seal their fate.

Meyer raises his head, though the effort of doing so causes him to groan with pain and his face is twisted with mortal fear. He looks at Anthing on his right, Herron on his left, and tries to gauge their temper. Unable to make the direct assault on the dying man, Jamka now turns his attention to Tyson, but there is more misery than menace in his scream now. Feeling no sympathetic rage from the sailors, but only embarrassment compounded by surprise, he shrinks. 'Why are we here? Why are we sitting on this shit-ice? Why are we not in shit-Disco?'

Tyson says nothing. He is looking past Jamka's right hip at the momentarily upstaged Kruger, who sits in scowling amazement, taken aback and uncertain, wondering how this intrusion affects his own position as spokesman for the lower deck, his own response to the crisis. For all of them, and most pressingly for Tyson, Kruger, Meyer and the natives, the situation has assumed a monstrous intricacy. What should have been a pellucidly clear problem of survival, of resisting the onslaught of a common enemy, has become a hotchpotch of conflicting perils. Tyson knows that aligning himself with Jamka's – and he guesses, Kruger's and the sailors' – attack on his main adversary will provide no guarantee of safety for himself or the eskimos. He looks at the shrivelled, vanquished figure of Meyer, the fellow-officer who has deserted him, has been chiefly responsible for his loss of authority over the men, has conducted a campaign of whispered scorn and denigration against him, and feels nothing. Coldly, he sees the unravelling of events: Kruger will reassert his leadership, continue the diversionary action started by Jamka, and the bloody venting of their anger on Meyer will be followed by a turning against the eskimos and against him, George Tyson, their protector.

But Kruger is no simple rabble-rouser. He steps toward Jamka and his touch on his friend's arm is comradely but tinged with contempt. From that contempt Tyson takes courage. He addresses Jamka in a voice as low as the grinding of the ice will permit.

'Frederick, don't think of Disco – Disco is gone. You'll dance with the Disco girls, but not this year.' He points southward. 'We're coming to the whaling grounds, and there is our salvation.'

Jamka leans against Kruger. 'Where are the shit-whalers, Mr Tyson?' he says. 'Where are your arsehole-friends?'

'Not long, Frederick, not long. But we must stay alive, and work as friends together. I have more to complain of than you, I guess, but this is not the time.'

Kruger puts his arm around Jamka's shoulder. 'Sit down, Frederick,' he says. Jamka is wordless now, his misery and rage doing battle in convulsive sobs that he can do nothing to hide.

The ice growls, Meyer emits a low groan, and no-one knows what to say, or how to act.

In diverting their attention to himself, away from Tyson, Kruger, Meyer and the eskimos, Jamka has shown what they least wish to see: failure and impotence and profitless rancour, a cringing acceptance of death. Kruger is not yet ready for that.

'When do we leave?' he asks Tyson.

Joyously, Tyson seizes upon that 'we,' spreading his arms to include all of them, then stepping back till he is beside Puney, his right hand touching her shoulder. 'We watch and listen, Robert. The ice grows thinner every hour, and if there is a sudden gale the way might be open ahead of us before this day is over.'

Jamka has not yet sat down. He resists Kruger's soft pressure on his arm and from somewhere finds the charge for a final salvo against Meyer. 'He's lied to us. All the time, lies. He's killed us.' The crisis has not yet passed. A single sailor's voice in his support could unleash the monster. It is possible, Tyson thinks, that Meyer is protected by his plainly evident feebleness, that even in this extremity they will hesitate to assault a sick and dying man. Tyson now places himself between Meyer and the two standing sailors,

173

and before he speaks to Jamka he briefly nods his gratitude to Kruger.

'He has not lied to you, Frederick. He has tried to deliver you from the ice as he saw fit. And now we must work together.'

Finally defeated, Jamka sinks slowly to the ice, until he squats between Kruger and Tyson.

Now Tyson feels the difficulty of subduing his own rage. As Kruger's eyes offer the prospect of comradeship, a new alignment, there is a sudden desperate need to triumph over him, over all of them. Death is still the likeliest outcome of their adventure – a communal drowning some hundred miles short of the whaling grounds – and he wishes to die smugly, wishes to meet the Great Planter justified and smiling, his delight in the aromas of peacock pie and French brandy uncomplicated by guilt.

'I tried, sir – oh, how I tried,' he will tell the Great Planter.

'Eat, George,' the Planter will say, laying an avuncular arm on his shoulder.

But he sees the Eskimos now, huddled compactly together in their fear, and banishes the vision, shuts his ears to the Louisiana drawl.

'We must be together, Robert,' he says to Kruger.

As March comes to a close there is movement in plenty. The ice is driven by northwestern gales and the floe is buffeted with such violence it seems impossible it can hold together. There is no sleep, but even now at the height of their terror diversion is provided; and a change of meat.

In the small hours of the 29th the wind eases, and they lie listening, alert for the next assault of the ice. Then there is a new sound, a businesslike crunching, insistent and regular, soft at first but increasing steadily, creeping along the ice and under the igloo walls.

'Dear God, we're breaking up,' Anthing says.

But none of the sailors has the courage or strength to investigate. It is Joe, not yet in bed and fully dressed, who crawls through the tunnel. Within seconds he is back, his fat behind foremost, his voice a wonderstruck whisper: 'Nanook! A bear in the kayak.'

The kayak sits a mere four paces from the door. Joe has smelled the great beast's farts, felt the hot wind of its breath in his face as it raised its head in irritation at his arrival.

The rifles are propped against the outside wall of the hut, within six feet of the bear's haunches. Tyson sends Joe through to warn the sailors and crawls along the tunnel to confirm that this is indeed the long-awaited nose-to-nose confrontation with the king of the ice-hummocks. The bear is devouring their laid-out sealskins, and the kayak rocks as it brushes carelessly against its sides. Tyson creeps alongside the wall to the guns. Lifting the Remington, he knocks over a shotgun, and the bear at once stops its chewing and listens, waving its head to sniff the air. They peer through the gloom at each other, while Tyson cocks and raises the rifle and the bear reads the scents. Hoping to find the heart, Tyson aims at the centre of the grey mass. He squeezes the trigger and the hammer clicks ineffectually. Stirred to curiosity, the bear begins to waddle toward him at an unhurried but steadily quickening pace. A second time the rifle misfires and Tyson runs for the hut entrance. He ejects the cartridge, reloads with a fresh one, crawls again to the end of the tunnel. This time the hammer does its work, and even in the near-darkness he can see that he has had a lucky shot. Struck in the left shoulder, the bear wheels to face him directly, but stumbles and rolls on to its side when it attempts to step forward. While it struggles to raise itself, Joe steps to within three paces and finishes it with a shot into the heart from his rifle and two more from his Colt revolver.

The meat is light and porky, a relief to jaws, teeth, palates and digestions after the constant diet of seal. Removing the heart, Joe puts his finger into the hole made by Tyson's ball. There is a moment of embarrassed but blessedly good-natured laughter when he offers to hand the liver to Herron. Their recovery from the oogjook poisoning has been swift enough, but the memory of the sickness and the grisly images of their peeling faces have remained.

They celebrate the end of March, then, with full bellies, but in the midst of their laughter the gales return screaming from the north, and the floe begins to rise and fall and crack in a manner that plainly spells disaster. On the first morning of April they find themselves adrift on an acre and a half of thinning ice with the main pack a full twenty miles to the west.

Braced for a life-or-death argument, Tyson warns Joe to stay close by his side with the Colt loaded and handy, but the sailors nod when he presents his view of their situation: the platform is no longer safe, and they must abandon it forthwith and make for the main pack. This will mean four days battling through the pashy ice, pulling up for rest on whatever more secure fragments they might come across. He dismisses as too dangerous Meyer's proposal of a southerly tack into open ocean, and finds ready support, but there are cries of anguish when he argues that they will have to dump most of their stock of meat – a month's supply – and a good proportion of their ammunition, if there is to be genuine hope of the six-man boat carrying the nineteen of them across the heaving waters to the comparative safety of the pack. His bitterest struggle, a serious flirting with mutiny, arrives when he insists that they keep Hall's writing-desk, the last tangible remembrance of the commander – but even in this he is successful.

For the whole of the first day they struggle through wild seas, perpetually awash, their bodies so tightly packed together that Tyson cannot handle the yoke lines without cuffing the heads of the children. As darkness falls, they haul up on a floe smaller again by half than the one they had abandoned. The following day they make five miles westward in twenty hours, battling against a hurricane. They land on a floe, attempt some repairs to the battered gunwales, fit canvas washboards. They are drenched and exhausted and some are on the threshold of accepting defeat, welcoming the rest that death will bring. Yet there is exhilaration of a sort; a joy in struggle and a rekindling of comradeship. Starvation is no longer the threat: the bladdernoses strew the ice so thickly that they can kill them with oars and paddles.

On the fourth day, when they are within ten miles of the main pack, they begin to sink. The eskimos, never content when out of sight of land, howl their terror, and when Christiana sees Kruger crawling aft she pulls the children to her body and lodges them between Hans and herself. Kruger pushes past her to come within reach of Tyson.

'Mr Tyson, we're sinking.' His voice is dangerous in its penetrating calm.

Tyson too, maintains a tone hardly removed from the conversational. 'No, Robert; but there is some danger. We have to lighten the boat. We have to cast away the meat, the pots and pans. We have to throw off all the unnecessary weight.'

Christiana tightens her embrace on Succi, but when Kruger looks downward it is clear that his attention is fixed on Hall's writing-desk. He points, and Tyson nods.

'But not only that, Robert. The meat, the pots, the useless tools, the extra blankets – everything except the weapons.' He hands the steering oar to Kruger, takes the arm of Joe, who assists him in heaving the desk clear of the washboard and into the ice-porridge. It is instantly engulfed, invisible – a single bob of dark oak, a brief glint of brass, nothing.

Tyson turns to the sailors. 'Now the meat, quick!'

For men who have lived intimately with starvation for half a year it is a terrifying thought: they hesitate, looking to Kruger for guidance. Tyson lifts a slab of sealmeat as big as his own torso and staggers to the side; Kruger nods, and the men set to, their mariners' fear of drowning finally erasing the memories of hunger. Divested of four hundred pounds of meat and twice as much again of excess wood and metal and hide, the boat rises in the waves. Tyson returns to the tiller and the sailors use the few remaining meat tins to bail out the water that has added another quarter-ton to their burden. They will reach the pack, but they will reach it soaked and worn out and haunted yet again by the ghost of starvation, and their hatred of Tyson returns, more bitter than ever before.

For his part, wilting under that hatred, Tyson is ready to embrace the ghost, be welcomed by him. His hands grip the oar, responding somehow to each toss of the waves, and his eyes search out the pack whenever the boat is hoisted above the heaving pash; but hand nor eye – neither seems to have a connection with his brain. He dreams again of God's bounteous board, of Burgundy and peacock pie. The ghost, a skeleton in gold-trimmed livery, gestures toward the shimmering spread with open right hand. Cunning in his triumph, the ghost does not gloat, does not belittle their six-month ordeal. 'You must be tired, George; you must be hungry,' he says.

Tyson smiles, sniffs the air, identifies the rich peacock gravy, the onions, the hint of cigar. His fingers relax, begin to loosen their grip on the oar. He is dying, and the thought pleases him.

Then his head, dropping suddenly to his chest, meets Hannah's ungloved fingers as she offers him a piece of bear-meat. Surprised, she drops the meat into her lap. Tyson shakes his head, and the ghost leaves.

'Hannah,' he says.

Hannah has recovered the meat, is pushing it gently against his lips. 'I do beg your pardon, Mr Tyson,' she says, with the shy smile that has charmed the Queen of England and the President of the United States. The meat passes between his teeth and he tastes her smoky oily fingertips. She withdraws her hand to strip off another piece. With his tongue, Tyson squeezes this scrap hard against the roof of his mouth and swallows the blood as it oozes free. The boat rises and he sees the pack, grim and jumbled and awsome enough in its jagged indifference, yet suddenly welcoming – and hardly two miles distant.

'Ah, Hannah,' he says.

The floe does not offer enough snow for a serviceable igloo, but Joe and Hans shape a wall that deflects the worst of the wind from their tent. Hans and Christiana and their three children occupy the boat. Then the wind shifts to the north and rises to a hurricane that would have instantly swamped them if they had still been on the waves. It brings thick snow that allows Joe to build a shelter and relieve the pressure of bodies in the tent.

The shelter, however, does not see a full day of existence. Throughout the fifth day of April the platform bobs madly, grinding against the pack, splitting and snapping and fraying at the edges. At noon they drag everything into the new centre as a third of the ice breaks free.

Joe and Hannah, carrying Puney, a pemmican-tin, a rifle and their three remaining oxhides, scramble across the widening crack and stand lamenting with the others as Joe's brief essay in ice-architecture splashes off on a fragment hardly bigger than itself.

Joe laughs and summons Hans, now clearly the junior partner, and together within a half-hour they have put up a new hovel which stands proudly six paces from the tent. Even Kruger smiles, pats Joe on the shoulder and lays his hand on Hannah's head in a gesture that might almost contain a promise, an assurance.

No protocol and no distinctions now as they occupy their village: Kruger and Anthing share the snowhouse with Joe and Hannah and Puney and the arch-enemy Tyson; Hans and Christiana stow their children in the boat and lie on top of them; the remaining sailors encompass the weakened Meyer in the tent and he mumbles his gratitude for their soldierly solicitude. Hans leans on the gunwale clutching his Remington, ready to fight off the attack which he regards as inevitable.

Joe, the builder, stays awake and keeps watch at the igloo door, and his alert presence allows the others the luxury of surrendering to their exhaustion. With the unconscious skill of seasoned igloo-dwellers, they dispose bodies and limbs so that nothing touches the walls, that warmth is shared, that the child is protected from draughts. An occasional monster-wave tilts the floe and they have to cling to the floor to avoid being hurled through Joe's clever ice-wall; and as they cling they laugh, and Kruger again compliments Joe on his craft.

'We're holding together like Heidelberg Castle, Little Joe.'

Tyson lies brow to brow with Hannah. Puney is a small still bundle, scarcely enough to separate their bodies. When she needs to cough, even in her sleep, Hannah turns her head away from Tyson's.

Ah, Hannah. Adrift on his dreams, Tyson marvels. This Hannah, this dying Hannah, whose breath whistles. A god-fearing married man, he nevertheless has no regrets that his skin has been intimate with hers, that his foot has nestled in the flesh of her thighs, that he has sucked her nipples, bitten her ears, clutched her smooth buttocks, rocked between her knees, moaned out his pain and delight under her wonderful cunning hands: no regrets that he will die now embracing her sealy warmth.

Tyson has visited this Hannah as he has never visited his own soft-voiced wife. This Hannah, this Tookolito, will smile when the icy waves engulf them – not because she expects shortly to stand in awe before the radiant gates of the Holy City: but simply because she smiles. He has thought her as ugly as a walrus, as simple as a stone, as savage as a wolf – but in their checkers, when he has stood in for Joe as her opponent, she has allowed him, too, as she frequently allows Joe, the occasional victory for his manhood's sake.

A lurch of the floe causes their heads to collide; he apologises and laughs into the darkness. The same lurch wakens Kruger.

179

'Dear God, I think we're finished,' he says.

'No, Robert,' Tyson says, 'We'll see the morning.'

Out of her sleep Puney says, 'The hunters of Ootgoolik.'

Kruger laughs. 'What is she saying, little Hannah?'

'The hunters of Oogoolik,' Hannah says. 'They were lost at sea, Mr Robert. Long ago.'

Anthing stirs. 'How lost?'

'It is a story,' Hannah says. 'A man's story.'

Still facing the entrance tunnel, Joe says, 'They were hunting by the aglu, they were watching by the seal-holes.'

Then conceding Hannah's superior command of the *kabloonas*' language, he grunts, allowing her to continue.

'They were on the sea ice, far from the shore, and the wind came suddenly, and the ice broke, and the fog came, and they could not see their village.'

'And they died?' Anthing asks

'No. Two of them were angatkut,' Joe says.

'Korvik and Kudlaluk could make magic,' Hannah explains. 'They could lean against the ice and stop it from crushing the hunters on their floe. But all the ice was salt, and they were all dying of thirst.'

Now Puney wakes. 'They have to please the spirits, they have to give their knives.'

Tyson strokes her head. 'Their knives?'

Hannah becomes the storyteller again, 'Yes. Each one gave his knife to throw into the sea, with a piece of skin around the handle, as a gift to the spirits. And Ringalorkana had the most beautiful knife, and they kept it till the last. When he threw it on the sea it floated for a long, long time, then the spirits took it, and the wind blew the hunters back home.'

'Lucky devils,' Kruger says. 'We have given up our knives too, little Hannah, and our guns and our food.'

'Yes,' Hannah says. 'Some of the hunters' wives had new husbands when the hunters came back home, but they were happy to see their old men alive, and the new husbands gave them back to the old ones.'

Into the silence that follows the end of the tale, Tyson says, 'Oh, Hannah.'

Hannah adds, 'The men were changed. The time on the sea stayed in their bones, like a spirit, and when they lay down to sleep the sea waves rolled in them and their bodies rocked. Forever.'

'Dear God, I understand that,' Anthing says.

Kruger laughs and says, 'Thank God for Joe's strong little castle.'

But this igloo also disappears: while dawn breaks the roar of the wind is split by the snarl of the ice as the floe parts across the middle and Hannah and Puney again have to scurry to safety and look back to watch their home being carried off.

There can be no discussion now, and no action. On each side it is a matter of five paces from the tent to the sea. Sleep is out of the question. They load their final few possessions into the boat with the children and stand clinging to the gunwales, ready to leap when the ice disappears from under their feet. They break into two shifts – half snatching rest in the tent while the other half perches on the edge, waiting and watching. On the morning of the seventh a crack runs with polecat speed straight across the tent floor, and their breakfast is lost. With the weight of their bodies they prevent the tent from being swept away, and when they pitch it again there is not room for a man to pass between it and the boat.

Finally, at midnight, comes the moment of wonderful, exquisite terror. With a noise like cannon fire the floe is ripped asunder along a precise straight line that passes between tent and boat. Five of them have been on watch, clinging to the boat, and four leap backwards to the wall of the tent, but Meyer has been asleep on his feet, and stays hanging on the gunwale. Within ten seconds an impassable twenty yards of pitching sea separates the two fragments: on the one, eighteen bodies and the tent: on the other, the boat, the kayak and Meyer. With any but he there might have been hope, but the handling of the boat is hopelessly beyond his strength and he cannot remain past five seconds upright in the kayak, the management of which has remained a mystery for all but the natives. Yet it is their thin thread of hope, their main hope of recovering the boat, without which the end is certain. Responding to their cries, he casts the kayak into the water in a wild hope that it might find its way back to them, but the wind is against him, and the paperweight craft is picked up and borne off into the darkness.

Only Joe and Hans, the seal-men, will do for the adventure that now beckons – the last remote prospect of saving their lives.

181

Hans takes the ice-spear and a line, Joe a pair of paddles, and they launch themselves into the gloom. Their tubby bodies are silhouetted against the dim grey of the northern sky as they leap from one shifting plate of ice to another. After an hour they are dimly visible on the same piece as Meyer and the boat, and the sailors cheer. Yet the situation has barely improved: the launching of the boat is still beyond the combined strength of the three of them. Tyson calls to them to rest up until the dawn, and sees them clamber into the boat. On the bigger fragment Jamka and Anthing stand guard while the rest crowd into the tent, though everyone knows that the gesture is a useless one, that they have no recourse against a further cracking of the ice.

The dawn will be mercifully early, and the gale is easing. Inside the tent no-one speaks, and the whimpering of the children is lost in the wind. They wallow in their separate, private sorrows. Pressed against Hannah, as he has often been throughout their drift, Tyson wonders yet again if she feels as he might feel, grieves as he might grieve for the loss of his life-companion, the imminent death of his only child, fears as he fears the coming death. He knows she is not asleep, hears her soft comforting croon in Puney's ear, but can think of no words of like comfort that he can offer her. His own consolation he takes from the thought that now, on what will surely be the last night of their ordeal, there is no recrimination, no rage, but an almost serene resignation to their shared end. As he drifts in and out of feverish sleep, he reviews the whole miserable tale of the United States North Polar Expedition and writes in his head the wise, wise book that will never be read – his guidance for future questers:

The vessel – a steamer of course – which is expected to prosecute with any hope of success the search for the Pole must be built as strong as wood and iron, properly combined, can make her; sharp bows and stem sloping, so that on striking ice she will run on it. If the stem is straight or perpendicular, the vessel brings up with a heavy thud, which is very damaging to her. The hull should be so modelled as to allow ...

Literary nothings, he knows, offered merely to establish his authorial and maritime credentials. Honest penmanship comes only when he begins to expostulate on the composition of the crew.

Twenty-five picked men would be enough to man her. These should be reliable, well-tried men … a good ship, a united company, and a calm, courageous leader will yet do this thing … this crew should, as far as possible, be men of a single nation, a shared language …

He tightens his arm around Hannah's shoulder, whispers in her ear, 'And God damn them, Hannah. God damn them, they should know George Washington's birthday.'

But it is not to be their last night, nor their worst. Tyson opens his eyes to whisperings of daylight, and crawls out to Jamka on the floe. Jamka points to the three men clinging to the boat a mile eastward and to the kayak locked in the ice the same distance to the south. 'They've been trying to move the boat, but she's too heavy, and Mr Meyer is looking bad.'

Kruger, who has approached without Tyson noticing, says, 'Then we have to go to them.'

Tyson nods, and touches his shoulder in gratitude.

Tyson and Kruger reach the boat as Joe and Hans have done, scrambling, crawling, leaping from plate to plate, while the sailors watch in subdued terror. Meyer is spent, lying on his back and rambling of death, and the combined efforts of the two eskimos and the two sailors is hardly enough to rock the boat, far from enough to launch it. Anthing and Jamka watching their failure, rouse the others. 'We all have to cross,' Anthing says.

Herron shakes his head. 'Dear Christ, there is no way I can cross that.'

'Then stay with the women,' Anthing says.

Johnson looks across the heaving ice, measuring the distance, searching out a route.

'Oh, dear God,' he says.

Jamka grips his arm and says, 'You stay too – we need somebody here.'

Jamka and Anthing, following the path forged by Tyson and Kruger, reach the boat party, but even after they have rested up, their added strength enables them to rock the boat, inch it toward the edge of the floe – and no more.

Lindquist and Jackson and Nindermann are hideously afraid,

but the remaining two, Herron and Johnson, are in a state of paralysis and there is clearly no need for discussion or negotiation. As the three cross, their own terror is hardly less than that of the watchers at either end of their crazy dance among the ice.

Joe, rousing their wonder, comes to meet them in the middle, takes the arm of each in turn, steers them across to the safer fragments; and when they are within a hundred yards, Kruger joins them, laughing hysterically. The five collapse by the boat, recovering their breath and their nerve.

Then they heave for dear life, all nine of them – Joe and Hans, Tyson, Kruger, Anthing, Jamka, Nindermann, Lindquist and Jackson, and the boat slips inch by dreadful inch until her bow touches the water. Refusing to be lifted, Meyer tries to climb over the side and falls into the sea, and as they drag him out he pleads to be left. But they claim him from the pash and launch the boat, and Kruger and Anthing row them back to the bigger floe where the women are waiting with dry clothes for Meyer and bear's blood, warmed inside their jackets, for the others.

They drag the boat to the centre of the floe, pitch the tent beside it, sit in a despairing huddle and begin to notice how hungry they are, how bare of life the ice has suddenly become, how ominously the wind is rising.

By midnight they are buffeted by a screaming gale again. They fix the boat to the ice with boathooks and leather lashings and pack the bigger children inside. Charlie Polaris whimpers perpetually, announcing his hunger from inside Christiana's hood. The sea washes over their heads, through their hut; it demolishes another of Joe's igloos and worst of all, it carries off every drop of fresh water from the floe, so that thirst becomes their most desperate affliction.

As dawn breaks the wind slackens, and they sleep. The ice closes, and the floe begins to groan under the pressure of the surrounding pack. The brightening sky reveals that they are jammed between two monstrous bergs, one threatening to topple from the north, the other from the south; either one would end their misery at a stroke. The day of April 12th is windless, sunny, mild. Tyson reads their latitude as fifty-five degrees, thirty-five minutes. 'We are south of Copenhagen,' he says, 'south of Dundee.' He points upward, at a circling black form. 'And there is a raven.'

UNITED STATES NAVY BOARD OF ENQUIRY, WASHINGTON DC, OCTOBER 16TH 1873, NAVY SECRETARY GEORGE ROBESON PRESIDING

Testimony of William F. Campbell, Fireman

Q   You saw Captain Hall immediately upon his return from the sledge journey?

A   Yes, sir. I was walking behind the observatory when I saw him with Mr Chester and the two natives.

Q   Did he seem to you in good health?

A   No, sir. I thought he looked unwell, and asked him as much. He replied that he was pretty tired, but quite well in health and quite raised by his journey.

Q   Did you accompany him toward the ship?

A   I did. As we passed the observatory Dr Bessel came out and shook hands with him, and walked with us to the ship, speaking to the captain about the sledge-journey, and about future plans. The captain seemed to recover some of his spirits then. When he stepped on board the ship, he requested coffee, and Mr Herron the steward went downstairs to fetch it.

Q   Was that coffee specially made for the captain's party?

A   Yes, sir, I believe it was.

Testimony of Joseph Mauch, Seaman

Q   Did you see the captain on his return from the sledge-journey?

A   I met the captain at the doorway where I complimented him on his appearance and enquired after his health. He said he felt well, but a little fatigued. I told him I had kept a full record of events during his absence, and he thanked me and promised to read it as soon as possible, after his coffee.

Q And was that coffee purposely made for the captain and his party?

A Yes, sir. I heard that the captain's can, at least, was freshly made.

Q And by whom?

A That I cannot say, sir. I heard that Captain Budington personally brought it to the table.

Testimony of William Morton, Second Mate

Q Did you enter the cabin with Captain Hall?

A Yes, sir. I helped him to remove his wet boots then I went to get him some dry clothing.

Q And how long were you getting the clothing?

A Twenty minutes, I would judge.

Q What did you find when you returned to the cabin?

A I found the captain very sick, and vomiting, after his coffee. I asked him what ailed him and he replied, 'Nothing at all – a foul stomach.' Then I assisted the doctor in getting him to bed. The doctor said it would not do to give him an emetic, he was not strong enough.

Q Was the doctor present when Captain Hall drank his coffee?

A I believe he was, sir, but I am not certain of it.

Testimony of Captain Sidney O. Budington

Q How did you first learn of Captain Hall's illness?

A I think it was shortly after twelve o' clock. Chester roused me up and said, 'Captain Hall is dying.' I ran up as quick as I could. He was sitting in the berth with his feet hanging over, his head going one way and the other, and eyes very glassy, and looking like a corpse – frightful to look at. He wanted to know how to spell 'murder.' He spelled it several different ways, and kept on spelling it for some time. At last he straightened up and looked around, and recognised who we were, and looked at the doctor. He said, 'Doctor, I know everything that's going on; you can't fool me,' and he called for some water. He undertook to swallow the water, but couldn't. He heaved it up. They persuaded him to lie down, and he did so, breathing very hard.

Q Was the coffee that he drank made expressly for him?

A Yes, sir. I made it for him, as my welcome to him.

Q And did no one else drink that same coffee?

A They might have done. I did not stay to see it all consumed.

Q Was it not the cook's responsibility to make coffee, and the steward's to serve it?

A It was, sir. But I wished to particularly welcome the captain, to see him safe, and to assure him that all had been well in his absence.

CHAPTER FIFTEEN
QUESTING: FOLLY BAY

Nathaniel Coffin ceased his rantings and began to eat, but he remained sedately mad. The liverdeep gloom of the first winter visited all of them with madness of some sort, as if the *piblotka* were no mere sickness, but a presence, a malign insect that crept out of the blackness and into their skulls. Hall's death-delirium had been relayed to the forecastle, to be translated into German and feed hours of frightened gossip. Coffin's fear of assassination now rebounded upon his own head as the sailors complained of the danger that he might attack them in their bunks, nail their heads to the planks in the night. Refusing the request that he be put in irons, Budington assured them that he would be carefully watched, but would be harmless.

'I've seen it before,' he said. 'I know the breed. We'll see him walking straight in Brooklyn.'

The weather itself, a week after the burial of the commander, seemed to catch the infection. The wind rose in the north, became a sixty-mile-an-hour gale that drove the pack of Robeson Channel with thunderous rage into Hall Basin . The *Polaris* began a rocking and a creaking in every beam and nail, and their ice-wall, the labour of weeks, crumbled, leaving them utterly naked before the fury of the gale and the churning ice. Providence Berg, shuddering but still firmly grounded, was their barrier against perdition. Nindermann, by the light of a burning rope, heroically clung to the ice and drove an anchor into its edge, then the *Polaris* was secured to it with hawsers. They were able to warp the ship along the side of the ice-mountain, and there they rested for three days before their preserver became their destroyer; on the night of 28th November the wind shifted southward and rose to hurricane strength, driving the floe ice against the berg and splitting it. The nearer half, ungrounded at last, began to drift toward them. They stared in impotent horror as it approached: fifty feet high, two hundred wide, it would not have been slowed in its drive for the land by the four hundred puny tons of the *Polaris*. Then with the wall of ice still forty feet distant, the ship began to rise stern first out of the bay and ease northwards toward the shore. Providence Berg was cradling them on an underwater spur, bearing them with slow inexorability landwards. No heroics, no derring-do with anchor or rope, could save them now. Their bodies they might entrust to the ice and to the shore, but the *Polaris's* doom seemed settled, until the errant half of Providence Berg grounded once more and the little ship, intact but careering desperately to port and with her bow raised six feet above her stern, came to a shuddering halt.

Budington, who had stayed below during the crisis, surveyed their predicament from the starboard rail. 'It might be wise to put the women and children ashore,' he said.

Hans and Joe had had enough of the sailor's life. They shifted their entire households to the shore and camped by the observatory.

Tyson, foreseeing the need of the carpenter's skills, resolved to nurse Nathaniel Coffin through his dementia. Relieved of the immediate peril of drowning, Budington dismissed the pleas of Tyson and Chester that the *Polaris* be warped off the spur and dragged to a safer berth, assured them that she was safe and snug enough where she sat, and declared that he had pressing business below. In ignoring the carpenter's madness and discounting his officers' assessment of the ship's danger, he began to apply the principle which was to guide him throughout the time that remained to the North Polar Expedition: that they should survive with the minimum of bodily effort. If the threat of the ice were to become acute, he would act: otherwise, he would sit. He would return the ship to Brooklyn with her spars intact and himself in command and lacking as little as possible of his two-hundred-and-ten pound frame. Not the North Pole, not the transits of stars, not the unravelling of the mystery of the Open Polar Sea, not the depths, currents and temperatures of the Arctic Ocean, not a single enjoinment of the United States Congress or the Academy of Science would propel his thoughts beyond that aim. If it could be accomplished with a healthy and undiminished crew, so much the better, but in this matter he was no fanatic.

The winter set in, and the *Polaris* rose and fell with the tides while the spur, the excrescent foot of Providence Berg, slowly rocked her prow in and out of the thickening ice of Thank God Harbor and the sailors slept through an endless creaking, a perpetual steady rocking, and wondered if she would split amidships, physically confirming the division between officers and crew that had arisen since Hall's death.

At no time were they oppressed by an overbearing command, or irritated by paternal interference: they caroused above while the leaks widened below, and they traversed the blackness of January with cards and rum and much moonlight firing of rifles, shotguns and pistols at passing shadows. It was manifest in their captain's bearing that escaping the bay-ice and steaming south at the first opportunity was his single aspiration, and so they grew daily more reckless in their consumption of the provisions, their wastage of fuel and ammunition.

Friendless and isolated, Budington was never less than tipsy, always surly, always suspicious, as if every remark addressed to him or about him was an accusation that he had murdered Hall. Bessel, likewise a target of the commander's dying imprecations, cocooned himself in scientific busyness, exchanging courtesies with the other officers, but venturing nothing that approached comradeship and eschewing confidence even with Meyer, his countryman and principal scientific colleague. In the occasional necessary performance of medical services for the sailors he twitched under their glances, knowing that for them he was the prime suspect, the expert poisoner.

In the middle ranks, where there might have been a harmony of equals, the misery of lost command, the failure of trust in the naval and in the scientific direction of the vessel, the desperate purposelessness of the whole adventure – all of these combined with the polar gloom to stretch friendships beyond the breaking point. Tyson and Chester rode into and out of intimacy: moments of shared resolve became scarcer and shorter as petty differences swelled into quarrels, small sarcasms into plain abuse.

Through the unremitting darkness and frequent gales of January their resentments festered. Only the scientists had the distraction of work: they observed, measured, argued, made notes. Lovingly Bessel and Bryan and Meyer checked and rechecked the chronometers, established the precious verticality of the transit instrument, called out the crossings of circumpolar and equatorial stars, solemnly debated lunar distances, cheerfully risked their lives to ensure that three times in a single week the theodolite magnetometer might be set up to record the wonderful fluctuations of absolute horizontal intensity, rocked their heads with the pendulum and compared the gravity of Thank God Harbor with the gravity of Washington DC. Assisting them on rare occasions with the coarser tasks, Joe and Hans frowned at Mr Bryan's patient explanations, tried to pronounce 'theodolite,' laughed till their ribs hurt, and smelled the moon.

They laughed too with the joy of futile hard labour when Tyson organised a gang to attempt the release of the *Polaris* from the ice-spur that perpetually threatened her stem. As they increased the dosage of powder, so the showers of surface ice and snow rose higher into the darkness, but the little tug settled all the more tightly into her ice cradle and rocked with the tides. Sensing Budington's scorn, Tyson pleaded with him to issue orders for the repair of leaks during neap tides.

'When the time is right,' the captain said in a tone that clearly spoke forth his contempt for the project and his anger at the impugnment of his authority.

Most of the time the natives were ensconced in their igloos, enjoying the customary enforced idleness of *kammaliak*, the moon-month. Joe and Hans emerged sometimes to minister to the dogs, sniff the air, scan southeastwards for signs of the returning light, listen and feel for the movements under the bay-ice that might hint at seal meat. Their abandonment of the groaning and trembling ship removed a main source of winter amusement for the sailors, who now had to rely increasingly on ever coarser gossip and speculation for their carnal relief. At the end of a five-day blizzard during which no one had stretched a limb out of doors and few had stirred from their bunks, Kruger returned from a raid on the galley with a bottle of Cognac, almost two-thirds full.

'I persuaded Mr Herron to part with it, for a small something,' he said. He burped. 'It was full, but a fellow gets thirsty, walking.'

He was dangerous. Noah Hays, the only American in the group, never more than half understanding the talk of the Germans, rose and announced that he would be required to assist Mr Campbell at the coal store, the storm having shifted the load. Joseph Mauch, who spoke English and German with equal facility and had served Hall as his secretary, offered to accompany him: his value as a source of gossip had dwindled, and he found himself daily more scorned, more excluded from the forecastle cliques.

191

As the door closed behind them, Kruger said, 'Maybe there will be time to read the little arsehole's journal.'

'Which little arsehole are you talking about?' Jamka asked. 'They both write journals.'

'Little Joseph. He thinks he' s a scholar of some distinction.'

'The little Yankee's worse,' Jamka said. 'He isn't happy shovelling coal. He deserves better, in his own opinion – he's a learned fellow too.'

'Yes, two learned little arseholes.' Kruger took a large swallow from the bottle, then handed it to Jamka and signalled with a nod his permission for it to be passed around the cabin. Spurred by his liberality, the others – Lindquist and Johnson first, followed by Anthing and Siemens, brought flasks from under their blankets.

'Maybe we should drink first to Mr Herron, our generous and understanding steward,' Kruger said.

'And to Black Bill, our little cook,' Anthing added.

'I have mine from the second mate himself, the famous Mr Morton,' Johnson said. The bottles passed around the circle – Kruger, Anthing, Siemens, Lindquist, Nindermann, Johnson – and with gloomy joy they swallowed Cognac, Bourbon, claret, rum, preserving fluid and laudanum, and let their gossip, their main prop against the blackness, expand.

'The little arsehole...' Kruger did not have to name Joseph Mauch, '...will have some wonderful stories to tell them in Washington.'

'Dear Christ, the stories!' Jamka said, 'Oh, the stories!'

This was Johnson's cue. He fell back on his bunk, raised his legs, and began to writhe and moan in obscene parody of Hall's death-agony. They had seen the pantomime a dozen times before, and their amusement and discomfiture at it had increased in equal measure: fondness for Hall had waxed and taken on a sentimental tinge during the two months of indiscipline and feeble leadership that had followed his death, but January and alcohol were a reckless mixture. In a passable imitation of Mauch's stiff posture and boyish voice, Lindquist took his place at Johnson's head and sat with his pen poised – the commander's amanuensis. Polyglot Swede, he offered a convincing enough version of Mauch's south-western drawl: 'Awl raaght, cep'n, ah'm ready.'

From the writhing wriggling Johnson came a succession of

fevered gasps, the rantings of a man staring his Maker in the face. 'Write, Joseph, write! Get this down!'

'I'm wraatin' Cep'n Haahll, see!' He waved his hand against the dying man's face, showing him the invisible pencil.

'They're killing me, Joseph, they're poisoning me – write it down – they're killing me.'

'Yeeeaas, Cep'n, but who's pizenin' you?'

'All of them! Budington, Bessel, Meyer, Schumann, Chester, Tyson – only Hannah is not killing me.' Lindquist scribbled rapidly, listing the malefactors.

'Haaow aah they killin' you, Cep'n?'

'Gas, Joseph, gas and poison. They are poisoning my socks and my pipes of tobacco. They are filling the cabin with blue vapours.'

Lindquist wrote: 'Saahcks, paaaps, vapours, yeaas, Cep'n.'

Jamka mincingly approached the bed and spoke in the high refined tones of Dr Emil Bessel of Heidelberg University. 'It is time for your medicine, Captain Hall; time for your preparation.'

The self-directed amateur theatrical was their safeguard. They laughed with unnatural loudness, forcing the embarrassment under, as the dying captain screamed and threshed and tried to fend off the murderous physician, who injected him with arsenic-laced quinine, plunged his head into vaporous vats, changed a poisoned sock for another yet more potent, while the high-pitched scribe meticulously set it all down, listed every treacherous act, transcribed every syllable of the assassin's evil reassurances, the victim's cries for mercy. The captain released his dying howl, and Kruger entered the cabin, stooping from Budington's six-feet at the imaginary door, stopping by the bunk, swaying drunkenly.

'I heard the noise,' he said, in the ice-master's habitual querulous bark.

Bessel was oily and foreign. 'Nothing to fear, Mr Budington. I have been administering the dear captain's medicine.'

'Ah.' The ice-master grinned knowingly, put his hand on the victim's head. 'How are your socks, Captain Hall?'

There was a rattle in the captain's throat. The ice-master nodded. 'Excellent, sir. I've brought you some coffee – good and strong, just as you like it. I'm afraid there is no sugar left, so I've used the prussic acid.'

The other two raised the dying man and propped him up while the ice-master tilted his head and poured three cups of poisoned coffee down his throat.

'There,' the ice-master said. 'No sugar, but sweetened with plenty of molasses and some whisky and some arsenic and plenty of prussic acid and a small drop of eskimo-piss – a little present from Hannah.'

They watched for a silent and tense half-minute while the assorted poisons began to work. Then came the death-call, a low rumble from the chest; the captain sat bolt upright, eyes wide in terror, clutching his throat with his right hand, waving his left wildly above his head. His voice was a hideous gurgle:

'Damn you, Joseph – write! The blue vapours!'

'I'm ready, sir.' Lindquist, an eager young Mauch hardly less fevered than his captain, held the imaginary pencil an inch above the imaginary notebook.

'This…' The patient sank slowly back on his bolster. He coughed. When he spoke again the words came slowly, formed by a tongue twisted in mortal agony.

'This … is … my … last…'

The scribe bent over the bunk, brought his ear to the dying man's mouth. 'Sir?'

'These … are the last words … of Charles … Francis … Hall, explorer. Write!'

'Sir, I'm wraatin'.'

'They have mur…' The voice faded. Gently, the scribe tapped the cheeks.

'Sir?'

A last desperate effort: 'They have murdered me!' The tongue rattled in the throat, and the entire body began to shake.

'Who hez murdered you, Cep'n? Ma paincil is ready.'

There was a final bout of twitching, a roar of despair that at last became a word – 'MURDER!' – and the explorer was suddenly rigid.

Jamka was again the birdlike little doctor. He bustled the scribe gently to the side, bent to listen to the patient's chest, felt his throat, held a mirror to his lips. 'There has been much sudation,' he said, drawing his finger across the forehead of the corpse, then holding it up for the others to see. 'Our dear, dear captain is dead, my friends. Of natural causes.'

'God have mercy,' the ice-master said, and wiped his eyes with his sleeve.

'His last word ...' the scribe held the pencil still poised above his book.

'He did not finish,' the doctor said. 'Alas, we have no way of knowing what he wished to say.'

'Alas,' the ice-master said.

The doctor shook his head sorrowfully. 'You are now our leader, Mr Budington. I congratulate you. You must now take us to the North Pole; you must plant the Sacred Banner.'

The sailors roared, and the louder they roared the more bitter their sorrow grew, and with it their contempt for their officers and themselves and their abject fear of the surrounding ice, the enveloping darkness.

'Oh God, there will be fun in Washington,' Siemens said.

Lindquist squinted in the darkness and read from the imaginary book. 'MURDER – whatevah cen he mean?'

'Nothing at all,' Jamka-Bessel assured him. 'An apoplectic shock; an act of God.'

'A natural cause,' Kruger-Budington said.

Lindquist-Mauch spoke in a terrified screech: 'But what shell ah tayll thaym in Waashinton?'

The doctor looked at the captain, and they shared a smile for the naivety of youth.

'Nothing,' he said. 'The captain was struck down and taken from us by an apoplectic shock. We did everything we could to save him.'

'I gave him coffee, fresh and specially made,' the ice-master said. He reached out for the notebook, snatched it from the scribe's hand, and said 'Now, go to your cabin, little mouse.'

The scribe left.

'Little arsehole,' Kruger said in his own voice, ending the performance. 'Little arselicker.'

He was murderously drunk now. He did not sit down when the other actors did, but lifted his woollen helmet from his bunk and announced that he was going to visit the natives. 'I'm missing the little louseballs. Who would like to join me? Who wants to see the little rats that have left the sinking ship?'

195

They recognised it as an invitation heavy with danger. In lifting his helmet Kruger had revealed his Colt, always loaded, lying on his bunk; and they were all familiar with his rages. Siemens, his closest friend and his equal in weight and bodily strength, assumed the burden. He rose from his bunk and said, 'I'll come with you, Robert, but you must promise to be courteous.'

'My dear Hermann, I am always courteous,' Kruger said. 'Now come.' He lifted the revolver and tucked it into his jacket. 'There may be bears,' he said.

The gale had subsided, and they climbed over the side of the *Polaris* into a balmy minus-thirteen. A dusting of cloud obscured the stars, but revealed a hint of dawn-grey in the southeastern sky.

Siemens put his arm around Kruger's shoulders and spoke into his ear. 'Remember, Robert, be courteous.'

Kruger was laughing. 'Hermann my friend, courtesy is the law of the igloo. I'm bringing Joe a little drink, and I hope he might offer me some eskimo favours in return.'

Siemens's grip tightened, stopping their progress across the snow. 'Dear God, what do you mean?' he asked.

'You know what I mean, friend. We've heard so many fairytales about the generosity which the little men show to their guests. We've heard all about their hospitality, but have we seen the proof?'

'Dear Christ, come back to the ship, Robert!'

Kruger had planted his feet hard in the snow, resisting Siemens's pull. He gave Siemens a playful punch in the chest. 'Don't get excited, Hermann. We are two wanderers in the night, seeking refuge from the storm, seeking shelter and warmth and food for our bellies.'

'They'll give us tea,' Siemens said.

'Fuck tea – we need something warmer.'

'Fish and seal-flipper.'

'Fuck seal-flipper – I need heat. I am a wanderer in the storm.'

'Dear Jesus, Robert. You're drunk, and little Joe can see in the dark better than you, and shoot better.'

'Little Joe is my friend. I have no fight with little Joe. Don't shit yourself, Hermann.'

They gave no signal before they bent to crawl through the entrance-tunnel, but their ritual comments about eskimo slovenliness as they stumbled over cast-off bones was warning for Hannah. Kruger passed first into the living-area. The grimy yellow light revealed nothing at first but a patch of grey that was Hannah's face and the brighter yellow of her eyes, wide with suspicion and alarm. Kruger crawled a little sideways to let Siemens join him inside the hut. He remained on all fours, grinning into the murk, waiting for his eyes to accustom themselves before he spoke.

'Good morning, little Hannah. Do we disturb you?'

Hannah said nothing, offered a thin smile. He eased himself into a sitting position, maintaining a respectful distance from her and the mound of oxhides which he knew must be covering Puney, then he peeled off his mittens and reached into his coat for his bottle.

'We've come to say hello to our friend little Joe, because we are not seeing him since so long. We wish to give him a little stuff to warm his toes.'

Siemens, in a voice gently modulated to calm her fears, added, 'We wanted to see that you and little Puney were well.'

In the weeks since the eskimos had taken to the shore the sailor's had almost forgotten Hannah's voice. Now it tickled them afresh with its delicate music, its wonderful intimations – not lost even on their uninstructed ears – of Boston and Cambridge, Massachusetts, Washington DC and London, England; porcelain and silver forks and sugar in lumps.

She spoke to Siemens. 'Joe is not here, Hermann. Would you like some tea? Joe and Hans are hunting, and I expect them home very soon.'

The absence of the men touched Siemens with relief and fear in equal measure. He removed his gloves, as Kruger had done.

'Tea, Hannah, yes: I would like some tea, and Robert would like some too.'

The water was simmering above the lamp. Hannah removed the pot and replaced it with the bottom half of a pemmican-tin. She ladled water into this, then reached behind her back into another tin for the tea. In the darkness her movements were deft and accurate. She dropped three fistfuls of tea into the decanted water. Now she handed a tin mug to Kruger, who she suspected might one day eat her child, and smiled at him.

'I have some sugar, Robert.'

Reaching behind again, she took a handful of sugar from somewhere and dropped it with easy skill into the boiling tea. Meekly enough, responding in his drunkenness to her prim authority, her Bostonian finesse, Kruger held out his cup while she ladled the tea into it. For Siemens she scooped a cupful of the treacly concoction directly into a mug and passed it to him.

'Thank you, Hannah,' he said.

While they sipped Kruger allowed his eyes and his nose to take in the surroundings: cast-off clothing draped on a rack above their heads; on the floor, a promiscuous litter of bones, cans, knives, harpoon-shafts, ropes, ox-skull bowls, pipes, deerskin rags, Puney's dolls – some carved for her by the sailors – buttons, a checkerboard neatly fashioned from deerskin, fish-heads, dog-traces, nails, fragments of wood, inexplicable stones, tin plates – the customary eskimo clutter, and the customary soup of oily, sooty, fishy odours. From under the soft mound that disturbed the even line of the sleeping-platform, Puney's soft child-snore established an air of domesticity reassuring to Siemens, who knew Kruger's sentimental attachment to his two daughters. Kruger sniffed.

'God in Heaven, Hermann,' he said in a near whisper that betrayed some recognition of Hannah's sensitivities and of her knowledge of German. 'I'd forgotten how it smells. You can hear the smell; you can chew it; you can cut it.'

'We shouldn't stay, Robert,' Siemens said.

'I like it,' Kruger said. 'I like to chew it and swallow it, like dear Captain Hall. Hannah liked dear Captain Hall, no?' He gulped loudly, proclaiming his relish of hot sweat, thick tea, tobacco, fish, seal, musk-ox, rancid fat, blood – and the other thing, the ever-present sharpness of soot which decreed that these people who lived under the clearest skies and breathed the purest air on earth should cough and spit and hack from chronically sick lungs and should die young. He poured a tot of Cognac into his mug and passed it to Hannah and she placed it on the floor without drinking from it. The brandy and whisky on his breath and in his sweat pierced the igloo-smells and frightened her. She had long feared what might happen if the *piblokta* should grip any of the sailors, and Kruger was the worst, the most brutal and reckless of them. And whether the return of Hans and Joe would calm the situation or inflame it she could not guess – Real Men excited by a successful hunt or disappointed by a failed one were no more fathomable than drunken *kablooonas*.

Kruger moved closer to her and turned so that like her he faced Siemens and the entrance tunnel. His shoulder brushed against hers. She was not naked, as she might have been if they had arrived ten minutes later, after she had trimmed the lampwick and crept under the blankets beside Puney; but the calico shirt she wore was thin, its neckline low, its front closed by a single button. She could feel his stare as he looked across her shoulder at her left breast, and sensed that any gesture of self-protection, any turning away or fastening of buttons might rouse his anger. He drank from the bottle and offered her a swallow. Diplomatically, she touched the rim with her lips, and he laughed.

'Sweet little Hannah, Joe is a lucky fellow, I too would like to live in this shithole with you to keep me warm.'

Siemens spoke softly, 'Robert, remember your courtesy.'

It was the wrong word. Kruger laughed again, dangerously. 'Courtesy, yes courtesy, that's what I've come for, a little bit of eskimo courtesy, a little bit of the hospitality of the old kind.'

His arm rose to embrace her shoulders. She smiled, calculating the several risks, and resisted the impulse to withdraw or protest. With her habitual blind ease she reached behind her back. 'Would you like some tobacco, Robert? And you, Hermann?' Cleverly, she made the appeal to Siemens, and cleverly he read her intent. In her hand were three clay pipes and a leather tobacco-pouch. Siemens moved across the carpet-skins until he was close to her left shoulder and hard against the sleeping-platform where Puney lay still undisturbed and gently snoring. Taking one of the pipes, he gently prised Kruger's fingers from her shoulder and pushed it into his hand.

'And now one for me, Hannah,' he said. 'Robert, we will smoke a pipe with little Hannah, and we must be quiet so that we don't disturb little Puney.'

Hannah smiled in acknowledgement of his support. She handed him a pipe then removed a bowlful of tobacco in her stubby fingers before handing the pouch to Kruger.

'After you, Robert,' Siemens said.

But Kruger pushed the pouch away. He had left the ship with a purpose, and was possessed with a drunken recklessness that was not to be lightly dismissed.

'Hermann first, little Hannah.'

In reaching toward Siemens with the pouch, she again offered Kruger the view of her left breast. His arm passed behind her shoulders once more, enclosing her, and continued further than last time, not stopping until his fingers were under her shirt, resting on the softness of the breast, two inches above the nipple. She bristled, but did not attempt to escape.

'Take some tobacco, Robert,' Siemens said.

Kruger's laugh was halfway toward a snarl. In the silence that followed it, all three knew the importance of that final two inches of flesh, knew that they were dancing on a cliff-edge.

'Take it, Robert.' Siemens offered the handful of tobacco which Hannah had given him, pushing it against Kruger's impudent left fingers. But Kruger was brandy-soaked and stubborn, and had not braved the polar night for a pipeful of Virginia shag.

He kept the hand in its place on Hannah 's breast and gently tapped Siemens's knuckles with the bowl of his pipe.

'Lick my arse, Hermann,' he growled. 'You keep the shit-tobacco.'

And instantly he raised the stakes, slipping his hand deeper into her shirt, cupping her breast in his palm. 'My hands are cold, little Hannah,' he said.

'Robert,' Siemens said.

Hannah did not speak, but dropped the pipe she had been filling and reached yet again behind her back. And again there was no fumbling, no searching among the skins. Her hand returned and rested on her lower throat and in the dim glow of the lamp the half-moon of sharpened flint was a new brightness. The Real People were richly supplied with implements of good Pittsburg steel, but both the women favoured their flint *ulus* for slicing meat. A peculiar woman's skill it was, the swift snick-snack and rock of the crescent blade, the barely visible wrist-twitch that could reduce ten pounds of seal-meat to a tidy heap of identical chewing-strips in a few minutes.

It was a moment rich in possibilities. Hannah did not doubt that Kruger could, and if pressed would, break her neck with ease, with a small quick jerk of his left arm. And she knew from long experience how brandy and rum robbed the *kabloonas* of their brains, their fear of all consequences. But the *ulu* had become an object of some wonder to the sailors: skilled enough themselves with fillet-knife and darning needle, they appreciated with connoisseurs' sincerity the cunning and precision of Inuit handiwork, had grinned their astonishment that such speed and delicacy of touch could originate from the lumpish seal-bodies, the short arms, the podgy sausage-fingers. They had seen the clumsy Hans pluck tiny darting dovekies out of the air with his outlandish fowling-net and the thickset, languorous Joe flick a designated dog's ear with his whip at fifteen paces while the sledge careered and bounced madly over the ice; but above all they had marvelled at the women, whose effortless dexterity with needle and *ulu* in the darkness of the igloos seemed more than, and less than, human. The *ulu*, and the damage it might inflict, had featured in a hundred coarse jokes.

They waited, all three, listening to Puney's child-snores, pondering whether Hannah's fear of death was less than Kruger's fear of losing four fingers.

And it was. The sailors removed their gloves only for operations whose delicacy made unencumbered fingers strictly necessary, and they had grown unused to the sight of their own hands. Each had known moments of horror, of slowly opening his eyes after some accident, some small muff with knife or spade or axe, to confirm that fingers numbed beyond all feeling were still present in the requisite number, in the appointed places. Most had lost skin through the lightest touch of fingertips on gunmetal, and images of gangrenous toes, detached noses, crumbling ears, haunted their dreams. For Kruger, the nakedness of his hand against the glint of blubber-light on Hannah's *ulu* did battle with the fumes of alcohol – and won. When he softly squeezed her breast she recognised it as mere bravado, the permissible last gesture of a defeated enemy preserving a shred of his manhood.

He lifted a pipe. 'Come, smoke, my friends,' he said. 'Tonight it will be frigging again, but tomorrow I'll ask little Joe for permission.'

As the days lightened and there were whispers of relaxation in the encompassing ice, they began to go through the motions of justifying Congress's fifty thousand. Budington, it was clear, thought only of the report to the Navy Department. With the onset of perpetual daylight and benign soft snow in May, Bessel, Chester and Tyson in their turn asked for the sledges, and each was rebuffed with the assurance that the equipment would be put to good use when the opportunity presented itself and that he, the captain, had his own plans for its deployment. He dispatched Tyson northwards to survey the ice and report on the prospects for a boat journey, and nodded slowly, with assumed sagacity, when Tyson reported that nothing could yet be attempted by sea.

'But with sledges, sir ...'

'I have my own plans for the sledges, George,' he said.

The first days of June brought real warmth and a softening of the pack that raised the *Polaris* and exposed a dozen leaks. The sailors reported that they could hear the flood tide rushing through the planks in the forward end.

But the main pack remained almost solid, and with the ice conditions clearly unpropitious, Budington allowed them to form two boat-parties. In their desperation for movement of any kind, for the achievement even of honourable failure, they pointed the boats toward the Pole and pushed. Chester and Meyer led the way in the largest of the boats, named *Grant* after the president, with Jamka, Anthing Siemens and Kruger as crew. Tyson and Bessel enlisted Hobby, Jansen, Nindermann and Lindquist for the second boat, christened *Robeson* in honour of the Navy Secretary.

Budington was below on the afternoon of June 7th when the first party left, so Bryan offered a prayer and led the cheers. The captain came up on deck two days later, before Tyson's boat had been launched, to watch with the rest as the six returned to Thank God Harbor wet, hungry and boatless, their brave foray against the ice a disaster more complete than even he might have hoped for. Dryly, not attempting to lower his voice, Tyson said, 'It would seem that prayers can be answered.'

A mere two miles from the ship, camped on a floe between two grounded icebergs, they had been forced to leap from their sleeping bags and scramble for the shore when Anthing, the night watchman yelled, 'The ice is coming!' And from the shore they had watched in shamefaced impotence while their floe, driven by the loosening pack into Robeson Channel from the great Polar Ocean itself, rammed against the bigger of the two bergs and brought a thousand tons of ice down upon tent, boat, logbooks, guns, clothing, provisions, everything. For the walk home most of them had been unshod.

The months of simmering irritation had frayed nerves and friendships. Angry at the captain's unconcealed satisfaction, his indifference to the loss of the boat and the abject depression of the returned voyagers, Tyson destroyed whatever lingering comradeship might have remained between himself and Chester, the First mate, by proposing that the Cape where the *Grant* was crushed be christened Cape Disaster, the bay from which they watched the catastrophe unfold, Folly Bay.

Meyer, sharing the humiliation, said bitterly, 'Light as ever with your drollery, Mr Tyson. I hope your own venture fares better.'

Omens were bad: lost with the *Grant* was the Sacred Bunting, the history-soaked starry banner which Hall had accepted from Horace Grinnell before the departure from New York.

For twenty miles northwards Tyson and the doctor found open channels through the pack, then they hit the barrier of ice at Newman Bay, and saw no sign of a fissure. They made camp on the shore and waited for movement. Bessel, immobilised by snow-blindness, lay in the tent and cursed, venting his self-pitying rage on the captain, the sailors, the insouciant icebergs. For a week they sat and watched, and no serious breach occurred in the wall of the northern pack in its slow progress through Robeson Channel. On the seventh day, Chester and his crew arrived in the canvas boat after five days of desperate toil, rowing and dragging it the scant twenty miles from the *Polaris*. The absurdity of the frail, square-nosed little pleasure-tub as it bobbed amid the fearsome pack provoked them to laugh through their exhaustion, and Tyson and Chester recovered a morsel of their former friendship in their shared embarrassment.

The wind remained day after day in the north, packing the fifteen-mile width of Robeson Channel with monstrous hummocky floes, yet for all the perpetual heaving and groaning and the constant wonderful transformations of the landscape, no gap appeared that could admit even a kayak. Seeing the uselessness of the boats, they abandoned all naval propriety and raged openly against Budington for his cowardice, his incompetence, his drunkenness, his determination to ensure that the North Polar Expedition should fail wretchedly to fulfil its originator's dream or honour any of its promises to Congress.

Tyson proposed that they haul the boats to a safe position and set off Polewards on foot, and Chester agreed that they must at least attempt the eighty-third parallel, but the men were sour and thoroughly infected with the captain's disinclination for adventure, while the doctor, despairing in his pain and blindness, added his voice against and recruited Meyer to the do-nothing cause. While they were still arguing Johnson arrived, on the afternoon of Independence Day, with a written order from Budington: the ice was loosening, the ship moving and leaking prolifically. On the instant that repairs were completed he would attempt to free the *Polaris* and steam south. The presence of all officers and hands was immediately required.

Chester sneered. 'Damn the man. If we don't at least pass eighty-three north we'll be laughed at for fools and cowards. I can hear Hall turning; I can see his wife's eyes.'

He dispatched Jamka and Anthing with a request for provisions and a message that ice-conditions promised fair for a northward foray within a few days, for an attempt on the eighty-third parallel that would bring honour and glory to the Expedition and the memory of its dead commander.

Receiving it, Budington spat, stamped his foot on the deck, and threatened to clamp him in irons. He sent the provisions with a peremptory insistence that the boat-parties return forthwith to Thank God Harbor where their services were urgently needed. Behind Jamka and Anthing came Hans with a reiteration of the directive, couched in still more imperious and admonitory terms. Bessel returned with Hans, while Tyson and Chester, seeing nothing but hard-packed ice to the south, hauled the dinghy and the already hopelessly damaged canvas boat into a ravine, wrapped them as securely as their equipment permitted, and made ready to tramp the twenty miles.

They were an angry and depressed party, and when Lindquist eight miles short of Thank God Harbor pointed to a patch of incongruous red-white-and-blue spread across a slowly drifting floe and they recognised it as the lost flag, there was no marked enthusiasm for the risky business of recovering it until Tyson swung them with the argument that it might be useful in shaming the captain, and he and Kruger set off to hop-skip-and-jump across the bobbing pack into the treacherous middle of the channel. It was two hours before they joined the main group again, soaked and exhausted and laughing at the folly of it all. They wrung out the ice and water and folded the Sacred Bunting into a long strip which was wound around Lindquist's waist for transportation to the *Polaris*.

Budington greeted them with contempt and anger and bland indifference to their bedragglement, their hunger, their disappointment, not deigning to look up from his chart table as he addressed them, 'Your adventure, gentlemen, has cost us three boats and a quantity of provisions whose loss we might yet come to regret. I trust I can rely on your undiluted cooperation in the main business.'

The United States North Polar Expedition was over with no serious threat to the inviolacy of the Pole. Yet, even now, when the only cause that remained was the saving of the ship and the sailors' lives and all were bound together in horror by the prospect of another winter trapped in the bay-ice, there was rancorous disunity and recalcitrance that came to the very brink of open mutiny. They protested at the command to man the hand-pumps and deliberately opened stop-cocks to flood the engine-room and necessitate the employment of the donkey engines. Investigating the crime, Budington found the engine- room door shut against him until threats of courts-martial and hangings persuaded the sailors to release the bolt on the promise of a general amnesty.

Budington took to dining alone and emerged from his cabin only to cast frowns on the operations to free the ship from the ice, or to remind the officers that all other plans were now subservient to these operations.

Lost in his impotence, lonely in his sobriety, Bryan the chaplain said private prayers for their deliverance and marvelled that there could be so much drink still flowing on board the *Polaris*.

The ice at last succumbed to the heat of a high July sun and began a cracking, a crumbling, a singing, an easing, a rapid retreat from the sides of the ship. Chester led a northward foray to recover what was worth saving from the abandoned boats.

As their respect for Budington withered, so their affection for the dead Hall bloomed afresh, and in solemn twos and threes they made their pilgrimages, secured the grave and Schumann's headboard against the polar wind, and unashamedly released their tears.

And in the very midst of their humiliation, while the commander ranted against their disloyalty and their chief scientist and doctor lay moaning in self-pity with compresses on his eyes, there were fair omens. On 12th August the sun was hot, the Sacred Bunting was raised on the observatory flagpole, Charlie Polaris uttered his first sour squawk at the world – and the ice opened.

CHAPTER SIXTEEN
DRIFTING: HANS JABBERS

Their dying begins with Meyer's toes. The ice closes, the wind slackens. They can neither launch the boat nor drag it across the pack and to abandon it will be certain swift death. On every side they see frolicking seals but are unable to approach close enough to risk ammunition on shooting at them. Rations are reduced to a handful of pemmican three times a day and most of them have gross difficulty in chewing it. Meyer can grasp nothing in his enormous deerskin gloves, so they take turns in placing minute scraps of pemmican between his lips. They can do nothing for his feet – he cries with the pain in his rotting toes. In the tent they cluster for warmth while two keep watch in hourly shifts, ready to warn them of movement in the ice, changes in the wind. On Easter Sunday Tyson, on watch with Herron, drifts out of a dream-strewn doze and feels again the blazing splendour of the aurora. He rouses his snoring companion.

'Dear God, John, it's surely a promise. It's surely a message that we have not been spared this long and come through these trials only to perish at last, within sight of land, among this abundance of game.'

'Oh, dear God,' Herron says, as they stare southward. The heavens are ablaze with silver yellow streamers that dance and gyrate and shoot upward toward and beyond the zenith until the whole dome of the firmament is lit, and the all-enveloping ice shimmers with reflected glory.

Tyson touches the Herron's shoulder. 'A promise, John: a promise.'

Herron's voice is grave. In the stillness of the coruscating night he whispers his awful warning. 'They're talking, Mr Tyson. They're blaming you for dumping the food, and they're talking.'

Tyson, too, whispers. 'What are they saying, John?' The steward shakes his head then bows it, pressing his chin tight against his chest, bunching his shoulders, saying nothing.

Tyson puts a hand on his arm. 'Tell me, John.'

Herron does not look at him, but stares upward, at the golden sky directly above his head. 'I think you know, Mr Tyson.'

Tyson knows. 'I cannot believe it,' he says.

'The hunger gets to their brains, Mr Tyson. It's not the natives now, it's Mr Meyer.'

'No, John. God will not allow that. Look up.'

The fireworks are almost spent, the dance almost finished. Herron turns his head to face Tyson. 'They're waiting for him to die, and I think he knows it. I think he knows what's on their mind, and I'm not sure that he cares much.'

'No, John. God won't allow it, and I won't either.'

Their watch is over. He signals Herron to crawl ahead of him into the tent. Jamka and Anthing go unbidden and cheerfully enough on to the floe, glad of the chance to flex their limbs. They gasp at the fading glory of the aurora, and Jamka cries out, a wordless cry of delight.

'It's a promise from the Almighty,' Tyson calls to them through the canvas. Then, to the silent huddle of bodies he says, 'We won't be abandoned now – we're being watched.'

'Shit,' Kruger growls. He and Nindermann, as Tyson impotently knows, have been pilfering from the bread-bag. Tyson presses. 'We have only to stick together, only to see it through.'

'Shit,' Kruger says again.

Through it all, through the wildest darkest moments of their storm-tossed nightmare, Tyson has kept the loaded Colt 45 wrapped in a piece of softened sealskin inside his shirt, secured with a strip cut from his buffalo-blanket, painfully tight against his left ribcage. Kruger, stronger than the rest to begin with, has benefited from the fruits of his perpetual thieving and is better muscled and less diseased than any of them except the natives. There can be no court-martial, no warning, no formal or informal challenge, no hearing, no exchange of views; when the thing becomes necessary, Tyson will place the muzzle of the Colt at the back of Kruger's head and blow his brain out. Justification will have to come afterwards, and will not be easy because Kruger has friends on the floe while Tyson has none – or at least none whose testimony will be heeded.

Throughout the day of April 20th, the wind quickens and the swell of the sea rises, then at nine in the evening the main assault begins. Jamka's cry gives them time only to brace themselves, to cover the children and cling to the canvas as the monstrous wave washes over the floe and carries off everything but their bodies, the tent and the boat. They load the women and children into the boat now, cover it, lash it with boat-warp and oogjook thongs to whatever projections they can find in the ice, and agree that they will cling to it, in four-man shifts, while the gale lasts.

The waves batter them at seven or eight minute intervals, bringing not only water but fragments of the pack, some as big as dining-tables, others fashioned into scimitars that tear the coats from their backs, slice the spars of the boat, rip the tent to shreds. And when finally the mighty one arrives, they are too weak to save anything but themselves: tent, skins, guns, ammunition, pots and pans – everything is swept into the sea. The boat breaks its makeshift moorings and careers to the far edge with the women screaming and the watch clinging to its sides. It stops, lodged against an ice-mound, a yard from the water.

It is the presence of the despised eskimo women and their brood, Tyson realises, that gives them the strength to fight. Despite their exhaustion, they cannot lie passively watching for the next wave to carry the boat off, and their response to his commands is immediate and disciplined, with even the half-dead Meyer lending his meagre weight. They drag the boat back to the windward edge, fasten her again wherever they can find a projection, and cling. With a tenderness that astonishes Tyson, Jamka and Anthing lift Meyer and drop him into the boat with the women.

If till now their bitterest horror has been the night of the separation from their ship, the events of the next ten hours cause them to revise the catalogue. The sea becomes a malevolent beast: they tune themselves to its pulse, resting while it rests then bearing down with every ounce of their weight in answer to Tyson's shouts as the thunderous waves crash upon their heads. The fragments of ice bruise them through their layers of deerskin and wool, and the boat, laden with seven bodies, threatens to leap across the floe and take to the air.

Precisely at midnight comes the true monster, a wave that stands a moment gathering strength then drops from sixty feet and engulfs them; the moorings are torn loose and the boat is swept to the far edge again. Hannah and Christiana climb down to the ice and help to push and drag it back to the safer side, and for the rest of the night the two women stand with the men, bracing themselves against each assault, roaring with the effort of holding the battered little tub fast against the ice. Twice more the boat is dislodged, but the knowledge that its loss can have only one end for them all – after the instant death of Meyer and the children – sustains them in their struggle.

The grey dawn reveals amid the tumult of grinding pack and clashing bergs a larger flatter floe riding comfortably a mere quarter mile from their own crumbling and unstable platform. Exploiting the new authority he has gained during the desperate exertions of the night, Tyson convinces them that a final mustering of strength, a shove through the mush to this bigger platform, might yet save them all. He issues the last morsels of pemmican that have been preserved under the planks of the boat, then orders the launch. The final heave into the sea leaves Jackson the cook stranded, and he has to leap for the boat and cling to the gunwale until they haul him on board. They reach the bigger floe, and although wind and wave are still violent, the centre is secure for the moment and they can allow themselves a few hours of rest. The temperature is above zero – ease and luxury for people who have endured as they have – but there is no sun to dry their clothing, no tent to shield them from the gale, and no food. Tyson again tries to comfort them with pious logic: it is not possible, not compatible with any system of belief, that they have been spared through the night gone by, bruised and battered but alive to the last man woman and child, alive even to the baby Charlie Polaris and the crippled Meyer, only to die of thirst and starvation south of the fifty-fourth parallel, in clement temperatures, surrounded by game.

Kruger dismisses his teleology with his customary retort: 'Shit.'

They are in latitude fifty-three degrees, fifty-four minutes. A day of relative peace serves only to underline the pain of their bruises, their exhaustion, their hunger. The driving sleet penetrates to their bones. Their only nourishment is a sheet of dried sealskin, intended once for boots; they divide it into strips. Meyer, who hungers most, is unable to chew. Hannah bites off small pieces, softens them in her mouth, and feeds him. Christiana performs like service for the children, and Herron asks her to chew his strip for him, in a gesture of trust and dependence that amazes even himself.

Soaked though they are, they are tormented violently by thirst. The solidarity of immediate danger has passed and Tyson again fears the worst. The Colt at his breast and the eskimos' rifles are the only weapons left. He knows that Kruger and his allies are aware of this, that an attack, if there should be one, will be an unannounced swift clubbing to the ice, a stab to the heart, a dismemberment rapid enough to outflank doubt, conscience, love, religion, duty.

He knows with his whaler's experience that the pure turmoil of nature cancels all memories of firesides and chintz, that there are in the end no rules governing the imperative to survive, no gods outranking the god of the belly. The urge to act first becomes pressing, but if he kills Kruger, how many of the rest must follow if he is to avoid instant bloody atonement?

Then, out of the pack, comes a smell of deliverance. Joe, on a routinely hopeless reconnoitre, climbs a hummock and finds himself staring across a hundred yards of ice at a thin bear that is waddling purposively toward them, clearly drawn along a scent-line, clearly with meat on its mind. Softly he creeps back to the huddle of bodies, touches the shoulder of the snoozing Hans, and whispers, 'Nanook!'

It is the one native word they all recognise. The children are silenced. Hans lifts his rifle and follows Joe to the hummock, where they lie on their bellies and take aim. Now they can all see the bear, and they fall flat, becoming basking seals.

It waddles on, bandy and preoccupied. It is as hungry as they, and its hopes are high as it short-sightedly pads from floe to floe, pausing occasionally to raise its head, swaying its scrawny neck, sniffing, reading the wind. The eskimos agree without discussion that Joe, the better marksman, will fire first. And Joe lets nothing – not his gnawing hunger, his fear for his wife and child, the ghastly threat he reads in Kruger's glance – distract him from the task or diminish his patience. A missed shot or one that does not find a vital organ might drive the bear into the safety of the water, where it will be as confident and secure as a narwhal and well beyond their reach within a half-minute. Not until its plod brings it to within an easy twenty paces of the hummock does Joe squeeze the trigger, and providence rewards his patience: the bear's left eye is a sudden red explosion; the bear staggers, its hind legs paralysed.

Hans's ball rips through the heart, and the bear slumps forwards, nose grating on the ice, then rolls on to its right side. Knowing there is no need of further shots, the two hunters leap to their feet and cheer, a signal for the others to do the same.

Again, there is laughter on the floe.

A stringy half-starved creature it is, to be sure, but the meat is the better for that – tender and digestible – and the blood, expertly drained and husbanded by Joe, is instant fire in their stomachs. For the first time in six days Meyer stands unaided, and grins.

Yet they are still in desperate peril. Their floe is withering fast, threatening at any moment to flip them into the pash. The boat has been damaged by the cascading ice and they have no means of repairing it, but they launch it nevertheless, and eight hours of crippling labour at the oars brings them to a section of the pack which offers the prospect of a night's camp. Built for six and carrying nineteen, the boat is now pounded into a condition that would spell danger on a summer lake. The bear-meat, it seems, has simply added a few days to their agony. Two nights of thick snow soak them through and prevent all chances of taking observations to establish their position.

When the gale rises again from the west they take their positions willingly enough on Tyson's order to stand by the boat, and even Meyer calls out encouragement and grips the sides with his oversized deerskin gloves. They have to leap over the sides as the floe buckles and cracks under their feet and the boat launches itself into the ice. An hour of frantic paddling gains them less than a hundred yards, and they haul up on the biggest section of their fragmented platform for a few hours of rest.

Tyson is shaken out of sleep by the frightened hands of Jackson, whose voice is not loud, not urgent, but final and resigned to death: 'Sweet Jesus, Mr Tyson, we's surely damn finished now.'

Following Jackson's pointing finger, he sees the icebergs, the nearest of them a mile westward. There are a dozen at least, but the immediate danger is from two clashing monsters approaching the final stage of a duel that may have begun a thousand miles to the north. Their millions of tons are tossed in a general eastward drift by wind and wave and current and they continually crash and grind together beneath the heaving surface.

'The boat,' Tyson says.

A fly trapped in amber, he thinks as they drive through the mushy ice, will struggle until it dies, but men can see the hopelessness. His grip on the steering-oar begins to slacken, his eyes to close. Overwhelmingly, he feels the urge to flip backwards into the sea, into instant absolution and rest.

Then Hannah's hand, ungloved, appears under his nose, offering a piece of bear-meat. As he opens his lips to receive it, Puney yawns; her outstretched arm strikes her mother's wrist and the meat falls. Hannah's mouth purses with mild motherly irritation, then widens in a sociable smile as she says, 'I beg your pardon, Mr Tyson.'

Yet again, the grotesque and wonderful Park Avenue politeness of her 'beg your pardon' makes him laugh, and his grip on the oar tightens again.

'Ah, Hannah,' he says.

The small floes are festooned and weighted down with bladdernoses. Joe, sure in his aim even from the rolling boat, kills three of them.

And the wind at last dies. The sky clears long enough for Meyer to take a reading from the sun and confirm that they have crossed the fifty-third parallel. They row toward a piece of ice that will bear the weight of their nineteen shrunken bodies and their battered boat, and light a fire in its centre. With food in their bellies, no wind, a balmy spring breeze rippling the waves between the floes, they settle unbidden into the old factions: Tyson with the eskimos; the six sailors and Meyer in a grumbling German-speaking clique; Herron the Englishman and Jackson the negro in some ill-defined neutral territory.

Tyson cradles Puney on his lap and together they look into the flames of the blubber-fire, deep yellow against the indigo night. Hannah brings a piece of seal-meat for each and settles beside them. Tyson squeezes the meat against his teeth, savouring the warmth of the blood, raising his head to let it run into his throat.

'Hannah,' he says, 'I believe we are now in the latitude of London, England.'

Not sure if she understands, he says, 'London England, Hannah – not New London, not New England. I mean that great London where you drank tea with the queen and where Joe bought his

213

gentleman's gamp.'

Hannah splutters. Trying to reply, to offer her stately thank-you for the intelligence, she is seized by a fit of deep coughing. As she strives in her ladylike fashion to stifle it, her lungs whistle and her eyes water. Tyson pats her back. 'There will be boats soon, Hannah,' he says.

The following afternoon Jamka, on watch at the bow, points northward and cries out, 'A steamer! Dear God, a steamer!'

They hoist their colours and row for dear life. They shout, they wave, they howl, Hans and Joe fire their rifles into the air. But there is no return of signal. The ice closes around them and their arms capitulate and they roar their anguish to the sky as it darkens, while the steamer – Tyson recognises her as a sealer – disappears into the night.

Camped again on the ice, they cannot sleep, but they talk, and eat, and the bitter loss is transformed into a source of new hope.

'We've come through, my friends; we're in the sealing grounds,' Tyson tells them.

The morning after they chase another but get no closer than seven miles before the ice renews its grip. They haul up on a floe barely big enough to accommodate their bodies with the children in the boat, hoist the colours on two lashed-together masts, fire three rounds each from the rifles. After twenty seconds there are answering shots, and the steamer turns her head toward them. Afraid to make a sound, they watch for three hours, during which she comes no closer.

'Damn her, she can't be held fast in ice as thin as this,' Tyson says, and orders another volley. They listen, each turning his good ear toward her. There is no reply, and the sealer turns broadside to them and heads rapidly southwest.

'They haven't seen us,' Tyson says.

Meyer is sobbing. 'The shots, Tyson. We heard the shots.'

'Not for us.'

The last morning of April is cloudless and calm. They see the Labrador coast not forty miles distant: and nine miles to the north the smoke of another steamer. Again they yell and leap and wave their arms; they fire the rifles, raise the colours on the masts, and when the thick wet fog closes in they sink into despairing inaction, cursing the fog, the ice, the steamer, the Arctic, the President, Congress, Uncle Sam and all his ways.

The fog teases them, sometimes thick enough to drink, sometimes allowing them a view to the far horizon. Tyson and Jackson, their two-hour watch completed, sit propped together on the ice, drifting into sleep. They have been silent and brooding during their watch, but now Jackson needs to speak. 'Mr Tyson, you reckon they's all dead now?'

Tyson does not have to ask what he means. 'I don't, Will. I reckon they're safe now in Washington, and the Navy knows of us.'

'How you reckon that, Mr Tyson?'

'Budington knows these parts, and he's careful, Will.'

The naming of the captain is what Jackson needs. 'Who done done this, Mr Tyson?'

'What, Will?'

'Who done done it that we's here dying without no ship, and Captain Hall's dead, and whatever you say them boys is most likely all dead, all dead. Was that Captain Hall done that? Was it Captain Budington?'

Tyson yawns. 'Sleep, Bill.'

But Jackson is awake, and Tyson feels the trembling where their bodies touch. 'Who was it done all that, Mr Tyson?'

Drifting, Tyson leans against the rail of the witness stand. He musters his thoughts, then straightens up and spreads his arms wide to recreate the scene for the lawyers and the reporters.

'Ice,' he says. 'Darkness and drink, ice, *piblotka*, the Flag, the stars, ice, science, Congress, Budington, peacock-brains, madness, Prince Albert.'

Enjoying his downstage moment, he pauses for effect: 'Ice, gentlemen, ice.'

He yawns again. 'Sleep, Will.'

Jackson stops trembling, and his body is rigid with decision. 'If they's alive or if they's dead, Mr Tyson, I ain't planning on saying nothing.'

'Nothing, Will, nothing. Now sleep.'

'I don't know what I seen, and you don't know what I seen, and you and me we sat a whole damn year and we done said nothing. Seems we all killed Captain Hall, seems it was no more Captain

Budington done it than you and me done it.'

'It may be, Will.' For Tyson, the banquet beckons.

'Is we dying here, Mr Tyson?'

'No, Will.'

'Seems to me this is dying, seems to me I feel it.'

'No. You must stop feeling it, Will. You must not think of it.'

'What goddamn thing does I start thinking on, Mr Tyson? What does I think on to stop me thinking on dying?'

'After. There will be after, Will, and we'll drink rum and laugh, and we'll chase whales.'

'Is they dead, is they dead with the ship?'

'I think not.'

'Why, Mr Tyson, why you think not?'

'God. I trust in God to deliver them.'

'Like he deliver us?'

'Yes, Will.'

'Well, I ain't sure. Seems to me he ain't doing so good by us, and seems to me the ship was holed, and a holed ship goes down, and it goes down God or no God. I seen holed ships, and they go down and them poor sailors go down with them, and God, he ain't got so many lifebelts, seems to me.'

'Oh, he has lifebelts aplenty, Will. Don't think of dying.'

'I does think of, it, and I thinks of Captain Budington dying, and the doctor dying, and all them boys dying.'

'We'll sail into Brooklyn again, Will.'

'If'n we does, and them boys is all dead, I ain't saying nothing, I ain't speaking no evil of the dead.'

'I hear you, Will.'

'Mr Tyson?'

'I hear you.'

'Don't be asking me, I won't say nothing.'

'I hear you.'

'But seems to me we's all dead, damn soon, we's all fishfood.'

The need to enlist him stirs Tyson. He holds Jackson's wrist. 'Will, a time might come soon when we have to be strong, strong against despair.'

'I don't know that I feel so strong, Mr Tyson.'

'Not for ourselves, Will. You hear the anger against Meyer. There will be more of that, and there will be anger against the natives, and we must be strong, we must defend them.'

'I ain't feeling too strong. I don't like Robert: and Fred, he's damn running crazy, he's damn making like to shoot somebody.'

'He won't, Will. Robert will manage him.'

'Robert? Sweet Jesus, I's always scared of Robert, he's the craziest of us all.'

'No. There's decency in Robert, and we must use it. Have you spoken to Herron?'

'I's spoke to him, oh yes, and he's damn scared too, Mr Tyson.'

'We're all scared, Will.'

'Yes, but he's scared out of his head, and he won't say nothing neither, and he ain't seen nothing neither. Them boys most surely, dead, Mr Tyson.'

Tyson's head sinks. Shyly he approaches the banquet. Hall has arrived before him and sits with his broad back toward him, his elbows spread as he carves a peacock-wing. Tyson is drifting in clouds of savoury steam; from somewhere above an orchestra plays welcoming airs but he dreads what he will see when Hall turns, fears to look the commander in the eye, knowing he will have no answer to the accusation that will be hurled at him.

The Host speaks first. He is laughing, pointing with his out-stretched finger along and beyond the table, and his drawl is softer, more patrician than ever: 'Steamer off the starboard bow, George.'

Lindquist, on watch with Johnson, has seen her first, has given the call in a voice that begins hardly above a whisper, then becomes a shout that echoes among the bergs. And now they are all gathered on the edge of the ice – their starboard bow – waving, roaring, weeping.

She is hardly two miles off, but the fog is closing again. Hans leaps into the kayak with the wonderful speed that his dumpy body commands in extremity, and they push him off. Joe and Tyson fire the rifles. The fog drifts in eerie shreds, at times obscuring the ship, then revealing her black against the grey sky. Her head turns and she begins to steam in their direction. Hans waves his paddle and yells,

'American steamer, Yankee steamer, big *Polaris*, big sailor, big Cap'n Hall!'

They see her clearly now: a barkentine, her mainmast and rigging festooned with men. They watch as three seal-boats are lowered and are rowed rapidly toward the floe.

Squinting, Tyson reads her bows: the *Tigress*. He knows her – a Newfoundland sealer – and he makes the first joke of his nine-month drift. 'She's the *Tigress*, boys – let's give her a tiger!'

They raise a cheer, the sailors in the rigging echo it, and all at once the men of the United States North Polar Expedition are sailors again, men bound by rules: the women and children are lifted into the first of the seal-boats, and Meyer after them. The others climb into their own boat and begin to row. Hans reaches the side of the *Tigress* and is hoisted over the rail jabbering unintelligibly to the astonished sealers.

Tyson climbs aboard and identifies himself to the mate of the *Tigress*, who asks him how long they have been on the ice.

He does not have to calculate. 'Since the fifteenth of last October, ten o'clock in the evening.'

In their six months on the ice they have drifted eighteen hundred miles as the crow flies; and Meyer will lose none of his toes. The young sailor who has helped Tyson aboard and whose hand is still clutching his wrist, steps back, looks at him in wonderment and says, 'And was you on it night and day?'

And Tyson grins.

UNITED STATES NAVY BOARD OF INQUIRY, WASHINGTON DC, OCTOBER 16TH 1873, NAVY SECRETARY GEORGE ROBESON PRESIDING, SURGEONS GENERAL BEALE (US NAVY) AND BARNES (US ARMY) IN ATTENDANCE

Testimony of William Jackson, Cook

Q   Did you make the coffee specially for the sledge-party?

A   No, sir, it was taken from the galley, the same as everybody else had.

Testimony of Joe Ebierbing, Eskimo Hunter

Q   Was Captain Hall in good health when your party returned from the sledge-journey?

A   Yes, sir, but tired.

Q   And were you present when he was taken ill?

A   No, sir. I did not see him that night. I saw him next morning . He remained abed. After breakfast he asked to speak to me. He says, 'Very sick last night, Joe.' I asked him what is the matter. He says, 'I do not know. I took a cup of coffee. In a little while very sick and vomiting.'

Q   Do you recall that he said anything about poisoning?

A   Yes, he say something. I can't tell sure. He ask me, 'Now, Joe, did you drink bad coffee?' Him feel it after a while; burn stomach. Later he told Hannah the coffee made him sick, he never see anything so bad as the coffee he took on coming aboard.

WASHINGTON DC, DECEMBER 24TH

Testimony of R W D Bryan, Astronomer and Chaplain

Q   Were you in the cabin when the captain drank the coffee?

219

A   No, but I was present soon after, and was told by the others what had happened, that he had suffered a bilious attack after swallowing his coffee, and had said, 'I feel sick,' or 'something is the matter with me,' or something of that kind. He made some such remark as that he was very weak and might be sick, and he asked for a basin to be brought.

Q   Was this within half an hour of his coming into the cabin or coming on board the vessel?

A   Yes, I think it would be correct to say it was within that time.

Q   And did you hear him associate the coffee with his illness?

A   Yes, I think he chided himself for drinking it too quickly.

Q   And his attack followed immediately upon swallowing the coffee?

A   I cannot be sure about that. He might have given the cup back, and he might have spoken a while, but from what I heard and saw I associated the two facts in my mind, that just as soon as he took the coffee he complained of feeling sick, and blamed the coffee, and went to bed. It might have been more or less of an interval, I could not tell you exactly how long.

Q   You say he blamed the coffee?

A   That was my understanding, but I was not present in the cabin.

Q   Then how is it that you know he blamed the coffee?

A   I cannot be entirely certain, but it was my understanding, from the account I was given by those who were present.

Q   And did you receive that account from any particular person?

A   That I cannot recollect sir. There were several men present, and I believe that most of them had something to say.

Testimony of Dr Emil Bessels, Chief Scientific Officer

Q   Did you have differences with Captain Hall at Disco?

A   No, sir.

Q   Did not you offer to resign your position?

A   At the time of the difficulty between Captain Hall and Mr Meyer, I told the Captain I preferred to go on shore myself if Mr Meyer was dismissed. I personally had no differences with Captain Hall.

Q   When the vessel was beset, did you work in harmony with him?

A   Complete harmony. The captain was always interested in our scientific endeavours, and we had many discussions.

Q   Did you not belittle the aim of the Expedition, namely the attainment of the North Pole?

A   No, sir. I was always for achieving as far north as possible, but I did say that much of the scientific work was independent of the North Pole, and Captain Hall agreed with me on this.

Q   Did you not express relief at the captain's death?

A   No sir, I did not, but it might be that some remark of mine was misunderstood.

Q   Were you present when Captain Hall and the sledge party drank the coffee upon their return to the vessel?

A   No, sir. I was sent for at the observatory.

Q   You were not present in the cabin?

A   I was not sir; I was sent for.

Q   And how did you find him?

A   I found him in his bed. The cabin was very warm, and I had the door opened. He told me he had been vomiting. His pulse was very irregular – from sixty to eighty – he all at once

became comatose. In twenty-five minutes he regained consciousness and I found a condition of hemiplegia – the left side of the
face, and the left arm and side, were paralysed, also the muscles
of the tongue, the point of which deflected to the left. I gave him
castor oil, and three or four drops of croton oil. He slept during
that night, but complained the next day of difficulty of
swallowing and numbness of the tongue; part of the time he
could not speak distinctly. I gave him more castor oil and croton
oil, and he recovered pretty well from the paralysis.

Q   How did you know he was paralysed? He was lying on his
berth?

A   Yes sir.

Q   How did you ascertain he was paralysed? Was it a paralysis
both of motion and sensation?

A   It was only paralysis of motion at first after the recovery
of consciousness, then it became both.

Q   Motion and sensation both?

A   Yes, sir. I tried the sensation in the first attack with a needle
and for the motion, I lifted his hand, and as soon as it was lifted,
it would fall.

Q   You had no doubt then that it was a case of this kind, that
the Captain had suffered an apoplectic shock?

A   Oh no, sir. There was not the least doubt about that.

Q   What was the further course of his illness?

A   On October 28th I saw the first signs of his mind
wandering.

Q   What were these signs?

A   He thought someone was going to shoot him, and accused
everybody.

Q   Of seeking to injure him?

A   Yes. He thought he saw blue gas coming out of people's mouths; would not take clean stockings from Chester, for fear they were poisoned. He seemed to trust Joe and Hannah most, and had them taste all his food, even when it came from sealed cans opened in his sight. From October 29th to November 4th he would not let me treat him, but took pills and medicines of his own. His tongue was all the time deflected toward the left. When I tried to bathe him on November 6th he thought I was going to poison him with the bath.

Q   When you say he accused everybody, do you mean there was no-one he seemed particularly to suspect?

A   He may perhaps have named myself and Captain Budington most.

Q   Why do you think he particularly named these two?

A   I cannot say, sir.

Q   Were you present at his death?

A   I was not awake, sir. Mr Morton was beside him, and he woke me at 3.30am of the 8th of November. Captain Hall had become comatose in the early hours of November seventh. I had tried with a pin and found some sensation on the right side, but none on the left. There were spasmodic motions of the muscles, mostly on the left side. After Mr Morton woke me, I examined the Captain and confirmed that he was dead.

Q   What do you consider to be the cause of the captain's sickness and death?

A   My opinion of the first attack is that he had suffered great fatigue and very low temperature during the sledge journey. He returned and entered a very warm cabin without taking off his thick fur clothing, and then he took a warm cup of coffee, which produced a sudden reaction, and finally an apoplectical insult.

Q   Do you find that all the symptoms and manifestations you observed are consistent with such a diagnosis?

A   I do, sir.

Q   Were you aware of suspicion among the crew about the circumstances of Captain Hall's death?

A   No, I was not.

Q   Did you not hear talk about the coffee that was served to the captain on his return to the ship?

A   I did not, sir, but I do not think it likely the men would have discussed such things in my presence.

Washington DC, December 26th, 1873

Sir,

We, the undersigned, were present by request of the honorable Secretary of the Navy, at the examination of Dr Emil Bessel, in regard to the cruise of the Polaris, and the circumstances connected with the illness and death of Captain Hall. We listened to his testimony with great care and put to him such questions as we deemed necessary.

From the circumstances and symptoms detailed by him, and comparing them with the medical testimony of all the witnesses, we are conclusively of the opinion that Captain Hall died from natural causes, viz, apoplexy; and that the treatment of the case by Dr Bessel was the best practicable under the circumstances.

Respectfully, your obedient servants

W K Barnes, Surgeon-General, United States Army
J Beale, Surgeon-General, United States Navy

CHAPTER SEVENTEEN
THEY KNIT

There is complicity: to begin with: a simple coming together of sufferers, the necessary concomitant of growing well; then as the scurvy leaves their bones, so too does much of the rancour. They are famous people; they have come through. The fourteen who abandoned them to the ice are again their lost shipmates, and not only Tyson and the eskimo men, but Kruger and Jamka as well sign on when President Ulysses S Grant orders the purchase of the *Tigress* for sixty thousand dollars and its refitting for a rescue journey.

Before that, the Navy will have its truth and Congress will have its story, the justification for its first fifty thousand; but nobody seriously cries for blood. The complicity becomes complicities: of sailors; of Yankees; of men who have seen the darkness. For each of them, grievance against the others is displaced by guilt, by shame, by self-contempt.

They are allowed a decent three weeks to recover their strength then summoned to Washington where the Navy Secretary institutes and conducts the official inquiry. If the talk is all of rescue, still the prevailing supposition is that that all or most of those aboard the stricken vessel have perished with her. No-one is enthusiastic to prove that the fifty thousand has been squandered; no-one will seriously besmirch the names of dead comrades; above all, no-one wishes to rekindle his self-loathing. Things must be said, but not such things as will blacken; not such as will offend Hall's ghost or distress his wife. Events on the floe are excluded from the main business: for the moment, officialdom seeks only to justify its dollars with the story of the besetment, the death of the commander, the separation, the probable loss of the ship; and it prefers a compendium fit for the New York Herald and the illustrated papers, uncluttered with sordid human failings. For the nineteen who travelled on the floe, these are distant happenings, the stuff of an earlier existence.

Yes, they will carp, but none will overstep the boundary of customary sailors' gripes. A few will relive the bickering, settle scores, overturn imagined defeats, exact revenge for perceived insults delivered by men now assumed dead, but none will speak of murder. The questioning is tentative, shy of encouraging too much revelation, and the responses are dutifully bland. Carpets and tablecloths and polished wood and frock coats jar against the passions that seethe in their hearts; exposure of these passions would be an exposure of personal failure, an admission of share in the guilt, an insufferable fanning of the flames of self-hatred.

So the year of miserable anarchy between Hall's death and the separation is, by a merging of needs, stripped of its madness and rewritten in a style that mollifies guilt, allows the Navy Department to assure the President, Congress and the public that their cash was well used. Every straw is clutched at: the Sacred Bunting now flutters at eighty-one degrees eleven minutes – above all others banners on earth; Americans have gazed upon the Polar Ocean itself and have established the route to the top of the world. The newspapers will swallow and disgorge the necessary pap, will relay the heroic saga of the Great Quest inaugurated by Kane and gloriously continued by Hall – the forging of the American Way to the Pole.

And a little later, the sideshow of Tyson's Drift will install new heroes, evoke new wonders of Yankee endurance. Scrubbed clean of carping, pilfering, insubordination and rancour, refashioned into a grand symphony of ice and storm and manly passion, it will feed polite conversation in parlours across the land, and make of Tyson a famous American. Things are said, but only small things: Budington drank and did not love the North Pole; Bessel despised the commander and his substitute alike; Meyer strutted; but the United States North Polar Expedition had a good ship and a doughty crew, had penetrated to the very edge of the Polar Ocean, had borne the Sacred Bunting with patriotic fervour toward the ninetieth degree.

They are finally bound, their collective guilt knitted into a single garment of shame by the comradeship of self-disgust. Secretly, in their memories and in their several diaries, they relive the rotting of their manhood, recoil from the twisting of their souls. Their shifting hatreds are charted and the shame gnaws at them, so that the touch of their wives and sisters and mothers and children hurts them.

They have little to say on the particulars of Hall's collapse, and even less on the treatment he received. There is vague agreement that he ranted, that he discharged accusations wildly and indiscriminately at everyone close to him except for the natives, that the doctor cared for him with some tenderness, that there might, however, have been relief in some quarters at his death because some were fearful of the ice.

Questioned about the coffee, Jackson admits only that it was fresh-made for the commander and not poured by himself, but by Herron or possibly by Budington, that he was not informed who drank it, whether the commander himself or others of the sledge party, that he was feeding the dogs when he heard that the commander was not well. He is not asked about the period of Hall's sickness and ventures no statement about it. After him, Tyson cannot forbear from criticising Budington's command, from unloading a store of bitterness, from voicing some of his long-rehearsed animadversions on the composition of the crew, but he reveals nothing of what he has learned from the cook, and knows nothing of coffee or of medicine.

Of the natives, only Joe, sad desolate Joe, is called to testify, and he has little to say.

For those who return to the ice in the Tigress the journey is an exorcism and a longed-for expiation. A tough tub the Navy makes of her in Brooklyn, encasing her three-foot sides in iron and bracing them with stout oak beams, renewing her masts, her rigging, her sails, setting her propeller low for working under the pack, running steampipes through her cabins for heating her against the possibility of a winter in the ice.

Tyson is commissioned as acting lieutenant and ice-master, one of eleven officers. Joe boards as interpreter. Oppressed by the heat of New York, Hans and Christiana and their children embark as fare-paying passengers but Hans enjoys less than a day as a gentleman-traveller, because Joe convinces him that deck-drudgery is a condition of the passage. As they make sail from Brooklyn the family is a focus for the crew's curiosity; the children are again chubby, smiling, and despite the ninety-degree heat of the East River, comically swathed in the garments gifted to them by the sentimental housewives of St Johns. But two days at sea puts an end to the sailors' interest, as the eskimo smell fills the cabin. Freshly afraid of the scornful kabloonas, Christiana remains shut up with the children, while Hans toils for Joe, and Joe smirks.

The *Tigress* is top-heavy with titles – even Lindquist can strut a little as Captain of the Maintop – and undercrewed, with a mere fourteen deckhands.

This speeds the healing. Daily Tyson and Kruger find themselves face-to-face, shoulder-to-shoulder. Each has a hundred times projected the gross and violent destruction of the other. For Tyson, rage against this recalcitrant crewman has been a main element in his staying alive. The thought of testifying at his court-martial, of seeing him strung up in Navy Yard – these things have sustained him through his darkest misery; he has chewed them in the absence of food, and in the absence of oil they have lightened his sunless polar days. For his part Kruger has shocked even himself with the exuberance and variety of his planned revenges against the man he counts as the author of all his suffering: he has clubbed Tyson's skull to a bloody mash, strewn his severed part across wide acres of drifting ice, pumped rifle-shells into his body till it was more lead than flesh, eaten his liver, violated his wife in front of his eyes before gouging out those same eyes with a marlin-spike. Now they exchange the comradely half-smile of men set apart from the rest, shipmates again, partners in the great quest for their lost friends.

The *Tigress* is light, too, in rubber coats, and the bitter rain of Bergy Hole soaks and chills them. But they are well fed, and the cabins are warm. Returning over his nightmare seas, Tyson weeps and laughs in turn. July ends with a glorious aurora, August opens with an accident: a medicine chest, dislodged in the tossing of the ship, crashes not an inch past the ear of the assistant doctor and breaks the floor-planking. 'How strange, to be almost killed with my own drugs,' he drolly muses. They call him puke-jerker, and marvel at his ugliness.

At Disco they dance with the beautiful half-breed girls, the blonde eskimos, and fumigate Hans and his family, ignoring his gentlemanly outrage.

Tyson is in his old whaling grounds, and there are fellow-whalers at his elbow on the watch. 'There she blows!' cries his ice-assistant, Mr Chipman, and he humours him with:

'Where away?'

On August 13th they are off Northumberland Island, and they see the sun at midnight. The captain sends a message to Tyson:

Sir – Having this morning passed near to Northumberland Island, affording a good view of the same, I desire you to state to me in writing whether in your opinion the said island was the one which was seen by you when you were separated from the Polaris, *in October 1872. If in your opinion it is not the island, you will state to me in detail the reasons why you form that opinion.*

Respectfully, etc., Jas. S. Greer

He has rehearsed his reply a hundred times in his head:

Sir – My reasons for thinking Northumberland Island is not the island where the Polaris *separated from me are as follows, viz.: the island is much larger than the one I saw the* Polaris *go behind; and Hakluyt Island, off the north-west end of Northumberland Island, is larger than the island – or rock – off the island where I last saw the* Polaris; *and the surrounding land in the vicinity of Northumberland Island does not correspond with that I saw at the time of separation.*

Very respectfully,

Geo. E. Tyson Ice-master, United States Navy

Signing his name, claiming that ice-master's authority which none in these planks, on this floating piece of the United States, will ever dispute, he feels the bitterness afresh, relives a hatred that penetrates to his very bones; and lacking Meyer, he wishes his officer's dignity were taken away, so that he might run to the tweendecks and find Kruger and grab him by the collar and shake him and force him to look, to tell all the others, with Lindquist his seconder and Joe nodding by his, George Tyson's side, that Mr. Tyson was, right, right, always right, that their nine-month agony might have been averted if they had but listened.

And before the day is over, in the late evening of 14th August, they are there. There is soft summer twilight, grey rock, open water, a squawking of birds, but he recognises in every nerve the spot where he was tossed into legend. The bow of the *Tigress* points northward toward Kane's famous Basin, Kennedy Channel, Thank God Harbor, Hall's grave, the Polar Sea. Leaning on the starboard rail, Tyson looks on the features of ancient enemies finally unmasked: the grim rock of Littleton Island; beyond it, Cape Alexander standing sentry at the entrance to Smith Sound; behind them the rise of Humboldt's Glacier and the Greenland ice-cap; on the port side, glowering through the rigging of the *Tigress*, the cliffs of Cape Isabella and the mountains of Ellesmere. He hears their laughter, and laughs himself.

A boat is lowered and is still two miles off the Etah shore when they hear voices. The rush of excitement subsides when it becomes clear that they are not about to meet Budington and the *Polaris* survivors, but only the local eskimos. Yet there are stories; there is news. The fourteen have wintered here in some comfort, have built themselves a pair of boats from the spars and planks of the *Polaris*, bequeathing the remnant to the village elder, the most distinguished of the natives, and at the loosening of the ice have headed for the whaling grounds, healthy and strong and well-supplied with food and fuel. The natives howl and hint at compensation for their unseaworthy inheritance, for it has sunk without trace in the first winter gale, while they helplessly looked on. The sailors understand why when they find the wooden house, still intact at the margin of the settlement: between it and the boats the bulk of the *Polaris* has been consumed, and the gift to the hosts has been a sorry scrap.

In the house they find tools, utensils, mugs, plates, books; and the diaries, wrapped against the damp. From every one of these the pages that relate to the death of Charles Francis Hall have been cleanly excised. Reading them, Tyson again is steeped in gall, humiliated at the recollection of the smothering resentment and paranoia – his own as strong as any – of the dark days between the burial and the separation.

Their own mission is now over and their hopes for the survivors high. When the *Tigress* ties up at St Johns, a year and a day after the separation, the pilot tells them that the party has been rescued, that all its members are safe and well. He carries with him the New York papers from a month ago, and all of them report the telegram from London:

The Dundee whaling-steamer Arctic *has arrived at Dundee, having on board Captain Budington and the crew of the* Polaris.

They have been rescued by the *Ravenscraig*, and transferred to the *Arctic* and the *Intrepid* – fit in body, high in spirit, entirely destitute of means.

With all safe, the stitches tighten, complicity becomes unspoken conspiracy. More thousands of dollars have been spent, and a rescue has been made. Yankee fortitude has again triumphed over savage nature; Budington has brought the ship party home without the loss of a single toe. Within a week they are officially examined on board the USS Talapoosa. There are more revelations, further tales of insubordination, drunkenness, pilfering, intertwining hatreds, Arctic dementia. There are clear lies and loud contradictions, yet no-one, least of all the United States Government, wishes a scandal; no-one can stomach a hanging; no-one probes after the final answer to the awful mystery. The diarists are not questioned about their missing pages; the precise composition of Hall's last mug of coffee is left unexplored; the whereabouts of the doctor when that coffee was swallowed are allowed to remain obscure. Budington is not invited to confirm or deny the burning of papers relating to his drinking. He will not make the lecture-tour that befits an American hero. It is a pale and stricken man who faces the inquiry – a man with guilt in his bones, pleading for forgiveness. 'I wished to welcome him as a friend, and congratulate him on his safe return,' he tells his questioners, with the sad ring of truth in his voice; and they are content.

Jackson, who knows most, says least, and when Joe ventures into the dangerous territory, they quickly bring him off.

UNITED STATES NAVY BOARD OF INQUIRY, WASHINGTON DC, OCTOBER 16TH 1873, NAVY SECRETARY GEORGE ROBESON PRESIDING, SURGEONS GENERAL BEALE (US NAVY) AND BARNES (US ARMY) IN ATTENDANCE

Testimony of William Jackson, Cook

Q   Did you not make the coffee for Captain Hall and his party when they returned from the sledge journey?

A   No, sir. Captain Budington made the coffee for Captain Hall.

Q   Captain Budington made it?

A   Yes, sir. He said Captain Hall liked it fresh-brewed, he said the others could have the old coffee that was laying on the stove.

Q   And did you see him brew the fresh coffee?

A   No sir, I did not. I got him the coffee can from the store, and I gave it to him, and I went out to feed the dogs that had come in with Captain Hall.

Q   Was it the custom for Captain Budington to brew coffee?

A   It was not, sir.

Q   Then what did you make of it?

A   He wanted to welcome Captain Hall, sir. He wanted him to know he was glad he come safe home, he was his friend.

Testimony of Joe Ebierbing, Eskimo Hunter

Q   Was Captain Hall in good health when your party returned from the sledge journey?

A   Yes sir, but tired. He wanted rest.

Q   And were you present when he was taken ill?

A   No, sir. I did not see him that night. I saw him next morning. He stayed abed. After breakfast he asked to speak to me. He says, 'Very sick in the night Joe.' I asked him what is he matter. He says, 'I don't know too good, I took coffee and in a little while I'm very sick and vomiting.'

Q   Do you recall that he said anything about poison?

A   He said something, I can't tell sure. He asked me, 'Joe, did you drink bad coffee? Feel it after a while; burn stomach, burn inside.' Later he told Hannah the coffee made him sick, he never saw anything so bad as the coffee he too when he come aboard.

Q   Did you see him during his illness?

A   Sometimes. He was bad. The doctor gave him medicine, but he said Captain Hall was too sick, he would die.

Q   Do you wish to return north now?

A   No, sir, not any more. With a man like Captain Hall, maybe. With a man like him.

Q   Is there anything else you wish to tell us of?

A   Captain Hall was my friend, Hannah's friend. Very sorry when he die. After he die, very sad, everybody sad, and there was no get north after that. Don't know nothing else, sir.

Marvels are broadcast: the Glorified Sacred Bunting is drawn for the illustrated papers flapping against a background of Hall's grave and Greenland's mountains, closer to the Pole than all other buntings; wheat can sprout to a height of three inches on the Arctic shores; the machinery of the *Polaris* functioned admirably well; the eskimos are intensely curious about cats.

233

EPILOGUE – 1879

Joe sits. When he fires Schwatka's Evans rifle the butt jars his right shoulder joint, and the pain passes like a telegraphed message to his right hip. But the rifle is a wonder: on his best day he has brought down eight caribou with ten shots, and Schwatka has given him honorary ownership. His own beautiful Treadmore twenty-six shot he has lent to Tulugaq, who has several times used its swift quiet power to kill two beasts with a single shot, though only last year he was making do with a pitiful antler-and-driftwood bow. Tulugaq wishes to exchange wives next month when he crosses to Kikertak to recover the *kabloonas*' cast-off supplies, because his own wife is nursing a son. Joe will agree to the arrangement: he needs a woman to massage his shoulder, to provide warmth under the qipik, but any woman will do.

Over beef, when the formal business of the Inquiry was finished, he told the Secretary for the United States Navy again that he was finished with the north, he was a Connecticut Yankee, a Groton man. 'Do you not wish to return to your own people?' the Secretary asked him, and there was the promise of a free passage in the tone of his voice.

But, no, he was a Yankee now.

He farmed and fished and talked to reporters and tourists, while Hannah stitched and Puney became Sylvia, a Yankee school-girl. But Puney died, and the *kabloonas* needed him, and money became scarce, and he was back in the ice two years after the Inquiry, vainly seeking the Northwest Passage with Captain Young in the *Pandora*. Later, as the *Jeanette*, she will sink beneath the ice, like the *Polaris*, and become famous because many of her crew will die.

When he returned to Groton he found Hannah coughing bright blood, and soon she joined Puney and there was nothing in Connecticut to hold him. Once he met Tyson, who told him he had come from the house of Captain Budington, having found there a grey, bitter man, finished with ice, finished with the sea, finished with society. Budington, he said, had sworn solemnly that the coffee was good, untampered with, a true peace-offering; but faced with the bread-pellets, had shrunk into himself and wept.

Jackson, the lonely bearer of the secret, had gone awhaling,

234

though Tyson did not know the name of the ship – with the loss of so many in the winter of '71, most of the whalers were new.

And they wept together, Tyson and Joe, for Hall and Hannah and Puney and Budington and dead dreams.

Now in the summer of '79, Puney dead and Hannah dead, Joe is back on the ice again, gazing across the strait to the forsaken wasteland where it all seriously began: Kikertak, King William's Island, where ten years ago Hall blundered over the ice looking for bits of the old man Franklin and his poor sailors, and complained bitterly when the Real People refused to stay beyond the spring melting.

Before Hall it had been hardly more than play – Captain Budington, Mr Bolby, the Queen of England, the Prince Regent, Bond Street – it had been a flirtation with the *kabloona*, an interlude from living. The whaling men who visited them in Cumberland Sound became creatures of the ice, whose preoccupations were barely different from those of the Nussarmuit who sheltered them and hunted for them: to fill their bellies, store oil in their ships' holds – and these things accomplished, to fuck and to dance.

In Hall, he met the other breed of white man – the *aglooka*, the long-strider, whose aim was the ice itself, whatever he might say about Flag and King and President, whatever High And Sacred Cause might provide his immediate pretext and his dollars. Joe intimately knew the catalogue of highminded crackpots, because it filled the heads and hearts and conversations of the *kabloonas* while they chewed fat and smoked in the igloo: Davis, who danced with the Real People and gave them knives; Frobisher, who baited them with bells and abducted two of them; then the chain of beplumed commanders whose stories he knew even from his own relatives: Ross and Parry and the old fool Franklin and the many who came to find his bones. After them, the Yankees: Kane, Hall, and now Schwatka.

Whatever the avowed goal – the Northwest Passage, the North Pole, the Polynya, Franklin's concrete coffin – the thing that drove them was the sickness. They ached in their bones for silence and piercing starlight, and for many their yearning could end only in death.

There are small pains everywhere on his body, stiffness wherever his skeleton is linked, and a chronic hard knot of agony at the base of his spine. The men of these parts, the Utkuhikhalingmiut, nod wisely when he describes the symptom. For them it is almost universal, a condition of growing older, born out of the endless hours of waiting by the seals' breathing-holes. With interlocked fingers they sculpt the pain, mime the eternal friction of the last vertebra against the sacrum. Their women know it too, and a significant bargaining point in the exchange of wives is their relative experience and cunning in manipulating the afflicted joints.

Joe has a new wife who is not without skill, but he supplements her ministrations with increasing doses of morphine. This new wife is plump, past the suppleness of girlhood, a widow who asks little of him; his father-in-law is no more than ten summers older than himself, but a man of some authority among the Netsilingmiut. While Joe has been laid up, able to walk only with a stick, this father-in-law has laid in meat for the absent *kabloonas*. Neither he nor his daughter wishes to move to Groton, Connecticut, and Joe accepts.

Joe has been instructing this settlement of Real People in the joys of Thanksgiving, Christmas, Easter, Independence Day, but they shake their heads and wish he would be quiet, especially here, where their ancestors are buried. The Utkuhikalingsmiut are a miserable tribe, a remnant, poor fisheaters whose arrows are futile against the caribou hide. The Netsilingmiut, better versed, tell Schwatka stories, serving up the titbits which they know the *kabloonas* like and will pay for. Translating, Joe exchanges secret glances with the storytellers: are they offering recollections, hearsay, or mere conjurations for the willing, gullible, ever-generous explorers? From all around they have come to the camp with their tales, good, graphic tales, of Franklin's crews dying as they dragged their boats through the hunting grounds of the Utkuhikalingsmiut toward the Great Fish River, rotting slowly among their spoons and plates and books and brass buttons. Joe does not enjoy interpreting; he has never mastered English, despite thirty years among the *kabloonas*, and the dialect of these Netsilingmiut is obscure. Hannah and Puney spoke like New England ladies, but New England killed them.

When the white men are gone and the fat is being properly chewed in the lamplight, the Utkuhikalingsmuit tell real stories, sad winter stories that catch the heart. His father-in-law has told him that the cliff he now faces, Ootgoolik, is a famous killer of children. Long ago an old bent hunter, a man known and avoided for his shamanistic powers, was enraged at the noise of some boys and girls who were playing under the cliff. Time and again their shouting and laughter drove away a seal he had been stalking for hours. Finally, as a sudden gust of laughter foiled him at the very moment when he was about to launch his harpoon, he lost patience, and invoked the spirits. 'Let those children be buried under the snow,' he said. Whereupon the cliff moved, and a great avalanche of snow and ice engulfed the children – twenty or more of them. Running from the village to investigate the noise, the parents saw the disaster as it happened. They fell upon the mountain of snow, digging frantically as the cries of the children grew steadily weaker. Long before they reached even the first child, there was silence.

Out on the ice they descried the old hunter, crouched again at the breathing-hole, determinedly ignoring them. They realised at once that he was responsible for the deaths of their children, and set off across the ice brandishing their snow-knives, ready in their rage and grief to cut him into pieces as small as a gull's liver. Hearing their cries, the old hunter turned to face them. He squatted by the breathing- hole, stiller than a stone, his face fixed in a smug malevolent grin, watching as they narrowed the gap. He was feeding his hatred of them, churning it in his spirit and transforming it into a last mighty surge of magical power. Calmly, arrogantly, he waited until they were within five paces, then he rose straight into the air, laughing aloud at their bewilderment and terror, and again cursing their dead children. They stared in baffled rage as he rose ever higher, until he became an indistinct spot in the darkening sky, and finally disappeared in a silver streak.

'And you'll see him still,' the father-in-law said, 'on any clear night, if you watch long enough.'

Joe has seen many a shooting star, many a dead child.

He looks up. His life with the *kabloonas* has rewritten the book of the sky. Now he reads names: Vega, Capella, the Seven Sisters, Deneb, Aldebaran – and the meandering Jupiter, whose satellites he could once, to Hall's delighted astonishment, distinguish with unaided eyes. And bleakly, obscurely, modestly twinkling – Polaris, the *kabloonas'* Grail, the navel-star. He sighs. Schwatka and the other three *kabloonas* are on the desolate marshland of Kikertak, finding and burying bones, tracing the footsteps and opening the cairns of previous searchers. Joe and his father-in-law have stored up salmon and deer for their return. The angekok has given Joe a healing rock for his joints. He places it under his pillow and the old woman, his wife's aunt, removes it three times daily for resanctification, but the pain laughs.

He has things to show them, for he has been doing some searching of his own. At Navertaroo – the *kabloonas'* Starvation Cove – opposite Keeanu where Hall buried the remains of five sailors, he has found buttons, shoes, scraps of clothing. And he has found his friend the Prince Consort. The medal is hardly as wide as his thumb, and the portrait of Albert fills one side. Lifting it, he at once recognised the high-domed forehead, the thin nose, the sidewhiskers; and he remembered tea, and stately conversation, and Hannah smiling. On the other side is a six-masted steamship, sails full-set:

> The Great Britain: *length 322 feet, breadth 50 feet 6 inches, depth 32 feet, six inches, weight of iron 1500 tons, 1000 horsepower. Launched July 19th, 1843, by HRH Prince Albert.*

He recalls the carpets, the gilt, the chintz, the bowing footmen, the little Queen, who yawned. He looks across at the landmark mound, Ogbuk, where Kikertak rises to its highest point. Beyond it the *kabloonas* – Schwatka, Klutschak, Gilders and Melms – are wading through clouds of mosquitoes, and Tulugaq is inwardly cursing.

Joe is not at home here: not comfortable. The Netsilikmiut and the Aivilingmiut have a long-running feud that could flare up on the instant, notwithstanding the peace-parleys and the warnings of the *kabloonas* that bloodshed would put an end to all trade. Nor is he comfortable about the exchange of wives with Tulagaq, because the practice sits unhappily with his New England Christianity; and Tulugaq's wife, if the truth be confessed, is a carper with a voice like the scraping of stone on sledge-runners.

Hall dead, Puney dead, Hannah dead.

Joe slips his arm from his sleeve, rubs his back inside his kulitsak, searching out the inflamed joint. He groans wearily, and squints again at the soft distant mound of Ogbuk. By now the *kabloonas* might be at the northernmost headland – Toonoonee, the Back of Beyond – burying more bones. He presses his backbone with the knuckles of his clenched right hand, finding the spot and pressing it to enjoy the agony.

He squints at the great purple circle of the midnight sun. Its lowest point almost brushes the summit of Ogbuk. He eases the pressure of his fingers, releases his breath slowly, watching the cloud of it rising above his head. Then he presses again, harder, until the pain fills every corner of his body and drums in his skull.

Bones, he thinks. Bones.

Fiction from Two Ravens Press

Love Letters from my Death-bed
Cynthia Rogerson

There's something very strange going on in Fairfax, California. Joe Johnson is on the hunt for dying people while his wife stares into space and flies land on her nose; the Snelling kids fester in a hippie backwater and pretend that they haven't just killed their grandfather; and Morag, multi-bigamist from the Scottish Highlands, makes some rash decisions when diagnosed with terminal cancer by Manuel – who may or may not be a doctor. Meanwhile, the ghost of Consuela threads her way through all the stories, oblivious to the ever-watching Connie – who sees everything from the attic of the Gentle Valleys Hospice.

Cynthia Rogerson's second novel is a funny and life-affirming tale about the courage to love in the face of death.

'*Witty, wise and on occasions laugh-aloud funny. A tonic for all those concerned with living more fully while we can.*' **Andrew Greig**

'*Her writing has a lovely spirit to it, an appealing mixture of the spiky and the warm.*' **Michel Faber**

£8.99. ISBN 978-1-906120-00-9. Published April 2007.

Parties
Tom Lappin

Gordon yearns for a little power; Richard wishes reality could match the romantic ideal of a perfect pop song; Grainne wants life to be a little more like Tolstoy. Beatrice looks on and tries to chronicle the disappointment of a generation measuring the years to the end of the century in parties.

Parties, the début novel by journalist Tom Lappin, is a scathing, insightful and profoundly human commentary on party politics and the corrupting effects of power. But above all it is a satire: a black comedy about young people getting older, and learning to be careful what they wish for, lest they end up finding it.

'*Compelling and absorbing: the story of four friends growing up in the '80s and '90s, through the voyage from idealism to disillusion that was left-wing party politics through the turn of the century.*' **Paul Torday** (author of *Salmon Fishing in the Yemen*)

£9.99. ISBN 978-1-906120-11-5. Published October 2007.

Prince Rupert's Teardrop
Lisa Glass

Mary undresses and wades into the boating lake. She dives and opens her eyes. In the blur, she perceives the outline of a head – she reaches...

A dead bird. But she will keep searching. Because Mary's mother, Meghranoush – a ninety-four year-old survivor of the genocide of Armenians by the Turkish army early in the twentieth century – has vanished.

Mary is already known to the police: a serial telephoner, a reporter of wrongdoing, a nuisance. Her doctor talks of mental illness.

But what has happened is not just inside her head. A trail of glass birds mocks her. A silver thimble shines at the riverbed – a thimble that belonged to her mother.

A glassblower burns a body in a furnace and uses the ash to colour a vase. Rumours circulate of a monster stalking the women of Plymouth. A serial killer who specialises in the elderly.

Has Mary's mother simply left – trying to escape the ghosts of genocide in her mind – or has she been abducted? It is left to this most unreliable and unpredictable of daughters to try to find her, in this moving, lyrical, and very powerful work.

'Lisa Glass writes with dazzling linguistic exuberance and a fearless imagination.' R.N. Morris

'A virtuoso stylist of the calibre of Rachel Cusk, Lisa Glass has created a powerful murder mystery, whose violent undercurrents flow from the bitter inheritance of the Armenian genocide.'
Stevie Davies

£9.99. ISBN 978-1-906120-15-3. Published November 2007.

Nightingale
Peter Dorward

On the second of August 1980, at 1pm, a bomb placed under a chair in the second class waiting room of the international railway station in Bologna exploded, resulting in the deaths of eighty-five people. Despite indictments and arrests, no convictions were ever secured.

Exactly a year before the bombing, a young British couple disembarked at the station and walked into town. He – pale-blue eyes, white collarless shirt, baggy green army surplus trousers – and twenty yards behind him, the woman whom, in a couple of years he will marry, then eventually abandon. He is Don, she is Julia. Within twenty-four hours she'll leave for home, and he will wander into a bar called the *Nightingale* – and a labyrinthine world of extreme politics and terrorism.

More than twenty years later their daughter Rosie, as naïve as her father was before her, will return to the city, and both Don – and his past – will follow...

'Nightingale *is a gripping and intelligent novel; it takes an unsentimental and vivid look at the lives of a small group of Italian terrorists and the naive Scottish musician who finds himself in their midst in Bologna in 1980. Full of authentic detail and texture,* Nightingale *is written with clarity and precision. Peter Dorward tells this tragic story with huge confidence and verve.'*
Kate Pullinger

£9.99. ISBN 978-1-906120-09-2. Published September 2007.

Short Fiction from Two Ravens Press

Types of Everlasting Rest
Clio Gray

From Italy and Russia in the time of Napoleon to the fate of Boy Scouts in Czechoslovakia during the Second World War, Clio Gray's short stories are filled with intrigue, conspiracy and murder. Laden with sumptuous detail, each story leads the reader directly into the compelling and sometimes bizarre inner worlds of her fascinating characters.

'Clio Gray *is a master of atmosphere and sensuousness. She combines historical realism with the bizarre, whimsy with the macabre. Reading her is like being at a sumptuous feast in a palace, just before it is stormed.'* **Alan Bissett**

£8.99. ISBN 978-1-906120-04-7. Published July 2007.

RIPTIDE
New Writing from the Highlands and Islands
Edited by Sharon Blackie & David Knowles

This diverse collection of new fiction and poetry from the Highlands and Islands showcases the work both of established writers and of new names to watch.

Contributors:

Pam Beasant, Sharon Blackie, Robert Davidson, Angus Dunn, Eva Faber, Alison Flett, Yvonne Gray, John Glenday, Clio Gray, Andrew Greig, Nicky Guthrie, Mandy Haggith, Morag Henderson, Elyse Jamieson, Laureen Johnson, David Knowles, Morag MacInnes, Anne Macleod, Kevin MacNeil, Daibhidh Martin, John McGill, Donald Murray, Alison Napier, Pauline Prior-Pitt, Joanna Ramsey, Cynthia Rogerson, David Ross, Mark Ryan Smith, and Peter Urpeth.

'...a force of creation, the kind of irresistible tide into which we should dip.' *The Scotsman*

£8.99. ISBN 978-1-906120-02-3. Published April 2007.

Highland Views
David Ross

Military jets exercise over Loch Eye as a seer struggles to remember his vision; the honeymoon is over for workers down at the Nigg yard, and an English incomer leads the fight for independence both for Scotland and for herself... This debut collection of stories provides an original perspective on the Highlands, subtly addressing the unique combination of old and new influences that operate today.

'I'm a big fan. A fine organic collection that advances a viewpoint, culture and history quite other than the urban central belt that still lopsidedly dominates recent Scottish literature.' **Andrew Greig**

'A view of the Highlands with a strong element of political and social comment. Ross explores these concerns in convincingly human terms through the lives of his characters.' **Brian McCabe**

£7.99. ISBN 978-1-906120-05-4. Published April 2007.

Poetry from Two Ravens Press

Castings: by Mandy Haggith.
£8.99. ISBN 978-1-906120-01-6. Published April 2007.

Leaving the Nest: by Dorothy Baird.
£8.99. ISBN 978-1-906120-06-1. Published July 2007.

The Zig Zag Woman: by Maggie Sawkins.
£8.99. ISBN 978-1-906120-08-5. Published September 2007.

In a Room Darkened: by Kevin Williamson.
£8.99. ISBN 978-1-906120-07-8. Published October 2007.

For more information on these and other titles, and for extracts and author interviews, see our website.

Titles are available direct from the publisher at
www.tworavenspress.com
or from any good bookshop.